CW01261921

MONK'S GATE

A Historical Time Travel Romance

Matilda Scotney

Copyright © Matilda Scotney 2022
National Library of Australia registered
All rights reserved.

No part of this publication may be reproduced, stored in a retrieval system, or transmitted in any form or by any means, electronic, mechanical, photocopying, recording or otherwise, without the prior written permission of the copyright owner The work cannot be parodied or passed off as the work of another author. Short passages of text may be used for the purposes of a book review or discussion in a book club.

This is a work of fiction. Any similarities between the characters, situations within the pages, places, or persons, either living or dead, are unintentional and coincidental. The political views presented are not necessarily the views of the author.
Matilda Scotney asserts her right to be identified as the author of this work.

The Monk's Gate: An Historical Time Travel Romance
ISBN: 9780648754596

Cover Design: 100 Covers
https://100covers.com

Many thanks to Eluned Bevan who invented Llanbleddynllwyd as a place name and kindly allowed me to use it in the story.

I would also like to thank The Welsh Society of Western Australia for filling in the gaps in my memory!

"Mi gerddaf gyda thi dros lwybrau maith"

"I'll walk beside you over many paths."

CHAPTER ONE _

Llanbleddynllwyd Historical Society

Calendar of Events for March/April 1956

Friday, March 16th. Historical talk by MR AND MRS ALFRED PARRY of Swansea. MR PARRY will provide an entertaining and informative talk on the role of coal in the Bronze Age and our village's place in history. Following MR PARRY'S words, MRS PARRY will give a brief speech on the following topics:

1/The Roman invasions.

2/The English Kings war on the Welsh and our position as a jewel in the English crown.

3/The effects of the Industrial Revolution and anthracite mining in the area.

As this is an all-evening event, there will also be an opportunity to discuss the colliery closure and how the old section of the village will move forward.

Admission: 3d. Light supper to follow.

~~~~~~~~~~

Monday, April 9th - General Meeting of the Llanbleddynllwyd Historical Society. This is a members-only event….
~~~~~~~~~~

Bethan Davies stopped reading, took her lips from her steaming cup of tea, and blew an inelegant and disparaging raspberry. A speech on the Roman Invasions? How many invasions were there? She thought there was only one. Also, what was it with the out-of-place capitalisation and grammar?

The offending pamphlet, reproduced dozens of times with the aid of carbon paper, arrived after she went to bed. She found it lying on the doormat this morning and wondered why people were sneaking around the village after dark, shoving their irrelevant propaganda through unsuspecting folks' letterboxes?

"I would have told them 'No thanks' if they'd given me a chance," she muttered.

Bethan had never once attended a historical society meeting. They knew it. So why would she waste an entire evening listening to the history of a town she couldn't wait to leave? Every resident knew about Llanbleddynllwyd's part in the Industrial Revolution. Posters and pamphlets featured everywhere, from the local primary school to the library across town. She could recite its history if she had a mind to. The remnants of its dirty old railway, the sub-canal used for transporting coal, were all around them as constant reminders. Now the pit had closed, the town clutched the history to its bosom as if it were a prize they feared to lose. For Bethan, she couldn't face an evening of fuddy-duddies who lamented progress as they hearkened to the town's glorious past. Short memories, Bethan thought. There was no glory in the depressing legacy of death, lung disease and exploitation that Llanbleddynllwyd shared with all other mining towns.

She returned to sipping her tea. These thoughts were ungracious. Most historical society members had been friends of her parents. Good people whose families had lived in this part of Wales for generations. Like her mam and dad, they were passionate about the village's history and viewed the grimy houses and failing infrastructure through rose-tinted glasses. The truth was the village was in decline. Now, only the oldest residents clung to their small, outdated cottages for the sake of nostalgia.

Apart from some time away at school in her early teens, Bethan lived in her widowed grandmother's house with her mam and dad. As a child, she hadn't noticed the cottage's cramped dimensions until she returned from boarding school. Going back to sharing a room with her gran, until the old lady went into a nursing home, made her want to run for London even then. Except she was still underage, and by the time she turned nineteen, lung disease had struck down both her parents. She devoted herself to their care, watching and learning from the district nurse on her visits. It kindled an ambition, a purpose in Bethan. Before, all she could think of was escaping, but she had no idea where or what to escape to. Now she knew her calling in life. She would become a nurse.

After several years of dedicated care from their daughter, Bethan's parents passed within two months of each other. She missed them, but as her grief lifted, so did her freedom to revisit her dreams of a future that didn't involve this house or this town.

She scrunched the leaflet with one hand, not interested in reading more of the perceived merits of this soul-destroying, joy-sucking place. She would save her threepence, light supper or not.

While she read, she'd been ignoring the slurping noises at her elbow. Now, they intruded enough to make her look at the overweight tabby cat, busy licking butter from a slice of half-eaten toast. The kitchen was too cold, and the hard yellow butter was impossible to spread. Bethan thought the hot toast would melt it, but the partly charcoaled bread cooled as soon as it came out from under the grill. The thought of spreading marmalade on those greasy slices made her shudder. Even the cream on the milk was sticking out the top of the bottle where the liquid froze. It was her fault. She let the boiler go out.

Bethan gave the cat a gentle shove. She didn't want the toast, but it was still disgusting to allow such liberties.

"Puss. Get off the table!"

The tabby ignored the reprimand and honoured Bethan with a stink eye before returning to its breakfast. The furry feline roamed this street for several years as a stray that moved in on this row of cottages, expecting food from everyone, hence its robust physique. Each morning, the cat graced Bethan's kitchen with its fluffy presence because, in the cooler months, she kept the boiler going low to warm the kitchen.

Except for this morning. Last night, she'd collapsed into bed after a packed two-day trip to Cardiff with her boss, Mike, and she neglected to stoke up the boiler. The cat had made a beeline for the warmest spot and waited for Bethan to give it a saucer of warm milk. After spending the night scrapping with local toms, it appreciated these minor considerations, but today, it was to be disappointed. Bethan lit the gas oven and opened the door, but the single row of burners was far too meagre to warm up the cold linoleum the same way. Today, the cat felt Bethan's hospitality sadly lacking.

Unable to settle on the cold lino, the cat jumped onto the table while Bethan read the leaflet. With catlike reasoning, it decided the distraction made this a perfect time to stick its tongue in her breakfast. When it finished, it stalked across the table, beady eyes scanning the kitchen in search of food, then curled itself around the old brown tea cosy to extract some warmth. Bethan's mam knitted the cosy during the great war, and she was not prepared to share it with the local moggy. She moved the teapot away, although she understood how the cat felt. Her only dressing gown was thin and inadequate, and the coldness of the floor chilled the soles of her feet through her slippers.

Wrapping her hands around the teacup, she tried to warm her cold fingers. The steam thawed her nose, and she wrinkled up her face. How long could she string out the entire pot before she had to brave the cold, have a wash, run to the post office, and on to work?

She eyed the cat, then tossed the leaflet in its direction.

"Puss. I said, get off!" The cat blinked. Why on earth was the woman making such a fuss?

The leaflet missed, but not to be bested, Bethan picked up the cat and scooted the ball of fluff outside, allowing herself a hint of guilt as frosty air blasted around her knees.

The cat would doubtless go next door to Mrs Higgins, who encouraged the animal's opportunistic tastes more than anyone in the entire row. Besides, it would have to get used to her not being here. In a few months, she would be in the nurses' home at the Alice Maud Hospital in London. This house, its memories, narrow stairs, historical society, and stray cat would be left far behind.

The tin pail Bethan kept for kitchen rubbish beckoned, and it received the toast with a single toss from her plate. She took a biscuit from the biscuit barrel and dunked it into her tea. Half got soggy and slopped off, and she fished it out inelegantly with her fingers. The other half teetered precariously before almost meeting the same fate, but she saved it with an uncouth slurp. Just one of the little idiosyncrasies a woman living alone could afford without worrying about manners.

Despite her tiredness after her long trip, Bethan had not slept well. Tossing and turning, she couldn't stop glancing at the clock on her nightstand, groaning each time she did, and measuring how much sleep she could manage before the alarm.

Bethan hated oversleeping. Losing minutes in the morning found her chasing seconds later in the day, as if she had to make use of every moment of her waking hours. She had a strict habit of never forgetting to set the alarm, even on days she didn't need to go to her job as a secretary. Last night, she finally dropped off to sleep in the small hours and didn't hear it. Now, her routine disrupted; she felt disordered and last minute. A feeling she hated.

Her kitchen reflected her neat and ordered life. Plain

blue curtains covered a sash window that suffered a residual griminess impossible to scrub clean. This morning, lacy ice patterns from the morning frost adorned the window, framing the face of a disgruntled cat that had perched itself on the windowsill.

The kitchen was Bethan's favourite room and cosy enough, provided she remembered to stoke up the boiler. If she stood at the sink and reached out, she could almost touch the wall near the back door. If she leant the other way, she could not quite touch her gran's Welsh dresser, a veritable museum of good porcelain pieces, all attractively arranged with her granddad's Davy lamp in pride of place.

The house was for sale, so Bethan saw no point in making changes. It was fine like it was. The dresser, the table and the tatty fireside chair fitted well enough, and Bethan rather liked the set-up, even though you could only take a couple of steps in any direction before you knocked into something. In a few months, she would leave for London. Travelling would be the fulfilment of a childhood dream, not just the opportunity to get away from the village. After completing her three-year training, she planned to join her brother in Australia. Owen suggested she just come and not bother about nursing, but her ambition had turned into a burning passion.

Besides, she had no desire to be a burden to him, and the nineteen-fifties were shaping up to be the dawn of a new era for women. No longer requiring a man to direct their fortunes, they were now forging ahead with their independence, and Bethan refused to be under anyone's thumb. So far, she avoided any romantic entanglements that might lead to marriage.

Self-sufficient and modern. That's how Bethan saw her future, and with the weeks ticking down until she left this godforsaken place, she looked forward to London sweeping her old life away.

Still, these last few months before heading for London felt like a prison sentence, so she concentrated on the few loose ends she still had to tie up. As with all her habits, Bethan had them all knotted together to deal with in order.

Today though, her mind and body felt troubled and out of place. Even the surrounding air seemed to ripple with—she couldn't put a finger on the feeling—impending change. She put it down to the upcoming move, which might have convinced her if the dream hadn't returned the previous night. A dream she'd had since boarding school.

It started the same, here, in this house, as she was now, a woman in her twenties, dark hair, well-dressed, but it always moved backwards in time. As the dream progressed, filthy rags replaced her clean clothes. She couldn't stand upright, and her knees ached. The surrounding village was Llanbleddynllwyd, but the cottages were wrong; set out where the park should be rather than up the hillside. The people's physical condition, and those of the street, filled her with horror. She never lingered in this scene because as the stench of sickness assaulted her nostrils, it moved on, only long enough for her to get a sense of being a pretender there. Other scenes, unfolding like a carousel, transported her to places unfamiliar. Some were grim and dark, with terrifying images of castles and dungeons, war, armour, and the clashing of swords and spears. Each time, sticky fluid spattered against her face and the salty taste turned her stomach. Then, with a silent scream, she would step back, her fingers running with the thick blood that trickled from her neck and soaked into the brocade of her courtly clothing.

She willed herself not to linger there. The violence was almost beyond her comprehension, and sometimes the dream allowed her to move on. At others, like a captor, a jailer, it forced her to observe. It should have brought her comfort, knowing it was not real, that she could not be witnessing a terrible event, but the unforgiving visions seemed to gain pleasure in making her relive the experiences.

There was always one part her sleeping self never failed to anticipate. The most vivid, terrifying, and detailed images that came right at the end. Even when she woke before the scene, nerves tingling, the dream would bookmark that point and continue as soon as she closed her eyes, urging her on to its conclusion.

It never varied. Rather than observe the events, Bethan became a player. Choking ash and an acrid stench of sulphur drove so far down into her body, she felt her sleeping self try to dredge her lungs of debris and clear her airway. The fear and confusion always remained well into the following day, but despite the intense physical component, never once did she find an escape in waking up during the dream. The single, familiar thing was a lucky charm she held in her hand.

Last night, formerly vague aspects of the dream sharpened in their focus. The fish market on the edge of the water, the face of the man, Tullius, who begged her to save his infant. This time, she heard her own voice as he laid the baby in her arms. The voice of a child, alone and terrified.

"Master…"

Bethan paused in her analysis to fetch another biscuit and tip the last of the tea into her cup. Instead of steaming liquid, a slurping sludge of tea leaves slid out of the spout. Disappointed, Bethan shoved the entire biscuit into her mouth. She just had to dismiss the dream, as unpleasant as it was, and the fact it was recurring. It was plain foolish to give it too much air. If she examined the reasons it happened, it was likely a result of memories of the dust-laden breezes that wafted her way from the spoil tip.

Bethan pulled the tea cosy off the pot and tipped the remaining leaves into the sink, idly watching them scatter up the side and make funny patterns before she swilled them around the plughole. Then, humming a random medley of tunes, she rinsed the last leaves away and waited for the kettle to boil for her morning wash. As a rule, there would be hot water left in the boiler, but without a fire under it, the boiler couldn't contend with the fact that winter had declined to give way to spring.

The kitchen was too cold to expose any skin, so Bethan performed her morning wash under her dressing gown with a certain amount of awkwardness. As she washed, her stockings and underwear warmed in front of the oven. She dressed hastily, applied a dab of lipstick, and combed her smooth, shoulder-length black hair. Almost ready to step out the front door, Bethan arranged her pillar box-red everyday hat on her head and pulled her coat from the peg in the hall. A grey and unsettled Welsh morning greeted her outside. A dissonant overture to whatever the day might bring.

CHAPTER TWO _

"Step back, Phildre. Step back!"

The comms echoed with only the roar of the volcano, and Chief Jardin had no way of knowing if the interventionist heard him or not. It was like Phildre to ignore orders, but she underestimated the timing of this event. It should not have progressed so rapidly, and he heaved a sigh of relief when he heard muttered cursing and "Stand by…" A woman's voice, her commentary drowned by the deafening crash of the exploding mountain. For an agonising second, Jardin prayed to any gods who might listen that Phildre had not stacked the odds against herself. She never lost a wager against any disaster she came up against, at least until now.

He yelled again. "Phildre! Step back! It's too dangerous!"

No matter what Phildre did now, it was too late to change the outcome of this eruption altogether, but that wasn't important. Whatever happened down there, Jardin had to get the interventionist out of harm's way. Her reply, unlikely to be compliant until she accomplished her task, became lost amid the shattering rock and magma.

Chief Jardin took a deep breath, suspending all movement while he directed his senses towards the communication relay. He didn't breathe again until he heard a muffled, *"Almost there. Something's happening… Chief, the pennant…"*

He would have words with the lieutenant about protocol, not that it was likely to do any good. She did things her way, and any moment now, she would step from the spiral onto the deck, a little singed perhaps, and more than a little angry a pennant played up. A first. And he could imagine Phildre's irritation that it happened on her watch.

He moved to the spiral conduit landing to await her arrival in case she needed help, but in the single heartbeat between Phildre's last words, Jardin moving to the landing, and the spiral returning, the interface lost sight of her.

The spiral conduit's task was to deliver an interventionist to the volcano to complete her work. At her command, it would retract to the ship with her aboard and direct its version of the mission to the interface. Except no-one issued a retract order, and the spiral returned empty.

From the spiral's local view and the interface's wider sensors, the two versions of events should match. This time, they conflicted. The interface had lost sight of the interventionist, but the spiral considered her to be retrieved. It deposited the equipment and pennants Phildre took with her on the deck, intact.

At a loss to understand why the spiral was empty, Jardin turned to the interface for an explanation.

Unfortunately, it had none, so together, they reviewed the data the spiral relayed to the interface. While it reported safe retrieval of the pennants and the interventionist, plus a potential sixty percent reduction of the catastrophe, it did not concur with the interface's data from the same time frame. The interface could only assure Chief Jardin that Phildre's life signs still registered.

Previous losses of interventionists usually resulted from falling during contact with the planet. If such a fate befell Lieutenant Phildre, why couldn't the interface establish a physical location? Jardin also speculated flying debris knocked her a distance outside the spiral's scope. Both were valid theories, but neither explained the life signs at the original coordinates. Also, Phildre was not like other interventionists. And this didn't add up.

Jardin ran through several scenarios with the interface. Could the inhabitants have observed her on the mountain and perhaps used a weapon against her? What is the possibility unknown technology detected the spiral and her presence? The interventionists did not routinely follow the planet's technological advancement, but as this world had not yet achieved space travel, they were confident the civilisations were still primitive. The spirals possessed phase technology, so until Phildre made physical contact with the planet, she would be hidden, therefore only vulnerable to scans or weapons during those few moments.

In Phildre's hands, the calamitous event unfolding on the world below should have been little more than a squeak and a puff of smoke, but it represented a failure on the interventionist's part. To be fair, not a total failure but far more than Phildre would find acceptable. Despite this, the events could have nothing to do with her not returning to the ship nor her steady life signs.

On the face of it, there was little to separate this geological event from other catastrophes Phildre attended. It was routine and unremarkable, except for the glaring discrepancies with the more comprehensive sensors of the interface and Phildre's apparent, albeit brief, struggle with the laying down of a pennant. Even on repeat examination and diagnostics by the interface, the spiral continued to affirm the interventionist's delivery back to the ship.

Jardin summoned his second officer, Lieutenant Merris, who viewed the array of information on display.

"What happened?"

"Phildre's missing."

Merris pointed to a data tile. "Not according to her life signs."

"Yes, but she's not at the site. Corky can't find her."

Merris checked out the spiral data, ignoring her rising sense of panic because there might be a simple answer. Although she couldn't think of one. In her years on this ship, she had not encountered a malfunction, although anything that involved Phildre had the potential to be out of the ordinary. She asked the chief if something could have interfered with the spiral report, suggesting it might be Lyran tech left on the planet or sabotage by another species. It was a thought. Jardin told her the interface found nothing out of the ordinary in orbit and showed her the contradictory spiral report.

Interventionist crews were well acquainted with spiral

technology. A simple construction, much like an interior elevator used in buildings on many worlds, spirals possessed superior speed and phase capability. Its purpose was to deliver organics and carry-on equipment to preset planetary coordinates. Spirals also performed narrow-beam view recordings of proceedings at a deposit/retrieval site and monitored the organic's position. At a signal, either from the interface or the passenger, the spiral would return to the exact location where the passenger embarked. On arrival, it correlated its narrow-beam data with the ship. In this case, the command to retract came from neither the interface nor Phildre herself.

However, they agreed on one point. The spiral data was incomplete or inaccurate. The interface reported Phildre's life signs remained steady despite her absence and confirmed they stemmed from her last known coordinates, which would mean she was in the eruption's path. Jardin and the interface went through every data tile received directly to the ship, then dissected the slices of information received from the spiral. None provided any answers.

The time frame exceeded only a few minutes after Phildre made her preparations. Most of the work took place on the ship before contact with the planet, and the act of spiralling down to set the pennants took mere moments. Once on the planet and pennants set, it would be job done, disaster averted. It should have been that simple. Phildre never failed to accomplish her task, and although she sometimes liked to clown around before returning, she would do nothing to worry her crewmates.

Jardin just didn't understand how Phildre physically

disappeared from sensors. If she fell or suffered an injury, locating her would be easy. If she were dead, perhaps because of the burning rocks, her life signs would register as extinct, not pulsing away steadily on her profile. He reran the options and data. Phildre's life signs gave him considerable hope, but the inconsistencies confused him. Even the interface's assurances it found no evidence of a retract request to the spiral and no interruptions to the operation offered no clues. Regardless, Jardin ordered several diagnostic reruns. Each time, all ship's systems returned as functional throughout.

The rapid progress of the eruption was another puzzling development. Phildre detected its coming to life at the first rumble, and it was still quiet when she stepped onto the spiral. So why did all hell break loose seconds later? Jardin had seen many volcanoes and witnessed Phildre set the calming pennants to soothe. Never once had a mountain behaved in this way. She didn't stand a chance. There wasn't even time to ignite a positional beacon that might lead them to her if she found a hiding place amid all that geological might.

Phildre's profile continued to draw his gaze. It reassured him she was not dead, but with such conflicting data and the evidence of the eruption in progress on the world below, it undermined his confidence in the interface. Still, the quality of her life signs made him once again comb through the spiral data.

He ran his hand through his hair. What were they missing? Phildre never used the term "stand by". She got in, did her work, sometimes made a few amusing observations, and left. Why did she need him to "stand by"? Was this because of the pennant? She never officially reported it malfunctioned. That was just an unchecked assumption by him as he searched for clues. Perhaps her suit suffered damage? That would certainly put her at risk. Or the pennant itself could have connected with an unknown external data stream not recognised by the ship's sensors.

None of it seemed likely. Jardin was clutching at straws, but he knew Phildre was a gambler. She liked to pit herself against the catastrophes, often spiralling into the depths of where the chaos would arise, to strike at its very heart, testing the limits of her courage while she saved the planet from disaster. She was not averse to risk. In truth, she was too confident even to see some of her behaviours *as* a risk. That made Jardin wonder. Did the risk-taking Phildre encounter something unexpected on the mountainside, causing her to hesitate? Did it mean her luck ran out? These were possibilities, as were others they might still discover, but Phildre's stable life signs told Jardin this was not the day she pushed her luck as far as it could go.

Phildre's sense of the sabotage left on the planet by the Lyran Monks was matched only by her impeccable timing. On so many occasions, she single-handedly saved entire societies that would otherwise suffer devastation by a volcanic eruption or swallowed by an earthquake or tsunami. None of the other eight interventionists had Phildre's sensitivity, and the fact this mission had such a measure of failure added to the puzzle.

The volcano spilled its boiling anger down its sides and towards the civilisations at its base, and the interface recast its sensors in an ever-widening arc. It could offer no explanation why a link between the lieutenant's new coordinates and her biosigns could not be established. It concurred with the chief's appraisal. The lieutenant had to be somewhere in the vicinity.

In considering the conflicting data, Jardin tried not to doubt the interface's competence. Corky was his best bet in locating and rescuing Phildre, so he examined every second of the mission, tile by tile.

Phildre analysed geological, topographical, and habitational information immediately sensors alerted her of a change in gases and movement of magma. Following her deliberations, she identified the precise positioning of the calming pennant vaults with her usual uncanny knack. This would offer optimum efficiency to the erasure beams that penetrated the heart of the mountain, spreading balm deep into the planet's layers and displacing the energy into the vault.

Laying the pennants took less than fifteen minutes, but when Jardin considered Phildre's comment before she disappeared, it sounded like one pennant had become compromised. Without more information, it could have been in detecting the plate or shifting the energy as designed. Judging by the result—he glanced out of the viewport—at least part of the mountain's force escaped and now unleashed destruction and death on the local inhabitants.

Phildre had sent him a cheery salute as she stepped into the spiral. For her, it was just another pennant placement, another day at the office. Had she become complacent? Too *certain?* The scale of this catastrophe had the potential to split the continent in two, but between Phildre and the pennants, the rumblings should have been barely noticed by the locals. An explanation for the failure could be that only one pennant absorbed and contained the mountain's power, but there was no way of finding out if the second pennant malfunctioned. Only the Nobles, the pennant keepers, could disassemble the pennant housing.

Overconfidence, arrogance, recklessness, Jardin dismissed them all. No matter how this turned out, a tragedy was spreading throughout the world below. Not least the potential loss of Phildre.

CHAPTER THREE _

"How many interventionists have miscalculated, suffered injury or become lost on a volcano, Corky?" Jardin asked the mainframe interface that ran the ship from its most basic propulsion to life support. Phildre had named it "Corky" because she decided "interface" sounded unsociable.

"No miscalculations, Chief," Corky replied. "We have lost one hundred and thirty-nine interventionists to mishap over the last sixteen hundred years. Forty-seven have been on volcanos."

"Does this volcano contain elements capable of shielding organics from sensors?" Jardin said before adding, "Nooks? Crannies? I'm asking if she could have found shelter."

"No, Chief, the volcano is a basic compound of…"

Jardin raised his hand to stop the interface from giving him a science lesson.

"I need to know how flesh and blood, caught up in a catastrophic event at the mouth of a volcano, still registers life signs. Ergo, not dead. According to scans, not injured either." He highlighted Phildre's bio tile. "The lieutenant appears to be in as robust good health as when she left the ship. I'm sure you understand why I have little confidence in the initial reports, so scan for any crevasse or elements that may shield her. Also, discount the location of her life signs and broaden your sensor arc to look for signs the spiral tossed her away from her coordinates. She could be injured at the base of the mountain."

"I have, Chief," the interface responded. "I can't trace the lieutenant, but I will reiterate that her life signs remain at the coordinates. It is improbable she is at the base or anywhere else on the mountain, and I cannot explain why her life signs are steady and emanating from her original position. Visuals inform me she is not there."

"Check again."

The interface expected the chief to explore every avenue for an answer. It was protocol, even if it was to ultimately prove unsuccessful. The interface had no answers either, only identifying the interventionist did not fall in the few moments it took her to connect with the mountain and lay the pennants. She did not step back onto the spiral either, but as per the chief's instructions, it went through the changing environment on the mountain, even extrapolating likely scenarios. Each time, it came up with nothing. The interface considered every probability, but a missing organic in a field of lava, exhibiting life signs, had never happened before.

An interventionist ship's interface was designed for independent thought, but at their most fundamental, they dealt with data. Verifiable data. The interface would have preferred any explanations it presented to have a foundation, but it had none, and in its experience, humans sometimes made mistakes.

"Lieutenant Phildre may have become distracted, Chief. If the pennant failed…"

Jardin had discounted interventionist error and scoffed at the suggestion. The interface had highlighted another unusual circumstance, which was the possible failure of the pennant. There was not a single incidence of pennant failure recorded throughout history, but they had to be missing something. He swiped to the spiral tile that showed Phildre attempting to set the second pennant.

"The event is diminished," Jardin said, "but the effect of this eruption will be devastating. From her comment, I think Phildre experienced difficulties with the pennant, but Phildre error and pennant failure are as inconceivable as the probability of sensor malfunction." He shook his head. All this was just so… *inconceivable.* "Let's go with the life signs for now and assume she has either found shelter or, as unlikely as it sounds, somehow removed by persons undetected by our sensors."

For ten years, Jardin had been commander of this vessel. He believed himself a clear thinker, not easily rattled, but the speed of the volcanic activity on the planet below contradicted and stretched everything he knew. Phildre's life signs gave him hope, but it would be only a matter of time before magma ripped the mountain apart, and that hope would be lost. He tapped the last two data tiles. Phildre was there. Then she was not. How could she just vanish?

Jardin and Merris worked through the mission

parameters. It was straightforward. Phildre performed computations for the depth of the energy rods that linked the pennant to the mountain, detected a suitable zone and transported via the phase spiral to the mountain to lay the pennant vaults. The pennants should have reduced the effects of a significant volcanic eruption to a mere grumble and minor shaking. While it seemed uncomplicated in theory, it required someone with sensitivity, an instinct for timing. Phildre had that instinct.

Jardin looked towards the viewport as if it would reveal more about the situation than the most sophisticated instruments in the galaxy could. But he was human. Sometimes it was simpler to believe his eyes. The mountain spewed forth tephra, and the flaming clouds now billowed into the atmosphere. Even in an environmental suit, if one of those rocks now battering the surroundings hit her, it would be like a missile. She couldn't survive, yet her life signs told them otherwise. He muttered under his breath. *Where in the hell is she?*

"If she stepped up to re-engage the spiral at the exact point it retracted," he asked the interface, "where else could she have made planetfall?"

"I scanned the region, Chief," the interface restated. "A reflex spill from a spiral would only result in a rebound of three local sectors at most, no more. She followed all protocols, except when she ignored your orders to step back, but she never listens to orders, so that is not unexpected."

Jardin knew that only too well. "Rescan for bio-traces on the spiral, unexpected posture, single footfall. Then, try scanning the area further out from the volcano's current reach, at a distance of one hundred zones."

The interface saw no point in the exercise unless Lieutenant Phildre had inexplicably learned how to fly. "Chief," it said. "It is futile to attempt a reconciliation between a physical location within such a broad environment and the lieutenant's life signs. She can only be in one place."

Jardin knew that. "She didn't reconnect with the spiral," he said. "But we know she is alive, although we can no longer assume her location. Your sensors and what I can see through the viewport tell me it is impossible. As you say, you are functioning at optimal capacity, so we must turn our attention to the possibility that something on the planet is causing this disparity. Keep your search ahead of the event."

Merris, who considered herself Phildre's best friend, allowed herself to follow the events with increasing dismay. While she had unfailing faith in the interface's competence, she busied herself examining every slice of sensor log. Phildre's life signs read as normal besides an elevation in pulse, cortisol, and adrenalin, but that was expected given the nature of an interventionist's work. No-one could go into these situations without an element of fear, or in Phildre's case, adventure, but the progress of the eruption and Phildre's presumed proximity to the mouth of the volcano brought the sensor's results into question. Phildre was remarkable, but she was still flesh and bone. No life could withstand direct contact with that heat.

Fighting mounting sadness and resignation that she

might have lost her friend, Merris pushed aside each tile, confident the chief and the interface had reviewed each in painstaking detail. She couldn't match Corky's thoroughness, but for the woman she looked on as a sister, she had to satisfy herself.

The only element out of place on the data tile was that the mission logged as a single degree behind time. That might have troubled Phildre, who liked timetables, but with no external signs of an eruption, Merris could disregard that degree. Besides, Phildre never turned up late for any party. She listened to Phildre's commentary during her positioning of the first pennant, then her cursing as she contended with the second. Merris grinned a little. Phildre had a store of lively expletives, but that struggle gave the mountain just enough time to come to life, resulting in Phildre having less time to complete her task.

Merris was also an interventionist who understood this world, perhaps not with the same affinity as Phildre, but how could a mountain go from simple volcanic deformation to a full-blown eruption in minutes? None of this made sense. It was as if time itself had sped up.

Phildre's success rate in alleviating these disasters, and there was no way of knowing which were Lyran sabotage and which were natural, held an unbeaten one hundred percent. Her success as an interventionist was legendary. None had ever been as intuitive or as effective as Phildre. It was shocking to think she might join the ranks of those lost over the centuries. Phildre possessed such a drive to help the human world, to defeat the inhumane legacy of the Lyrans. And so far, she had never failed.

Tears pricked behind Merris's eyes, but she would not give in to despair, not while Phildre's life signs remained steady. The tiles gave her nothing, so she froze the tile sequencing and closed her eyes so she might think with no distractions.

The three crewmates had been friends for the past three years since Phildre's assignment to this ship. Merris couldn't imagine any existence without her outgoing, funny, unpredictable, and colourful friend. The three had become close, even spending their off-duty time together. What if she was really gone?

Merris realised she was losing hope. Thinking of Phildre in the past tense would do no-one any good, so she blinked open her eyes. Phildre did not belong in the past. Not yet.

Sniffing, Merris wiped away a single tear with the heel of her hand. The last tile she viewed hovered before her. It gave no clues…

She leaned forward and narrowed her eyes.

"What the…?"

How could she have missed the almost imperceptible smudge that obscured the outline of her friend? She had studied the tile before closing her eyes and was sure she missed nothing, although maybe in her distress, she hadn't paid sufficient attention.

No, that smudge wasn't there before. She flicked back to the preceding tile. No smudge, but it was on two following tiles, so she checked the timeframes. The blemish's appearance corresponded with the exact point Phildre appeared to struggle with the pennant. Then, with the rest of her commentary lost, she disappeared from the ship's sensors. So why didn't the spiral or the interface sensors register this blemish?

Merris overlaid the spiral data from the corresponding timeframes. The first showed no smudge, but it appeared in front of Phildre on the second and again on the next. When Merris examined the tile where Phildre vanished, the smudge remained. So, why did the spiral report her as retrieved? Could the spiral view the smudge as organic and think it was Phildre? Whatever happened might have been beyond the spiral's scope to record, but one thing was for sure, it wasn't a sensor ghost. Not on this ship. She pulled back the tile and called out to Jardin, pointing out the shadowy mark.

"Chief, what do you think this smudge is?"

Jardin peered at the tile and tried to make sense of the ill-defined, ghostly image. It was small, occupying only a tiny section of the tile and covering like a patch on Phildre's shoulder. Yet, he hadn't seen it prior.

"Corky," he said. "Explanation?"

Corky enlarged the image. "An anomaly, Chief. An artefact from the volcano. It appears insignificant. Lieutenant Merris's description is adequate. It's a smudge."

Merris folded her arms. "From what, Corky? A fingerprint? Did someone put their cup on it? And why wasn't it there before? Under the circumstances, nothing is insignificant. Artefacts are common on drag trader sensors, and we might expect them from low-level sensors on bottom-of-the-range shuttles, but on the most sophisticated technology in the galaxy, you dismiss this as an artefact? Do me a favour! Could this 'artefact' be an echo of Lyran technology?"

Jardin agreed. It warranted investigation.

"It will be an enormous coincidence if it's not related to Phildre's disappearance," he said. "The mark overlays her in the seconds before she disappears. There is no evidence she, the pennant, or the volcano is generating this anomaly. Corky, repeat the analysis."

Corky hesitated. He needed to examine how the smudge got past his initial examination, although it was as it appeared, a smudge, a blemish. He made a visual analysis to humour the crew so they might arrive at a like conclusion. Humans liked to suppose they didn't need to rely on an interface's superior results.

He came up with nothing specific to report.

"As you can determine for yourself," he said, "The information it yields falls below the parameters for further inquiry. It has no technological or geological attributes I can work with, and while I concede it overlays Lieutenant Phildre, the irregularity does not possess human attributes either. It could be a simple concentration of vapour arising from the volcano, but I determine this anomaly has nothing to add to the prevailing situation."

"Vapour clouds have properties you can analyse."

"Yes, Lieutenant Merris, but this does not have the attributes of vapour. I was offering a comparison."

"Then what attributes does it have? It has to be something."

"I can speculate it is from the volcano. It might be '*something*', but under the circumstances, further investigation might distract us from locating Lieutenant Phildre."

"The spiral also recorded these tiles before it retracted," Merris said. "So if 'something' snatched Phildre from the spiral landing or the planet, wouldn't it have recorded an unauthorised movement?"

"It would, Lieutenant Merris," Corky yielded, "but if she had already stepped back, therefore concluding the mission, there would be no recording."

"And there is no evidence Phildre called the spiral to withdraw?"

"Correct. Something else prompted the response."

"We all agree there is a 'something'," Jardin said. "Corky, let us suppose that whatever this is exists as something other than an artefact or vapour. Is there any way you can extrapolate from its coordinates where it originated?"

"Chief, it might just be a sensor ghost, not of Phildre, but a glitch, an artefa…"

Jardin glared. Sometimes he wondered about interfaces, why the Nobles made them so they could argue back. He knew it was because the interfaces could enter debates, but they didn't need it on this ship.

"I *know*," he growled. "An artefact, a shadow, vapour. Please don't run through everything it *might* be. I want to know what it *is* and why it turned up right when we lost a crew member and, at the exact point a pennant supposedly failed. Merris is right. It can't be a coincidence. While you're at it, find out how the hell we missed it in our first analysis."

Hope of finding Phildre alive on the mountain began

to fade, and Corky could not locate her at any distance. Phildre would have been glad she at least partially mitigated this event. No doubt the Lyran Monks would have made sure this eruption had the potential to inflict widespread devastation on the planet. Just one more disaster averted that this planet had to thank Phildre for, along with all the interventionists who went before.

The humans of this world didn't know the Nobles were looking out for them, ensuring their civilisation continued with as minor inconvenience as possible. However, interventionists didn't stop all volcanic eruptions or earthquakes because there were certain natural events in which an interventionist had no place. The civilisations below would never learn of the care taken by the Nobles and their human fleet to undo the work of the Lyran Monks, the human-looking, silent invaders that harvested the early humans as slaves before the Nobles intervened. As payback, and in their dying days, the Lyrans placed devices in weaker, sensitive areas that would, over time, magnify many natural disasters and wreak havoc on the planet. The Nobles never discovered those devices, and even now, their locations remained a mystery. Still, the interventionist fleet's vigilance had reduced those threats for the last sixteen hundred years.

As the minutes passed and the volcanic plume rose higher into the atmosphere, neither Merris nor Jardin came up with any theories about the anomaly. They both refused to accept Corky's suggestion of a sensor glitch or artefact, although they conceded they didn't have a better explanation. Meanwhile, despite that sector now suffering a deluge of tephra, sensors continued to list their missing colleague in vigorous good health at her last known coordinates. Considering the unexpected discovery of the "smudge", they reviewed the spiral data and found nothing changed, continuing to list Phildre as on board. The interface repeated its assertion that evaluation of the sensors showed them to be operating at peak efficiency.

While declining to concede the possibility of the volcano affecting sensor data, the interface suggested Phildre's disappearance may relate to the failed pennant. However, as far as could be told, the pennant appeared viable. In simple terms, calming vault pennants, an invention of the ancient Nobles, could transmit a beam that reached far below into the planet's crust. The beam, or the erasure, assimilated the energy that calmed the heart of an angry mountain and settled the hidden world below the planet's outer surface. It displaced the rampant energy into a vault, moving it out of phase as it calmed. The energy would not be recovered from the pennant vault, nor did it need to be disposed of. Some speculated the pennants were time machines, a theory never confirmed nor denied by the Nobles. Only they knew what happened within the vault, and they weren't telling. A race that revelled in their enigma, the Nobles perpetuated their mystery, reducing anything any other race believed of them to the level of myth or supposition.

Ship's interfaces, also designed by the Nobles, did not have pennant specifications in their program. Because it had little else to offer, Corky suggested the possibility, while realising the crew would consider it preposterous, was that the pennant did not fail. He speculated that somehow, the extraordinarily accurate Phildre got careless—she had been consuming alcohol the previous night—and Phildre entered the vault. Of course, the interface did not factor in how the pennant would channel a flesh and bone individual, but given they knew so little of the pennants' other capabilities, could it be possible?

Merris and Jardin's incredulous looks spoke reams, and Jardin voiced his scorn. Yes, it was preposterous, reminding the interface that first pennants took energy, not physical matter, and second, the pennant had returned to the ship. Phildre's life signs emanated from the planet. That's where she had to be. Last, and just as importantly, Phildre could drink them all under the table with no ill effects.

Merris nodded. The interface must be struggling to come up with that suggestion. Still, she hadn't seen Jardin this rattled in a long time.

"That's not a theory we even need to explore, Corky," she said. "I propose we take the spiral as close to the planet as possible for a manual visual."

For what seemed like the thousandth time in the past hour, Jardin looked out the viewport at the carnage on the planet below. He turned to Merris.

"Look for yourself. I cannot risk either of us, just as I can't figure out why the mountain was quiescent one minute, then exploding the next. Phildre doesn't make those kinds of mistakes in her timing. I don't understand how it progressed at such a torrid pace." He frowned. "I've never seen anything like it."

"I will remind you, Chief," the interface cut in, "Lieutenant Phildre does like to wager. Perhaps, as she likes to say, she 'backed herself' regarding her timing and lost."

"Lost, Corky?" Jardin pointed to Phildre's profile. "She doesn't look 'lost'. She just isn't found."

Merris saw for herself the progress of the eruption.

"If we believe the sensors, Phildre has to be located—" she touched the tile, "right there, in the heart of all that chaos, all that fire. I'll risk a manual survey, and I won't leave the spiral."

Jardin refused to entertain the prospect that Phildre had become absorbed in the pennant or was waiting to be rescued from a field of flowing lava. If he chose the pennant theory, how would she even have life signs if the pennant dispersed her energy into some time void before today? And a lava field? It was too fantastic. He would not sanction Merris's volunteering for a mission that he could see with his own eyes could not succeed.

After a further hour of considering and poring over the data tiles until their eyes glazed over, and notwithstanding the life signs, none were closer to an answer. In addition, the interface had not submitted its analysis of the smudge.

Phildre's profile tile was audible, reciting its report of her life signs until her crewmates fell to silence and their own thoughts. Jardin picked up a glove and threw it at the tile, but the interface deleted the audio before the missile hit its target.

Five hours after his interventionist disappeared, five long hours of deliberating, formulating and reformulating, Jardin rubbed his hand over his face to dispel his grief and confusion.

Although her life signs still registered, and he didn't understand how, Phildre was gone. The smudge defied analysis, and a sensor sweep of the area turned up nothing. There were protocols to observe when an interventionist went missing, but Jardin had never needed to enact them. However, he doubted existing life signs in the interventionist's absence were a feature seen before.

Defeated, he called out to the interface.

"Corky, contact the Noble homeworld. We need guidance."

CHAPTER FOUR _

The modest craft that docked with the interventionist ship was of Noble design intended for use by senior police fleet officers. Unusually, it was phase enabled and modified for high manoeuvrability, suggesting a ship piloted by a hierarchical Noble. Little was known about the Nobles other than they settled their homeworld thousands of centuries before, never revealing their origins to the neighbouring star systems. Although some regarded them as xenophobic, the Nobles answered a call to aid the ten sectors in centuries gone by when that corner of the galaxy was under siege by pirates and cartels. In response to the crisis, the Nobles created and maintained a police fleet to protect the ten-sector region, an undertaking it continued at the request of the ten-sector council, even after the greatest threats were subdued or eliminated.

The interventionist fleet was not part of that agreement and operated outside the ten-sector governance. The planet the Nobles protected wasn't even in their region, but they secured an undertaking from the ten-sector council that no ship other than those displaying a Noble flag could approach. They agreed to this in gratitude for the Nobles making the sector safe.

The Noble homeworld also had a secondary culture, the tribal ordinaries, from the same genetic pool. Tribal ordinaries were charged with maintenance and management of Noble ships, including those used by the interventionist crews and the police fleet.

Jardin expected a tribal ordinary, so a hierarchy ship was an unwelcome surprise, as was the pilot.

Typical of a Noble, the man was tall, wiry, with silvery hair that stretched from his face in a half-braid, exposing a pallid complexion. Dressed from neck to foot in black, the Noble stepped from the spiral onto the bridge, his unblinking gaze shifting between Chief Jardin and Merris, then to the view of the world below. For several minutes, expressionless and silent, he studied the fiery scene unfolding on the planet.

Interventionists seldom interacted with Nobles, although in an official sense, the Nobles were their employers. The hierarchy selected each member of their interventionist and police fleets, but the contact ended there, except in rare, formal meetings. Tribal ordinaries carried out all training, even with the pennants, which were only ever accessed by touch through a housing, never by sight.

Tribal ordinaries did not suffer the same hierarchical cultural attitudes but acknowledged the hierarchy as the ruling class, an attribution all hierarchical Nobles accepted. The hierarchy claimed admiration and honour for all technological advances, even though it was widely believed the development and application of those technologies became the domain of the tribal ordinaries. The truth was, no-one knew. Most was rumour, but a common saying among the interventionists was that tribal ordinaries may not always be the brains behind the operation, but they were always the builders. Not enough was known about the structure of the society to judge the hierarchy as no other species had ever visited the Noble homeworld. Instead, a vast pontoon attached to the shipyard orbited the planet as a place to receive guests and dignitaries.

Jardin was one of those who considered the hierarchy unfriendly and xenophobic. The ten-sector council built a colossal image to honour the Noble clan father who established the Grielik Police Fleet. Standing in the government's palatial forc-quadrangle and carved from local whitestone, the image was supposed to be a close likeness. If so, it was a good one because, in real life, the Nobles looked like chiselled smoothness. Like white statues. Jardin couldn't quite find an apt description for them, but if he had to choose a single word, it would probably be, well…*tight.*

Tribal ordinaries, although some had similar physical characteristics to Nobles, went out of their way to be helpful while remaining tight-lipped about their homeworld. And today, because he expected a tribal ordinary, a hierarchical Noble was enough to add to Jardin's angst, particularly as this Noble carried the distinguishing bold red stripe of the ruling house of Anevan over his shoulder.

Only on rare occasions did an officer request assistance, but just as rare was a Noble of any rank to appear in response. To the Noble hierarchy's mind, the duties of an interventionist were well suited to humans. This was their heritage world, and they ably carried out the Noble covenant to preserve this planet. Beyond the supply and maintenance of vehicles and equipment, contact was neither expected nor encouraged, and they tasked the tribal ordinaries with dealing with any issues the humans could not.

Jardin knew as much about the Nobles as anyone else, which was next to nothing, but he was sure they liked to cultivate the mystique surrounding them. Some worlds viewed them not only as a species but as a cult. Others feared them, and history saw them, at least since the Lyran problem, as the saviours of the ten sectors.

While Jardin found the Nobles visually bland, they possessed a startling, distinguishing feature seldom observed in the tribal ordinaries. A distinction Jardin found disconcerting. The tribal ordinaries had standard eyes, an iris, a reactive pupil, and sometimes tiny vestigial retinas. However, the eyes of the Noble ranks reflected a curious liquid goldenness, speckled like a sparrow's egg, each tiny speckle a retina that saw far more than the single eye of a human. These unique compound retinas enabled the Nobles to view the "chak" of any species except their own. It gave them the capacity to gauge desire, fear, guilt, and the effects of the previous week's events on a person's psyche and well-being. This ability did little to allay the concern of those species who mistrusted the Nobles. Jardin didn't like to be read without his consent, and he'd never met a Noble who asked first.

This Noble was different, and Jardin saw something in him he'd never encountered before. Although difficult to approach, members of the hierarchy were never rude, unlike the man before him, who appeared distracted and irritated. He didn't acknowledge Jardin and Merris, just watched the volcano from the viewport, arms folded. From what the two officers could tell, he seemed far more interested in the event than Phildre's disappearance.

"Do you believe this is a Lyran sabotage or one of your altruistic interventions to save the planet from a natural disaster?" he asked finally, the curtness of his tone making both Jardin and Merris bristle.

"It fits the scale of a Lyran sabotage, Noble," Jardin answered politely. He would have liked to have taken snideness up a notch, except those nuances were invariably lost on Nobles.

The Noble nodded towards the viewport.

"Then this volcano should not have erupted."

"We lost our interventionist during setting of the pennants."

The pale man flicked a glance at Jardin. "You report the interventionist failed to return with the phase spiral, that her location is at present unknown, and her life signs remain stable. Now you advise you 'lost' her? Do you wish to change your statement and inform us of a death?"

Jardin shook his head. "It is true we couldn't retrieve her, Noble, but we do not believe she is dead. The interface confirms she is not at her last known coordinates, but that is where her life signs arise. We can't explain why she appears to have vanished."

The Noble kept his eyes on the viewport, and Jardin fancied he lifted his chin a little as he delivered his condescending response.

"Chief, there are two outcomes from an intervention. Death or retrieval. There is never 'vanished'. Interface, display the relevant data tiles."

"Yes, Noble. These are the events of the last twenty hours. Lieutenant Phildre prescribed two vault pennants for the intervention. As you will see, she provided an incomplete commentary which implied complications with the second pennant. The spiral reported a sixty percent reduction in the volcanic event, but with two pennants, it should have been at least ninety-nine point nine. I cannot ascertain if the pennant failed, which might have led to unanticipated and reduced effectiveness."

The Noble watched the spiral conduit's perspective as the events unfolded. The mountain had already awoken as the interventionist carried out the task of laying the pennants. Despite the escalating and dangerous conditions, she slipped her hand into the housing of the first pennant to follow the plexus language and initiate the sequence. The spiral offered an excellent perspective of the procedure, and the pennant functioned as expected, reducing the mountain's power. As the interventionist turned her attention to the second pennant, she appeared to become distracted, glancing over her shoulder and raising her arm in a sweeping motion. The data from the spiral and data recorded by the ship's sensors differed from that point.

The Noble arranged each peripheral tile from both the spiral and the interface around the individual tile, which showed the interventionist's moment of distraction. Jardin and Merris also examined the tiles in silence, attempting to follow his train of thought.

The Noble spoke first.

"There was insufficient time for the two pennants to complete the calming before the spiral retracted," he said. Then he pointed to the blemish on Phildre's shoulder. "What is the origin of the mark overlying her upper body?"

"At our first and subsequent viewings, Noble," Jardin nodded to Merris, "neither we nor the interface noticed this smudge. The interface believes it to be irrelevant."

"Smudge? Chief Jardin? That is a scientific term I am not familiar with. Perhaps I can see where you cannot."

Oh, shut up, Jardin thought. *Even with all those retinas, you can't see what an interface can.*

With a sudden movement that pushed the two men apart, Merris shoved her arm between them to point at the anomaly. This was a surprising breach of protocol. No-one shoved superior officers, but she had spotted a critical development.

"Chief! Noble!" she cried urgently. "The smudge has changed. It doesn't have the same characteristics. Corky," she ordered without referring to either the Noble or the Chief, "Measure and compare the two tiles."

Corky complied. There were differences, minor but recordable.

Merris huffed out her breath at the interface. "You still say this is nothing?"

It drew a reaction from the Noble, who raised his eyebrows. That piqued his interest.

"The interface concluded this anomaly to be 'nothing'?" he asked.

"Yes, Noble," Jardin said, feeling a need to stick up for Corky. "In the absence of any supporting evidence, it came up with 'nothing to add to the current situation'."

The anomaly had no distinguishable features and no organic properties. The Noble saw that, yet it existed at this site. Why here? Why now? How could something grow or change on a data tile? *Unless…*

"Interface. What is your diagnostic status?"

"In nine hundred and forty-two diagnostics over the last twenty hours, Noble," Corky reported, "I have detected no malfunction."

The Noble had never met an interface that owned up to a malfunction. The unit had to be decommissioned to find any faults, and even then, it was rare. He ran back the data tiles.

"The interventionist appears distracted in the moments before her disappearance," he said. "Chief Jardin, I see you have investigated the possibility of other technologies, but there is no doubt she encountered something. Or someone."

Jardin had registered the slight movement of Phildre's head, but it would take a Noble's eyes to see what took place within her helmet. And she did move her arm. Merris thought it looked like she was catching something.

"I do not have your visual acuity, Noble," Jardin said, "But a simple movement of her head and arm would not necessarily be relevant. Just prior, I assumed she encountered difficulties with the second pennant, that given the outcome, perhaps did not activate, or if it did, failed to absorb."

"Have you considered other possibilities?"

"Such as further covert Lyran sabotage?"

"I meant geological variations in the underlying plate or planetary core. Lyrans were not precise with their science, and I doubt they had time to install a secondary device."

When he arrived, the Noble saw the concern and agitation of the two remaining crew members, although they tried to keep level heads, perhaps to avoid showing their emotion. Contrary to Jardin's belief, their visitor rarely read chak. He simply never bothered unless he had no alternative, and with these humans, he knew it would be natural they hoped their crewmate had survived. Their uncertainty about the anomaly's relevance to her disappearance was evident, heightened by the interface's erroneous assumption it was "nothing".

The interventionist was at least partially successful from what the Noble could see. Had she not, he would now be witnessing the destruction of half a continent. His change in focus gave Jardin a natural opportunity to speak. It felt foolish to voice Corky's suggestion after he so roundly dismissed it earlier, but Noble technology, at least what they shared, was as remarkable as it was unknown. It was worth a shot.

"Is there any way the second pennant took Phildre rather than drawing in the energy?"

Merris looked across at the chief, her eyes wide with disbelief. She would have kicked him in the shins had she been close enough.

The Noble was glad he had his back to them at that moment because he had to bite his lip against a grin. Smiling, grinning, laughing; such displays were the most un-Noble actions he could perform in the company of another species. So instead, he turned and fixed his gaze on the chief, delivering his retort with superior loftiness.

"Chief, never has a pennant 'failed' or confined an interventionist within its vault."

He kept his gaze on Jardin long enough to make the chief's blood boil. Jardin didn't even care if the Noble's all-seeing eyes saw it because so far, for all his cleverness, this Noble had no more answers than they did.

Merris shifted her position to look the Noble right in his remarkable eyes.

"I know it sounds crazy, but if not the pennant, if not the anomaly, then what? Noble, you have examined all the circumstances since she left the ship. She didn't fall, nor was she knocked to the ground or from the tray by the spiral. I believe that whatever caused this smudge has something to do with Phildre's disappearance, so why can't we define a source?"

The "smudges" presence troubled the Noble as much as it did the two crew members. He could not ignore its contribution. The interface had misinterpreted the gravity of the irregularity, but the second officer's outburst told him, without needing to check her chak, that both crew members were too emotional, so he directed his questioning towards the interface.

"The anomaly is first seen at the interventionist's right shoulder less than three seconds before her disappearance," he said. "Were there any changes in her life signs during the gathering of these two data tiles?"

"The lieutenant's life signs remained steady throughout, Noble."

"I see, just as they are now. Considering the changes in the anomaly, Interface, do you still report it as 'nothing'?"

The interface could make complex calculations far more efficiently than any living being, but its function was to be the ship's heart, keep everything working, and not unravel cosmic conundrums. This was outside its programming, and it was stumped.

"Noble," Corky said. "Anything I offer now is conjecture only. The data on the anomaly is inconclusive. There is no record of a similar phenomenon, and despite the obvious change, the anomaly could be a shadow, an artefact…."

The Noble turned his thoughts inwards while the interface rattled off its conjectures. To reach full potential, an interface required isolation from the central matrix, and authority for that did not lie with a chief interventionist. As it stood, the interface could not extrapolate a theory about the anomaly without further freedoms. No matter, he agreed with Merris and Jardin. This was not an artefact. The evidence was not clear enough for him to evaluate, and he could not attend the surface of this world to search for answers, but there was one thing Nobles shared with humans. Gut instinct. Only a fool would suppose there was no link between the two events, so he would investigate, but that investigation could not include the crew. Further, to rule out his suspicions of the anomaly, he needed this interface. So he ordered it to implement an immediate exchange with his ship.

Jardin and Merris exchanged bewildered looks.

"Why are you removing Corky?" Jardin asked. "You can transfer the data."

The Noble didn't need to justify his reasoning. He could do as he pleased with the technology.

"I understand that this is irregular and that you have suffered a personal catastrophe," he said. "If your distress is not too great, please return to your duties while I investigate."

Another bewildered look passed between Jardin and Merris. This Noble certainly knew how to dish out surprises. If he investigated, then he would need them as witnesses. Besides, Phildre was a crew member, so protocol demanded that they be involved. When Jardin protested, the Noble raised his hand.

"I have isolated the entire data stream for this incident. You will speak of it to no-one."

"Noble, we were here when this took place," Jardin pointed out, unwilling to back down. "Phildre is one of my crew, and we should be part of any investigation. So how can you ask us not to speak of it when I sent the notification to your homeworld? They will expect an update."

The Noble appeared untroubled. "Leave that to me."

Merris knew the Noble would have the final say in what went down, but she didn't like it either.

"Are you silencing Corky as well?" she demanded.

The Noble blinked. The crewman need not concern herself, but to say so might be inflammatory. Still, she made it clear she wasn't happy.

"And how will you mount a search? Nobles can't go to this planet…"

The Noble took a sharp breath, and Merris put a lid on her passion. Nobles rarely reprimanded, but she might have overstepped by making a personal comment about one of the few things his species couldn't do. But he didn't reprimand. Instead, his voice softened as if he realised the strong attachment between the three.

"Her life signs give confidence, Lieutenant Merris. I will do all in my power to locate her."

They had no option but to be satisfied with his assurances, except for one more thing. Phildre's family.

"She has an aunt," Jardin said. "Shall we notify her?"

The Noble didn't respond. His work here done, he turned on his heel and stepped into the spiral. Jardin and Merris watched him leave, and Corky transferred to the Noble's ship. Its counterpart linked, with no knowledge of the events of the last few hours.

"I suppose that means 'no'," Jardin said as the spiral disappeared. "Confidential it is. I don't think he even cares."

Merris watched the interface go through its reboot. She would miss Corky. Phildre gave it so many programming quirks it seemed almost human but was glad the Noble was gone. She asked the new interface for his name.

"Yi, heir to House Anevan, Lieutenant," it responded.

"House Anevan? Isn't House Anevan top brass Noble hierarchy?"

Jardin had recognised the Noble's insignia. He nodded.

"Not just hierarchy. The ruling house. He looks young

to be a clan father, so he must be an heir. I didn't think they ever left their homeworld. What was he doing here?"

"Perhaps he escaped. It would be tough being an heir. No wonder he's so frosty."

Jardin snorted. "The unified Grielik police force would hunt him down if he did that. His dad would never let him out of his sight. But he seemed to show a bit of sympathy in the end. Interface, can you tell us why Yianevan—" Jardin used the informal address of a Noble, "travels alone?"

"Negative, Chief. If anyone asks, the Noble programmed me to tell them to mind their own business."

That brought a cynical smile to Merris's face. "A Noble with a sense of humour? I would never have guessed."

But Jardin couldn't shake his puzzlement. "I don't know what's going on, Merris. Why would he swear us to secrecy? I don't get it. The past day has been a nightmare, and I thought he'd relieve us of duty while the investigation took place, but…."

He stopped to collect himself, then patted Merris on the shoulder. "It looks like you're the resident interventionist now."

Merris would have preferred a few hours off to collect her thoughts and garner some trust that the Noble had Phildre's interest at heart.

"He saw something in that anomaly, Chief," she said. "The way it… I dunno, *grew*. First, it wasn't there, then it was, then it got bigger, or at least more noticeable."

"Yeah, like it was forming or transitioning into something else."

Merris agreed. Forming, yes, that was a good word, but

it didn't make either of them feel any better.

"I think it was an alien."

Jardin rolled his eyes. "Merris, truly? An alien?"

"Well, you saw the way Yianevan studied it. The Nobles are inscrutable, so how would we know what he saw?"

"We wouldn't, and we answer to him as our current authority. So we will have to get on with our jobs and hope he does what he says he's going to."

"Don't you trust him?"

"It's not a question of trust, but I've never known a Noble to lie."

Merris rubbed her eyes and sat in the command chair. She felt almost too weary to continue and just wanted to sit here to gather her thoughts. Fortunately, Jardin wasn't territorial.

"I don't know if I can concentrate if we get another disaster," she sighed. "I'm not in Phildre's league, and I might make mistakes." She looked up, unsurprised to see Jardin looking every bit as weary.

"Chief," she said in a small voice. "I hope Philly's okay."

"All we can do is hope," Jardin said, trying to allow his professionalism to gain some ascension over his sadness. It wasn't working too well.

"The Noble took Phildre's pennants with him. If there's an issue, he'll find it."

"You don't really believe a pennant could displace an unphased person?"

Jardin threw his hands up in exasperation. He was such

an ass. Whatever made him mention it? And to a Noble of all people.

"I don't even know why I said it, Merris. We might work with them, but all we know about the pennants' construction is rumour. Pennants have power, and no-one knows how one might behave if unexpected circumstances present themselves."

"The Nobles know."

"Yeah, their big secret."

They both had to trust there might be answers that would only occur to a Noble, and even just to honour Phildre's commitment to her work, they had to continue. Besides, Yianevan was doubtless right to not include Jardin in an investigation. Everyone knew he was more than a little fond of Phildre.

CHAPTER FIVE _

The interface integrated into Yianevan's ship, anticipating its services would be the first thing the Noble would call for. After observing the change in the anomaly, it revised its opinion of being "nothing" or something easy to explain. It was indeed a problem never placed before an interface of the hierarchy. Interfaces often exchanged assignments, but they downloaded each other's databases before the exchange. On this occasion, the Noble isolated Corky's data, so not even the central matrix had access. Adding to that mystery was the Noble's advisement to the crew that the incident was not to be discussed.

COQ interfaces, slender, elegant, bevelled-edged transparent ovals, a metre high, mobile, and designed as a physical unit programmed to merge with Noble ships. All ship's functions and life support linked to the interface. It could synthesise food, liquid, materials, and some equipment. Its holographic appendages could fetch and carry if one or more crew became incapacitated. It also possessed autonomous command functions if the entire crew were disabled. Or if they all died, then its program sent it home to headquarters on Chabin.

The interface that had now transferred to Jardin's ship had been Yianevan's only companion for a considerable time. It didn't take long for Jardin and Merris to discover it had no personality.

Yianevan escaped the Noble homeworld twenty years before with the help of his mother and a ship from her clan house. His father traced him but did not demand his return if he complied with a raft of restrictions, the main one being that he remained in disguise and never demystified the Nobles. Non-compliance came with a threat of harm to his mother and brother. One rule was that Yianevan must not return unless he wished to bring his self-exile to an end. The ship the mother secured from her clan was range-restricted but of distinctive Noble design and speed. It would be recognised wherever the son went, so they created a new persona for him, disguised as a Grielik police fleet supervisor. A meaningless designation because he didn't often interact with Grielik's, but one that would not be questioned.

However, something changed in recent months, and the clan father now wanted his son to return, citing familial duties as heir to the rulership. Yianevan believed he had shed the position as heir, but as those requests turned to demands and threats, he feared for the well-being of his younger brother. When the Noble homeworld received the transmission about the missing interventionist, Yianevan's father diverted him to "deal with the situation" as he was the closest and already mobile. The homeworld advised that life signs were present, so it should be a simple locate and extract. In twenty years, this was the first time Yianevan had contacted another ship without assuming a false identity and appeared as a Noble.

However, a warning and a curfew came along with his father's communication. He had indulged his son's waywardness long enough. If he did not return within four days, he would visit his sin of betrayal upon his younger brother.

As a youth, Yianevan rebelled against the rigid traditions of his society, but his father knew him well enough that he would not let his brother bear the burden of his rebelliousness. Despite his son's rejection of tradition, he was sentimental, like the mother, and would return home.

Yianevan envied other species their sovereignty. Few in the galaxy imposed such obligations on their children or such constraints as the hierarchy did on theirs, but he had memories. Experiences. Would they be enough to sustain him through the long years to come? He doubted it. His yearning for freedom may have made his prison a worse place. The thousands of star systems throughout the ten sectors became his sanctuary. He knew he should feel grateful for those few years of liberty not afforded to any heir before but felt cheated, robbed of free will, and wished with all his heart he had been born a tribal ordinary or even an amoeba. That would be preferable to what lay ahead.

The interface isolated all the data concerning the interventionist and the anomaly, and Yianevan was confident the hierarchy would not request it during his investigation. Meanwhile, he needed as much background as possible.

"Interface. Display the full sequence of events from the moment the interventionist left the ship."

The interface again imaged every data tile, overlying the inconsistencies between the spiral view and the interventionist ship's sensor log.

Yianevan studied each frame. Not a single sector, colour, or movement went unchecked. The possibility of a spiral failing to make a complete recording at the time was unlikely, so was this an act of deception by the anomaly's creators? He built a portrait of the events leading to the interventionist's disappearance, then narrowed the view to the moment Jardin ordered her to step back. Cross-checking with the ship's log record, he lingered on the tile where she glanced over her shoulder. She appeared to look into the anomaly.

Chief Jardin believed this was unlikely to be interventionist error. Yianevan agreed. The woman showed neither panic nor fear. Her line of sight was to the north when she glanced behind. What did she see? Did she hear a noise? Did whatever made her turn communicate with her? What was it that made her lift her arm in defence? Or, as Lieutenant Merris suggested, to catch an object? If so, what?

No answers. Only more questions. The Nobles did not possess knowledge of all Lyran technology, so Yianevan contemplated the possibility of a trap left by the Lyrans. But for whom? He gazed at the shadowy mark. Where did it come from? He turned the mystery over in his mind. This was not a random event. Had the interventionist triggered it?

Lieutenant Phildre's personnel file read like any other, except she displayed a one hundred percent success rate with mitigating Lyran sabotage. Yianevan would have liked to know what set her apart from other interventionists. A Noble would not survive many hours of exposure to that world's soil, and a human could not survive the conditions on that mountain. But what if she wasn't human or had access to hidden technology?

A question mark hung over every possibility, but each question returned to the anomaly playing a part in the disappearance. The smudge, the blemish, took on a quality he found almost impossible to define. As he watched and considered, "almost impossible" changed to "what if?"

The Nobles regarded themselves prepared for any Lyran sabotage, although Yianevan thought such a notion imperious. If his suspicions were correct, they had ignored a crucial piece of history.

CHAPTER SIX _

The terrified girl ran as fast as her young legs could carry her. In her fear and despair, she sought to shield her eyes from the stinging smoke and heat that scorched her nostrils and lungs. Breathless and desperate for relief from the falling ash, she stumbled through a doorway into an antechamber. Gulping mouthfuls of contaminated air, she searched for water to soothe her parched throat. Outside, men choked and gagged, and womenfolk scurried from their doorways, a fearful child in one hand, treasures clutched in the other. All about her, homes turned into crematoriums. Exhausted, the girl slid to the floor. She didn't recognise this house, nor this town in its turmoil with wailing and terrified inhabitants. Neither did she see how the chaos began, nor did she witness the earth's groans or its violent shaking. Did the people not see the first signs of the smoke that threaded its way from the yaw of Vesuvius? At their peril, they ignored the warning, and now they would pay for their blindness. All the girl remembered was a river and a metal bead she clasped in her fist and almost dropped when a balcony collapsed under the weight of ash.

"You, girl!" A man dragged her to her feet and thrust a newborn infant into her arms. "Take the child, run…"

He pushed her towards the entrance, but she had no courage to brave the heat.

"Master…!" she protested.

The word felt alien to her tongue, but he ignored her fear and draped her and the baby in a paenula, wrapping the thick coat around them, hoping to provide some protection from the ash. She resisted. This seemed to be the only sanctuary, but he barred her way back into the atrium

"You must save the infant. Her mother is weak from the birth, and I cannot leave her. Now run. May Apollo keep you both safe."

The girl darted an anxious look at the doorway, then forced herself back out into the pressing throng, spurred forward by a desire to survive and a curious realisation this was not a place where she belonged. The baby's little head bobbed against the girl's neck as she ran, but there was no time to secure the infant.

She scrambled over walls, flesh tearing from her knees and her shins grazing against rocks as she bumped and jostled against the other terrified, fleeing refugees. The shawl slipped somewhere along the way, and she had to continue with no covering for the baby. The girl's feet burned at each step, but she willed herself to run, fearing her newborn charge might perish as it breathed in the dense smoke and airborne debris. Without a covering to protect the baby, the girl used her sleeve to cover its little face, but too small for anyone to notice, she had to use her free arm to force a path through the crowd.

The sky blackened as sulphur-laden ash hid the sun, but still, the girl ran, a slight figure alone with a tiny child held against her. Too young to bear the responsibility for such a new life, she feared she may not save either of them. Her throat and eyes burned. She coughed and retched, and although she stumbled, she didn't dare slow her pace. Each time she glanced down, the baby seemed uninjured, not yet smothered by the smoke or from being held so close to her saviour's body.

Ahead, other refugees were climbing a hill, and the girl saw that if she could make it to the top, the other side might shield them and give her a moment's relief. She urged her feet to move forward, but the climb proved arduous for the weakened child, and with lungs heaving to purge themselves of ash, she fell to the ground.

For a moment, she lay still, then summoned all her strength to check the infant and look behind to see what might be left of the doomed city. All was gloom and smoke, and around her, bent in supplication and suffering, people were on their knees in lamentation to Minerva, Apollo or Venus, any god, to spare them. Others were like the girl, stopping only to catch their breath, unable to pray, or grieving that their god had forsaken them. The girl knew few would survive the wrath those gods were about to unleash.

Shielding her mouth with her hand as a filter, she tried to draw a deep, sustaining breath and then began running again. After only a few steps, her mouth and throat became fouled with ash, and gasping, she sank once more to her knees. The baby howled, and fearful its gasping wails would fill its tiny body with dangerous dust, the little girl held the baby against her neck, desperate to soothe its distress. She knew nothing about infants or how she got here. Finally, the anguish and hopelessness became too much, and the girl stretched herself on the ground, ready to abandon them both to their fate.

Without gentleness and with all the urgency of a saviour, the girl felt herself pulled upwards, the action so violent, so sudden, she almost dropped the infant. She snatched the babe to her body as a large hand slammed her onto the pommel of a saddle. The action startled the baby to quietness, and the girl had a moment to tuck the little body into her tunic.

Glancing upwards, she tried to glimpse her rescuer, but with the sun hidden, she could not see his face. She understood the rhythmic movement under her body, the ring of hooves against the ground, and the massive hand that held the two children in his protective grasp as they rode before the prevailing destruction. Other horses thundered past, and the cries of people on the ground who still hoped to outrun the fire clamoured in her ears. The man did not speak, only kept one powerful arm about them until the air cleared enough for the girl to view him. A soldier from an army she did not recognise wore a metal helmet framing a grim, unsmiling face, focused on taking them all to safety.

As they reached a valley, the soldier reined in his horse and slipped the girl and the baby to the ground. Grey powder covered them, but the air here still had some freshness and a little more light. There would only be a brief reprieve; soon, more ash would reach them, and not even the fleetest horse possessed sufficient speed to outrun it. The soldier looked back in the direction they travelled, then knelt and placed his hands on the girl's shoulders.

"We were fortunate indeed not to be hit by boiling rocks. Who is your master?"

The girl shrank from him and his strange accent. She didn't recall having a master, even though, perhaps on instinct, that was what she called the baby's father. The soldier looked big and fierce, and her little girl voice trembled.

"I—I have forgotten. This..." She dusted off the baby's face as if it would make a difference to the soldier's recognition. "A man committed this babe to me."

The soldier rubbed the infant's swathes between his thumb and forefinger and examined the crest he found. He studied the girl as if seeking to recognise her.

"The swathe displays the emblem of Tullius. Were you his slave?"

The girl shook her head. She remembered nothing other than running from the river, but the soldier didn't ask again. Instead, he sat the girl on the ground and checked the wounds on her legs. There was no time to treat them now, but he frowned at the burns on her feet and wondered how they carried a child so far. The gods were smiling upon her, and he would keep her with him, then they would smile on him as well.

"We were following our routine circuit of the towns," he told his young charge. "We were headed to Misenum when I came upon you." He nodded to the infant. "It seems your master could not escape."

The girl would have told him the baby's mother was sick, but the soldier's horse harrumphed and snorted to clear its nose from the effects of its ash-laden exertion. The soldier turned away and patted its neck to calm its distress.

"She needs water," he said as he lifted the girl onto the horse's back. "And the babe will need milk, but we must continue for as long as the horses can stay their speed. At our next ease, I will find a nurse." The soldier blew on the girl's grimy face and grinned. "There, I thought to blow away the ash, but I fear I made it worse. Can you at least remember your name?"

He waited a moment for her to answer, but she didn't remember her name either.

"No? Then I will call you Valentina," he declared. "Master Tullius had a slave called Valentina, but you are too young to be she. I do not visit his house often, so she may have had a child, and I am unaware."

The girl had no other identity, so humbly, she lowered her eyes and accepted the one given her.

As they rode, other centurions joined them, riding towards hope and safety with refugees who fled the town. In her heart, Valentina believed it was fitting to save and show compassion for the plight of the people. These men were soldiers who might have tried to preserve only themselves, but they risked their own lives for others. Even a slave girl, if that was what she was, had much to thank them for. Yes, she thought, the soldier showed mercy on the day the gods of these people rained down their displeasure.

The horses pushed on with spirit, but in time, fatigue overcame both animal and rider. They had made good progress, and the cloud was far enough behind to allow a brief respite. After, they would proceed on foot to allow the horses to rest.

Valentina sat down on the ground, and the baby made squawking noises as though it was trying to speak to her. Its tiny mouth made sucking movements as it struggled within its swathes. She didn't recall ever holding a baby, but she knew they needed milk and hoped the soldier would know what to do.

Spitting on her fingers, she cleaned around the baby's nose, gently removing ash from its nostrils and hoping the tiny body could expel any that had entered. At her touch, the baby stopped its squawking to fix unfocused blue eyes on her. It looked wise and new, and Valentina wondered if the mother would have survived even without the mountain's fury.

Do people die after childbirth these days? Valentina didn't know. She didn't even know what these days were, only that she felt constrained in a body and place unfamiliar to her.

All around, the displaced wept, and soldiers spoke to one another, some in hushed tones, others loud and authoritative. Valentina understood what the soldiers were saying, but when she said the words herself, they moved around on her tongue as if she had never spoken them before. Yet her soldier understood her.

Valentina held the baby close, its hot little body

bringing comfort. They made it this far alive, but right now, they only had each other. If the soldier could not locate a nurse, Valentina did not know what she would do. Where would she find the strength and knowledge to save them both?

But the soldier stayed true to his vow. He returned with a young woman carrying an infant. She sat with Valentina to feed the baby along with her own. While the baby fed, the soldier told Valentina about his own family, safe, far away from the volcano. She paid close attention to the rhythm of his voice, to the cadences, and attended to every word. She somehow recognised this language, its layers and nuances, but she also knew she didn't belong here.

"The sea is up in Naples," the soldier said when the babes finished nursing, and the two little cherubs' dirty faces looked serene in peaceful slumber. "We will head inland until the mountain calms. Valentina, one of my men will take the nurse and the infants. I promise I will reunite you both when we get to Misenum, but we have a long journey ahead."

Valentina didn't want to part from the baby, but what else could a child, an enslaved girl, do but obey an officer? The officer turned to her as a second centurion lifted the nurse and both babies onto his horse and led the horse away.

"You are a mystery, little Valentina," he said as he wiped away the tears she couldn't stop falling. His large thumb smeared ash across her face. "Pray now that the gods continue to smile upon us."

In Misenum, women cared for the refugees, attended to their wounds and burns and offered food and shelter, with no distinction between slave and freeman. The centurion, Tiberius, reunited Valentina with the baby and kept her together with the wet nurse. He told her the infant had a relative in Naples and that they would ride there as soon as the seas settled.

Several days passed before they could make the journey and every step filled Valentina with dread. She did not wish to part from the baby. Even in those moments when the wet nurse took it from her to feed, her arms felt empty and bereft. Without the infant, she was alone in this strange world.

In Naples, Tiberius brought Valentina before the prefect to account for herself. She feared for the future, for the baby, but Tiberius, although he was never unkind, always called her "slave". And she knew that meant obedience.

The prefect was tall, and he watched her with bulging eyes. His large, slack mouth looked as if it never stopped ordering his soldiers to do terrible things. Valentina felt afraid, and she stepped back, only managing a few shuffling steps before her soldier planted his hand firmly on her shoulder. The baby slept in her arms, and she tightened them protectively, fearing the moment they would tear from her the only comfort she had in the world.

Tiberius held her hand as they entered the Prefect's rooms. "The prefect will help you, Valentina," he said. "There is no need for fear."

Valentina trusted her soldier, who had kept her close,

and if he said the prefect would treat her well, she would believe him, but it was hard for a child to transition from terrified to trusting, so she held her breath and shut her eyes as the man who would decide her fate faced her. But even a child cannot hold her breath forever nor keep her eyes so tightly closed, not when tears pushed themselves under her eyelids. When she opened them, the man towered above, and she only reached as high as his belt buckle.

After peering down from his great height, he dropped to one knee. Valentina didn't look at him. She knew he had done terrible things as a soldier because she listened to the stories of the centurions at Misenum. They laughed as they spoke of gathering slaves and waging bloody battles far across the sea. Sometimes, she had to put her hands over her ears to shield herself from the temptation to listen.

The prefect waited until Valentina took the courage to look into his eyes. She saw no cruelty there. Whatever this man was to others, his eyes held sympathy for her.

"Valentina?" he said. "Master Tullius was my cousin. You will be part of my household from this day on, and I will raise his child as my own." He frowned then and took Valentina's chin in his large hand, turning her face from side to side. "Hmm, so young. It is unusual to find a female slave of your age. Was your mother of the house?"

Valentina nodded. She didn't know her mother, but it seemed wise to agree. The prefect pinched her cheek as he stood. He had already decided her fate.

"We travel now to Britannia. You have the look of the Briton about you, Valentina, so we are returning you to the land of your forefathers. Tiberius, take the child to my servant and the infant to my eldest daughter."

Valentina resisted when Tiberius tried to take the baby. Her chin quivered, and she couldn't speak of her fear at the parting. But he understood, so he did not scold or insist. She had been through an ordeal that no child, no person, should suffer.

"Child. You are not yet ten years old. Master Tullius commended his newborn daughter to your care, and you carried out your duty with determination and honour. The prefect does not mean to part you from her, as you will also be under his protection. Valentine, I must take the infant."

Tiberius was right. How could she care for a baby with no possessions or home? A child would need so much more than she could give. Weeping, she placed the baby into Tiberius's waiting arms, then followed him from the cabin onto the ship's deck. Night had fallen, and the smell of the burning mountain still wafted in the air. Above her, a ghostly moon struggled to peep through the tarry night, and all around, tall ships pitched and rocked as their timbers creaked over the angry waters of the bay.

CHAPTER SEVEN _

During his twenty years in the ten sectors, Yianevan divided his time between observing other worlds and societies and basking in his solitude. A situation that would be in stark contrast to his future, where he would spend almost every hour of every day in the company of others. These years of quiet reflection gave him focus. He studied, paid attention, and became an expert on many cultures within the ten sectors, which were a fascinating study, but he couldn't absorb himself into any society because of his father's restrictions. Now it seemed the knowledge he gained would benefit his world. As rulership was to be forced upon him, he intended for his people to become part of the broader regional galactic community, and he would dispel the Noble mystique.

Throughout history, his race drew mixed reactions from the thousands of inhabited planets within the ten sectors. Some lauded the Nobles, and others accepted them only for the restricted technology they sold. Still others regarded them with suspicion. A few societies exhibited hostility towards anything from the homeworld. How could they trust a species that would not welcome a friend into their midst?

Yianevan understood. He watched those worlds through ocular prosthetics that concealed his compound retinas and vowed that now he had to return home, he would offer those people a hand of friendship.

The universe was a marvel to Yianevan, but his homeworld was a potential prison to his enquiring mind. He wondered if that was why he planned to instigate change. He dreaded tedium and lack of purpose, but most of all, he feared the loss of freedom to choose his path. If the clan father learned of his heir's future plans, Yianevan believed he would not be in such a hurry to forgive him. Even with all his bold ideas, he recognised many Nobles were mired in centuries-old traditions they would not relinquish, which meant the reformation he desired might take far longer than the years he had left.

This mission to locate the interventionist was the only assignment given to him by his father, but it represented the end of Yianevan's self-exile and a return to responsibility and culture. A full stop at the conclusion of a chapter.

"Why do the crew call you 'Corky'?" Yianevan said suddenly as they viewed the data tiles.

"A human attribute, Noble," the interface responded. "They like to give an identity to the equipment they work closely with."

"Why 'Corky'?"

"C.O.Q, Noble. My interface designation. They didn't

want to call me 'Coq'. Nor add a 'y' and call me 'coqy'. Lieutenant Phildre is quite inventive and, I might add, a little eccentric. She decided I must appear 'cute' and 'friendly', so she came up with a name to reflect those attributes. She also assigned me a gender. I am male."

"Phildre? The missing crewman?"

"Yes, Noble."

"Display her image."

Yianevan looked through Phildre's biographical profile, a well-detailed compilation from her submission to the interventionist programme several years before. Important milestones, character, and intelligence assessments were all documented. The file also included commendations collected over her years of service. He found not a single criticism or black mark against her record. The stringent entry requirements into Noble service deterred many humans, the only species accepted. Even if a candidate made it as far as the program, they seldom progressed to completion. Accordingly, it wasn't too hard for the Nobles to select the best of the best.

An Elbis national, Phildre came from a minor planet in the Covarantuum system, a place Yianevan knew well. The Nobles received her into the interventionist program at age eighteen. A recent visual of a woman in her mid-twenties appeared. Black hair, grey eyes, slim build, around one sixty-eight centimetres tall. Yianevan considered her unexceptional, but he found it difficult to distinguish between human females. He spent some time among the pockets of humans dotted about the ten sectors. A few lived beyond the boundary, a place his range-restricted ship could not visit. Humans came in all sizes and skin colours, but in telling them apart, Yianevan found it was less their facial similarities than they all seemed so similar in temperament. If his burgeoning suspicion about the anomaly was correct, it would be worth imprinting the image of this human on his mind.

Corky expected the Noble to clarify the need to study this information rather than work on a rescue strategy. He didn't know what direction the Noble was heading with this investigation or even if he had a plan.

"Lieutenant Phildre lives in a fleet commune on the Chabin annexure," Corky said, changing the view to the Chabin system to indulge the Noble's interest. "She migrated there after recruiting into the Nobles' service seven years ago."

"Show me her living quarters."

Corky complied without question, or at least that he voiced. An irregular request, he didn't understand what a visual sweep of Phildre's apartment would accomplish. He assumed a recovery mission wasn't on the cards because too much time had passed.

Each accommodation within the communes had a security interface at the entrance. They permitted access only in exceptional circumstances and then only under the authority of a Noble or one of their police. The Chabin annexure had several of these constructions built by the Nobles for their interventionist and police fleet. Grieliks, a humanoid species similar in physiology to humans, only more muscled and less physically refined, made up the police force. Yianevan considered Grieliks less intelligent than their human counterpart, but they were industrious and trustworthy and made excellent law enforcers throughout the ten sectors.

The annexure apartment buildings comprised a central pole, with ringed constructs threaded atop one another from ground level. The pinnacle rose several hundred metres high, with each ring divided into two halves. A single officer received an allocation of one half. The individual suites had their own docking bay and private access via the stem.

The apartments afforded glorious views of the lakes and mountains of Chabin, which Yianevan had to admit, offered a spectacular way of life for those inclined to solitude and the beauty of nature. He liked these accommodations. The Nobles called them communes, but you could close your door and not be bothered by another soul. Unlike on his homeworld, where the hierarchy scorned seclusion, privacy was unheard of, and personal choices discouraged. The only opportunity to be alone was in your bed at night, provided you were in an unmarried state. In Yianevan's case, his father would have selected betrotheds, and in keeping with tradition, they would also need to be considered.

In his society, cleaning the body was communal, meals communal, recreation communal, and as he grew up, the constant clamour of voices proved agony. His mother protected him as much as she could but knew one day, her son would rebel.

As a youth, Yianevan stole a ship and tried to flee off-world. When the Grieliks captured him and returned him, they placed him under guard, only for him to repeat the exercise when he regained his father's trust. Later, he circulated a document renouncing his heirdom, but his father intercepted it. Knowing such an act would bring dishonour, Yianevan again attempted to escape. That time, they apprehended him before he even made it to the shipyards. Under threat of banishment to the Southern Climes, the clan father secured his son's compliance. It wasn't to last because Yianevan continued with his rebellious ways. His mother watched the uneasy truce between father and son. Her son challenged everything the clan father, indeed everything the Nobles stood for, so she secured a small space-going vessel from her clan house and sent him away. She did not tell the clan father, and when he discovered her deception, she made a case that time might purge the boy's restlessness, suggesting his second son Bo as heir.

Yianevan was unlike other Nobles. He didn't fit in, couldn't conform, and he knew no amount of indoctrination would change that fact. Now the time was upon him where his differences would need to be set aside, at least for a while. If he must inherit rulership, he would rule on his own terms.

As he thought of his younger brother, he considered abandoning the interventionist to her fate or requesting his father to assign someone else to find her. However, the anomaly aroused his curiosity and, in the end, his inherent thirst for knowledge and desire to prolong his absence from his homeworld won out.

The visuals gave Yianevan a panoramic view of the

interventionist's apartment. Now committed to the investigation, he felt no compunction about intruding upon her privacy. With his belief in the anomaly's nature firming, he required to learn as much about the woman's personality as possible. He wished to draw his own conclusions, not rely on the emotional input of her crewmates.

Arranged in tiers, the apartment's upper level housed the designated sleeping section. The usual things adorned it. A bed, although this one was a little different because it had turned posts at each corner, custom-built, and an ornate lace bedcovering which Yianevan recognised as a human affectation. Lacy accoutrements and personal design beds were not standard issue. A reference to the woman's individuality.

Three sweeping steps below the rest area, two oversized armchairs with seats that would make someone as tall as him hard-pressed to place his feet on the ground were positioned to take advantage of the scenic view through the window. Bright multicoloured cushions adorned the seats, with a scatter of handwoven fabric squares tossed haphazardly over the arms and headrests. Yianevan knew which part of the exclusion zone at the frontier these items hailed from. Not a place for the faint-hearted. This interventionist either enjoyed risk or was supremely confident in her ability to handle herself.

Regulation soft coverings in neutral tones covered the floor, but the tenant had randomly scattered rugs of different widths and colours with the same carefree abandon as the cushions and squares. Strange ornamental images crafted from wood and clay stood guard around the semicircular walls, and an exotic, white, furry creature slept in a basket, its flat face and whiskers twitching as it dreamed.

A further three steps below the mezzanine on the veranda area, the interventionist had constructed a garden terrace, forgoing the sparse furnishings usual to these window spaces. She had also installed a mini-ecosystem, invisible to a human eye, but with his enhanced vision, Yianevan could see a generated forcefield. Insect life buzzed and flitted, living in companionable harmony with the plants in the field. He nodded in approval. Very innovative. Only registered individuals were allowed in, but the beetles and flying insects that lived there could not get out.

Each apartment came with a basic strip of artificial grass and a few shrubs that could tolerate the indifference inflicted on them by absent or disinterested fleet officers. The interventionist made good use of the area because every plant flourished, glossy and robust, with the massive windows as gleaming backdrops complimenting those spectacular views.

An unexpected addition was an ancient concierge interface that rattled into view, unaware of the apartment's silent surveillance. It headed towards the fluffy feline, making swishing noises to wake it up. The cat yawned, stretched, then took its time to follow the concierge to the garden, making a show of resistance to being ordered around. Once through the forcefield, it stuck its face into a food bowl, purring between mouthfuls to show its disdain for the insects that buzzed over its head. The interface engaged in a one-sided conversation with the cat while busying itself with the tending of plants in what presented as a most natural and pleasing environment.

Yianevan had never seen a home interface employed in this way. It looked like a museum piece, a relic, and it surprised him to find an interventionist with a personal concierge. It brought him a moment of amusement, and he smiled at such a pastoral scene. Corky saw his expression.

"Phildre received it for her ninth birthday, Noble," he explained. "A reconditioned unit to help her with her schoolwork. She had it reprogrammed to keep it with her. She calls it 'Betty'."

A picture built of the woman. Sentimental. Reckless maybe, given where she acquired some of her furnishings. Compassionate because she likes animals. Individualistic. Not neurotypical. Interesting.

"Interface," Yianevan said. "According to her profile, her parents had no distinctions and are now deceased. I understand she has an aunt?"

"A great-aunt, Noble. On Elbis. She is very elderly."

"I see. Go through the timeline from when the officer left the ship to when she disappeared," he told Corky. "Also, detail every biological report the Noble hierarchy has on her and her family."

While Corky carried out the request, Yianevan re-visualised the missing interventionist's home. Humans were not known for putting down strong roots, and as far as Yianevan was aware, the only humans in stable positions were the interventionist fleet and a few administrators in the police force. So, it surprised him to see Lieutenant Phildre's apartment much less austere than most officers.

Contraband from the frontier or outlier systems involved considerable changing of hands, not to mention money, and if it was just to secure furnishings, also foolhardy.

But the workmanship of the merchandise was unrivalled and to a discerning eye, not available anywhere within the ten sectors. Clearly, home was an important aspect of her life. Yianevan might add she appeared a little gregarious, a trait he ordinarily detested, but perhaps, in this case, better characterised as "colourful". No doubt she liked to talk. Humans were irritatingly cheerful and spoke incessantly about inane subjects. Of course, that was a generalisation. He knew only a handful of humans, but if he went by the ancient interface that rattled about the apartment, followed by the cat, something set this one apart.

The cat's sudden yowling distracted him and stung his sensitive hearing. He didn't much like cats. For reasons best known to themselves, when the Lyrans abducted humans, they also took a few of the useless fluff balls. Both species spread throughout the ten sectors, and while the humans proved a valuable addition, he couldn't think of many uses for cats. This one vocalised at the top of its lungs as it followed the concierge around, and peace was only restored when it received a satisfactory response to its demands for attention.

Yianevan decided that if the interventionist's interior design skills, combined with the illegal hand weave, were clues to her personality, he would revisit his earlier observation she might be a woman who threw caution to the wind. Learning this about her made him wonder if he should consider the possibility the incident on the volcano was a gamble that didn't pay off, even if it didn't explain the anomaly or her life signs. He examined three years of Phildre's missions and discovered that the more he read, the more he realised this interventionist was a risk-taker. She often sought the most precarious landing places but always with the strategic expectation of optimum results. Possessed with a knack for perfect timing and balance of the pennants, those results were consistently dramatic.

The Nobles didn't lay down criteria for the interventionists to follow as they entered a sabotaged zone, allowing each operative to establish the merits of an event. With an instinctive sense of the sabotage, the lieutenant developed a unique method of determining those merits. Yianevan couldn't help feeling impressed. The woman had intuition, and she had empathy for the planet. The scale of the Lyran sabotage horrified him, as it did all Nobles, but how much worse would it be for the humans whose distant posterity may still dwell on that world. Designed to devastate, the Lyran Monks devised a cruel punishment to visit upon a civilisation innocent of any wrongdoing as a rebuke to the Nobles and leave the Lyrans with the last word. An interventionist's task was to locate the Lyran Monk's sabotaged sites at the first sign of planetary change. A task that required vigilance. Looking at the lieutenant's records, she was remarkable at preventing the major catastrophes that befell the small blue planet. The still primitive inhabitants had much to thank their unknown benefactress for.

The Lyran Monks were thorough in their treachery. There was no distinguishing between Lyran orchestrated or natural disasters, so the Nobles had no way of knowing how long they would need to watch over the planet. Unless they developed technology to detect the sabotaged sites, their covenant would last forever.

Despite their name, there was nothing godly about Lyran Monks. A ruthless, selfish, and dangerous cartel, in ancient times, they were a scourge across the ten sectors. So when the Nobles caught the Monks red-handed abducting humans from this undeveloped world, they had no choice but to intervene. It was the humane thing to do.

Generations before, the ten-sector council had begged the Nobles, a race who guarded their privacy but had advanced technology, to help with policing the sectors against pirates and the Lyran Monk Cartel. Other marauders plagued the ten sectors from across the boundary and outlier worlds, so the Nobles, still relative newcomers to the region and not yet established, agreed to help. It was also an opportunity to put their superiority on display and cement their place in the region. The Noble hierarchy drew up an iron-clad agreement with the ten-sector council that all Noble technology and its use remained under Noble management. In addition, crews were to be approved only by the hierarchy. They equipped a police fleet with fast, armoured ships and employed men and women from the neighbouring system of Griel as law enforcement officers

This act by the Nobles rendered the ten sectors safe, and the sheer might of the police force drove many pirates, including the Lyrans, back across the border. In time, other cartels rose, and other pirates chanced to take on the police force, but thanks to the Nobles, the ten sectors became a peaceful place to live.

When the Nobles learned the Lyran Monks had recommenced their collection of human slaves, they engaged them in war above the remote human planet. The Lyrans relied on the Nobles' well-known preference for seclusion and aimed to continue their illegal dealings away from the ten sectors without fear of discovery. However, before the Nobles could crush their enterprise, the Lyran Monk Cartel laid timed traps to devastate the human world that would last for centuries.

When the ten-sector council learned of the Lyran sabotage and their subsequent defeat, they acknowledged the Nobles' selfless determination to watch over the planet, where they would undertake to mitigate the effects of the sabotage. In establishing such a presence, the Nobles would safeguard the natural evolution of the incumbent civilisations. The human planet was well outside the council's jurisdiction, but they agreed to mandate that no ships from within the ten sectors might approach that world. For a time, the Nobles' charitable deed thrust its xenophobic culture once more into the planetary spotlight, and despite the vague terms of friendship enjoyed with the ten-sector council, the hierarchy continued to refuse access to their own planet. Any Noble who left the homeworld remained aloof from other societies, and this air of superiority promoted less than cordial relationships with other worlds. Even their management and provision of the police force to protect the outposts and less defended planets did little to elevate the Nobles in many of the ten-sectors residents' esteem. It had been this way for centuries, and the Nobles never deemed it necessary to change the status quo.

Yianevan knew the history. As a much younger man, he spent some time in the archives reviewing the war. He recalled one brief entry, written without care or with supportive testimony to attribute to any author. It didn't capture his interest then, but now, he was glad of the memory. The words, written centuries ago at the time of the Lyran war, told of a gate into time that the Lyran Monks constructed on the human planet. The gate was a portal through which they could collect more humans from some future time, a time when civilisation was more advanced than the primitives they were abducting when the Nobles arrived. The existence of this so-called Monk's Gate was never proven. The soil of the human world contained toxins that could kill a Noble in a matter of hours, so a direct investigation was not possible. That was all the information the entry offered.

It seemed rather fabulous to Yianevan, almost a fairy tale. His Noble forefathers had developed the ability to phase energy backwards in time to a minute degree with the pennants, but they deemed the concept of future time travel preposterous. He was unaware of any science that advanced the theory or current research on his homeworld, but he had not returned there for twenty years.

Now, the anomaly made him ponder the myth anew. If there was a portal to the future, even in theory, why didn't Grielik scientists investigate? The human world was not toxic to Grieliks, and while their scientists might not be as advanced as Nobles, they worked well under direction.

Presented with such a fascinating possibility, why did the Nobles relegate it to the status of a myth and not investigate it further? A portal might mean the Lyrans were taking refuge somewhere in the planet's past or future, so now Yianevan had to consider if the Monk's Gate, if he wasn't being fanciful, somehow seized the woman. Just as worryingly, given her remarkable sensitivity to the sabotage technology, she might have Lyran heritage. Despite their rigorous medical evaluations, the Nobles were not infallible. It begged the question; could the Lyrans be amassing on the borders of time?

Yianevan had no choice but to follow the assumption the anomaly might be proof the gate existed. It would be prudent to contact the Noble hierarchy, yet he felt constrained. An idea, a gut feeling, was not sufficient to mobilise a Noble armada or to draw them into armed conflict. If the Lyrans were in the future, the battle might already have been waged, and the hierarchy defeated by superior firepower. No-one knew the future, and his people could already be doomed and living on borrowed time.

It was a gloomy train of thought. If the Monk's Gate appeared, it was more likely the Lyrans planned to return to the here and now, bringing their ships and weapons procured from the future of the human world. Historically, his people dismissed the gate as a myth and were unlikely to rekindle their interest or raise an army on the say-so of an errant son.

Yianevan's hand hovered over the communications tile. Then he curled his fingers into his palm. If he contacted his father, it would all be over. He would have to return home. No Lyrans had emerged from this planet in centuries, and this anomaly may have appeared before but gone unnoticed. He closed his eyes and cleared his mind of thoughts of his homeworld, relaxing into a vision of the anomaly, and allowed it to flow into his mind, dark, quiet, abandoned. He opened his eyes. Abandoned? *Abandoned?* Why would such an idea be amongst his thoughts? Were Lyran warriors trapped within the gate? Were generations deserted by the Monks, and somehow, he sensed them?

Despite the Noble's ability to see into a person's emotions, they did not consider themselves psychic. Their visual skills were part of a practical evolution and, like so many species, viewed psychic abilities as soothsaying and charlatanism. He recognised the irony that while he discarded supernatural powers, he was at that point considering a portal to another time. Why should that be more believable? However, if he brought it back to a commonly used device, the calming pennants fell into that category. They displaced energy to the past. The Nobles created that technology, and as it existed, why was it so unbelievable that moving into the future could not be achieved?

No doubt minds greater than his had already pondered that question, so he pushed his thoughts to the side and focused on the tiles that bore the image of the anomaly. His eyes stayed motionless, allowing the changing dimensions to bring clarity and cohesion to his mind.

He blinked. This didn't require scientific analysis. It went beyond that which was immediately visible, even to the interface, but it could mean the Lyrans still had a means by which to return. Unable to ignore the burgeoning sense that the answer to the interventionist's disappearance lay with the anomaly, he came to realise that future or past, she was on the planet. A place he could not go. *Unless…*

Corky interrupted him.

"Noble, the tile shows another change in the anomaly's dimensions. I am endeavouring to locate other discernible features, but so far, I have been unsuccessful."

Yianevan mentioned his new theory to the interface. "Could this be a time portal built by the Lyrans?"

"You refer to the Monk's Gate, Noble. It is a myth. Unproven."

"You know of it?"

"Mention of the myth in my database extends to little more than a few lines entered by a historian," Corky said. "The scientific community considers the entry hearsay. There is no foundation to the theory."

It sounded like the same paragraph Yianevan read years before.

"I believe we have found it, Interface. If the Lyran Monks created this gate through time, the ten sectors are in danger, and it needs to be destroyed."

"The Lyrans are gone, Noble," Corky pointed out. "Their species is extinct and cannot return."

"A remnant might be hiding out in this planet's future. That makes the gate's appearance concerning."

Corky took a nanosecond to react, long enough for Yianevan to know it believed his conclusions absurd. However, the Nobles programmed their interfaces to respond with tact to all proposals.

"Unlikely," Corky said. "The Noble's abandoned the notion of future time travel."

"Yet, our forebears mastered time displacement to the past with the pennants."

"The hierarchy does not disclose the nature of the pennants, Noble, only that the technology to recreate them is no longer available to your people."

None of that mattered to Yianevan. "I am satisfied the woman has travelled to either the future or the past, by accident or design. She is not caught up in the eruption."

"The probability is she is either deceased or preserved on the mountain."

That earned a raised eyebrow from Yianevan. "Preserved on an erupting volcano?"

Corky knew it sounded extreme. "The lieutenant's life sign coordinates are metres below a flowing lava field, Noble. I have several theories. First, she is dead, and her life signs are an echo of earlier data. If so, that might require further investigation of my programming. Or she continues phased and therefore escaped the pyroclastic flow. My final theory is that persons unknown have removed her. Of course, that does not explain her life signs within the anomaly, located at her last known coordinates."

"It isn't possible to phase without close contact with a spiral, Interface," Yianevan said. "The interventionist would have to be in a physical condition. Further, your sensors would detect a phased organic, and we can disregard your theory of a rescue."

"Yes, Noble. I concede we are amidst the inexplicable. I cannot discount she is somewhere in the future or even the past, but I do not believe your theory to be any more credible than those I put forth. On a more simplistic level, I might be malfunctioning, although diagnostics appear to refute that."

Yianevan disagreed. The interface hadn't come up with answers, but it wasn't malfunctioning.

"More likely, there are gaps in your programming, although I am not clear why. However, I am neither an engineer nor a scientist, and I must ask you to put aside logic until we solve this puzzle." Yianevan stroked his chin. "You have developed human-like traits in your time with the interventionists."

Corky wasn't sure about developing "human-like traits". It was his job to offer alternatives, and he would continue to do so. Next time, he would just modify his delivery, but the Noble had moved on, wishing now to set up a dialogue about the vagaries of time travel.

"In a new timeline, would she forget her real identity?"

How would Corky know that? Still, he had to answer. "Without evidence of a window into time, Noble, it is conjecture."

"Interface, if she is dead, there is no point in expending resources and energy retrieving her. However, if that anomaly is, as I suspect, a Lyran time portal, then it demands to be analysed."

Corky would have said again there was no evidence, but that would mean engaging in pointless debate. So instead, he gave a more measured response.

"We would first need to establish that is the case, Noble," he said. "It is a task I do not know how to accomplish. Although I can narrow Lieutenant Phildre's life signs to the anomaly, it does not mean she is contained within the phenomenon."

Yianevan disagreed. "I believe we should give credence to the possibility of a portal."

"At your request, Noble, I will place logic to one side, but as an interface, I am also programmed to make observations. Therefore, I cannot concur that this is the only explanation."

Yianevan understood. The interface was only doing its job.

"Very well," he said. "Find a better one, other than those you've already come up with."

Corky continued to run diagnostics since he interfaced with Yianevan's ship. The systems were running at optimum, but the anomaly had taken on a different perspective as it changed dimensions on the data tile. This was a mystery, but nothing about it implied a pathway to the future unless the Noble knew something not in Corky's program. The interface exhausted every possible angle, and despite the Noble insisting on a time portal, it believed the notion as improbable as Phildre surviving a lava flow. He decided not to further question Yianevan's orders, just do as he was told, but had to admit he had no other theories.

"As illogical as the theory of a time portal is, Noble," he said, "I agree we must explore all possibilities. If you are considering a forward time displacement, should we discard the possibility she moved backwards through time within a calming pennant?"

Yianevan suppressed a smile. An interface clutching at

straws. Rare indeed. He should report the humanising of this interface to the tribal ordinaries, but he rather liked that it was so personable. It never occurred to him to interact with his previous interface and help it develop a personality, and it certainly didn't develop one on its own. An interface like Corky might have assuaged the periods of loneliness and melancholy he experienced over the years, separated from his mother and brother. Too late for regrets now.

"I initiated the pennant," he told Corky, making no attempt to hide the fact he found the notion amusing. "I am pleased to report that a wraithlike Lieutenant Phildre did not emerge."

"Yes, Noble," Corky said. "I do not know if calming pennants displace time. It is rumoured only. However, perhaps the technology might afford us some clues."

"Except the pennants do not disperse energy to the future, Interface. By reputation, if it exists, the Monk's Gate does."

That gave Corky an idea. He replayed the sequence that showed Phildre setting the first pennant.

"It may be useful to examine the possibility the pennant triggered this anomaly when Lieutenant Phildre initiated the calming sequence," he said, displaying to the Noble the results of his subsequent scans of the planet's atmosphere. "I found no technology, even Lyran, but I continued with the theory it could originate from elsewhere. Therefore, I did not consider the effect of our own technology."

"We would have detected another ship, Interface. Perhaps the pennant did play a part."

Corky still had reservations. "Our theories have weak foundations, Noble. In pursuing the gate theory, I fear we might waste time making leaps from a myth to a legend to a fact, particularly now so much time has passed since Lieutenant Phildre went missing."

Yianevan had thought of that. "All we have are theories, Interface. What do you propose instead? That we concentrate on the anomaly and abandon the interventionist?"

Corky's circuits twitched at the idea of leaving Phildre to her fate and not getting answers. Perhaps "abandon" was a little premature. He revisited the possibility local inhabitants had rescued her.

"We do not study the societies," he added when he saw the Noble's sceptical reaction to the suggestion. "It might be a culture that would view someone kitted out like Lieutenant Phildre with mistrust and fear. She may be at the mercy of barbarians, and rescue warranted. Otherwise, the short answer is we could indeed abandon her. The locals would soon forget, and she might become a myth herself."

"And if we refer to the theory of a time portal as a likely location for her?"

"I have no data, Noble," Corky said. "And I am uncertain how any species could create a portal to something that does not yet exist, then exercise control where they or anyone went upon entering. I regret this sounds unsophisticated, but we are not speaking of known technology. Even hypothetically, I am not programmed for this situation.

"But you *can* hypothesise, Interface," Yianevan

pointed out. "You do it all the time. Work on this assumption and leave others to the side. If this is a window to the future, and the woman is there, how would we get her back?"

Corky indulged himself with another nanosecond to consider. The Nobles discarded the Monk's Gate theory centuries ago, leaving only a brief mention in their interface's databases. The unconfirmed rumour was the Nobles had command of time travel with the pennants, even to a minuscule degree. If the ancient Nobles could harness time enough to move energy, then reasonably, another species might also discover the specifics. Corky knew the Noble had already considered this, thus his confidence he had found the fabled Monk's Gate, but he was just an interface. What did he know? And the Noble was in charge.

"The anomaly appeared on only two sensor tiles, Noble," he said. "I cannot determine if it is a movable point. But I have this to offer; in the ancient Noble's brief study of future time travel, they assumed a single entry and exit. Therefore, if we follow their deduction, Lieutenant Phildre would need to exit the anomaly where she entered. As you can see, if she were to exit now, she would be incinerated by the eruption."

Yianevan agreed. Could the anomaly somehow be protecting the woman? It would explain her steady life signs, but why would Lyran technology protect her? Why would it need to? Unfortunately, he didn't have the luxury of a leisurely investigation, so he had to think on his feet.

"I believe she has moved beyond the anomaly and into

time. If this interventionist is Lyran, would it not be reasonable to assume she would be in the company of Lyrans on the other side?"

Corky had nothing of substance to add. "Noble, I can only speculate…"

"Speculate then…

"As time is in constant motion, a portal that exists as an entrance and exit may not occupy the same point. Further, Lieutenant Phildre is human. She does not possess any Lyran DNA, and there is no evidence she entered the anomaly willingly."

"And if it displaced an unsuspecting human in time?"

That was easy. "The unfamiliar environment, language, technology, and topography would disorient," Corky said. "The human may face a hostile environment or have reverted to childhood or extreme old age."

"Are you saying her memory of her true self might be disrupted, Interface? If she is human, confusion may cause her to seek help and draw unwelcome attention from the Lyrans hiding out in the future. However, if I am correct, and she is Lyran…"

Yianevan paused. He'd decided. "I am convinced the lieutenant is no longer on the mountain. We need to find a way into the anomaly. Although you say she is human, there can be no doubt something connects the woman to the gate. She may be the key to destroying the time portal…"

Corky interjected before the Noble got ahead of himself and issued a caution.

"It would be wise to alert the homeworld, Noble. Our scientists…"

Yianevan stopped the interface mid-sentence. "I will contact the homeworld when I consider it necessary."

That was clear enough. Corky wouldn't argue. Instead, he suggested that if Phildre suffered a memory lapse due to time differences, she would need to be guided back through the gate to return to this point. The Noble accepted that might be the case but suggested the anomaly might possess similar properties to the calming pennants. If so, there would be no opportunity to return.

"We need to locate the gate within the anomaly before carrying out a thorough investigation," Yianevan said. "It may require a physical presence."

"You cannot withstand the environment on the human planet, Noble."

"Then we need to send a human. If Lyrans still exist on the planet, perhaps in the future, would they be aware she came through?"

Corky would have rolled his eyes if he had any. What part of "no information" did this Noble not understand?

"They will either know, Noble," he replied. "Or they will not."

"Then our priority must be to decipher the anomaly and locate the interventionist and any Lyrans."

Yianevan knew the interface wanted to search for facts it could verify, and he had asked it to go against its programming. Something curious and exciting was unfolding on the planet below, and he could not explore it without the interface's help. He commanded Corky to increase monitoring to include every type of Lyran technology from ancient right through to their extinction.

Corky reminded him his programming did not include a Monk's Gate or any form of time travel technology.

"I think this gate is not to transport humans, Interface," Yianevan said. "I believe it is a hiding place until the Lyrans reach such numbers they can rise again. We do not know the future of the human planet. Perhaps in time, they will rival the Nobles in technology, which may be technology the Lyrans helped develop. We cannot ignore the possibility of a portal that gives the Lyrans an advantage over the galaxy and beyond."

"Assuming this is a portal that leads to the future."

If that came from an organic, it would have been a very dry comment, and it made Yianevan laugh.

"Interface, you have doubts! We program you to give opinions, and I would expect nothing less, but I am directing this investigation, and the anomaly's continued effect on the tile convinces me of its nature. It has depth, more like a well than a gate. Perhaps the Lyrans placed the generating device deep in the planet's crust, and the erasure beam from the calming pennant created a disturbance." He looked for an apt description for the possibility. "Perhaps the lieutenant woke it up."

"Noble, the only conclusive way to tell if this is indeed a gateway to elsewhere is to send someone through who can report back. That is if they *can* report back."

Yianevan agreed. It would be a risky mission, with capture by the Lyrans a definite possibility. Merris or Jardin might be suitable candidates. Both were enterprising and no strangers to risk. He suggested them as possibilities to the interface. Corky was tight-lipped about the goings-on aboard ship, but under the circumstances, the Noble might need to reconsider his choices.

"I do not wish to burden you with information about the crew's private lives, Noble," he said, "but Chief Jardin has formed an attachment to Lieutenant Phildre."

The crew had been together for several years, and Yianevan saw how there would be potential for deeper relationships. He hadn't considered it, always feeling removed from any emotional bond with other people, save perhaps his mother and brother.

"Attachment?" he echoed. "Friends? Or something more?"

"Something more in the chief's head, Noble. The lieutenant has never shown signs of encouragement."

"Then there is nothing to be concerned about."

"Yes, Noble, but without further information, Chief Jardin will contend she remains on the mountain, somehow concealed and protected. Of course, he will follow your orders, but unless you are prepared to share your theory, tasking him with this may present significant difficulties. A somewhat more malleable species, such as a Grielik, might be a more appropriate choice."

"We have already discounted the lieutenant surviving on the mountain," Yianevan said, cursing his limitation on time. "Summoning help from the ten sectors is a waste of resources. Jardin will surely agree that it is a physical impossibility for her to avoid burning lava or conceal herself in a crevasse. Will he also contend that an enterprising local saw her plight and dashed up the mountain to rescue her?"

Corky believed Jardin might contend many scenarios

without the full background, which the Noble was unlikely to provide. Yianevan's sarcasm was not lost on the interface, but it struggled with the probability of a Lyran-created time portal.

For Yianevan, he knew that if Lyrans had this technology before their extinction, and there was no evidence it did, such a creation could have dire consequences for the galaxy. He discounted Jardin and Merris as candidates, but it meant the only way was to approach the anomaly himself and see where it led. He would not allow the Lyrans to rise, and the interventionist had to be a key player.

The interface stood by, awaiting orders that would include contact with the homeworld.

Without another word, Yianevan turned and headed to his quarters.

CHAPTER EIGHT _

In need of a few minutes to collect his thoughts and consolidate the germ of an idea he conceived while speaking to the interface, Yianevan watched the developments on the planet below. The loss of life could have been worse. He could be witnessing the destruction of most of this continent. Upon checking the second pennant, he found the interventionist had not completed the initiation sequence. The event would be too catastrophic for one pennant to handle alone, yet he did not feel the interventionist's actions were deliberate. Why set one and not the other? Did she fall into the portal before she had time to complete the task? Was she pushed, or was she drawn in?

In his mind, Yianevan formulated a plan. If it failed and he perished, then his father would not take out his dissatisfaction on his younger brother. Of course, the clan father might retrieve the information about the anomaly from the interface, but Yianevan would most likely have to report it, anyway.

He poured and drained a glass of Birn, the rugged

liquid concoction the humans brought from their homeworld. Discovered early in his exile, he appreciated the sense of relaxation and clarity of mind the brew offered.

The flicker of a communication visual registered, but he didn't turn to acknowledge his elder sister's signature. She always turned up uninvited, purporting to be his father's envoy, but it was more to delight in plaguing her brother.

Aaris, the clan father's first-born child, resented Yianevan's position as heir. Her interest in her brother was only to hope that one day, she would turn up and find him dead. It was to her bitter disappointment that so far, he hadn't obliged. If the weak, rebellious heir died without a son, she could manipulate the younger brother until his majority, some five years hence, long enough to implement change that would favour her own sons.

There was little to rule within the hierarchy's strict traditions, but Aaris craved authority. As Regent Advisor, she would have power over the lesser houses. Even as a token figurehead, she believed governance was beyond her undeserving brother, whose selfish interests lay only in running from his responsibilities. To Aaris, the heir was a fool who didn't even deserve her pity. And it galled her that her only travels off-world were in holographic form. The heir's freedom only added to her bitterness.

If she only knew, her "undeserving" brother tacitly agreed that change needed to come to their society, except he possessed wisdom enough to be less vocal and not choose her as his confidante. Forced now into accepting his succession, Yianevan could not allow his father to learn of his vision for the Noble homeworld, or he might delay his abdication.

He poured another drink before addressing her.

"Sister," he said, aware even without looking, that her upper lip curled in condescension, and her chin lifted high with radiated and imagined superiority.

"Brother," she replied. "At leisure, I see. How goes the search for the interventionist?"

"She has strong life signs," Yianevan answered, "and we have her location. As we speak, I am working on a rescue plan."

Aaris's response dripped with sarcasm.

"How charitable to compromise yourself by attending an erupting volcano."

Yianevan seated himself before the comm-vis. Yes, there it was, the shimmering hologram of his sister, complete with the sneering smile that spoiled what otherwise would have been a beautiful face.

"As you know, Aaris, the Nobles' understanding of volcanoes is unsurpassed. This one holds no terror for me."

"Oh, but you mustn't contact the soil on your little sojourn, dear brother," Aaris replied with mock concern. "That would be a pity."

Yianevan sighed. "Is there a purpose to this interruption? Or am I just having a bad dream?"

"Our father sends his cautions, Yi. Retrieve the interventionist, but not at risk to your own life."

"I'm surprised you felt moved to come here with such a caution, sister." Yianevan gave a short, humourless laugh. "I imagined you languishing within the Marisene, awaiting news of my demise."

Aaris dipped her head. "That might yet be a welcome prospect. However, our father prefers outdated practices."

"He cares for the welfare of his people." Yianevan doubted the truth of that, but it was the right thing to say. "Tradition keeps them secure."

An impatient flick of her hand accompanied Aaris's reply. "You are not sincere. Retrieve the interventionist, or her body. That is the message. Or you may retrieve neither. It matters little to me. Our father awaits your return home. He has appointed your betrotheds."

"No doubt," Yianevan said. "For now, I am focused on this mission."

"Four days, brother," Aaris warned as her image faded. "You have four days."

Yianevan suspected it was not beyond the bounds of possibility that he would need to look over his shoulder for an assassin once he returned home. The idea made him grin. Aaris was too subtle for that. She would enjoy just making his life a misery.

Within the Noble hierarchy, the strongest relationships were between the clan father, his wives, seldom less than two, and their children. The first-born son, although Yianevan, up to now, believed himself excused from the tradition, was expected to succeed to the rulership of the homeworld when the father abdicated, which most typically came when the heir reached his majority at age forty. If the heir was under forty at abdication and there was an elder sister, they would appoint her as regent. It was the only form of governance permitted for hierarchical women and, even then, exceedingly rare.

Nobles were long-lived and could exceed one hundred and thirty years. Childhood ended at twelve, and adolescents spent the next eight years in intense study and education. Adulthood began at twenty, and majority came at forty. Yianevan's present age.

By tradition, the ruling clan father selected his heir's first two betrotheds. More commonly known as cleaveship, marriage only followed if a betrothed conceived a son. Once cleaved, a hierarchical woman enjoyed no change in her status. In contrast, a wife from a lesser house would become hierarchy only for the sake of any heirs she bore. She would remain free to pursue a career, receive acknowledgements for her achievements, and even travel off-world if her work demanded, provided all aspects remained under the direction of the ruling house. These wives from lesser houses were as valued as their hierarchical sisters, but they had more freedoms, an inequality Yianevan knew would need addressing sooner rather than later. The hierarchy did not grant females of the hierarchical houses off-world travel. If a member of the hierarchy wished to expand their mind, then the pursuit of knowledge was acceptable, provided it did not interfere with the social nature of the ruling house or wider hierarchy. However, any discovery, invention or achievement gained from this knowledge would become the domain of a lesser Noble or the tribal ordinaries. Women from lesser houses who married into the hierarchy could travel within the ten sectors if House Anevan endorsed such travel.

This demoralising and antiquated rule was no different for hierarchical males, even a clan father. They could never be acknowledged for an individual feat that might benefit the broader reach of the homeworld.

Accepting assignation as a betrothed was voluntary, but for some lesser Noble females, better recognition and access to greater technology was often an attractive proposition. Many females who cleaved with the hierarchical house of Anevan and its lower branches were physicians, scientists, and engineers. Any child born was raised within the sib, by aunts, uncles, cousins, and more importantly, the father, the natural mother and her sister-wife or wives. A perfect situation for a lesser Noble who wished to experience motherhood while maintaining her vocation.

Yianevan envied the freedoms of lesser Nobles. From now on, cultural and societal expectations would direct every aspect of his life. Because of his earlier rebelliousness, his father would watch him for signs of non-conformity. He would not abdicate until trust was re-established, so he could not allow his father any inkling of the changes he planned for the homeworld. He also envied the self-governance of the tribal ordinaries, so-called because of their inability to see into a person's "chak" to read emotional responses. It was an ability they seemed to have fared very well without, and one Yianevan viewed as a useless accessory considering the Noble's antipathy towards other worlds. He believed the hierarchy was wrong to not extend a welcome to other species. Other than the police force and covenant on the human world, his society shrouded itself in secrecy, resisting any overtures from other systems. This was just a tiny part of the stifling of the hierarchy's sons and daughters that Yianevan vowed to reform when he became ruler.

"Noble, I configured a program to align with your assumption the anomaly is a time portal," Corky said when Yianevan returned to the bridge. "As you have isolated the secondary privacy module, I now hold it in a separate file. I assume it is still your wish not to communicate your findings to the Noble homeworld?"

"You assume correctly, Interface."

"I directed all data to the new file. Therefore, it will not be discoverable should you wish never to share it."

"Very astute."

"Thank you, Noble. I spend much time around organics, and I have found that among their admirable traits, they are also capable of deceit."

Yianevan raised his eyebrows in surprise at the interface's somewhat pointed revelation, or perhaps, accusation.

"Deceit?"

"Yes, Noble," came the interface's matter-of-fact response. "I have 'fudged' reports on Lieutenant Phildre's authority when she wishes to explore a region not on our manifest. She describes these desires as a 'feeling'. The chief and second officer are complicit, and she frequently finds minor geological issues on the protected world with the potential to injure the local population. She uses a single pennant as a 'patch', and to hide her extracurricular activities, she 'fudges' the reports. This is her description of falsified reports. 'Fudged'."

Yianevan knew this interventionist was likely to move outside mission parameters, but she should not "fudge". Still, he acknowledged the slight ripple of guilt. It wasn't any different from what he was doing.

"Perhaps there is virtue in an unorthodox approach," he said.

Corky agreed. "Yes, Noble. Lieutenant Phildre is efficient."

"I have seen her commendations." Yianevan pointed to the tiles, where the anomaly now obscured each one. "Please report on your progress."

"I recreated the events leading up to the loss of the lieutenant, Noble. My findings were inconclusive, so I widened the spiral's input gain to improve visuals and then overrode its sensors. This is an illegal procedure, but it proved useful. I aimed the spiral at the lieutenant's last known coordinates and received this communication. I am attempting to clean it up, but there is no accompanying biotelemetry or audio."

With such crude and unfocused data, viewing the scene was almost like looking through a kaleidoscope of merging colours and shapes. Admittedly, it was incomplete, but as it cleared, it offered two things of considerable interest. First, it contained movement. Second, possible industrialisation.

"Industry and mechanisation…" Yianevan glanced at the interface, "… and life. Can you link the interventionist's biosigns to these images?"

"Not to the images, Noble, but they remain steady within the anomaly. As you have observed, this vision possesses both an industrial and mechanised component, but my sensors detect only population density on the planet. I cannot lock in to identify the technology. There are other inhabited worlds in nearby systems. It could be a projection."

However, Corky expected the Noble to presume he was looking into the future of the human planet and wouldn't accept the possibility of an echo or external transmission.

"The Lyrans appear to have exercised no influence over human technology," he said, isolating examples of the mechanisation. "At least not in this sample. If a portal to the future exists, it will be impossible to locate Lyrans in the timescape."

The images showed a backward civilisation, but if the interface could prove they projected from another world, how would it explain the anomaly's role as a receiver? Yianevan put the idea to Corky, who agreed he couldn't prove anything and only offered the vague suggestion that the anomaly might be a lens of some type. Yianevan's previous interface never had this many opinions or operated so much on guesswork, but then, he never asked it to take part in a project this remarkable.

"Interface," he said. "You will not accept that we have discovered the Monk's Gate. Only hours ago, you would not entertain the idea this was anything other than a 'smudge'. Lens or gate, call it what you will; whatever it is showing us is worthy of investigation."

Corky conceded events had progressed, but in the beginning, the parameters of the anomaly did not alert him to a threat. It was just that. A smudge. Now, in its evolution from its original state, he acknowledged it exhibited qualities he needed time to define. The Noble continued to assert his conviction his own theory of the gate was valid and that the analysis would proceed on that assumption. Corky would have preferred a more scientific explanation. Except he didn't have one. The theory of a gate into time required stretching what humans called "imagination". He reasoned that if the Lyrans planned to return, they would not experiment with the primitive four-wheel vehicles in the images. Instead, they would have transported their technology and resources to their destination to advance their knowledge.

As they discussed these possibilities, Corky pointed out that if what they viewed was indeed the mythical Monk's Gate, the images could be just one timeline in potentially infinite timelines. Yianevan saw Corky's point, but among those infinites, they had a focus; the interventionist's life signs still emanating from the anomaly. He told Corky to direct his search toward the images for the physical location of the interventionist.

"It might be just one possible timeline," he said, "but it also might be the most relevant. Meanwhile, I require your input on a different matter."

"Another hypothesis, Noble?"

Yianevan ignored him.

"The soil on this planet is considered the most toxic known to my species. If I were to apply a graft to suppress my Noble physiology, how long could I withstand the conditions?"

Corky checked his database before replying because a

graft that defied the toxicity of certain soils was new to him.

"As I have no data on such grafts, Noble," he said, "I can only advise that any physiological suppressant to override your DNA is likely to be disastrous. You may survive the graft. Then again, you may not."

Corky displayed the ratio of deadly soil fungi and bacteria before continuing. "If you survive the graft, you may also survive the soil fungi. Then again…"

"I may not," Yianevan finished for him.

"Yes, Noble. I assume you are contemplating an attempt to enter the anomaly. Even with further study, there is no guarantee I can retrieve you."

Yianevan listened to Corky's conclusions, but all the hypothesising and theorising weren't getting him anywhere. The interface assumed he would visit the planet and see for himself. Of course he would. The woman was there, and she was his lead to understanding the gate. He was sure of it.

However, Corky disagreed, and he had no choice but to issue another caution.

"If this graft, which I do not believe to be sanctioned by your government, protects you on the planet," he said, "your appearance is distinctive and would be apparent to a Lyran. If you are correct, and this is a Lyran time portal, they would detain you for certain and possibly execute you. Your presence may even precipitate a Lyran uprising. Therefore, I must counsel you to reconsider."

"My mother was a botanist and phytopathologist," Yianevan told him. "The graft not only exists but has aided me on other worlds. I believe it will offer enough protection for a brief visit. Keep monitoring my biosigns. As for being recognised..." He grinned. "Camouflage is my speciality."

Yianevan positioned himself before an imager. He looked like any Noble. Pale skin, straight nose, white hair, lean body, and long limbs. His face was proportioned but not as rounded as a human's. Still, it was at least a clean canvas upon which to work. He didn't have to add the random dermal bumps and moles sported by humans, nor the tiny facial horns of the C'aanastre, or even the extra digits on each hand of the Chabin natives. Deciding there was little to disguise, he set about enhancing some of his other features.

He considered Jardin's tall, muscled physique and bronzed skin. Unfortunately, the Nobles had no well-defined musculature, but there were also thin humans, so he wouldn't worry too much about that. Besides, not every human male looked like Jardin, and he didn't care for the short and spiky hairstyle the interventionist fleet officers favoured.

So, trimming his long hair up around his ears, he copied Jardin's hair colour, light brown with reddish highlights, then applied blue optical prosthetics to his eyes. These devices took several hours to integrate and interfered with his compound retinas. That made reading chaks problematic. No matter. When the interface located the woman, it would be a simple extraction and removal to his homeworld for interrogation. It would no doubt take the focus off him for a while. Besides, this disguise was only in case the Lyrans spotted him.

Hair and eyes meeting his approval, Yianevan adjusted his complexion a few shades darker. The unnatural result made him revert to a tint that did little to hide his paleness, but he found it more realistic. Then he darkened his eyebrows and eyelashes, which apart from his head, was the only hair on a Nobles' body.

Yianevan lamented that his mouth did not possess the fullness he observed with Chief Jardin and many other humans, but he believed he would pass for a human male on any planet. Oddly, it was a disguise he'd never considered before, even though the ten sectors accepted and liked the humans. All he needed now was suitable attire and a location.

As he caught sight of his reflection, he wondered if an attitude adjustment might also be called for. Overconfidence did not always guarantee a good outcome.

"Progress?" he asked the interface.

"I cannot narrow the technology in the vision to the Lyrans or any other known species, Noble."

"Have you made any further viewings?"

"Others appear within the original," Corky said, displaying a rather complicated and tangled visual. "I am attempting to isolate them, but my expertise is deficient, so I cannot say if it is one or many timelines. The spiral is communicating, but its telemetry is erratic. I also cannot determine from which of these points it is transmitting."

"Very well. Could we be viewing the Lyrans' hiding places somewhere in the planet's future, but not at a time where they exerted influence?"

"I can neither confirm nor deny that theory, Noble," Corky admitted. "I would fail in my duty if I did not express my doubt that what we saw was anything other than an echo from another place. The industrial advancement is inconclusive…"

Corky suddenly fell to silence, leaving Yianevan to watch and wait in confusion as the interface rearranged the datum.

"Interface?"

"Noble, I have located Lieutenant Phildre."

Yianevan drew a deep breath. At last.

"On the mountain?"

"No, Noble. At the point of the images. I can fix the link, but she appears to be moving."

At that moment, the anomaly disappeared from tiles, reappearing immediately on external sensors at the original site.

"How did it do that?" Yianevan flicked across the data tiles. They were clean.

Corky didn't know, but for what was still basically a smudge, it was a fascinating development because it restored the tiles to their initial smudge-free state.

"Could it be responding to the interventionist?" Yianevan said after considering the obvious answers, such as intelligence or programming.

"A possibility, Noble. The characteristics changed when I detected the lieutenant."

This confirmed to Yianevan that the interventionist and the anomaly were linked. He would not waste another second.

"Bring the spiral."

"I do not have a firm lock on her coordinates, Noble," Corky cautioned. "I cannot be sure where the spiral will deliver you. If the anomaly disappears again, it might not return, and you will be lost."

This was no time to heed a cautious interface's warnings. A brief visit to gain much-needed intelligence was worth the risk, but Corky thought it a pointless exercise. A visit to the planet might give information, and it might also task him with informing the Noble homeworld of the loss of their heir. Yianevan though was determined and continued with his preparations.

Seeing the Noble would not be dissuaded, Corky suggested inserting a language processor under his skin to gather syntax examples. Yianevan felt he would agree to anything in the face of his mounting excitement. The last twenty years had provided a wealth of experiences, but the prospect of experiencing time travel? Any risks to himself had to be a secondary consideration.

Language processors were a necessary adjunct in his disguises when visiting worlds where the dialect was unfamiliar, so this would be no different. However, the future would be unlike any other world he had visited before. His anticipation of the mission scaled up, and he became impatient to get started. Even the interface's gloomy predictions of how it might turn out failed to dissuade him.

While Yianevan self-administered the graft, Corky synthesised a bundle of clothing copied from the view through the gate. He couldn't guarantee the accuracy, and it might draw unwelcome attention. Still, it was not an interface's job to tell someone from the race of his creators what to do, even though he often commented. He attempted a tone that sounded more like a concerned colleague than an interface issuing another caution for the Noble to reject.

"Noble, it is not just your appearance that troubles me," he said. "If you step from the spiral, it may not locate you again. You would be stranded."

Yianevan dismissed Corky's concerns. "Set me down as near as possible, and don't worry about language. I understand several human dialects. We shall just have to trust it retains many of its distinctions. You can make adjustments when you analyse the processor."

"Noble, if as you insist, you will be in a later time, I respectfully remind you the very last of the abducted humans were from different continents with different languages. The language will have evolved."

The interface had a point, but Yianevan was like a child just granted an extra ride at the fair.

"It is all a risk, Interface," he declared.

There was little point in arguing. The Noble had made up both their minds.

"Yes, Noble," Corky responded as it once again tried to pinpoint the ghostly figure of the interventionist through the shadowy pages of the future.

CHAPTER NINE _

"Pardon me!" The tall man moved to steady Bethan as he collided with her on the post office steps. "I'm afraid my mind was elsewhere."

She smiled a "no harm done" smile. The man accepted her assurance, raised his homburg hat in a polite gesture and continued on his way.

Under other circumstances, Bethan would not have given such an event any thought, but his appearance caught her eye, and she watched him as he strode away. His brown worsted overcoat, polished shoes and homburg seemed out of place in a mining village. Most men hereabouts wore flat caps and well-worn jackets, so it was unusual to see someone dressed as smartly out and about on a chilly morning. Her curiosity was fleeting because she had so many other things on her mind and still so much to organise before she left for London.

Bethan's best friend, Ivy, looked up from behind the counter. She worked at the post office a couple of days each week as respite from caring for an ailing mother, an arrangement that had been in place since leaving school. Ivy's pretty face broke into a delighted smile at the sight of her friend, her bridge of pale freckles crinkling across her nose.

"Hello, Bethan," she said. "I haven't seen you all week! I was starting to think you'd already left for London!"

Bethan couldn't help smiling because Ivy's natural cheerfulness was always a tonic. She pushed an envelope across the counter.

"I need to send these certificates to Australia, Ivy. Owen asked for them."

Ivy fished around in the drawer underneath her desk to find the international postage stamps, a rare request in this village. While she searched, she asked, "Are you going to the social tomorrow, Bethie?".

Bethan was ready with an excuse. She hated gatherings.

"I can't, Ivy. I've got too much to do."

Ivy was a master at manifesting her emotions on her face. As she plonked the stamp down on the counter, Bethan saw she had skillfully woven massive disappointment into her expression.

"It's just a social, Bethie," she pleaded. "We may never see each other again after July."

Ivy had been Bethan's best friend in a world where she had few, despite the three-year age gap. Bethan didn't go on to the local senior school when she left primary, and for Ivy, they were the loneliest years of her life. With Bethan leaving for London, then on to Australia, she had to face that loss again, so she was determined to spend as much time with Bethan as possible.

Ivy had a point, even though Bethan had no intention of losing touch.

"Of course we'll see each other," she promised. "I'll be in London for three years before I go to Australia, and I will visit you. There's plenty of time."

Ivy smiled, but her shoulders drooped. Such tactics had worked before, and they did now. This meant a lot to Ivy, so Bethan backtracked.

"Okay," she said with a sigh. "I'll come."

Having got her way, Ivy brightened and clapped her hands together. She didn't seem to see she didn't need Bethan. Her popularity with the local lads and the others who came in for the dance from the neighbouring villages often meant Bethan walked home alone.

"I'm so glad, Bethie," Ivy exclaimed. "It'll be splendid. You might even meet a nice man and decide to stay here."

Bethan gave her friend an "as if" look and grinned. "You know what they say, Ivy. Nice men are like the number twenty-four bus."

Ivy looked puzzled. "We don't have a number twenty-four bus in the village."

Bethan gave her a knowing nod. "Come by at seven. We'll walk together."

Once outside, Bethan stood on the post office steps while she put on her gloves. March had arrived, crisp and clear. A sprinkling of snow still dusted the distant peaks, like icing sugar on rock cakes, and for a change, the air smelled sweet rather than tinged with the odours from the new industrial centre across the valley. She sometimes fancied she recalled the acrid smell of coal, but she left here when she was twelve, while the mine was still operating. It seemed so long ago, but the memories and the grime-covered buildings remained. The mountains gave a glimpse of beauty, but the snow-dusted peaks were so distant, they might as well be on the moon and only added to Bethan's sense of confinement.

As a starry-eyed teenager, full of hope and ambition, she had returned from boarding school bursting with dreams and energy. It turned out her freedom to dream was short-lived because of her parents' poor health. After they died, and to stop her feelings of pointlessness, she took the first job she could find, as a secretary to an electrical contractor with a small shop across town. Several years passed before she resurrected the idea of disentangling herself from the village.

That evening after work, Bethan let herself into the terraced cottage left to her upon her parents' death. She had been born here in one of the two upstairs bedrooms on her mam and dad's bed, a giant old oak monstrosity with a goose-down mattress that became the heart of a bonfire in a local field many years before. Mam and dad found the money to buy a new one and gladly donated the sagging sack for a Guy Fawkes Night ritual.

Bethan shared a bedroom with her brother and grandmother until she was four. Owen, eleven years her senior, ran away from home at fifteen. He surfaced in Australia at the beginning of the war, far wealthier than when he had left Wales years before. He offered to pay for his family to move to a "better" area, but grandma refused to budge, her determination supported by Bethan's parents.

All the Davies family lived in this village, so the argument went, and Bethan knew it well, having heard it many times, but she had no such attachment.

When Owen suggested joining him in Australia when she completed her training, Bethan agreed. She wouldn't be sad to see the back of the grimy, old, dilapidated house that reeked of lack of ambition, failure, even death, and would use the proceeds to fund her expenses in London. Determined not to live off her brother, despite his success abroad, she looked forward to independence. That word always made her smile because her mother warned her against it, telling her daughter often that a woman had no status unless she had a man.

That fact got hammered home when Bethan tried to open an account at the local bank when she started working. The teller told her a male had to countersign the application, and as her father was dead and her only male relative overseas, her new boss obliged. It was humiliating, and that single incident made Bethan swear she would never depend on anyone. However, her mother's primary goal before her death, even from her sickbed, was to see her daughter married, despite Bethan making it clear she had no such thing in mind. She adored her mother, so to keep her happy, she once accepted an invitation to the cinema with a local boy but refused the offer of a second outing.

Now Bethan had a problem. The house hadn't sold. The only interest was from the local council, but they were yet to make a firm offer. So, in a bold move, Bethan placed it in the hands of an estate agent in Swansea. It was a leap of faith as few people sold houses around here, and when they did, it was to the mine. Now, there was no mine to sell to. The agent sent a man to value the house, and he told her some young couples in London were looking for properties within commuting distance to larger towns and areas where the local industry was growing. That was happening across the valley, and there was a regular bus service, but the type of work available seemed too menial for someone to afford a house.

Still, renting out was another avenue to consider, but Bethan wanted rid of it. Making sure she had no reason to return was part of stepping across the threshold of her brave new world.

On Saturday, Bethan laid out her best dress on the bed. She'd packed it already, possibly a little prematurely, but she didn't expect to wear it again before leaving for London. She liberated herself of a lot of old clothes and sold some surplus furniture, ready for her move. The local children could use anything left for a bonfire, with the serviceable pieces going to charity.

A photo of her parents, looking very serious, sat on the bedside table. That picture always made Bethan feel a little disloyal about her chosen path, even though she could not see a life for herself in this village. The world beckoned. Anywhere away from the village beckoned. She missed Owen when he left all those years ago, but now she understood why he went.

Bethan stood beside Ivy, a glass of fruit punch in her hand, watching a handful of couples sway with self-conscious awkwardness to music too antiquated for anyone to recognise.

Bethan ungraciously called the dance a "stand" because a local reverend who dreamed up this gathering considered music written after the first world war to be "of the devil". He permitted only the slowest of dances where he could monitor any "hanky panky". Consequently, the small band of musicians played only Welsh folk tunes and improvised Bach or Strauss. When the newly incumbent rector took over, a man who inherited his predecessor's moral ideals, he took the rules one step further, insisting unmarried couples ensured their torsos did not touch while dancing. He sometimes even went to the trouble of passing a ruler between them to check.

"I'm not sure I'll come to these when you're gone, Bethie," Ivy said, although she grinned from ear to ear as she observed what she called "talent". Some lads came in from the surrounding area to "stand", and most regulars, like Ivy, seemed to find a way around the rules and danced all evening. Many bored young people from across the valley came here for recreation, and there was only one rector who couldn't be everywhere! Some only turned up to mock the villagers with their unmodern ways, but Constable Marley kept his eye out for troublemakers if they got too rowdy. Tonight though, the cold kept away everyone except the most dedicated, like Ivy.

"Of course you'll come," Bethan said. "You enjoy it. You'll have to get yourself a steady boyfriend to bring."

Ivy laughed. "And where would I meet a boy I've not known since we were kids? At the grocers? The butchers?

One of the toothless old men who've lived in this village since it was built? I don't want to get the bus on my own and go out of town to the other socials. Mam would have a fit if I did that. Still, I don't plan to be the girl who waits for the number twenty-four!"

"What about the boys from across town?"

Ivy nodded. "They're okay, but some are a bit rough, and I'd have to go to their socials to meet them. They don't always come here." She looked towards the door, then craned her neck to check the entrance hall. "I wonder if Jacob Barton is coming tonight?"

Bethan knew Ivy's determination not to go to another town on her own might doom her to eternal spinsterhood. Never marrying didn't worry Bethan. She had mapped out her future, which didn't include a man, but Ivy dreamed of a husband and children for as long as Bethan could remember. It's just there were such slim pickings in the village. If Jacob, Ivy's long-term crush, didn't start returning the interest, Ivy might have to wait for a random number twenty-four bus!

Each town around the valley hosted a Saturday night social on a monthly roster, and for Ivy, a pretty redhead with a curvy figure that reflected a love of bread and sweet things, they were her sole means of meeting people who were not as old as her mother. She would have liked to go to all the socials, but because of that late-night bus ride home, she wouldn't unless Bethan accompanied her.

Bethan's dad called Ivy "modern". Her mam, though, called her "loose" and used her as a caution to Bethan. Ivy was friendly and flirtatious around men, but Bethan knew her friend didn't warrant her reputation. Also, Ivy was generous to a fault and devoted to her disabled mother, a dedication that wasn't likely to end anytime soon because so far, her mother had defied all the grim reaper's attempts to claim her.

The local lads knew Ivy's home situation and that at least for now, she wasn't likely to trap a boy into marriage, so they felt safe at having a bit of harmless fun. The younger men from outside the village were more interested in Bethan because of her striking looks, grey eyes, raven hair and smooth skin with a hint of olive, but she was aloof, unapproachable, and older than most of them. And that suited Bethan just fine. She was only ever here to keep Ivy company, anyway. On occasions, she danced with Mr Griffiths from the grocer's shop or Mr Thomas from the bakers, and again, that was just fine.

Tonight, neither the grocer nor the baker were here, so when a couple of lads vied for Ivy's attention, Bethan found herself alone, wondering for the umpteenth time why she had agreed to come.

Finding a table where she could practice her wallflower skills, she waited until she could leave without anyone noticing. As she made to sit down, she heard a familiar voice.

"Good evening, we meet again."

Bethan turned to the man who had bumped into her on the post office steps. He lifted his hat in greeting, and she couldn't help but smile at his formality.

"Do you always wear a hat, even indoors?" she asked.

The man's eyes widened as if caught out in a social

gaffe, and he pulled the hat from his head, leaving his fine hair to stick up in a flourish of unruly wisps.

"I'm sorry," he said. "I've only just arrived here." He looked around as if trying to determine where he had arrived at. "I stepped in from the street when I heard the festivities."

His voice had a strange cadence, and Bethan couldn't place where he might be from. Not anywhere in Wales, that was for sure.

"Well, not very festive," she replied. "The piece they're playing right now is Y Gwcw Fach. It's a Welsh folk song and the fastest tune they've played all evening. It seems no-one wanted to brave the cold, hence the lack of support. Either way, I'm afraid most consider this social a little old-fashioned."

"Do you think that?"

In response, Bethan nodded toward Ivy. "I only came to keep my friend company. The girl with the red hair. She doesn't really need me."

The man glanced across, then turned back to Bethan. "My name is Ian Noble."

Yianevan had practised a friendly tone, but the words felt awkward on his tongue. He knew body language would accompany the initial greeting, but he'd only got as far as lifting his hat because he didn't know what else to do. Even to him, his voice sounded strange, something he hoped to avoid. The woman seemed receptive, but judging by her look of bemusement, it was fair to assume he'd already given her that impression.

After his first few failed visits to the planet, Corky

analysed the vocal processor. The syntax was not dissimilar to a range of human dialects carried forward, dialects which Yianevan had a vague acquaintance with. He still had to undergo subliminal tutoring, but the entire exercise was rushed, so not entirely satisfactory, and there was no time to perfect his conversation skills. The result was that to the ears of a native speaker, he might sound very foreign, but he had to proceed and bluff his way through. So he smiled and added,

"I've just moved to the village."

"Well, welcome to Llanbleddynllwyd," Bethan grinned. "I'm Bethan Davies."

She took in the man's soft white hands and manicured ultra-clean nails. He didn't look like he would have much to do with mining or the industrial area unless he worked in an office, and a clerk could not afford those expensive clothes, even if they were a hangover from the forties. Ian was tall, with light brown hair, a little longer than fashionable, and intense blue eyes. He had a well-educated air, so a solicitor maybe, she wondered. Something to do with the mine winding up? He also seemed awkward, as if he was expecting her to say more. Seeing he wasn't forthcoming, she took a stab at his occupation.

"Are you from the NCB?"

Yianevan gave Bethan a polite smile while he made a mental note to look up that acronym at the first opportunity. This NCB appeared to provide a valid reason to visit the village, so he would accept it.

"Yes. NCB."

"I assumed they were pretty much finished at the pit."

"They are," Yianevan said. It was essential to sound knowledgeable. NCB must relate to mines, and he hoped he hadn't painted himself into a corner. When Corky told him about the village, he studied at the book repository to appraise himself on local industry. The information was clearly not current as he had learned now the mine was not operating, and this woman had confirmed it. He had concocted a diverting lie about being a geologist and surveyor but so far had not come up with a workable story, leaving him to hope that between this mysterious NCB and surveying, he would convince her.

"My work is in geological surveys of the area," he said, flexing his lying muscles. "The pit and the NCB are minor features of my work."

"Well, you don't look as if you go underground much."

"No," Yianevan smiled. "Not very much."

The woman was quite open in her silent appraisal. Yianevan expected it and hoped his disguise and answers held up. So far, so good. She didn't appear to recognise him as a Noble, but he had never met a Lyran, so he had no idea how he would know. With the optical prosthetics, Yianevan couldn't read her chak, so he couldn't be sure of any differences. So far, his simple plan to remove her to the gate via the spiral encountered many obstacles, and he realised his confidence vastly outweighed his knowledge. Even making direct contact with her the previous morning had not encouraged the spiral to recognise her. He visited the planet several times before finding his target, but on each visit, he had not come across a single person who appeared to be involved in amassing weapons or developing technology. If these were Lyran Monks, the scourge of the galaxy, they were all somewhat predictable and ordinary.

Still, he needed to learn about the gate, and the interventionist was his best bet in gaining an understanding, as she was the last person, at least that he knew of, to go through it. From her, he might learn how to bring about its destruction before any Lyrans accessed it to renew the war.

So far, however, Yianevan's observations told a different story. The Lyrans within the interventionist's vicinity appeared to have technologically regressed. The machines used for transport and industry matched the technology he and Corky observed in their first imaging and corresponded almost to the pre-history of other cultures in the ten sectors. He also struggled with the lack of cultural advancement, making him wonder if another gate elsewhere led to a different future where society and technology had progressed. If so, why did the interventionist end up here? Did the Lyrans have a specific plan for her?

Like the few people he met elsewhere in the village and neighbouring town, the woman exhibited curiosity about him. She seemed accepting, even a little amused by his accent and manner.

"You aren't Welsh," Bethan said. "Where are you from?"

"I live and work abroad," he told her. "I am only here for a few months, then I plan to return home."

He seems nice, Bethan thought, attractive in a late-bloomer adolescent way. He didn't even look as if he needed to shave, yet he had to be older than fifteen to be a surveyor. His voice was deep and the accent unusual and intriguing, almost as if he'd only recently learned to speak English. And each time he answered, he didn't seem to know how to follow up. Shy? Maybe, but he approached her, so maybe not, and that only added to the intrigue.

"Are you going to ask me to dance?" she said, holding out her hand in invitation.

"Dance?"

Yianevan groaned inwardly and looked towards the dance floor. The Nobles' physical interpretation of music took a different form, so he had no choice but to admit, "I have never danced."

"Never?" Bethan almost laughed. Everyone in the world had danced at least once. "I can't believe that!" she said. "Put your hat on the table and take off your coat. Now they've got their one quick-paced piece out of the way, the band will only play slow tunes. Don't worry. There's no danger of me tripping you up."

Yianevan trailed Bethan out onto the dance floor. This wasn't how things were meant to transpire, being led and not in control. The interventionist had suggested an employer, and he'd agreed. She suggested he do this "dance" exercise, and he had followed. It emphasised Corky's warnings he knew too little about this society.

Corky had proved a significant resource. Over the last few hours, Yianevan could almost forget it was just an interface, but it had configured its systems to glean information about this place. Yianevan resolved to study more and not be caught out again. He had been too confident, waving away the interface's recommendations regarding the social environment into which he was to be deposited.

Fortunately, he had no difficulty mastering the controls of the primitive transport Corky secured from a farmer's derelict barn, employing repair bots to facilitate an adequate overhaul. As each bot depleted, the temperamental spiral refused to return them to the ship, so Yianevan had to bury them in a field.

The interface also discovered a learning repository in a nearby town called a library. Yianevan spent many hours there leading up to "bumping" into the woman to ensure she was who he sought. Corky removed him often, and he observed with interest that time passed at a different rate here than on the ship. There, he could still view the progress of Vesuvius's eruption. Here, on the planet, it was ancient history.

Now he had met the interventionist, he felt pressed to convince her he was human and could be her friend, and that meant learning human ways on a strange world with peculiar customs and inclement weather. He'd visited many worlds and civilisations, all with their idiosyncrasies, but none as unevolved as this Earth. All ten sector worlds had space travel, even in rudimentary development.

This was a first for Bethan to take the lead and ask a handsome stranger to dance, and she wondered what her mother would say about her being so forward. She wasn't sure Ian enjoyed being led because, like most novice dancers as they followed instructions, he concentrated too hard on what his feet were doing, unable to look up and go with the music. It made the entire experience just a little more untidy than necessary, and Bethan would have preferred he stepped on her foot now and then rather than take it so seriously.

Yianevan didn't notice these things, only that in his concentration, he felt foolish for causing the two of them to bump heads as he kept track of the progress of his feet. Rhythm escaped him to the point his analysis of moving to the music made her laugh. He was also still working on the human concept of humour and didn't know what was so funny.

Ivy monitored proceedings as she danced, then caught Bethan's eye to give her an approving nod. Bethan seldom gave herself permission to enjoy herself, so it was nice to see her friend with someone who made her laugh, for whatever reason.

Bethan's tolerance for Ian's clumsy efforts had limits, so she suggested they return to the table. Once seated, he found his voice, asking polite questions about the village, its history, and the people. All the while, she noticed he studied her face as if waiting for her to give away something meaningful or to declare a fact that he required before he ended the interview. Interview? Odd that she would think of meeting someone at a dance as an interview. That aside, Ian carried himself in the most gentlemanly and charming way. Despite that, Bethan hesitated when he asked to see her home. He put on his hat and shrugged himself into his coat without waiting for an answer.

"I have a vehicle," he said but then remembered what he learned about rules of propriety. "Or we can walk." Yes, less suggestive.

Bethan felt unsure. Although other women seemed to

get away with it, there was something not nice about being picked up at a dance. She looked across at Ivy.

"I can't just abandon my friend."

"She seems to have plenty of admirers. Why not ask her if she minds you leaving?"

While Bethan hesitated, Ivy took matters out of her hands by waving, then mouthing, *"It's fine, go on"*, before continuing her surreptitious canoodling with her dance partner. As a rule, Ivy left with a man, and Bethan was the one to make her own way home. It seemed odd to be turning the tables.

She smiled at Ian. How could she know her next few words would start her on a journey that would turn her world on its head?

"I'll get my coat."

CHAPTER TEN _

Yianevan knew where Bethan lived, but he couldn't let her know he'd been spying on her. That would be creepy anywhere in the galaxy, so he allowed her to steer him. He recognised the park leading to her street, a popular area for older people taking an evening constitutional and for dog walkers.

Dogs. Canines. The Lyrans overlooked abducting these delightful beasts. If Yianevan had his way, he would exchange every cat in the ten sectors for dogs. They came in all shapes and sizes and had an affinity with organics. Best of all, they knew their place. Not like cats, who believed themselves to be descended from gods.

Horses were also overlooked by the Lyrans but greatly admired by Yianevan. So far, his only encounter with the beautiful animals had been with one that pulled a filthy cart filled with what he could only describe as household garbage. The horse paused in its work to refresh itself at a water trough at this park. Despite its somewhat tatty appearance, the grace and intelligence of the animal inspired

Yianevan to spend an enjoyable morning studying the species.

Despite the primitive aspects of this society, there was much to enjoy and discover. He only wished he had more time.

The park had been the village's only green space for as long as Bethan could remember, spoiled a little because the pithead was part of the scenery. There was a separate field where men sometimes came to play rugby, but it was getting less use with the man-drain from the village and the closest towns. Ian asked about the village, and as he seemed interested, Bethan dredged up her not-so-modest store of knowledge.

In the olden days, she told him, this part of the village was filled with slums. Rundown cottages the miners called home. Substandard sanitation and poverty contributed to regular epidemics, which Bethan supposed kept the population down. But there were always families with young sons ready to take over when a father or older brother perished in the pit or succumbed to one of the many diseases prevalent to life underground. She worked through a condensed history of Llanbleddynllwyd's mining past and spoke about the anonymous benefactor who donated a pile of money to the village to improve conditions. The injection of these funds meant that at the turn of the century, they built new cottages further up the hillside. Once they demolished the slums and cleared the ruins, the mine owners established the green area, now managed by the local council.

Bethan pointed out features better seen in daylight, and

she grudgingly conceded the park was rather pretty. Established flower beds and trees and shrubs skirted the lawned area, and swings and a slide for any children who might visit. It was unfortunate they positioned the park close to the rear of the baker's shop. Further, some town planner with no creative vision placed a bench facing the pavement and the uninspiring faded yellow brick of the baker's back wall. This meant that upon sitting, instead of facing the grassed area, one's feet stuck out across the pavement. Bethan giggled as she showed him. Yianevan saw the humour. It was fine for this time of night, but during the day, when people were out and about and the flowers were bright and vibrant, it was odd to be facing away from all that colour.

Bethan surprised herself she discovered so much to tell him. Ian gave her little opportunity to draw breath. As soon as she answered a question, he came back with another. He was very prepared with each one, and she wondered if he saw her as a local historian. She was about to direct him to the library across town or even find one of those leaflets so he could go to the historical society's meeting, but there had been at least half a minute since she answered his previous question, so she didn't get the chance.

"Have you lived here long?" he asked.

Something made her hate to admit it. Living here most of her life made her feel insignificant, and judging by Ian's accent and refinement, he must be well-travelled, maybe even to exotic places. All she had was this life. That was the truth, and she shouldn't feel ashamed. His questioning, although rapidly delivered, had been polite, and his curiosity seemed genuine. If he judged her by her circumstances, then so be it. Honesty is always the best policy.

She shrugged. "All my life. And my parents before, and my grandparents before. I expect generations before that too. I don't really know."

"Do you have siblings?"

"Siblings?" Bethan laughed. "*Siblings*?"

"I'm sorry. Brothers or sisters."

"I know what it means, Ian, but I doubt many people around here would. I'm not sure if we allow people who say, 'siblings' into Wales!"

Yianevan stopped in his tracks. How could he make such a blunder? Corky's analysis of the processor had been thorough, but if a simple word was offensive and might draw the attention of the justice system…

Bethan giggled at his horrified expression.

"I'm joking, Ian. Your speech is a little unusual, but it's fine."

She was laughing and making a joke. The two things together. Yes, "fine".

"My sense of humour is a little rusty," he admitted.

"Don't worry." Bethan was having a rather fun time. "And to answer your question, I have a brother, Owen, who lives in Australia. He found village life and the idea of going down the mines confining and ran away. I also have my grandmother in a nursing home in Denbigh. It's a long way from here, but it is a private home, paid for by my brother, and she loves it. So I go by train." She held up her fingers. "Two trains."

"Do you see her?"

Bethan made a guilty face. "Not in a while. I used to bake pice bach for her once a month to take to her. They were such a treat when I was growing up. Then, a couple of years ago, every time I visited, she would get upset and say, 'You're not my Bethie'. It happened so often I decided writing letters would be less harrowing. The nurses read them to her, and they say she enjoys them. She's ninety, so perhaps her mind has wandered."

"Peekybark?"

Bethan bit her lip at his clumsy attempt to copy her pronunciation of a traditional recipe.

"Welsh cakes in English," she said. "They're like a flat scone with dried fruit and cooked on a bakestone. I still make them when the fancy takes me."

"I see. And you don't find this village confining as your brother did?"

"Yes, I do!" Bethan shot back. "I am utterly cloistered. Fit to burst!" Then, without trying to hide her pride and excitement, she added, "I'm going to London to become a nurse, then I'm joining Owen in Australia. It's all arranged."

For a moment, Yianevan wondered if he had the right woman. If she were Lyran, she would have a different focus. A focus that would take on galactic proportions, not these feeble ambitions. Then, of course, she wasn't likely to inform a stranger of her real purpose. She accepted him as human, and there would undoubtedly be other humans in this timeline. None of this made sense, yet he had to act as if he didn't know her true intent.

"Were you educated here?"

"Ian! You ask a lot of questions. Why don't you tell me

about yourself?"

Yianevan's face fell as if she had caught him in some mischief. Was she joking again? It was so hard to tell, so he tried smiling, which she seemed to accept and didn't press him for an answer. He didn't know it, but the streetlamps highlighted the paleness of his skin, and it served as a distraction. She hadn't noticed his pale complexion in the dance hall. Now, she wondered if he came from a cold climate, but she wouldn't ask. He seemed hesitant to offer anything about himself.

Again, an apology reached his lips, but she anticipated him. It was okay. She'll answer questions. Better than walking in uncomfortable silence.

"I went to a local infant school," she continued. "When I try to think of it now, it's just a blur. I obviously didn't learn much! After the eleven plus exam, Owen paid for me to go to a private school in Somerset. I had five years there, and I loved it, but the village seemed too small for me when I came back. I suppose the people I met at boarding school broadened my horizons, and back here at home, everything seemed to have shrunk." Bethan looked up at him. "Mam and dad, they were only in their fifties, but they had health problems, so I couldn't just up and leave. When they died, I took a secretarial job in town. I still have it."

"I am sorry you lost your parents," Yianevan said. "My mother died recently, and I was not at home when it happened."

He didn't wait for a sympathetic reply, which would have come had he not turned away to look towards the row of houses just above them on the hill. "The village is pleasant. I am from a large family, so accustomed to living close to others. There are fewer people here, so I do not feel 'cloistered'." Yianevan liked that word. "Not in the way I believed it would be."

"You have a unique way of expressing yourself, Ian," Bethan said. "Village life is fine for a while, but it gets stuffy if you've lived here all your life and have ambition. Do you live in a big city? If you do, I suspect life here will wear you down."

Yianevan fixed a blank expression on his face. "I do not plan on staying too long. I am here on assignment, and when it is completed, I will return home."

He wasn't giving anything away, so Bethan decided to fish, just a little. "And where is home? Not local, judging by the accent."

Yianevan shook his head. "Not local."

They stopped in front of a terraced house. "This is where I live," Bethan said. "Thank you for walking me home. I feel like I've done all the talking!"

Further down the row, the cottages were uniformly grimy and needed maintenance. Bethan's dwelling was painted light blue with a darker blue front door. Other houses in the row had attempted to relieve the griminess by painting the houses' facades. It worked to some extent, even though it made the unpainted houses look even sadder. Bethan watched him appraising the buildings, her breath steaming in the chilly night air. She was freezing but felt it impolite to dismiss him.

Then, as if he realised he had created a hiatus in the conversation, he lifted his hat and delivered an unexpected,

"I asked a lot of questions. May I see you again?"

Bethan took a second to respond. She wanted to refuse because she couldn't imagine what they would have left to talk about, but he was intriguing, so somewhere between her head and her heart, the answer changed to, "Thank you, that would be nice."

Yianevan waited until Bethan closed her front door before walking away. He'd suggested she go in the vehicle, but that was improper. It was not prudent for a female to get into a car with a stranger, implying the interventionist lived by local rules and adopted the cautionary approach.

The gate was still at the coordinates on the mountain, but they were a long way from Pompeii. Provided the gate did not move, it should be easy to access. If Corky continued to make no headway in convincing the spiral to remove the interventionist, Yianevan must use other methods to get her to tell him about the gate. Asking friendly questions was one thing. Interrogation another. If he could, he would try to get her to go through the gate and return to their own time. He scratched his head. What had he taken on?

CHAPTER ELEVEN _

Bethan made a pot of tea and sat at the kitchen table to agonise over the fact she had talked so much about personal things with a total stranger. But Ian was just so… unexpected. His accent, manner, even his pale skin seemed so out of place here.

One thing she didn't understand was his sidestepping of every one of her questions about his origins. In hindsight, she should have pressed him a little because she had been more forthcoming about her life than usual. He must have thought her a chatterbox. Perhaps he liked chatterboxes because he asked to see her again.

What on earth would bring a man like that to Llanbleddynllwyd? He said he was in the area for work, but off the top of her head, she couldn't think what surveying work he would need to do here. Not unless it was related to the mine closing. Ian said his work with the National Coal Board only took up a small part, so where did he do his surveying? Not in the village, that was for sure.

Okay, Bethan reasoned, a lot was going on across the

valley. He might be occupied there, although seeing him twice in two days seemed remarkable. Maybe it wasn't just work. Perhaps Ian was fleeing a sad past or broken relationship. Bethan didn't imagine this village was somewhere you'd escape to. Quite the opposite. No, it was probably as he said. Work. And she was just concocting a romantic story because he avoided speaking about himself.

Bethan seldom felt attracted to men, and while she didn't admit to it now, as she sipped her tea, her mind wandered to the unusual blue of Ian's eyes and his shining, baby-fine hair.

Then she shook her head, dumped the tea things in the sink and gave herself a good scolding.

Listen to yourself, Bethan Davies. You're like a teenager with a crush. Now is not the time to get involved with anyone.

In a few months, she would leave the village forever, and that was her focus. She had agreed to see Ian again, and he would likely wring all her local knowledge from her before he became just one more thing she left behind. Still, he made an undeniable impression, although right now, as she stifled a yawn, her bed called.

As Bethan passed the front parlour, she paused. She kept the door closed, never feeling a need to go in there, always telling herself it was because she preferred the cosiness of the kitchen. But it was really because on those few occasions she ventured into the parlour since mam and dad died, she felt like she didn't belong. Something about that room seemed to magnify that feeling, but tonight, she turned the door handle and stood in the doorway.

The lamp post outside the window cast eerie shadows

into the room. Bethan switched on the electric light, but it made little difference, only serving to highlight the gloom. She wished she could remember her life before boarding school with clarity, but it was just a glimpse here or a brief reminder there. It was like one of her strange dreams, with nothing solid for her to hold on to.

Her mam and dad would sit in here on a Sunday evening in days gone by. Bethan vaguely remembered sitting on the sofa with a book, her father puffing on his old pipe and his false teeth clicking against the stem. Mam liked to knit, and occasionally she counted stitches under her breath. The fire would flick its cosy warmth around the room, at least before the electric bar heater got installed. That still sat in the grate, dusty and unused behind the deep bowl dad used as an ashtray. Now, there was no fire, no mam and dad, and Bethan felt as if she were opening a tomb.

Forgetting her tiredness, she stepped into the room, glancing up at the single bare lightbulb in the middle of the ceiling. Bethan hadn't turned the light on since, well, since… she couldn't remember when—at least for ages—and she wondered why she hadn't noticed there was no lampshade. The room still smelled of dad's pipe baccy and evoked those hazy, distant memories Bethan found so hard to capture.

Running her hand over the mantlepiece, she disturbed months, no—years of dust. The odour of stale tobacco, an echo of knitting needles, and the naked lightbulb's bleakness only enhanced the neglect. To Bethan, this room wasn't hers. It belonged to her mam and dad. In their memory, she shouldn't have let it get to this state.

On impulse, she tossed the cushions onto the floor and shoved the two chairs from their place on either side of the fire. A modest couch stood against one wall, and Bethan sat on its arm, wary of the dust accumulating on the seats. Short of replacing the tired furniture, the only thing she could think of was a good do-over with the hoover. It would clean them up a bit, but the room was so dilapidated it would never be enough. She made a delicate track with her fingers down the old, stained wallpaper. At least it wasn't peeling off, so she could get away with not redecorating.

In this light, the sepia-toned pictures of long-dead ancestors that adorned the walls looked out at her from their ghostly perspectives. Bethan couldn't even remember who those people were. Above the mantlepiece hung an amateur watercolour, the canvas so discoloured with age and smoke, the subject was almost impossible to make out. Bethan recalled her father telling her it was Llyn Deron, a place he took her sometimes during school holidays, although the picture didn't reflect the visual glory of the lake. It looked out of place, as if someone painted it without ever visiting there and did not understand what made Llyn Deron so magnificent.

As she studied the grimy and warped picture, Bethan realised it was like her life, not yet magnificent, just a drab watercolour that lacked vibrancy. She didn't need a reminder, so after a moment's reflection, she reached above the mantle and took the picture down.

The lightbulb flickered, which was hardly surprising because it was decades old, so she made a mental note to get a new one on Monday when she went to work. Then she lifted one of the two layers of sheer netting that covered the window. The coal fire that preceded the electric heater had left dusty streaks and stains on the yellowed fabric. Mam had been too sick to wash them, and Bethan couldn't remember why she didn't wash them for her. She then pulled on the heavy drapes that were never drawn, only to discover they had broken off the curtain rings at one edge and now hung down with a giant dusty cobweb attaching it to the wall. Seeing it so forlorn filled Bethan with a sudden sadness. The room looked like a dump for old furniture. How could she ever expect to sell the house with it so cheerless and unwelcoming? She had to fix it up, even if that meant only improving the look of this room. It needed colour, a bit of life, although replacing the furniture was an expense she didn't need right now. Instead, hiding the old stuff with bright cushions, chair covers, and a few rugs would spruce it up.

Despite the lateness of the hour and the imminent failure of the light bulb, Bethan dragged the small sofa from its embedded position and heaved it across the threadbare carpet to the end of the room to face the window. The layers of dust that accumulated behind made her feel guilty she had never cleaned there. For such a precise person in so many ways, Bethan wasn't much enamoured by housework.

Next, she repositioned the small glass-fronted cabinet that held a few pieces of her mother's best china to the side of the fireplace. Then she rearranged the two fireside chairs so the focal point was the window. She didn't get much farther. The lightbulb flickered like stage lights in a theatrical drama, then pinged out. Bethan couldn't work by the dim light from the lamppost outside, so there was little more she could do. She brushed the dust from her hands, closed the door, and climbed the stairs to bed, promising the front parlour that transformation was coming.

The following morning, Bethan found a note on the doormat.

"Good morning," the note began. "I trust you slept well. Are you available this evening to see a film? If you are comfortable, we can take my car. I will stop outside your house at 6pm."

The note wasn't signed, but it had Ian's voice. She could almost imagine him standing there and saying it. There wasn't an address or telephone number, so she couldn't respond. Few houses in the village, or even over at the council estate, had telephones, so it was possible Ian didn't have one, but she would have expected a signature. Bethan caught herself smiling that Ian had made contact, but she still turned the note over in her fingers. What was she getting herself into? She wavered between going back on accepting another invitation and not seeing the harm. It was all such bad timing.

With a sigh, she placed the note on the kitchen table. There was no way of contacting him to tell him no, so she'd just enjoy this evening and leave it at that.

Despite her resolve this would be her only outing with Ian, Bethan felt a strange fluttering throughout the day. First, of course, she felt flattered he invited her out, but alongside, another sensation nudged itself around the edges of her excitement. Not a disagreeable sensation, but one she couldn't define. It was a feeling there was more to Ian's turning up than it seemed. Bethan was neither superstitious nor religious, but her mam always believed God or fate intervened in even the most cherished plans.

As six o'clock approached, Bethan went back to the note. Ian's handwriting was so precise. Without thinking, she stroked a finger over the paper, frowning as a ripple of strange remembrance flowed through her. For just a second, she felt something… *familiar.*

With a shake, she reined in her foolishness. She had never seen Ian before in her entire life, so how could she feel any familiarity? Reading any more into these feelings was absurd. Tonight would be pleasant. Then she would come home and not give Ian Noble another thought. Who knows, he might have an objectionable habit, like picking his nose or belching in public. In that case, she could righteously decline a second date.

It so happened Ian turned out to be a perfect gentleman. He held open the door of a dilapidated and unwashed Austin A40, which surprised Bethan, considering Ian's pristine appearance. She assumed the car of a surveyor who worked in outdoor locations would likely get a little grubby, even if its owner had turned up immaculately dressed. But to her horror, Ian was a terrible driver. The car's engine revved in anguish as it begged him to shift gear, and he displayed a blatant disregard for road signs. Fortunately, the village only had a few, and while Bethan expected the road out to the neighbouring town would be quiet, her nerves were too jangled to watch a film. Instead, she proposed they stop at a pub outside town where the landlady had a stash of homemade meat pies she kept in a warmer. It might be a nice place to have a snack and talk for a while. Talking seemed to be Ian's favourite pastime, anyway.

As Bethan expected, Ian had a list of questions about the village. She fancied he had them written down someplace and memorised them for tonight. It even emerged he'd read the leaflet sent out by the historical society, as some of his questions involved their topics. Namely, local heritage.

"Heritage, Ian?" Bethan gave him a thin smile but answered his question the best she knew how, telling him the discovery of anthracite and the dawn of the Industrial Revolution was the end of any heritage as far as she was concerned. In fact, that was the death knell for many Welsh villages once the mines moved in. Angular arches of pit winding gear grew beside vast mountains of slag. Tiny miners' cottages, unsanitary and ill-equipped, lined the valley sides, and almost overnight, even the greenest valleys turned black from smoke, soot, and grime.

"Mining was the greatest invasion of all time, even more so than the Romans," she said, not without bitterness because it was lung disease that carried off her parents.

Then, she painted for Ian a grim picture of the village in years past, how the mining invasion brought coal shafts, canals, and steam locomotives that bilged choking smoke from their stacks. She described the coal cars that carried away mountains of that blackish earthy rock the miners so often paid for with their lives.

"The village can recover, Bethan," Yianevan said. "If

the people who live here want it."

She shook her head. "I think only the old people want it preserved. After the war, the government promised a new council estate to house returning servicemen, but local authority funding ran out, so they didn't build as many houses. As a result, the temporary prefabs they put up turned into permanent homes and quickly became run down. That meant the promised extra facilities that would have buoyed the village didn't eventuate. The influx of families only added to the unemployment and despondency that followed the war years. So Ian, I say again. What heritage? A half-empty council estate, a village full of decaying buildings and a few Roman artefacts in the local museum? I can't see anything worth preserving."

Ian didn't answer. He'd read some booklets on local history, and they didn't seem to share Bethan's gloomy, although somewhat vivid, appraisal.

Bethan didn't view Llanbleddynllwyd as a place with a rich past. From her knowledge, destitution, poverty, death, and disease wrote its history. A place that went from disaster to misery. How could people forget? No, the village's days were numbered. The time had come to make way for new industries and let the council tear down the old cottages. Then they could use the site as a rubbish tip. She didn't say so to Ian because he still looked to be pondering her earlier discourse.

"Good things happened in this village too," he said. "You said someone helped the miners?"

A flush spread across Bethan's cheeks. She seemed unable to think or even speak about the village in any other way than ungraciously.

"Ian, I am sorry. I didn't mean to sound harsh. The people in the village are wonderful, all of them. I don't know why I feel I don't belong here anymore. Perhaps I never did. My mam always said we were one of the lucky families because no-one in our family died in the epidemics and cave-ins so commonplace in the village's mining history."

"Then, for you, history is not so bleak?"

"Not for us," she admitted. "There were a few organisations, housing clubs, that safeguarded the interests of the miners' housing. The one here used funds from a bequest to clear the slums and move the terraced houses further up the hillside away from the mine. The syndicate tried to identify the silent benefactor, but it was so tied up in legal paperwork they all went to their eternal rest, never finding out. My grandparents benefitted from those funds and purchased one of the new cottages under a mortgage."

"You see? Your family *was* one of the lucky ones."

Ian was right. Her family had indeed been lucky, and even though it all seemed vague, her mam and dad, her grandparents, were all happy here. So why couldn't she be happy here too?

Satisfied with sifting through Bethan's store of local knowledge, Ian shifted his focus to Bethan's own history.

There wasn't much to tell, and most of it she recounted the previous evening, but he seemed satisfied even with trivial facts from her childhood, school, and anecdotes about her life in the village. He neatly skirted her counter-questioning, which made Bethan revisit the idea he was running from some catastrophic or sad event in his recent past. If so, he might have taken this contract to forget or recuperate. She even thought he was pale enough to have had a serious illness, but Bethan felt that was too personal to ask about.

To his delight, Yianevan made a startling discovery at the pub. A bottle containing a golden liquid similar to Birn caught his eye, and he requested a sample. When he brought it back to the table, Bethan told him the story of her grandmother, who was a member of the temperance society. He learned then that unlike Lieutenant Phildre, Bethan did not drink alcohol, although she appeared not to be judgemental of those who did.

"Have you never had whisky before, Ian?" Bethan asked as she witnessed his delight at the first taste.

He nodded. "I know it by a different name, but I believe this has a superior composition."

"I thought whisky had the same name all over the world. What do they call it in your country?"

Yianevan gave her an enigmatic smile. It probably did have the same name all over *this* world, but not all over the galaxy.

Bethan would keep dropping hints about his background, so rather than an outright lie, he diverted the conversation towards geology. This was the practice the interventionist Phildre would call "fudging", but he felt he needed to offer something that would satisfy her other self's questioning, and it was an area where he had the most expertise.

Bethan's fascination with the subject most definitely ended her enquiries about him. Instead, the conversation turned into a lengthy question-and-answer session about rocks. Yianevan enjoyed sharing his knowledge. The woman had a lively and quick mind, and while many people's eyes would glaze over after a half-hour discourse on the life of a rock, Bethan hung on to every word. She then bent his ear with more questions, and they both laughed as she recounted, not always correctly, what he told her.

The evening concluded almost as before. Ian drove Bethan home, escorted her to her door, raised his hat, and expressed hope he would see her again but did not make a firm date.

As she did the previous night after their first meeting, Bethan made a cup of tea, but this time, she took her cup and saucer into the front parlour. She tried the electric light, but the bulb was long past resurrection. The light from the hallway and the glow from the streetlamp met around the middle of the room above the tatty armchairs, so she eased herself down into mam's old chair and rubbed her hands over the worn arms. She tried to relive how it was when her mother sat there, but the memory wouldn't stay, so she allowed her imagination to visualise the changes she would make to this room. It meant a bus ride across town, but she had some time to undertake the project this week, and in her head, she had visions of the parlour transformed.

At his lodgings, a little way from the village, accommodation he had found without Corky's help, Yianevan congratulated himself on his cleverness. He made it through the entire evening, giving nothing of himself away other than his knowledge of rocks. He had a vast store of information to draw on, but then rocks were essentially the same throughout the galaxy as far as he knew. The interventionist made lively conversation and listened to his answers with interest, so he concluded he made a good impression.

The other pleasing discovery of the evening was whisky, and it was even more palatable than the version in his own time. Yianevan recognised it sparked Bethan's story about her grandmother and the temperance society, noting she drank only tomato juice at the pub. Consumption of such a benign beverage would not see her "drink him under the table", the attribute alluded to by the interface when describing the interventionist.

He would advise the interface of this change in her character the next time the spiral removed him back to the ship. It had been over forty-eight hours between contacts. A longer interval than agreed and one that gave cause for concern.

Four days passed before Bethan heard from Ian again. The note had a phone number, so when she got to work, she called to invite him to Sunday lunch at her home. He accepted but sounded unsure when she told him Mike and Ivy were also coming. Wondering if his response was a simple case of shyness, she suspected that an afternoon with Ivy would knock that out of him.

Yianevan spent the days before the Sunday lunch studying human behaviour norms. Upon further reading at a library ten miles away from the village, Yianevan realised he might not be doing as well as he'd hoped. Social nuances continued to elude him, but he'd only spent time with the interventionist, who seemed tolerant, even amused, by his stumbling pronunciations and syntax. Before seeing her again, he needed to master inflexion and the display of emotions through body language to make him seem more human. For now, his only source of information was at the library, where he spent most of his time. Bethan had been forthcoming and pleasant, so he was confident she did not recognise him as a Noble. He wanted to keep it that way. Even his name didn't seem to prompt her to suspicion.

When the interface finally made contact, it advised him the spiral continued in its refusal to recognise Lieutenant Phildre, so it could not extract her through the gate and onto the ship. If they must retrieve the interventionist, the only option would be to present her in physical form at the gate's coordinates on the volcano. The interface further offered the possibility that a Lyran would know the gate's location, and if the Noble revealed it, she would discover his identity.

So far, Yianevan had seen nothing to suggest the galaxy was in danger of a Lyran invasion from the future. The interventionist appeared to be like all the other beings in the village, exhibiting no apparent recognition they may be part of a Lyran uprising. Yianevan accepted the possibility of memory suppression by the Lyran Monks, but with the evidence, it seemed unlikely. However, Yianevan was not yet ready to abandon the idea of a connection between the woman and the gate. As the planet's environment had not affected him so far, he told the interface the hierarchy would almost certainly approve of him returning her.

He enjoyed his last encounter with Bethan, dining on

meat pies and chatting about rocks, stones, and landscapes. Something set her apart from the other people he had met since coming here, a distinction that captured his attention. Perhaps it was because she was Lyran, or maybe because she wasn't, and he expected a specific type of behaviour. Did she know he was the enemy all along and was playing him? He might learn more at the Sunday lunch ritual. To keep up the subterfuge if he encountered Lyrans behaving like humans, he would have to act as if it was a ritual he understood. He had undertaken a single lunch at his lodgings and found the procedure arduous. Consumption of the food made his jaw ache, threatened to dislodge his teeth, and he resented his landlady hovering beside him to ensure he "ate it all up".

According to a Good Housekeeping book he liked to read, Sunday lunch appeared to have a greater variety of food than on other days. Yianevan lived on hard-boiled eggs and potato crisps because he found everything else either unpalatable or grown in soil, which he felt prudent to avoid just in case they compromised his graft. Potato crisps were so processed, he believed the manufacturer would leave no soil trace on the finished product. They always nestled a small blue "twist" of paper within the crisps. After some suspicious examination, he decided the object contained a seasoning agent to sprinkle on the product to enhance the flavour. It was a novel approach and one that meant the tiny blue pouch could not be a means of assassinating a Noble. The shop where he purchased them was owned by a friendly, white-haired elderly couple who did not appear to be Lyran fifth columnists.

Food concerns went further for Yianevan because he also took issue with the animal flesh consumed by humans in the village. His landlady served the rigid slab at that lunch ritual, and to his dismay, he was also served soil-grown produce, invoking concern they might contain fungal residue. Attending this planet already placed him at risk, and consuming even a minute portion of the soil would be foolhardy. He had nibbled at one pale orange-coloured circle, but fear of the vegetable killing him or stopping him from completing his mission won out, and he pushed them to the side of his plate. That action earned him a sharp rebuke from his landlady, who spent "hours" preparing the meal.

The morning after this disquieting repast, Yianevan consulted a guidebook on the technique of cooking vegetables. It left him in no doubt that Mrs Jenkins's vegetables had little in them of any description to either harm or help. Boiled to an almost white mush, he felt relatively safe consuming them if the need arose. He just had to hope the interventionist had at least a similar culinary expertise as his landlady.

CHAPTER TWELVE _

By the end of the week, another communication lapse with the ship left Yianevan re-evaluating his presence on the planet. These disconnects proved disconcerting because he could not keep apprised of the situation with the gate. At its previous contact, the interface advised signs of instability within the anomaly, so the prospect of being stranded to suffer the toxic spores became a possibility he couldn't ignore. This instability also interfered with the brief but reassuring audio transmissions the interface generated via the spiral. During the periods of silence, Yianevan had no way of initiating contact with the ship or even knowing if the interface continued to monitor his life signs. In effect, he was on his own.

With the comms issues, Yianevan reconsidered his options. He arrived here with no coherent plan and so far saw no evidence of Lyran activity. Previously convinced of a Lyran presence, he conceded the village and its rather quaint and backwards inhabitants continued to yield nothing of value. He wondered if it might be wiser to leave the interventionist and return to the ship when next the interface made contact. Then he would alert the homeworld and leave the problem of the gate to the scientists.

Except the interface did not make contact.

Yianevan read and reread many books in the social sciences section of the library. His ocular prosthesis didn't interfere with his eye movement or ability to process only the relevant text areas, but after several hours of reading, the words of a dictionary on etiquette blurred in front of his eyes. He had an open packet of potato crisps in his pocket and was taking them out one at a time to stave off hunger.

By their very name, crisps were noisy snacks, and if Yianevan wanted to munch them in a library, he had to learn how to do it without drawing attention to himself. Crisps were relenting in their crunchiness, so Yianevan sorted it by sticking his face close to the book he was reading and leaning his hand on his cheek. It wasn't always successful. One time, he earned a stern glance from the female librarian, who pointed to a sign above the desk. It advised "Tawelwch".

Underneath, for the benefit of non-Welsh speakers, was a translation.

"Quiet, Please,".

A sign such as this would be useful for when he returned home. It would only serve as an amusement. No sign would ever be enough to silence his clamorous family.

But he had produced a crunching noise, and although the librarian didn't realise he was eating crisps, he acknowledged her with a slight bow of his head and mouthed, *"My apologies."* It seemed to satisfy, and he vowed to mend his ways.

Yianevan had welcomed Bethan's invitation before she told him others would be present. If they were human, his appearance would fool them. After all, he was positive he'd fooled Bethan, although he felt confused about her because she was the one most likely to be Lyran.

He read up on group activities, but none mentioned Sunday lunch. The local accents also troubled him, although he understood Bethan and his landlady. Now he would have to deal with conversing with someone new. Yianevan spoke and understood languages and dialects that stemmed from many cultures and worlds, but he never encountered any tongue like Welsh anywhere in the galaxy.

Although somewhat archaic and extrapolated from the early abducted humans, Corky's subliminal instruction in English had provided Yianevan with passable language skills. The Welsh accent, though, had a pronounced rhythmic structure. He had to study the speaker to catch the nuances and the strong and weak stresses on various syllables. The cadence began as a song, perhaps because people here liked to sing, and came out the other side with a poetic lilt. Yianevan believed the accent, whether spoken in its native form or the English version, was unique in the galaxy. No matter how he tried, he could not get his tongue around the maddening Welsh pronunciations of place names or even names of local food products and everyday endeavours. He was glad the interventionist spoke English, albeit with a lyrical Welsh inflexion, and he didn't dare think what would happen if something as straightforward as language imperilled the mission. He didn't speak Lyran either, so Lyran might be mixed up in the Welsh, and he wouldn't have a clue.

Putting the book on etiquette to one side, Yianevan rubbed his eyes and turned instead to a publication on theatre and film. He enjoyed reading from a page rather than data folds or tiles, and he found the language easy to follow, although he kept a pocket dictionary at his side.

As on his world, human entertainment depicted icons and events from history or literature, a pastime defined as "acting". Yianevan looked up the term in the dictionary and what he found placed him in a philosophical frame of mind. He repeated the definitions to himself.

"Acting: Pretence. Make-believe." He looked up from the dictionary and frowned. *Isn't life an act, anyway?*

Every society he came across, including his own, required its people to behave in a way that made them acceptable and enslaved to custom. Even those he considered free. From what he knew of the galaxy, he rather felt his species was the worst, more so even than the primitive humans of this world, kept in line by a host of social mores and conformities not to be breached. He couldn't even let out an audible sigh in a library because of the "Quiet" sign, so he took a deep breath and let the air seep out through his nose and pores.

Feeling around in his pocket for the crisps, he was disappointed to find the bag empty, but his searching made the bag crackle. The librarian looked his way, but as he felt philosophical, he decided her sharp expression was justified because he wasn't supposed to be eating in here.

The book gave him the idea that he just had to learn how to improve his acting to get by until the interface removed him. It had nothing to do with reality. The word "pretence" showed up several times on the page. He looked up "pretence" in the dictionary and then repeated the definition under his breath.

"Make-believe. Nonsense. Fancy."

The terms concurred with "acting". Yianevan understood. To make the woman trust him, he needs to cultivate these skills. The other individuals he would meet on Sunday were her friends, but what if they turned out to be overtly Lyran and recognised him where she did not? What *was* overtly Lyran? Their race was extinct for hundreds of years, so how would he know? Sunday lunch might just see him handed over to the Lyran Monks and targeted for execution. He supposed he could hide until the interface made contact, but that made all this pointless, and he hated that feeling.

The Nobles maintained Lyrans wiped themselves out by their own excesses. What would be the probability they'd overlooked at least one genetic strain and let the interventionist slip through their stringent screening procedures? Nobles weren't infallible, although listening to his father, one might gain a different view. It made Yianevan wonder. Before the Nobles created the interventionist fleet and vetted the humans to ensure their human-ness, how many Lyrans fled through the Monk's Gate? Of one thing he was sure, they weren't hiding out en masse in this village, even if battalions of them lurked elsewhere across this world.

The postman passed by the library window. Could that man in the blue hat, trusted by everyone, daily pushing around his pile of letters in a cart, be a Lyran waiting for the day when he would return through the gate to wreak havoc on the galaxy? Could Mr Hopkins, the butcher across the way from the library, rotund and jolly under his blue apron, waken one morning to his memories and discover he was not a purveyor of fine meats but a Lyran scientist or warrior?

All these people. Were they biding their time until they could again flood the galaxy with their evil? It was absurd in the extreme, and Yianevan again questioned his reasons for being here.

A horse-drawn milk cart followed the postman along the street. Pondering the rickety vehicle brought a grin to Yianevan. It would never get to the gate; the wheels would fall off after a couple of miles. In ten sector terms, technology on this world wasn't much further advanced than the cart. Even his automobile would move faster if he pushed. So far, he had discovered no evidence of anyone developing technology that would suggest groundwork for an insurrection. If he judged their evolution, it seemed unlikely that the butcher across the road, the library patrons, or the baker who did his rounds with a cart in Bethan's village possessed the technical expertise to plan an uprising on a galactic scale. They just didn't seem to be heading that way.

Of course, they could hide their advancement, but where? If they were Lyrans, they could speak freely amongst one another, but they all seemed to know only this place they called the land of their forefathers. This was their existence, and they seemed content with what they had. Only Bethan was restless.

The other possibility was multiple timelines, and this one did not contain Lyrans. That begged the question he'd asked himself before. Why was the woman transported here through the gate if not to join other Lyrans? And why was it that the few people he encountered were so pleasant? They seemed like decent, ordinary people, and Yianevan found them to be some of the nicest in the galaxy.

And that made no sense. The only other conclusion was that the Lyrans in this time did not know their true selves. In that case, what threat would they pose? If they remained ignorant of their heritage, they would not differ from the humans they lived alongside unless some kind of trigger would awaken them to their true purpose. He revisited his idea of memory suppression. Were the Lyran Monks capable of that?

Yianevan had composed a list of suspects, which was so far empty apart from Bethan, and even she hadn't given him actual cause to suspect her as Lyran, apart from ending up here via the gate. His landlady, Mrs Jenkins, was elderly, grey-haired. Not Lyran. Those same instincts told him neither the man who sold newspapers nor the bus driver he met once was anything but human.

He looked about him. The librarian, a middle-aged woman who wore uncomfortable-to-look-at checked fabric skirts, looked human. He discovered the description of that fabric after consulting a book on fashion. Tartan. He didn't like it. Had he not been wearing an ocular prosthesis, he would have struggled with the cacophony of woven colours. She didn't come under his radar as Lyran, either.

So, what was the purpose of the Monk's Gate?

Yianevan's head pounded with all these possibilities, so he left the library, drove to the countryside, and parked the car in a quiet laneway. He brought a novel from Mrs Jenkins's house, a work of fiction about a private investigator who smoked a pipe and wore a strange hat that Yianevan preferred to the one the interface provided. He wished he'd told Bethan he was a detective. It sounded like a respectable profession and offered an air of confidentiality that would divert her from too many enquiries. Either way, he regretted his lack of preparation, which swept him up in her assumptions about his work.

It appeared he had to maintain the lie now and just had to hope Ivy and Mike knew nothing about geology and the duties of a surveyor.

CHAPTER THIRTEEN _

On Sunday, Yianevan wore his hat to lunch. At first, he didn't follow Bethan's signals he should remove it, but when she smiled and pointed, "Ian, your hat," he liberated it from his head, then allowed her to slip his coat from his shoulders. She hung the coat on the end of the bannister and plopped his hat on top.

Yianevan paid attention. Hats and coats were not welcome attire at the lunch table when visiting. He'd worn them when he and Bethan had pies at the pub and at Mrs Jenkins's house during the meals he couldn't avoid. She hadn't mentioned it, although he did receive a sideways look he didn't understand.

Specific garments had their place among the many layers of clothing the humans wore. They did not wear overcoats and hats at mealtimes, even when the wearer felt cold. Yianevan had observed many galactic species over the years. He was learning that perhaps a little more participation would have made sense.

One of Bethan's guests had already arrived, and

Bethan introduced the two men.

Mike Trent, a man of slight build, bespectacled and wearing an outdated and too large Sunday best suit, was Bethan's employer. Softly spoken and mild in manner, Mike had known Bethan since she came to work for him five years before, following the death of her parents. He believed Bethan had a destiny greater in life than existence in a forsaken mining village. Although he hated to lose her, he was glad she had the drive and ambition to move away and make a life elsewhere. She had mentioned her new friend, and Mike was glad to meet him, although it surprised him a little to find Ian aloof and uncertain when to smile. He also noticed his avoidance of any reference to his origins, only making vague noises about moving around a lot as he grew up. Not once did he give an answer that satisfied the question. Of note, when Mike politely pressed, Ian revealed his father was an archaeologist but again became vague when questioned further. He even countered direct questions about his mother by asking a question in return. Mike, an astute listener, later decided that if he were to evaluate any substance in Ian's entire conversation, he actually said little.

Bethan wasn't blind to it either. Twice she had been alone with Ian, and both times she noticed his tactic to turn around questions involving his family. She hoped Mike didn't think him rude, but Mike was not judgemental, although his regard for Bethan engendered a certain wariness that she had struck up a friendship with someone this secretive. However, as soon as Ivy arrived, the discussion turned far more general and livelier, drawing them all into village gossip.

To Yianevan's relief, Bethan proved far more capable in the culinary arts than Mrs Jenkins. The animal flesh, cut into thin slices rather than assaulted with a knife, posed no hazard to teeth, and the vegetables had distinctive flavours, quite unlike the nondescript sludge served by Mrs Jenkins. A pie followed, served with a yellow sauce Bethan called "Bird's custard". He had this concoction at Mrs Jenkins's table, who assured him the manufacture included no feathered creatures. Mrs Jenkins's version was in a pouring vessel, except it was not pourable, and slipped from the jug in a jellified clump, part of which hit the tablecloth like a missile. It earned him a look of reproof from his landlady as she mopped up the spillage, then another when he found the custard almost as challenging as the meat. Bethan's version was smooth and sweet and infinitely superior.

Later, after a pleasant and at times awkward lunch, due to Ian's social skills, Bethan waved Mike and Ivy goodbye. Ian didn't leave with the others, so she assumed he was about to offer to help her with the washing up. She was glad he hadn't hurried away and hoped he would stay for a cup of tea afterwards.

That was Yianevan's intention. Mrs Jenkins expected him to wipe up after meals, except her preferred topic of conversation during the ritual was other people's business in the village, often at the expense of those long dead. Ivy spoke in a similar vein but without the unkind undertones.

Mrs Jenkins's shrill voice assaulted Yianevan's sensitive ears and jangled his nerves when she gossiped about the village. While he didn't think humans could die of boredom, he wondered to what degree her inane chatter contributed to her husband's premature demise.

At least he had her to thank for showing him how to wipe dishes. Considering he only ate meals at his lodgings when Mrs Jenkins caught him sneaking out, he felt relatively well practised in its execution.

To his dismay, Bethan did not order her cupboards like Mrs Jenkins. He stood with a pile of plates in his hands, staring at shelves laden with glassware of different sizes. Mrs Jenkins stored her plates in a cupboard above the kitchen counter. Bethan did not. When she saw him hesitate, she took them from him.

"You're not very domesticated, are you?" she said with an indulgent grin.

Yianevan understood the word "domesticated". It meant Bethan did not consider him house-trained. He filed away the word to check the next day at the library and how it related to human behaviour rather than cats.

Bethan turned a knob on a brown box perched on the narrow mantlepiece.

"Do you like the wireless, Ian?" she asked as the device crackled into life. "On a Sunday, I listen to the local news and see what's happening in the world. Shall we? It's only thirty minutes."

Yianevan didn't mind. Broadcasting information to the residents here struck him as innovative, considering the village was overlooked by the rest of the world. The first time he heard the wireless, he assumed it was a communication network for the Lyrans but soon realised this was a human invention.

The wireless array was encased in an old housing which Bethan advised her interested guest was called "Bakelite". While she appeared oblivious to the hissing and scratching noises made by the appliance, Yianevan's ears buzzed as if he were listening to Mrs Jenkins. Bethan, however, paid careful attention to the transmission and made a few comments Yianevan didn't know how to respond to. Finally, with the delivery of information completed, the wireless was silenced by a second turn of the knob.

Yianevan ran what he heard back in his head. He learned nothing of value. The reporting was superficial, lacked evidence, and delivered in an English, not Welsh, accent. The news didn't relate to anyone or anything in the village. Bethan apologised. She only just noticed he didn't enjoy the program.

"You look bored, Ian. I don't put it on during the week. Mike has a newspaper delivered daily to the office, so I bring that home to read. It keeps me up to date."

Yianevan pointed to the wireless. "The apparatus is malfunctioning," he said. "I found it difficult to concentrate."

To Bethan, the wireless sounded like it always did.

"Malfunctioning?" She thought for a moment. "Oh, you mean the hissing? The knobs are loose, and I can't tune them. Mam and Dad got it donkey's years ago, and Mike says it'll be the wiring. He offered to look, but I haven't taken him up on it so far. There's no point now I'm going to London."

"Would you like me to repair it?"

The wireless was too old to bother with as far as

Bethan was concerned, but if he was offering…

"If you like."

Yianevan lifted the wireless onto the table. The back fell off, exposing its inner components and the mummified remains of a small rodent. He sat down and peered inside. A brilliant piece of primitive engineering, he thought. Small wonder humans made such a reputation for themselves in the ten sectors. Presented with a simple idea and the tools, they ran with it. Yes, a species to be admired. Even though they seemed slow to get going, the inhabitants of this world had a bright future if the interventionist fleet continued to mitigate the Lyran sabotages.

Bethan pulled up a chair beside him and peered into the wireless's innards.

"What are we looking at?" she asked first, quickly followed with, "How does it work?" then a barrage of questions. In minutes, with Yianevan as her instructor and using a multi-tool he stole from Mrs Jenkins's shed, Bethan became an eager participant in the device's repair.

Mike, as an electrician, first considered an electrical issue, but Yianevan, having spent many years out in space, knew a thing or two about communication devices. This was a crude example, but some principles remained in use on a few worlds. The knobs *were* loose, as Bethan diagnosed, but the fundamental problem was the antenna, which was tucked inside the set instead of being mounted on the back panel. The antenna was shredded, a possible last meal for the now-deceased rodent.

Bethan gave him an old fountain pen, and he used the rubber insert to fashion a stent for the aerial, employing leftover fragments to tighten the knobs. The task hardly stretched him, but she was impressed. When he completed the repair and switched on the wireless, it crackled briefly, then produced a clear and superior reception. Bethan clapped her hands together in delight and laughed.

"You are so clever!"

Yianevan secured the back and replaced the wireless on the mantlepiece. Her laughter sent a thrill through him, right down to his toes. Because of the warmth he felt in his face, he didn't turn immediately, just made a show of adjusting the position, embarrassed by her evident admiration.

"You helped," he said.

But Bethan decided he deserved the glory. "Ian, I held your pocketknife!"

He fixed on a smile and turned to face her. "And you made sensible contributions. This is old technology."

"Yes, it is!" she agreed, not knowing just how old it was for him. "At least from the thirties! If I'd taken the back of that thing off on my own, I wouldn't have made head nor tails of it." She stood and picked up two teacups. "Ian. Thank you. I think you deserve more apple pie and a fresh cup of tea."

This time, Bethan served dessert in the front parlour. She showed Yianevan to the small sofa and sat opposite him on her mam's old chair. Feeling rather proud of everything she had accomplished in this room this week, she hoped Ian might comment.

She had spent the day prior cleaning the parlour from top to bottom and laying the few covers she purchased on her trip to Llanfrydd over the back and arms of the seats. The chairs weren't as deep as she would have liked, wishing she could curl up and get lost in them. She recalled an armchair with broad seats, large enough to do that, but where she saw it escaped her. Probably in a magazine where rich people had such things made for them.

Bethan took ages to arrange the fabrics, but none of it felt right. Even adding the cushions she made on her sewing machine didn't satisfy her vision for the room. It might have been the drabness, or perhaps she had chosen the wrong colours, but none of it quite "fit". She just couldn't decide. The new lampshade looked nice, and washing the curtains and repairing the curtain pole made a difference, but for the rest, she had no choice but to let her irritation slide. Besides, the new rug Mike brought over in his van hid a fair amount of the threadbare carpet, which helped her disappointment.

When she finished, she had to admit, despite her misgivings, the room not only looked more cheerful but also felt a tad more homely. Mrs Higgins from next door gave her a couple of plants to set in front of the window, and although Ian hadn't seen it in its previous state, she was keen to get his opinion.

If this attempt at tidying up didn't attract a buyer for the house, she decided to approach the council, because this week, Bethan felt an urgency to sell. Her world seemed—that word again—cloistered. She even noticed she held her arms close to her body when she went downstairs, as if the walls pressed in on her. The sensation unsettled her, perhaps because it had only been since she met Ian.

Yianevan sat on the old sofa and felt a stray spring

poking into his bottom through the cover. He shifted, trying to balance his plate of pie on his knee and a cup and saucer in one hand. The spring's presence was uncomfortable but endurable, and it was apparent Bethan had overlooked it during her renovations. She told him she had been sewing cushions to brighten her parlour, and he looked around at the result.

Colourful matching fabric panels lay across the arms and backs of two old armchairs and the sofa. Bethan treated the floor to a bright, multi-hued rug and arranged far-too-large cushions on the armchairs. A picture hung on the wall surrounded by several faded patches of yellowed wallpaper, where other pictures had hung previously and since been removed. Under the window stood a tall plant with large fronds, and next to it a bamboo planter that held a solitary plant with long grass-like leaves, the tips of which had tiny replica plants of the host.

The room smelled of the same floral spray Mrs Jenkins used in her parlour, but it also had an underlying sickly scent of tobacco that Yianevan found invasive. The warm, spicy apple pie smell of Bethan's kitchen was so much more inviting.

He knew Bethan expected a comment about the room, perhaps even a compliment, but the underpinning furnishings were too drab, too tattered to carry the burden of such bright colours. The arrangement of furniture and plants brought to his mind the interventionist's apartment on Chabin. Bethan hadn't gone as far as acquiring a cat, but with her plans to leave in a few weeks, he guessed such an affectation would be frivolous and irresponsible, given felines were not independent and demanded daily care.

Even with the room's new accoutrements, Yianevan believed whatever change time had made to the woman's personality, she was no longer as outgoing as Lieutenant Phildre. He didn't know what to say about the room, so he stayed quiet, ate pie, drank tea, and pretended not to notice the spring. She allowed him five minutes before she prompted him.

"I suppose it was indulgent," she said, trying not to sound too eager for his response. "Spending money on a room in a house I am about to leave is extravagant. It's not as if I come in here often. I did it on impulse." She looked around. "What do you think? It's not quite right, but it is more cheerful."

Yianevan couldn't say it was garish and disturbing given the room's drab foundations, so he lied.

"It's nice. I think you put a lot of yourself into it."

Well, that was an unexpected observation. Multicolour décor was not Bethan's usual choice because of the dearth of decent print fabrics in the shops across the valley. He obviously saw something in the room that she didn't.

"I'm not sure about that, Ian," she said. "I tend to go for one colour at a time. Although I like these prints. Mrs Higgins from next door gave me the plants when I told her I needed to cheer the place up a bit to sell. Plants curl up their roots and die if I'm even in the same room." She laughed at her confession. "Mrs Higgins assures me these are hardy."

Yianevan had gained considerable knowledge from his mother about the behaviour of plants. To kill them by being in the same room was remarkable. Perhaps Earth's plants shared empathy with humans, although he couldn't imagine Bethan deliberately causing a plant's death.

So, he didn't laugh along. Instead, he recalled the interventionist's ecosystem and the health of the plants in her apartment. He doubted the garden suffered many fatalities. Of course, he couldn't tell Bethan that, so to distract himself, he plucked at the covering on the arm of the chair. There were elements of the room that reminded him of Lieutenant Phildre, but there was little else of her colouring Bethan's so far rather drab life.

"Will you miss this abode?" he asked.

"This abode?" Bethan grinned. "If you mean will I miss this house, I will have to say no. Owen offered to buy my parents a nicer house, but they, and Gran, refused to move. He suggested somewhere further south, but the area was too 'posh' for them and too far away from their roots."

"Is it problematic to sell a house?"

Bethan sighed and nodded. "It seems to be. The local government is interested, so if I can't get the price I want, I will have to let it go to them. They won't pay what it's worth."

"Do you mean in currency?"

"Of course I mean currency, Ian! I didn't mean in bananas!"

Hmm, Yianevan thought, at least she made a joke of his conversational errors, even though he didn't find bananas funny. He had seen them in a shop. They comprised an upper joint, from which protruded many curved pods, like a sneaky Dinolongian dirt spider. He didn't trust them.

"What is the house worth?"

Bethan tilted her head. "Do you plan to make me an offer?"

"I don't need a house, Bethan. I am not staying."

There. Ian had voiced that he would be here only for a while, and the confirmation stung. *This is only the third time you've seen him,* Bethan reminded herself. *Stop being silly.*

"Well, neither do I," she said, bringing her inner silliness under control. "It got painted and tidied up just after I returned from school, but that was years ago. I haven't done any more with it. A couple of people along the row had bathrooms put in, but I didn't bother. I still have the tin bath hanging over the coal bunker, and I cart it in twice a week. Whoever buys the house can modernise it how they want."

"That is sensible. Where did you go to school?"

"In Somerset." Bethan had become used to Ian's habit of changing topics midway through a conversation. "My brother Owen paid the fees. Mam and Dad were glad, but the neighbours thought it was a little 'posh' to be going away to boarding school. No-one else around here ever did."

Yianevan had not encountered that word before today.

"Is 'posh' unfavourable?"

Bethan wrinkled up her nose, remembering her reception from the villagers when she arrived home for her first school holidays.

"It can be," she said with a shrug. "Around here, if someone is trying to be better than they are, the locals might try to take you down a peg. Everyone knew our mam and dad weren't snobs, and Owen had the money to pay. They got over it, but I've always been a bit of an outsider. Ivy is my only friend. I call Mike a friend, but he doesn't come from around here, anyway."

"I see. Did your brother return to the village?"

"Never." Bethan hadn't seen her brother in over two decades. Thinking of him now made her sad that it would still be another few years before she saw him again.

"He's eleven years older than me," she said. "He ran away at fifteen to join the merchant navy. I expect he lied about his age, but six months in the mine was enough for him. I know he and dad had a huge row about it, and they didn't speak for years. He wrote to our mam from time to time, and each letter had a different postmark. Then he turned up in Australia in the early days of the war. He's done very well for himself."

"An enterprising man, then?"

Bethan shook her head. "To be honest, Ian, I know little, only that he went gold prospecting. He never said how wealthy that made him, but enough to buy property there and send me to school. He owns three small hotels in New South Wales and a shop like Mike's that sells electrical goods. In his letters, he said he got put off his ship in Sydney after an explosion just before the outbreak of war. It made him deaf in one ear, so they didn't require him to join the army." She smiled. "He's all I've got, him and his wife and my nephew. So that is why I want to go to Australia when I finish my training."

With his mother gone, Yianevan had no such pull towards his family. There was a sister born to his brother's mother after he left, but he didn't know her and were it not for his half-brother, Bo, he would choose to be anywhere else in the galaxy. As for his older half-sister, Aaris, from his father's first wife, she would prefer it if he never returned.

Bethan noticed his sudden introspection. Perhaps this talk of family was affecting him.

"You don't socialise much, do you?" she said.

"I avoid it, Bethan," Yianevan admitted, and it applied to anywhere he happened to be in the galaxy. "But I am keen to spend more time with you if you agree. I hope I said nothing to offend you or your friends."

"Not at all!" Bethan laughed. "Ivy finds you mysterious, and she's got a few ideas. A Hollywood actor, perhaps, here to see if you can make a film about the village." Then her eyes widened. "Or a *Martian!*"

Yianevan found these assumptions remarkable. Actor. Acting. Make-believe. Pretence. Accurate if you left out the Hollywood part. And Martian? A native of Mars. An uninhabited planet not reachable using the technology available on this world. How would the unsophisticated Ivy know about such things?

"I do not believe Mars supports life," he answered with a puzzled frown. "Is Ivy a student of astronomy?"

Bethan burst into laughter. "Ian! She didn't mean it! It's just a saying. You know…" She raised her hands and waggled her fingers to portray an alien. "Oooh! Little green men from Mars?"

He didn't know, nor did he understand the hand gestures. He was pale but not green, so how could Ivy make that comparison? It might be wise to steer the conversation to more comfortable territory.

"As I am neither green nor mysterious. I must own up and say I am rather dull. I know only how to ask questions, and I am afraid I get rather tongue-tied when required to answer them."

He'd looked for an opportunity to say "tongue-tied" after reading about it at the library. Considering the limited length of a tongue, it was an intriguing concept. And now he'd used it in context. Bethan wouldn't have described his dodging of questions as tongue-tie. She would describe it as simple avoidance, but he was her guest, and she would be gracious.

"Do you now?" she said. "Well, Mike and Ivy were strangers to you. Ivy has a good heart, even if she likes to stick her nose in people's affairs, but she means no harm." Bethan rocked her head from side to side, and her forehead creased a little in thought. "Mrs Jenkins, now…"

Yianevan guessed Bethan would know his landlady, even though Mrs Jenkins's house was away from the main village. The village was small enough for everyone to know everyone else, which was a concern while keeping a low profile. Still, it pleased him to learn from Bethan during their discussion that few people chatted with Mrs Jenkins for fear she may embellish their private business. A question to the wrong person might expose that he had never visited the mine and didn't possess surveying equipment. Not that Mrs Jenkins ever went looking in his car. It was one reason he spent his days either in the library in the neighbouring town or with a book and a packet of crisps out in the countryside. Keeping out of sight as much as possible prevented any

Lyrans, or those who *knew* they were Lyrans, from recognising him. It also stopped too many questions about the stranger with the foreign accent.

Contact with the inhabitants worried him because he hadn't quite got the mannerisms correct. He knew now he had blundered with this mission, and that disturbed him too. Even being here longer than expected bothered him. He also felt "bothered" because contact with the interface was long overdue.

The late afternoon passed into evening, and Bethan and Yianevan continued in pleasant conversation, mostly inspired by the plants that now occupied the space below the window. Yianevan was not acquainted with these plant varieties, but as in all the topics they discussed, Bethan soaked up his knowledge.

However, his concern about blowing his cover caused him to ask, casually, if Bethan ever went to the mine. The question came as a surprise, as she had only visited there twice in her whole life. The village women seldom needed to go to the pit head unless something terrible happened.

Her answer satisfied him, so he turned the discussion to Bethan's family, pointing to the patches on the wall where her forebears' portraits hung until recently. She had little to offer about them, but she mentioned the old picture of Llyn Deron she'd taken down, which led her to tell him her memories of the lake. After that, it seemed natural to tell him about her dreams.

She described the changing landscapes she encountered as she stepped backwards through the visions. Ragged clothes in the first, then she was a grand lady walking the corridors of a castle in the next. In another, a lowly field worker. At other times, she was a phantom gliding unobserved through other people's lives. She dreamt of a world with fantastic flying machines that glittered like distant fireflies. Some dreams had an element of humour, others fear and dread, but the most enduring was also the most disturbing. A dream in which she felt the most physical effects.

She had only ever read about Pompeii in books, but when she mentioned the name, Bethan noted Ian placed his plate beside him on the sofa and leaned forward to better listen with no distractions. His interest prompted her to reveal every aspect of the dream, so she detailed the lightness of the baby in her arms, the centurion, her terror, the sickening smell of burning flesh, the cuts on her feet and legs. She left out no detail, no horror unaccounted for.

"I even had a name," she said when she finished. "Valentina. The centurion said it was the name of a slave in the household of the baby's father."

It surprised Yianevan that she remembered such details when she had no memory of her true self, except for the firefly dream, which he believed was a glimpse of Chabin, Lieutenant Phildre's home. He wanted to discuss them further.

"Your dreams hold variety and excitement, Bethan. Dreams are often very slippery, yet you paint a detailed and provocative picture of a town caught in the throes of destruction. Is there a link between each dream? Can you identify a common thread?"

Bethan made a face. "Hmm, a common thread. Well,

now that you mention it. There is one."

She fished inside the neckline of her sweater and lifted out a metallic bead hanging from a chain. Undoing the clasp, she draped it over the back of her hand for him to view.

Yianevan pasted on a smile he hoped would disguise the alarm that sparked every nerve in his body. A pennant here on the human world? Possessed by someone who might be under Lyran control, if not Lyran herself?

Gleaming and unhoused, it shone against Bethan's skin. Only a Noble knew the power of the pennants. The beads were of exquisite craftmanship and powered every ship the Nobles manufactured. As an essential energy source on the homeworld, pennants were fundamental to the Nobles' superior phase and speed technology. Many species had tried to produce ships and technology of equivalent capability, but their efforts were doomed to failure. No other species save a few select humans, working as interventionists with limited knowledge, knew of the pennants' existence. Thus, the hierarchy's mystique and claim as the most technologically advanced species in the ten sectors remained unchallenged.

There existed a potential for a pennant's power to be harnessed to serve as a weapon, but that was never its purpose. In the right hands, it was a balm to soothe the heart of even the angriest volcano, calm a raging sea, and provide the cleanest energy to the Noble society. Yianevan knew that no interventionist or anyone outside the Noble homeworld had ever viewed a pennant or understood the extent of its power. A complex outer casing that allowed the interventionist's hand inside to "read" the plexus concealed the pennant but allowed touch to initiate the calming sequence when attending the Lyran sabotage sites. The Noble hierarchy was aware of the interventionist fleet's theories regarding the pennants' backwards displacement of time but never confirmed them. It was unthinkable that a pennant may fall into the hands of an enemy, yet here, one had become a trinket, and Bethan showed no recognition of the power she held.

Unless she was testing him, waiting for a reaction that would give him away as a Noble.

Yet it was like no other pennant Yianevan had seen. Although unquestionably of Noble origin, this pennant was of curious design. Fashioned more like a teardrop, it exhibited an unnatural language across the plexus filigree. He felt an inexplicable desire to touch it, run the plexus through his fingers, and hold it in his hands to unravel its message. He never felt that way about a calming pennant, which was an everyday part of his life. How could a pennant this unique have come into Bethan's possession?

He had to cover his surprise. So he gave an admiring nod.

"It is beautiful. This travels with you always? A token?"

Bethan tucked the chain back into her sweater.

"Yes, I *love* it. I can't remember a time when I didn't have it. Sometimes in the dreams, it's in my hand. Other times, it's tied around my neck or wrist on a strip of leather. I recall catching it in the Pompeii dream as if someone tossed it to me."

Yes, the interventionist raised her arm. Was that the moment the pennant delivered itself to her?

"I don't suppose it's got any value," she said. "My dad bought the chain for it. It wasn't expensive because he was only a miner, so he didn't have much money."

The chain was as important as the charm because Bethan hated that her father seemed so distant from her memory. It made her wonder about Ian's father, but there was no point in asking. So instead, she stood and gathered up the plates and cups. Yianevan followed her into the kitchen.

"Ian?" Bethan asked as she filled the sink. "What was so fascinating about my Pompeii dream? It's just a dream, so your interest surprised me." She wiped her hands and leaned against the sink. "In America, they research dream meanings. Is this a sideline occupation, Ian Noble? Am I to be featured in a book?"

Bethan didn't expect Ian to respond to the humour, but when he did, his eyes crinkled, and his lips parted in a smile as astonishing as it was unpractised. He had the most beautiful teeth, white, unstained, so… *clean*, like the rest of him. It was his best smile since they met, and it had quite an effect. She felt quite overcome.

"I am intrigued by humans… um, humankind. People," he admitted, unaware of the effect he had. "Fascinated may be a better word."

"Why? You are people yourself."

He had to concede that, although a different "people," to her. He nodded.

"Indeed, but I am sure you understand I am a solitary man and prefer to observe rather than integrate."

"Ian, you always have something to say. Or should I

say, ready with a new question? Besides, no-one can be just an observer of humanity. Even the shyest person has to take part at some point."

More's the pity, Yianevan thought. A man could disappear here. At least a man other than him, who would never fit in no matter how much he wished for it. Perhaps the Monk's Gate was an escape, a place not to wait until the Lyrans could rise again, but somewhere for dissenters to hide. He needed to give that angle some thought.

"Bethan, I merely ask, and others take over the conversation."

She raised her hand to her mouth, her cheeks flushing a faint pink.

"Ian, I'm so sorry. Have I been jabbering on? I know Ivy can say in ten words what the rest of us can say in one, but I didn't realise, now she's not here, that I was taking over the conversation."

"Not at all. That is not what I meant. It is my intention to learn as much about you as I can."

What a strange and unexpected response. In their few meetings, she noticed he did rather study her, although now his face gave nothing away. Bethan wondered why that didn't make her uneasy, but even though there seemed nothing ominous about him, she narrowed her eyes a little.

"Why? Why is that your intention?"

Yianevan realised he'd blundered. Think. Find the right words.

"As I said, I am intrigued. As a newcomer, I have met few people, but I enjoyed our walk and subsequent discussions, and I am keen to repeat them. There is little to report about myself, and you are far more interesting, so I plan on letting you do most of the talking. I am more comfortable asking questions, but I don't wish to make you feel out of place." There, that should work.

"Too late for that!" Bethan snorted. "I've felt out of place all my life!"

Unwilling to make any more blunders, Yianevan pulled a tea towel from a hook and held it up. Bethan turned back to the tea things in the sink, and they worked in silence for a few minutes, giving her time to study that earlier comment. Keen to repeat their meetings? Could his interest in her be romantic, but he was too clumsy or inexperienced to express it? She allowed herself a sideways glance at him as he put the cups on the table. Somehow, that wouldn't have surprised her. Ian was a little socially inept, but the thought threw up a measure of disquiet. She liked him a lot, but she had to be practical. Unless he planned to head for London too, maybe now was the time to discourage him. She tried to be matter of fact in her delivery, but she had little practice in discouraging men. It was usually a simple "no" when asked for a date.

"I can't believe I'm leaving for London in a few weeks," she said. It was the best she could come up with.

Untroubled by her announcement, he nodded. "I'm aware. I do not plan to be here much longer myself."

"Oh." Disquiet set aside and rapidly evaporating, Bethan realised their fledgeling friendship was doomed anyway, unless…

"Do you get to London much?"

"I can go anywhere I wish," he said. "It depends on

my assignment, on my commitment."

"What is your assignment?"

"Not for discussion, I'm afraid. I need to garner a little more information."

"About the mine?" Bethan asked, forgetting his earlier comment regarding learning about her. "Well, good luck there. The mine boss, Mr Trevor, has been there since nineteen-twenty. I've been told he's unhappy about the Coal Board's decisions, but I suppose you've met him."

Yianevan didn't answer. He hadn't met Mr Trevor, nor even driven close to the mine, nor had he followed up enough on the Coal Board. He unwisely assumed he wouldn't be here long enough for it to matter.

After he left, Bethan stood in the tiny hallway and gazed towards the parlour. Ian left a presence everywhere, something indefinable, like a reminder of someone she once met in those vivid dreams. What was she thinking! That was plain nonsense. She couldn't place Ian in any of them. The presence of the charm inside her sweater was a source of comfort. It was with her constantly. To her, it was more than just a piece of jewellery, a pretty trinket. It was intensely private, and Ian was the only person who had ever seen it besides her mam and dad.

She puffed out her breath in a long sigh. Ian probably thought her downright sentimental, but she had loved sharing the dreams with him. She didn't remember having them before boarding school, and the only other person she told was her mother. However, her mam's disinterest made her feel silly about attaching too much importance to them, so she learned to endure the dreams alone.

The Pompeii dream was the most detailed and, in a historical sense, the earliest. She identified the other dreams as historically later, except perhaps the firefly dream, where she had no point of reference. Often, she felt even her day-to-day life had a dreamlike quality, as if she were acting out her existence in a play. Or perhaps a puppet with someone else pulling the strings.

As she often did while preparing for bed, Bethan went over the day's events. She didn't know what possessed her to tell Ian about her dreams, even though she was glad she had. He didn't interrupt, just encouraged her with a nod when she wavered. Perhaps because he was a stranger and so private himself, she felt safe, although his comment tonight did highlight that his questions implied more than just a simple "getting to know you". How could it happen that she felt connected to him in only a little over a week? Even trustful of him? She didn't believe in love at first sight. She was far too practical for that, but couldn't deny that he affected her in a way no man ever had.

Tucking the sheet around her chin, Bethan tried to shut down her overactive mind. It was fanciful to assume he felt the same attraction to her. And she knew nothing about him. He would most likely complete his contract and move on without giving her another thought.

CHAPTER FOURTEEN _

Yianevan didn't make it to his car. Instead, moments after Bethan closed her front door, the spiral snatched him from the street and delivered him to the ship. Corky wasted no time in showing him the changes to the gate. Worrying changes that might foreshadow complete destabilisation. The gate now presented as a dark cloud shadowing Vesuvius, irregular at its edge and in places showed a rippling translucence that revealed the eruption underneath.

"Noble, I apologise," Corky said. "Your presence within the anomaly appears to create a destabilising effect. It seemed a safer option to bring you back. As you can see, it is settling down now you are here. I cannot even risk sending the spiral for routine contact."

"Why doesn't it react this way to the lieutenant?

Corky had tried to find an explanation for that himself.

"It appears to recognise her, Noble. This is opposite to the spiral, which continues to disregard any commands to collect her. I have conducted surveillance of the local technology but have returned no evidence of Lyran activity.

However, I have detected traces of the lieutenant's bio-signature throughout what might be multiple timelines. Apart from the one you also occupied, I cannot access them. They are closed to probes."

Yianevan suspected it all came down to the pennant. Had the Lyran Monks somehow obtained Noble technology? It seemed unlikely, but not impossible. Details of the Lyran war were vague, filled with individual Noble heroics to pass on to posterity, but otherwise with limited substance. The Nobles won. The Lyrans lost. That was enough to satisfy. Regardless, he couldn't leave the pennant on the planet, even though he was almost convinced Bethan was not Lyran.

"There was a development I must explore further," he advised Corky. "I need to return to the surface."

"Noble," Corky said, "Your safety will be compromised, so unless this development is significant, I propose we turn our attention to analysing the properties of the gate. As you failed to recover the lieutenant, an investigation on the ship would be a more productive use of our time. It would also be wise to alert the Noble homeworld."

Yianevan did not choose to share this development with Corky. Not yet. The configuration of Bethan's pennant, even why she had it, had to be investigated first. If he told his father, the mission would end, and he would order him home. He doubted his father would regard Bethan's well-being, and the pennant was yet another link in the triad. Bethan-pennant-Monk's Gate.

He shook his head. "They do not expect a report for

another three days. I will contact them. Just not now. Tell me, Interface, when was this interventionist's family abducted from Earth? She related to me a recurring dream she has of this volcanic event. She recounted the event from the perspective of a child."

"Earth", as the planet's designation, was first mentioned in records during the final abductions. Corky knew what the humans called it, but no-one made it official.

"As far as Phildre's ancestry is concerned," he said, "her lineage appears on Noble records from the outset of the war, thus predating this event. Her ancestors were known as Britons, but they didn't enslave her line because the Nobles intercepted the Lyran transport and sent them as refugees to the ten sectors. Returning her forebears to the planet was not an option because of technological contamination. Is this significant?"

Yianevan didn't know. He just wanted to understand, try to piece things together. So, perhaps yes, perhaps no.

"I wonder how she appeared to spring into life with no memory," he said. "I am also intrigued by the difference in the movement of time between the planet and the ship. After hearing of her dreams, it occurred to me that were her ancestors not abducted, she would have indeed suffered this disaster and has somehow taken on a life not yet led. Perhaps the Lyrans had a better understanding of forward time travel. It is still a concern, even though I do not believe the time period the interventionist inhabits harbours Lyran fugitives or soldiers."

"It would be impossible to tell by appearance only, Noble," Corky said. "According to records, the Lyran

Monks and their people were organised into groups and communities. Social only amongst themselves, they did not seek communion with other species outside their common faction. They are unemotional and self-serving. Are these characteristics you observe?"

The interface could have been describing Nobles. That description fitted them perfectly. But were the people on the Earth organised? From what he had observed, they were, but not dedicated to groups unless you consider the church or the historical society. And social? Mrs Jenkins lived alone. Bethan lived alone. Mike Trent lived alone, and none of them appeared desperate for daily contact with others. The interface described Lyrans as unemotional and self-serving. He couldn't say he'd experienced either of those traits. In fact, everybody he met in the village cared about what they did, and they cared about the people they met. If Corky's description was correct, the village's residents were not typical of Lyrans.

"I have met not a single person who displays the casual disregard for truth and law attributed to Lyrans, Interface," he said. "Neither have I encountered any of the dubious qualities you describe. So, I cannot find a reason for the interventionist's presence in that timeline unless she is a Lyran working alone. In that case, she is remarkable in concealing her character. I do not consider her deceptive. Rather, I think she arrived there in error."

Corky showed Yianevan the results of his investigations. "The other timelines branching off from her current position are unclear, Noble. I can detect similar technology in some, such as those in our original imaging. I cannot ascertain how time moves nor predict forward motion. At times, it appears circular and unpredictable. And Noble, may I remind you that the lieutenant is not Lyran? None of her ancestors had any form of Lyran genetic coding."

Yianevan knew that, but it made her presence on the planet more confusing.

"Interface," he said. "You advised Lieutenant Phildre is a regular imbiber of alcohol. I discovered a drink called whisky, which is superior to Birn. I have observed that overuse of this, and other distilled products, often leads to unconsciousness and unacceptable behaviour. However, the lieutenant rejects the use of all such intoxicating beverages. This shows a shift in her personality."

"Lieutenant Phildre favours Birn and floral-flavoured Micy, Noble," Corky said. "She becomes quite senseless, but not until everyone else is on the floor as well."

That didn't sound like Bethan, who possessed some of her grandmother's temperate notions. She wasn't highly social, and her ambitions, although perhaps a little more daring for her time, would not be deemed reckless. There was definitely a change that made Yianevan wonder how it worked. To be influenced by family values suggested being raised in a family environment, so she must have been a child at one time. Yet, going by her dreams and the interface's conclusions, she moved through multiple timelines in reverse chronological order. Could it be her intelligence possessed different bodies? If so, why does the version living in the Welsh village look like Lieutenant Phildre? He paused. Did the lieutenant look like her? In features perhaps, but Bethan's appearance was a little softer, her skin glowed, and she showed a little more moderation in her behaviour.

It didn't matter. Now Yianevan knew it was there, the pennant could not remain on the planet. There might not be Lyrans in Bethan's timeline, but there might be others elsewhere, and he couldn't let such sensitive and powerful technology fall into their hands. The difficulty he faced was getting Bethan to part with her "charm". He had to go back. He had to get the pennant, somehow.

"As the spiral cannot retrieve Lieutenant Phildre," he declared, "I will devise a physical removal to the gate."

"Is that necessary, Noble?" Corky knew there was little point in debating, but he did it anyway. "We have established you are not in a timeline likely to contain Lyrans, so I must counsel you to turn your attention away from the lieutenant. Another attempt by you to retrieve her is likely to destabilise the gate further, and we may lose the opportunity of study."

"I thought you liked Lieutenant Phildre?"

"I do, Noble. However, her position as an interventionist poses substantial risks of which she is aware, and she is dedicated to erasing Lyran threats to this planet. If she were the one deciding, she would choose to sacrifice herself rather than miss the opportunity to identify dangerous Lyran technology. It is easy to anticipate what course the hierarchy would prefer."

It didn't matter what the interface thought. Yianevan was returning to the surface.

"The interventionist may not have a direct connection

to the Lyrans," he said, "but she is connected to the gate. Of that, I am confident."

Corky continued to point out the problems the Noble might face if he chose that course of action; the dangers in the soil, destabilisation of the gate, loss of communication, not to mention the considerable distance between the lieutenant's location and the gate's coordinates.

Yianevan had considered them all, but he had to risk another trip to the planet to retrieve the pennant. Until he knew of its existence, he had considered leaving the interventionist but could only do that if he could persuade her to surrender her "charm".

Also, there was the slight possibility he and Corky were wrong. Bethan might still be Lyran. Either way, Noble technology had no place on the human world and certainly not as a charm around a person's neck. Removing the pennant by force was an option, but he didn't want to harm Bethan. He had an idea.

"From my learnings, Interface," he said, "travel to an overseas destination is an exciting and romantic concept. However, the interventionist has taken on some sensibilities of the time. This means, at least as a social norm, she would not accept an invitation to accompany me to the site of the gate unless she is cleaved to me. I believe that may be a solution."

Corky searched for a simpler and less time-consuming solution to minimise the Noble's time within the gate's confines. Finally, he came up with one possibility. He displayed the schematic of an archaic device. Yianevan had never seen it before.

"What is it?" he asked.

"A neurotryptojag, Noble. It would render the lieutenant unconscious and quicken the memory response. If it works, she will answer your questions about her involvement with the gate, and there will be no need to bring her back through. I can simulate one for you," he added helpfully.

Yianevan asked for more information.

"Its use was abandoned centuries ago, Noble. Of the two thousand human test subjects, they only recorded a dubious five per cent success rate. Even under controlled procedures, death or complete memory failure occurred in around seventy five percent of participants."

Corky watched as the Noble's expression went from incredulous to horrified.

"What! Who is responsible for this barbarity?" Yianevan demanded. "The Lyrans?"

Corky didn't want to admit the Nobles invented it. Given his response to the technology, the heir wouldn't like the rest of the story either, but he was committed.

"The Nobles, Noble. They suspected many human adults of being Lyran. DNA proved indeterminate as the two species appear to share a common ancestor, so they devised the test to stimulate memories. The children born to the human females on the Lyran freighter had Lyran DNA, but they didn't have memories of Lyra, so they didn't get tested. As you know, Lyran DNA was bred out over generations. The Nobles only used the mechanism in that one application and then abandoned it because it was unreliable."

Yianevan felt his body tense. This was unbelievable. "Interface, this is not common knowledge."

"I understand, Noble, but they stored it in one of my caches. I recovered it because I believed it might be of use."

"The hierarchy allowed you knowledge of this barbarism, but nothing about the gate?"

"I can vary my program as pathways of new information unfold, but in the beginning, the Nobles only gave me what they believed I required."

Yianevan shook his head. "I would leave the interventionist rather than risk her life, but there have been signs of some memories emerging."

He didn't mention the attempts at redecoration. It seemed pointless, and he doubted it represented a full recovery of Bethan's memories, which were unlikely to return before his inability to live on the planet took over.

"I have explored means of encouraging her to accompany me, Interface," he said. "I require identification and travel documents."

"I will need to sort through many layers of their legal system, Noble, and I cannot predict what effect a prolonged presence of the spiral will have on the gate. We have few opportunities left now to keep the spiral tether secure to Lieutenant Phildre's timeline, and the gate may deteriorate to the point where it is not accessible."

"Make the attempt," Yianevan ordered. "If it destabilises, we will consider the interventionist lost and concentrate on the evidence before our eyes."

While he waited, Yianevan examined the sensor readings of the gate. It looked fragile, and its earlier form of an encroaching blemish appeared shadowy, delicate, and fragmented. The gate and he had one thing in common; they had limited time. Had Bethan not shown him the pennant, he would not be returning, but unknown Noble technology on an alien world, one once invaded by Lyrans, who might even be responsible for its presence, could have unimaginable consequences. This would be his last attempt to bring the woman to the gate, but one thing was certain; when he next returned to the ship, the pennant would be in his possession.

He relayed a possible course of action to Corky; one he formulated after reading an old housekeeping magazine belonging to Mrs Jenkins. It had a section detailing a wife's duty, and it gave him an idea.

"Humans on this world expect in their lives to enter a marriage contract," he said. "If I can make this contract with the interventionist, she will come under my dominion, and I will command her to accompany me to Pompeii."

Corky responded with the brief silence he often displayed since the Noble began his investigation. This Noble's actions were unpredictable, but he had to answer, even if it didn't sound hopeful.

"I have worked with Lieutenant Phildre for several years, Noble. I have never known her not to question a command."

The housekeeping book was Yianevan's only frame of reference, and the interventionist accepted the laws of her new society.

"She will obey me," he asserted with far more confidence than he felt. "The law requires her solemn vow."

*CHAPTER FIFTEEN_*

Mrs Jenkins collared Bethan at the grocers to inform her that her new houseguest, Mr Noble, was a delightful and quiet gentleman. Then she glanced about her and leaned in, her voice lowered.

"He is a little strange, Bethie. He wears his hat at mealtimes, makes his own bed and never gives me laundry."

Strange? Not as if Bethan hadn't spotted that for herself, so she just made agreeable noises at Mrs Jenkins that seemed to satisfy.

Mrs Jenkins was a woman who inherited the busybody gene from her mother. She pressed Bethan for information about the previous Sunday because Mr Noble had revealed he was attending the Davies' residence for lunch. Bethan knew what poking about for details sounded like and wasn't prepared to give anything away. So she dismissed Ian's attendance at lunch as just welcoming a visitor to the village and bid Mrs Jenkins a good day.

Mrs Jenkins sniffed as Bethan made her getaway. The Davies family always thought themselves above everyone else, the fact of the son making good overseas and the daughter going to a posh school. She would have loved to know Bethan wasn't just welcoming a visitor. Ian visited the day after the Sunday lunch and again on Tuesday. Although they never went anywhere specific, they enjoyed strolling through the park or along the canal. Attracted by his intelligence, awkwardness, and puzzlement at humour, Bethan found he occupied much of her thoughts as she tried to unravel the enigma that was Ian Noble. While he didn't open up to her about his past, he spoke about the things that interested him, and he was clever, not to mention amusing, in how he shared his knowledge. It made her wonder if he was a man she could ever truly know.

That week, late-night work commitments on Wednesday and Thursday meant Bethan wouldn't see him. She felt a little foolish that she preferred to lock in a firm date when they would get together again, but she planned to see Ivy on Friday evening, so Saturday would be her first opportunity. She telephoned Ian from Mike's office on Thursday.

"Hello, Ian. Would you like to go on a picnic? There's a bus that goes up to Llyn Deron on Saturday mornings. It's a bit of a trip, but the scenery is wonderful."

A picnic was a new concept to Yianevan, and Bethan picked up the caution in his reply. He wasn't sure how to manage another unfamiliar social situation. Not if others were present.

"A picnic?" he echoed. "With Mike and Ivy?"

"No, just us. And, yes, a picnic. You know, where you take a flask and sandwiches and sit on a rug in a nice place?"

The "just us" aspect sounded appealing. Sitting on the ground, less so.

"Won't we get cold?"

"A bit," Bethan said, trying to dumb down the fact it was always cold at the lake if you didn't dress for the weather. "Early Spring is the best time of year up in the hills. You'll love it, I promise. Dress warmly. I'll organise a picnic basket."

"Would it be best to go in my vehicle?"

Bethan hesitated. She didn't want to get in a car with him but telling him he was a terrible driver in a phone conversation sounded unfair.

"We'll talk about it. Can you come by at eight?"

"Yes, will I see you before then?"

"It's Thursday, Ian," she laughed. "It's only the day after tomorrow." But she couldn't ignore how his eagerness to see her again made her feel.

"Yes, of course," he replied. "I will see you on Saturday."

Yianevan put down the telephone. Saturday? Well, at least that gave him a day to read up on picnics, but it was one more day wasted. He'd managed two more days of getting to know her, but her working late represented delays. After reviewing the marriage idea, it turned out not to be as simple as he imagined and required more planning than he had time for, even though it would offer a more certain outcome if he could execute it. If their friendship developed, he could make a casual proposal they visit Pompeii together. In the meantime, he had acquired a fascination for particular literature that informed him such forwardness was inappropriate.

He first encountered women's magazines in Mrs Jenkins's parlour, and the slim volumes rewarded him with the answers to all his questions about befriending a female.

The pages portrayed the ideal woman, although Yianevan did not believe them to be typical of this village. An "ideal" woman would wear a subtle smear of lipstick. The seams in her stockings would be straight, her hair brushed until shining, and rolled at night to give just the right volume of bouncy curls. He thought of Bethan. She didn't need any of these accoutrements. Her dark hair always shone, and he hadn't noticed seams in her stockings, but then, he hadn't paid attention to the back of her legs. He thought Bethan's mouth was perfect and natural, although he didn't know if the lovely rose colour came from a lipstick smear.

The journals cautioned women to be modest in their dealings with men. They further advised, a little unfairly, Yianevan thought, that males had an agenda and could never be "just friends" with a member of the opposite sex. He couldn't help but speculate how the people who wrote those articles would find life on his homeworld, with its sexual freedoms and informal attitude to modesty.

Yianevan found Bethan's front door open on Saturday morning, anticipating his arrival. He called out, and she poked her head around the kitchen door, a woolly hat on her head and a thick scarf around her neck. She wore boots and trousers, and he realised what she meant by dressing warmly. Bethan took in his suit, tie, and hat, all protected by his worsted overcoat. Why did that surprise her? Ian always dressed as if he was going to a conference. So she waggled her finger at him.

"Ian, you didn't listen. That's not suitable."

He glanced down. He paid attention to what she said, but he didn't have many clothes, so he made a half-hearted protest.

"I'll be warm enough."

Bethan went behind him and stripped him of his coat. Then she reached up and knocked his hat off his head, tossing it onto the peg of the hall stand where it landed first try.

"It's not just the cold, you goose," she said, half-grinning, half-mocking. "You're going to get muddy, and the breeze up there will blow that fancy hat off your head!" So saying, she ushered him into the warm kitchen.

"We'll be walking and sitting on the ground," she told him. "You should have worn something that won't matter if it gets covered in grass or mud. Wait here." Bethan headed for the stairs. "I'll find you something."

Yianevan wandered around the kitchen while he waited, taking a moment to examine the fancy china on the dresser. It was cosy in here. Comfortable and welcoming. Beside the boiler sat an empty dish and an enormous cat who looked pleased to be occupying the warmest spot. Front legs tucked under itself; it blinked up at its hostess's early morning visitor.

Bethan had spoken of a cat that came to visit. An opportunist cat, like every cat Yianevan had ever met anywhere in the galaxy. He bent down and scratched the feline behind the ears, and for a moment, it purred in condescension as it allowed the contact. Then it lashed its tail to signal the petting time was over. It didn't occur to Yianevan then that it was the first time he'd ever touched a cat's fur.

A small crate with a handle stood on the counter, and he couldn't resist looking inside. Cut into tiny peaks, a row of sandwiches stood like a miniature mountain range on greaseproof paper. He leaned forward and sniffed. Egg. Nice. A yellow oblong cake was another addition. Cake was a revelation to Yianevan. Bethan gave him a slice to take home after one of their evenings together, and he loved its delicate crumbliness.

A few circular objects were also in the basket. Emitting an enticing spicy aroma, he noted with some alarm they contained squashed insects. Compelled to pick one up for closer examination, he felt relief to find dried fruit. These must be Peekybarks. Still warm, Bethan must have got up early to make them for the picnic.

"Here," Bethan bustled back into the kitchen and dumped a bundle of clothes on the table. "I'd sorted out my dad's stuff, and it was ready to go to the jumble sale. They're all laundered, and they'll do you for today. He didn't have woolly hats, but here's one of mine."

She reached up and stretched the hat over Yianevan's head, then wrapped a matching scarf around his neck. Stepping back, she admired her handiwork.

"That's better," she said, following up by bundling him into an oversized old coat. "This was always too big for dad, but it will save your good coat from getting wrecked."

An awful smell assailed Yianevan's sensitive nostrils, but Bethan waved away his silent protest.

"Sorry about that. I had to put it in mothballs. Don't worry. The fresh air at the lake will blow it away."

"Are we taking the vehicle?"

Bethan felt awkward. It would take over an hour if they went by bus. Then they would have to leave by three to get the bus back, and she dearly wanted to see the sunset. This might be her only opportunity. When her dad took her there, they always left early for the bus. She heard from others about the glorious sunsets, but there was no guarantee they would get back at all if Ian drove. He misinterpreted her hesitation.

"You prefer the bus?"

"No, Ian." She summoned the courage to tell him the truth. "I'll be honest. Your driving scares me. We can take your car, but only if I drive."

"You can drive?" he said, his surprise muffled by the scarf. "I've only seen males driving cars."

"Ian, what planet are you from!? That's very old-fashioned of you. They taught us at boarding school. We learned to drive and do basic mechanics while the war was still on. The Queen was our example."

"The Queen?"

"Yes, well, she was Princess Elizabeth then. I took a driving test, and I even have a licence."

That was more than Yianevan had. He wasn't even sure what a licence was. However, Bethan's suggestion seemed like a good solution, so he handed her the keys.

"Good," she said. "Let's go."

With a beaming smile, Bethan shushed the cat out the back door and Ian out the front. Minutes later, Yi of the ruling house of Anevan, time traveller and heir to the Noble homeworld, sat in the passenger seat of the car, bundled up in a scarf and woollen hat, picnic basket on his knee, and settled like a small child at the mercy of an efficient and overprotective parent.

CHAPTER SIXTEEN

Bethan possessed a remarkable ability to chat and drive at the same time, a skill that impressed Yianevan because he found navigating a tiny vehicle down narrow roads took considerable concentration. Even at spacelight speed, the galaxy was far more straightforward, and vessels were mostly automated. He had mastered the car's simple controls, but without an interface, everything had to be carried out "manually". It also required a liquid propellant to ensure its continuous movement, which was an obstacle at first because he hadn't then grasped the concept of Earth's currency or inserting fuel.

Bethan also understood the meanings of each road sign. Yianevan determined them to be of human religious significance and was glad Bethan took a moment to explain. There were also place signs showing distance, but he could not make sense of them as they were in the native language.

As they travelled, Yianevan watched the passing scenery and listened to Bethan's commentary about the farmland. The morning sun lit the new spring pasture with green and gold, and newborn lambs frolicked with their mothers. Small birds darted in and out of the bushes, and a hedgehog narrowly missed being run over as it scurried home after its nocturnal meanderings. Dew glistened on spider's webs on the hedgerows, and Yianevan saw his surroundings through fresh eyes. He wound down the window and filled his lungs with the fresh air that smelled of morning gloriousness. He closed his eyes, but his unspoken delight made Bethan laugh. She thought she was witnessing a big city boy on a day trip to the country.

It turned out she was right about the hat. It wouldn't have lasted five minutes at the lake's edge, where the wind had yet to decide whether blustering or settling into a gentle breeze should be the order of the day. Bethan covered a grassy patch with a thick blanket and popped the basket on top to make sure it didn't blow away. The morning air had a definite chill, so Yianevan was glad of the overcoat, despite its stinky aroma that did indeed diminish as it aired out in the day's freshness. Either that, or he just got used to it. Bethan didn't ask him to sit. Instead, she suggested they take a walk.

Llyn Deron sat in a vast basin, cradled by soaring hills on one side and forest on the other. Despite the lingering effects of winter in the village, soft grass covered the lake's banks, and a profusion of trumpet-like yellow flowers grew as far as the eye could see. Bethan led the way. She appeared to know where to go.

"Do you come here often?" Yianevan asked.

Bethan stopped to admire the view. "Not in years. My father brought me a few times, but the bus doesn't always run. A car makes it easier."

Yianevan saw why Bethan loved this place. Apart from the beauty of the lake, the air was fragrant with earthy perfumes and woodland aromas that reminded him of his homeworld. Although he didn't recall ever needing an overcoat there.

"How did you remember the way here?" he said as he clambered over rocks, trying to keep up and wondering how he ever became so reliant on technology to find his way.

"I have an excellent sense of direction," Bethan giggled, puffed out from the exertion of climbing. "I'm vague about some details of my life, but once I've been somewhere, I never forget."

Yianevan smiled. Yes, like Pompeii.

Stepping up onto a boulder, Bethan held out her hand in invitation.

"Come up here and see the view. It's glorious."

He didn't take her hand. Instead, climbed up without her help.

It was indeed a glorious view. The lake sparkled in the hazy sunlight, and Bethan told him that heralded the promise of a crisp spring day ahead. The sun warmed his face, and he tried to not let her see when he glanced across to see what she was doing. Her eyes were closed, and he didn't realise she was wondering why he ignored her hand. She felt his eyes on her, and after a moment, what she saw as a rejection stopped hurting.

The trek took hours, and they returned to the picnic rug just as the sun found a suitable position overhead. They took off their woollen hats as the air warmed, and Yianevan had already discarded the coat. They talked, ate sandwiches and drank hot tea from a thermos before Yianevan made a startling revelation. He didn't like tea. Without a word, Bethan added a spoonful of sugar to his cup, grinning while she stirred.

"This'll fix it."

And it did. A complete and very luscious transformation. The Peekybarks were a perfect complement to the tea, and the cake was also superb. Yianevan's appreciative munching made Bethan smile.

"It's Battenburg cake. I bought it at Mr Griffith's shop. I can make a good roast dinner, but cakes usually sink. It's safer to buy them." She grinned. "I think you have a sweet tooth."

"It's all so good," he sighed. Then he examined the cake's yellow outer confection. "Do all cakes have an edible outer layer?"

"Outer layer?"

"Skin?"

"Ian, that's marzipan! Didn't your mother ever bake cakes?"

"My mother?"

Yianevan put the cake down. The question disconcerted him. He didn't doubt his mother could have prepared food if she wished, but tribal ordinaries were far more accomplished in culinary arts than the Noble hierarchy, most of whom gathered in large assemblies to indulge themselves and laud their own importance to the galaxy. His mother was from a lesser Noble house, so maybe she knew how to prepare food. He'd just never seen her do it.

"My mother didn't bake cakes. She didn't cook."

Surprised, Bethan wriggled herself around to face him.

"Your mother didn't cook? Did you have servants?"

Revealing even this minor fact about his mother invited further discussion. Yianevan realised he was getting too comfortable. He didn't want to spoil a pleasurable experience, so he lied with a bit of truth thrown in.

"My society has a caste system, Bethan. Females of my mother's caste do not prepare food."

Bethan made a face. "Females? You refer to your mother as a *female*? You sound like you're talking about an animal in a zoo. And a caste system? Ian, where are you from?"

A careless choice of words, and Bethan was too intelligent to let it go. Now she was intrigued.

"A community," he said, hoping it would be enough. "Other than that, I would rather not say."

She took a minute to digest the information, speculating he may have belonged to some kind of cult. She'd heard of such things, and people left them to become part of the world. It may be painful to talk about, and he said he'd rather not say more, so she would abide by that.

"Okay," she said. "I know. Touchy subject, so I'll not ask. You can tell me when you want to.

"Thank you, Bethan."

Bethan didn't revisit Yianevan's history for the rest of the day. Together, they enjoyed the sunshine and fed the waterbirds with the remains of their sandwiches, but Yianevan wrapped the rest of the cake, reluctant to donate it to the local wildlife. As the afternoon sun slipped into the west and they ran out of tea, Bethan seemed in no hurry to leave.

"We can stay to watch the sunset," she suggested. "Dad and I only ever came by bus, so we had to leave early. I've always wanted to see the sunset up here. I have a torch to find the car when it gets dark. It's just over there, anyway." She made a vague gesture towards the unsealed road as if not finding the car would be only a minor inconvenience.

That suited Yianevan. He was in no hurry for the day to end, either. Bethan had awoken in him a desire to be close to her, and her gentleness brought him a peace he did not experience in twenty years of near solitude in space.

Later, Bethan took out a book of Welsh poetry and read the verses aloud. Yianevan didn't understand the words, but he loved the chiming of the native dialect, coupled with the lilting rhythm of her voice. It occurred to him that even the mind-boggling, tongue-twisting language was an endearing aspect of this beautiful place.

Soothed and lulled by the poetry, he lay back on the picnic rug with a contented sigh and watched as tiny, happy insects flew overhead, their gossamer wings glinting in the late afternoon sun.

They stayed there until the sky turned red and gold, and the setting sun ignited the mountains with a fiery ambience. Too dark now to read, they sat side by side in silence. As the sun began to disappear, the small bedrocks at the base of the mountains lit like the glowing embers of a dying fire. The chatter of small birds punctuated the stillness as they flew within the branches of the trees to find their rest for the night.

Yianevan had witnessed spectacular sunsets on many worlds, but none overflowed into his senses like this one. A sliver of sunlight still peeped through a gulley between the steep hills, making the lake's surface ripple with orange-yellow light. He wished time would cease its inevitable path and keep them both in this moment.

Wishes, he thought. Why would he wish? Wishes never come true.

Bethan had catered for them staying late and brought a second flask filled with hot cocoa. The chocolaty goodness warmed them as they munched on the last of the Peekybarks and watched the splendid changes in the sky give way to a moonless night filled with a generous sprinkling of stars.

"You know that dream you have, the one about fireflies?" Yianevan said.

"I'm surprised you remembered," Bethan laughed. "We don't have fireflies in Wales, and I've only ever seen pictures."

"Shall I show you the planet where they live?"

It was dark, but he knew she was smiling.

"Go on then."

"Are you prepared to be blinded by science?"

"I don't think my eyes are in any danger."

"Okay." Yianevan pointed out across the lake. "Can you see the outline of the two hills that the lake runs between?"

Bethan wriggled closer and looked along his arm, so

close he could feel her warmth. She nodded.

"Draw a square," Yianevan instructed. "Make it around the size of a postage stamp from the top, and position it, so the bottom left corner is just resting on the highest point."

Bethan nodded again. "Yes, done."

"Now, divide the postage stamp into four sections, like a window. Can you do it?"

"It's small. But yes."

"In the top left-hand quadrant is the world you dream about."

"It's full of stars, Ian. How do I know which one?"

"Oh, it's there," he assured her. "Do you see the pinpoint of light?"

"They're all pinpoints of light," she giggled. "We're billions of miles away."

Yianevan stretched out his hand. "It's the one right at the end of my finger."

At that, Bethan slapped his arm. "You are being daft, Ian Noble."

"Well, don't say I didn't point it out."

"Okay," she said, attempting to challenge his creativity. "What's it called?"

"Chabin," he answered without hesitating. "And those aren't fireflies. They're ships that travel deep into space. There are tall buildings where the people who pilot those ships live."

Bethan hugged her knees. "Why are they going into space?"

"Because they need to go to other planets. They have

a society like yours."

"Do they look like us?"

He would let her think about that one. "You tell me."

"Hmm. I think they do, except they have an extra finger on each hand."

"That's right! How did you know?"

Bethan laughed, immersing herself in what, to her, was a game of make-believe.

"You gave it away when you said they were pilots. Everyone knows you need at least five fingers and a thumb to drive a spaceship."

It was Yianevan's turn to laugh because she wasn't wrong. Chabin natives had an extra digit they used in piloting their own transports. It seemed her memories were intact and in there somewhere.

"What other planets have you been to?" Bethan asked, surprised at his ability as a plausible storyteller.

He gave a non-committal shrug and grinned.

"Too many to name."

"Are there only humans, or are there some green blobs?"

"I've never seen a green blob," Yianevan confessed. "Most species resemble humans. Even those who look a little different walk upright and possess varying degrees of intelligence. The world where you were born is very multicultural."

"Really? What's my world called?"

"Elbis. It's ten times as distant as the system your astronomers call Sagittarius but in that general direction. There's a lot of water and high humidity, but amazing plant life."

"It sounds wonderful, and I'm glad I'm not a green blob!"

Yianevan laughed. "Nothing blobby about you, Bethan," he said. "You are beautiful."

The compliment slipped out without him thinking, although, in fact, he *had* thought about it. But he didn't know how she would react, so he could only hope he hadn't ruined the evening. She seemed fine, just waiting for him to continue, so perhaps the awkward silence that followed was only in his imagination.

"See that constellation?" he said, picking up where he left off. "Earth's astronomers call it Lyra. Pretty, isn't it? Where I come from, Lyrans were gangsters. They were the scourge of the galaxy until a race called the Nobles came along to stop them. This can't be the same Lyra. It's got too many stars."

Bethan found it hard to pay attention. She was too busy trying to stop her heart from racing. Ian told her she was beautiful, then carried on with the story as if nothing happened. Perhaps he just got caught up in the moment. Or Llyn Deron and the stars had woven some kind of romantic magic!

Stop it! Stop being an idiot, she told herself. *Think of something to say. You are being ridiculous!*

"The Nobles?" she said, surprised to find her voice sounded so normal. "You had to include yourself, didn't you?"

"Well. I am the one telling the story..."

Although neither one wanted the night to end, the ground became so cold, they had no choice but to abandon their storytelling and stargazing and retreat to the car. Bethan's heart had settled and was now brimming with happiness at how the day turned out. To have seen the sunset here at least once before leaving Wales was a dream come true. Sharing it with Ian made it perfect.

He guided them back to the car. Even without the torch, he had no trouble seeing in the dark. The ocular prosthetics didn't interfere with night vision, but he couldn't own up to it. He offered to drive, but Bethan flashed the torch upwards and pulled a face. She didn't trust his driving, daytime, nighttime, or anytime.

The picnic was a turning point in their relationship. Not a day went by that Yianevan didn't spend time at Bethan's home. She taught him how to play solitaire and do crossword puzzles. They listened to the wireless and engaged in lively debate about what they heard. Other times they sat on the sofa, the cat between them or on Ian's lap, while Bethan read poetry out loud. Bethan treasured these moments but wondered why Ian never appeared bored. He was obviously happy with their meetings because he always returned for more the next night.

Although Bethan laughed often, she didn't realise she built up for Yianevan a picture of a relatively empty existence, a far cry from the highly socialised life of an interventionist. Interventionist crews, possibly because of their hazardous occupation, were well known for playing hard in their free time. So far, all he had to marry the two personalities were a few bright cushions and a garish rug in her parlour. He supposed he could add that the two sorry plants in no way replaced the lush terrace garden the interventionist created in her apartment on Chabin.

Each evening, they drank well-sugared tea in the parlour or walked down to the park, where Yianevan described the heavens, pointing out the various constellations to Bethan and answering her questions. She liked facts, but sometimes, depending on how playful her mood was, she asked for a fantastic story, hoping it would prompt him to repeat that single compliment. But he never did, so she had to allow his knowledge of the stars to thrill her and not let disappointment colour the experience.

At first, her questions about the universe were simplistic; this society had yet to move a human beyond their own atmosphere, but she remembered everything he told her. The questions soon took on more complexity, to the point where Yianevan purchased a book on astronomy to feed her interest. A delighted Bethan received the gift and, in no time, impressed him with how much of the night sky she committed to memory.

Saturday evenings would find them eating fish and chips out of newspaper beside the canal and discussing the positions of constellations. Yianevan already knew the designations given by the Earth's scientific organisations, so it wasn't too challenging for him to point them out. She asked him if he believed people lived on those distant planets. She didn't wait for an answer, just told him she thought they did. Not blobs, but real people, with actual jobs, like the ones in his stories.

It made Yianevan feel sad when Bethan described her

small life. When she moved to London, she knew her life would get bigger. The prospect excited her. How could he tell her she already had an exciting life among the stars she found so fascinating? Out there was her true home. London would never compare.

Bethan appreciated Ian listened and never interrupted but often wished that when they strayed from other subjects, it wasn't always about her. She had given up asking questions about his family and instead rummaged through his vast knowledge of astronomy, plants, and rocks. But after every meeting and outing, she found his "thank you for a pleasant evening" and raise of his hat began to wear thin.

On the one hand, a relationship was the last thing she needed. It would simply hinder her plans. On the other, she doubted herself. If Ian didn't find her attractive, why did he tell her she was beautiful? Did he just say it in fun because she didn't want to be a green blob? If so, why did he bother? And why did it bother her? Ian was a good-looking man. Perhaps he thought he could do better, but then he could be holding back on becoming romantic because she was leaving soon.

Bethan needed to deal with her confusion and Ian's mixed signals. The prospect of her leaving the village might discourage him, but he had said he could go to London if he wished, so it didn't really need to end.

Now *there* was a thought. What didn't need to end? Nothing had begun. Not really. She couldn't deny her feelings for Ian were changing, perhaps more so since his compliment at the lake. Not that she wanted him to sweep her into his arms and smother her with kisses …

Or did she?

He had never touched her hand, never made inappropriate or suggestive comments, but neither did he seem cold or indifferent. The idea of just a friendship resulting from their time together made her feel oddly deflated, and she recognised that was a massive turnaround in her feelings about involvement. Ian's arrival had disrupted her ordered life, and she realised with a sense of alarm that leaving the village was one thing, but leaving Ian, unless he had only friendship in mind, was another.

At the library, Yianevan was thinking along similar lines. A platonic friendship was not exploitable in this society, at least not sufficient to get Bethan to accompany him abroad. They spent a lot of time together since the picnic, but he didn't attempt any of the romantic overtures he saw in films or read about in magazines, despite the temptation, for fear his inexperience ended up with him being shown the door. He still sensed Bethan's attraction to Ian Noble. If he could read her chak, he'd know for sure, but for now, he had to rely on signals. Did she give any? How would he know? Unless extending her hand to him at the lake was a signal, but wasn't that just to help him up onto the rock? Sometimes, often, he wondered what it would be like to hold her, feel her skin next to his, so for the life of him, he didn't understand why he didn't take her hand when she offered.

These feelings had to be put aside. Whatever he felt. Whatever Bethan felt, his presence on this world was for a purpose, and he needed a position in her life where he could influence where she went. Marriage would ensure her obedience, and with time running out, he had to move quickly. He had to take a risk.

Selecting several books on the subject, he manoeuvred himself back to his seat in the library and dropped the heavy pile onto the table. The resulting "bang" drew the attention of the younger assistant librarian, who had wondered about the pale, handsome man with the exotic accent who spent so much time here. She'd taken to applying a little lip colour just in case she was the reason for his continued attendance. Yianevan hadn't noticed. His grasp of human body language was still in its infancy. Besides, he was only interested in how Bethan responded to him.

As he pored over the conflicting views and advice in the various manuals on marriage, it occurred to him that everything he knew about the humans on Earth came from books, glossy magazines, fashion advice, and the TV interface apparatus in Mrs Jenkins's parlour. He assumed this must be the same for all humans in remoter parts because where would they find any form of stimulation if not for those mediums? The human interventionists who protected this world were descended from the slaves taken by the Lyrans. Those humans lived broader lives out in the galaxy, and it reflected in their levels of intelligence, confidence, and innovation.

Bethan was intelligent. Ivy less so. Mrs Jenkins, the senior librarian and her assistant topped Yianevan's list of non-people. Mike was bright and at least knew something of the planet, and Yianevan guessed the persona of Ian

Noble did not convince him. Did that mean it was easier to dupe a human female than a human male? It was such a small sample of people from which to draw any conclusions, and though the dynamics interested him, he had more important things on his mind.

He didn't realise he was staring at the assistant librarian. She gave him a shy smile, then turned away in mortification at her boldness when he frowned—not in response to her—but at his own thoughts. She couldn't read minds, but his off-hand dismissal would affect her behaviour around men for years to come.

As he read about the institution of marriage, Yianevan had to admit that establishing such an affiliation with Bethan had considerable appeal. However, she undoubtedly had a different perspective on it than he did. The other problem was his lack of familiarity with human mating rituals.

Even though he enjoyed the pastimes he and Bethan indulged in, their lively chats and playing of board games were just that. Passing time. Wasting time. Time he didn't have. He required traction in his relationship with her, and it was too late to lament his unpreparedness. He was a bumbling fool, and the interface showed far more wisdom than he did. On any of the occasions he visited her these past days, he could have reached for her hand or stroked her cheek, but having never made these kinds of overtures before, he feared acting "too forward". He wished he knew how far one could go before it was considered "too forward". However, if she was receptive, he would ask to marry her and remove her to the gate with the pennant.

Yianevan sighed. It couldn't be that easy. If Bethan hadn't shown him the pennant, he wouldn't be sitting here deliberating. He checked out a map of the world, but with a feeling of weariness, he pressed his fingers against his temples. From this library, Pompeii might as well be on the other side of the galaxy.

CHAPTER SEVENTEEN

Back in his room at his lodgings, Yianevan revised a stack of a dozen women's magazines. In his search for ways to approach the subject of the legal ritual of marriage, he read them all cover to cover, leading him to believe that soon there would not be another magazine or book left in Wales for him to discover.

One entry on marriage informed the reader that a dutiful woman, secure within the confines of the married state, would always submit to her husband's wishes. He read and re-read the lengthy article. The magazine was old and dated from the 1930s, but Mrs Jenkins kept a historical file of old publications. She was a hoarder of such things, and right now, Yianevan was glad of it.

The article claimed the last word on marriage and a woman's place within it. All very different from his world's cleaving commitments, but he only needed to get Bethan as far as the ceremony. She would recite her vows, and everything would fall into place. As Phildre, she might have been a nonconformist, not taking orders as an interventionist. As Bethan, a resident of Earth and complicit in its rules, he could reasonably assume she would go where he directed. Therefore, he determined he would marry the interventionist at the earliest opportunity and take the air transport to the Monk's Gate. Simple.

Simple until he stopped congratulating himself and read that a proposal of marriage needed to be preceded by a period of courtship. He groaned. It seemed a sudden invitation wasn't likely to get him anywhere. So he cross-referenced with a new magazine, one for the modern woman, which advised males that if they thought they were doing a girl a favour by marrying her and rescuing her from eternal spinsterhood, they should think again. The article stressed in no uncertain terms she could live her life her own way without a man, thank you very much!

Each magazine agreed that marriage was an important and once in a lifetime decision not to enter lightly. The term "woo" came up a few times, and Yianevan looked it up in his pocket dictionary.

He repeated to himself the definitions. *"To court. To entice. To pursue with a view to marriage."*

That was okay, but the entry omitted to mention "lengthy, pointless, and time-consuming." This new information meant he would have to manoeuvre Bethan into a position where she would accept a proposal without the frippery. It meant the friendship they'd already built needed to be enough to influence her decision in the positive.

Armed with a superlative knowledge of human females, Yianevan now needed to view a magazine taken from a male perspective to balance his learning. Unfortunately, Mrs Jenkins's hoard did not have such a publication, but it seemed reasonable he could acquire one from the tobacconists or grocers.

At the shop, he found the women's magazines displayed on a stand, but when he searched for something similar, there were only newspapers that contained little to add to his education about wooing and marriage. In innocence, he asked.

Fortunately, that day, Yianevan had varied his routine and driven to a different town where he was unknown. A wink and a nod later, the grocer handed him a publication in plain wrapping from under the counter, payment for the goods being slipped without comment into a separate cash box. He didn't understand why but sensed that unwrapping the parcel in the shop might be inappropriate, seeing as they hid it from view, so he waited until he got back to his car before exploring the pages. There were many pictures of women who looked as if they were going about their daily ablutions in various stages of undress, with unsanctioned images in the manner of listening to a private conversation. Ivy told him about this word as it related to gossip. Eavesdropper.

He checked the designation of the apparatus responsible for the images. A camera. This language had so many contradictions. An eavesdropper overhears. The camera sees. Was the camera operator an eyedropper? He searched in his pocket dictionary for the definition of an eyedropper. A medical device to administer medication to the eye. He eventually came up with a solution to the riddle.

A voyeur or peeping-tom. The camera device was a voyeur in this magazine, and he didn't like how it made him feel. Nevertheless, he learned a few things about human females and their anatomy. He also learned of the very minor and manageable differences between his own species and humans. The magazine had pages of articles to read and made vulgar jokes at the expense of women. Yianevan was still developing a human-like sense of humour, and he understood none of these references, but what he did come to understand was why the shop presented the publication in plain paper. Even holding it in his hands, he didn't feel he would be open about possessing it. He compared himself to the magazine. Plain wrapping. Hiding so no-one knew his true intentions.

Bethan was visiting Ivy that evening, so Yianevan forced down a worse than usual dinner with Mrs Jenkins, followed by an eye-wateringly sweet pastry dessert topped with rubbery custard slices. Afterwards, he went into the parlour to recover and switched on the brown televisual interface that sat in the corner.

TV was a concept that amused Yianevan. An interesting gadget linked to a central programming area somewhere in the ether, paired with a signal receiving hub that sat on the upper ledge of the box. Two long spindles emerged from the hub, often requiring lengthy adjustments to achieve efficient reception. If Mrs Jenkins had left him alone for five minutes, Yianevan could have made it far more effective by using the pocketknife and a few components from the late Mr Jenkins's shed.

Mrs Jenkins sat on the sofa beside him, her ample

bottom spreading across the seat and tipping up the cushions.

"What are you watching, love?"

Yianevan rearranged himself to accommodate her.

"Nothing yet, Mrs Jenkins. I thought to watch a love story."

"A love story, eh?" She handed him a magazine. "Well, look in the Radio Times. It'll tell you what's on. I suppose seeing Bethan Davies stirred up notions romantic?"

"I am not sure what you mean, Mrs Jenkins."

And he didn't, even after all his reading. And he had no-one to ask. Even if communications with Corky resumed, what would an interface know about human interaction from this time period? The 1950s hadn't even happened yet. They were still parallel to AD79, and the galaxy elsewhere was light years ahead in terms of technology. This world was a backwater, primitive, overlooked, except for the Lyran invasion, which he knew now could not have been to glean technology.

Yianevan scoured the Radio Times for a programme that would give him an idea for wooing Bethan. He felt confident that females saw men as the decisive leaders in a marriage partnership. Bethan seemed to have a grip on her life, but according to most of his information, marriage would change everything and make her compliant with his will.

That knowledge was sobering. If he took that attitude in his own society, the women would make an effigy of him and light a fire under it. Hierarchical females were the only women on his homeworld to fall under the command of the clan father. Lesser Noble females had far greater freedoms, and there were thousands of worlds throughout the ten sectors where subjugating a female would see you in prison.

In his own culture, members of the Noble hierarchy didn't woo. They didn't pursue a mate. Instead, they got arranged and expected. Yianevan's father would offer the betrothal assignment to two females, and at least one of those would need to produce a son before they sanctioned the betrothal. He needed to be human in wooing Bethan. He just didn't know how, so he relied on the TV to provide him with some visual clues.

The Radio Times was a slim, well set out pamphlet listing TV interface programming on any given day. Finally, he found a decade-old film that fit the parameters. Mouth to mouth contact was a prominent feature, an action he'd observed by a few species in the ten sectors and once between Ivy and an unknown male at a Saturday night dance. Personally, Yianevan didn't see the point, nor had he ever felt an urge to hold his mouth against another, but from the main character's interaction, he felt he got the gist of the technique. He also learned a new word.

Darling.

Mrs Jenkins fell asleep almost as soon as the film started, her gentle snoring making him bold enough to whisper the word aloud. It didn't sound as ridiculous and false to his ears as he thought it would, so he resolved to try this new endearment on Bethan when he asked her to marry him. According to his research, a woman expected lip contact before marriage but no mating. What about an embrace? No part of his body ever made contact with

Bethan. It would be nice, though. If she was agreeable. He found he often daydreamed about how soft her skin would be.

As the film, Now, Voyager concluded, Yianevan paid precise attention to the final, tender moment of the two protagonists. He didn't recall tenderness in his sexual dealings with females in the past. There had only been one or two in his youth and a couple of accommodating Grielik's in recent years. At best, he was perfunctory, but Bethan would expect more. He had to show sensitivity in all his actions towards her, and if he failed, it might come down to giving her one of his "alien" stories to convince her she should hand over the pennant.

Mrs Jenkins woke and took herself off to bed, but Yianevan stayed to view a second educational romantic film. Here, the man kissed the female's eyelids and the tip of her nose, then squeezed her so tight against his body that the pressure around her arms flung her head far back. Then, when the man had entrapped her, he engulfed her mouth with his until Yianevan felt had he been there, he would need to intercede to stop the woman from suffocating. Waiting with anticipation for her reaction, he expected her to emerge breathless and gasping for air. To his surprise, she seemed delighted, encouraging the male to repeat the exercise. He deduced from this that sometimes kissing might involve brutality. Did the males not fear injuring the woman they professed affection for? Did the female stagger back bruised and angry? Or was it just fantasy? If so, whose?

Confused, he returned to his room to re-examine the magazine he got from under the shop counter. If the voyeur's device was sneaking up on these women without their knowledge, it would be as they went about their day-to-day lives. He thought about Bethan's home. Her bath hung on a nail on the garden wall, and she dragged it in when she needed to immerse herself. Did a camera observe her through that tiny kitchen window? She would be horrified.

He looked at the women again. They seemed natural, playful, even in the group photographs. It could almost be staged. Acted. Realisation dawned. This was not substance. This was not reality. This was meant to be entertainment, and the women were models, paid to remove their clothes, and he was naïve.

Reassured this was not real life, Yianevan read every article in the magazine and examined the pictures cover to cover with detached impartiality. Then, with information extracted from the two films, he decided he was well-placed to offer more intimacy to Bethan. If he could encourage romance between them and then marriage, he was sure he could come up with an explanation about his lack of body hair and the nominal differences between him and human males. That is if she had ever seen a naked male. If he could accomplish all this over the next couple of days, he could be back on the ship, and both Bethan and the pennant would be where they belonged.

Provided he survived long enough. He wiped his forehead and looked at the moisture in his palm. Nobles perspired only during times of illness or duress, so he knew his body was changing. From this point on, he was living on borrowed time.

CHAPTER EIGHTEEN _

On Saturday evening, Yianevan met Bethan for a fish and chip "picnic" supper in the park, followed by a stroll along the canal. He enjoyed the informality of outdoor eating at the lake and now viewed any form of dining in the open air as a "picnic".

Bethan loved viewing the world from Ian's perspective. Everything was so fresh to him, and he treated new information with a kind of restrained wonder. He even made the village seem less dismal, as he created his own fantastic version of its history for her, always set someplace else in the galaxy. She became more and more curious about his origins and why he seemed to know nothing about Wales. It wasn't so remote it wouldn't feature on a map of Europe, but then she often wondered why a surveyor didn't have more knowledge of other places.

Ian only mentioned mining once in passing when they were discussing the formation of rocks, and she asked him if Mr Trevor, the mine manager, had been welcoming. He didn't give a direct answer, but in the coming weeks, Bethan would have cause to reflect on that conversation.

Yianevan designated that evening to advance their relationship. He showed up well-prepared, anticipating the success of the encounter. Bethan possessed the sweetest nature of any human he ever encountered, so the tender approach would be the one with which to "woo" her. He decided the brutal method, with its near suffocation and possible mouth bruising, was unrealistic and designed only to arouse or titillate in a fictional setting. Still, if she rejected him, he supposed he could try it, but she might slap his face, like on TV when a male made advances that were not welcome. Then all this would be for nothing. Bethan would hate him, and he'd never get to be with her again to make her laugh with his stories about the cosmos, which were actually true. In addition, he would lose the pennant.

Yianevan had practised kissing on the back of his hand and against the door until his lips became numb. Despite his anticipation of being close to Bethan, he discovered no matter how much he tried, he didn't see the point in joining two pairs of lips in this manner. He tried opening his mouth like he observed in the second film, but the door tasted of paint, so he abandoned it, leaving him to wonder why such a simple act was turning out so complex.

Nevertheless, it was a prerequisite, and he told himself one he could navigate. He was well-rehearsed and understood that approaching the kiss would be critical. He had to ensure he located Bethan's mouth on the first attempt or risk looking ridiculous. Appearing self-assured and masterful was essential. Otherwise, she would not submit to him. This mission's success depended on the result, and thoughts of what was to come distracted him throughout the evening as they finished their meal and began their walk along the canal. Bethan was chatty about her busy week, and Yianevan stole sidelong peeks at her, which he liked to think went unnoticed. They didn't. He wasn't as clever as he thought.

Tonight, it struck him again that Bethan no longer looked like other human females. When he reviewed her profile back on the ship, they all looked alike. They still did, but Bethan's hair was silkier, her complexion fresher, her grey eyes clearer and without secrets. Even when they weren't together, thinking about her brought a smile as he remembered how she waved her arms around when trying to make him understand something that escaped him. And those funny side-to-side movements she made with her head that she claimed aided decision-making. And her wonderful laugh. All his life, Yianevan found little to laugh about, but now, in the strange and temporary world of the future, he had reason to smile.

While anxieties about returning to his homeworld were never far from his mind and his natural apprehension about the kiss, he would not let his fears spoil this evening. Spring had pushed away the remnants of winter, and although it wasn't overly warm, Bethan had traded her usual winter coat for a floral dress and cardigan. A sure sign spring has sprung, she told him.

"You're quiet this evening," Bethan said, wondering why the glances and lack of questioning. "Is everything alright?"

Yianevan took a deep breath. It was now or never.

"Yes, of course, it's just that…"

The kiss surprised them both. For Bethan, because it was unexpected and not accompanied by an embrace. Ian just leaned down and planted the kiss on her lips. For Yianevan, the surprise came because he hadn't considered that kissing someone after fish and chips had a two-way taste and smell; rather startling for someone with enhanced olfactory senses. The kiss was brief and left them both speechless. Yianevan couldn't decide if it appalled him, appalled Bethan, or if it had gone well.

"Have you kissed lots of girls?" Bethan asked after she recovered from the surprise.

He went to shrug. He read in the journal that keeping an enigmatic silence about one's romantic conquests was attractive to women, but even though he lied his way into Bethan's life, he wasn't quick enough with his expression to hide the denial. Caught out, he admitted that no; he hadn't kissed lots of girls.

Bethan grinned. "I would say none."

He offered a sheepish nod. Somehow, he hated it being that obvious, even though kissing had no real meaning to him. But when Bethan stepped closer, he knew it had not been a total disaster. The technique might need work, but not the gesture. Her smile was soft and inviting as she asked if he would like to try again.

Yianevan couldn't deny the sensation of his mouth on hers didn't feel as pointless as he imagined it would. He'd never felt an attraction to a human before Bethan, but it felt natural to wrap her in his arms and close his eyes, better to feel her warmth and softness. This time, as he breathed in the floral notes of her perfume, he paid attention.

Bethan parted her lips ever so slightly. Shifting her arms over his shoulders, he felt the play of her fingers over the back of his neck, gently twisting a lock of hair she found there. He loved the sensuality. In the splendour of that moment, he saw precisely the point of kissing, so much so he didn't want it to end, didn't want her to stop touching him. When it did, he felt an overwhelming urgency to do it again, but Bethan put her hands against his chest and giggled.

"Ian. People are passing. I don't want a reputation!"

He hadn't seen the couple who stared as they passed by. Mortified by his lack of control, he released her and shuffled backwards a few paces to create a distance. What happened to sensitivity? He gushed out an apology.

"Bethan, I'm so sorry!"

She slipped her hand into his and watched the couple head towards the park, then she turned to him with a smile.

"Ian, don't you dare apologise. You know you can't put a lifetime of not kissing into one evening, don't you? Now, be honest and don't come over all mysterious; how can a grown man never have kissed a woman?"

That was a question Yianevan didn't expect.

"Have you?" he asked.

"Kissed a woman?" Bethan said in all seriousness. "No. But I have been kissed by men a couple of times in the past."

The feeling of her small hand in his made him feel protective of her. Everything had changed now. He wanted them to be together, even if only for a short time, and he wished he could tell her the truth.

"I never had the opportunity, Bethan," he confessed. "I'm afraid my family was very vigilant."

"You should tell me about them."

"There's not much to say. To be honest, Bethan, we are estranged."

She knew there was something Ian found too painful to speak of, and now he had said it, she sensed a sudden tenseness from him. That tenseness had nothing to do with her question and everything to do with Yianevan's sense of urgency. The recognition of time running out tempered his euphoria, his desire to be worthy of her. He could not delay, even for another day. Bethan liked the kiss—at least the second one—so he prayed she would respond as favourably to a proposal.

Bethan interpreted his tenseness as her straying into unwelcome territory. A few kisses didn't give her the right to pry into areas Ian felt were private. How could she know that by the end of the evening, she would be engaged to be married.

Although they'd known each other only a little over six weeks, Bethan was over the moon at Ian's proposal, even though she knew it would mean renouncing her plans to become a nurse.

When he asked her to marry him, her life turned in a heartbeat, and she knew she wanted to be with him always. Marriage and a family had never formed part of her plans, but the feelings he stirred in her were like nothing she'd felt before, so with no comparison and in a childlike way, she translated them into feelings of love. Every moment spent together brought her happiness, and every moment of their time apart gave her a sense of longing. Her priorities were different now, and she had no misgivings. Everything seemed to fit together perfectly. With his absurd stories about other planets and his funny accent, which he sometimes altered just to make her laugh, Ian Noble had, in such a short time, become her world. Her mam would say their meeting was meant to be, and for Bethan, she couldn't imagine any part of her future without him.

She didn't go straight to bed the night of their first kiss. Instead, she sat in her oddly ordered parlour amongst the colourful cushions that provoked a memory of something she'd once seen, or maybe of faraway places and imaginings she had since childhood. She thought about Ian's stories. They fuelled her imagination and made her consider a life beyond her other ambitions. She lifted her hand and admired the solitary diamond in her engagement ring, sparkling like a star in the dim light.

"Look, Mam. Look, Dad," she said with pride. "I'm engaged. And I am so happy!"

No-one she knew ever had an engagement ring, not her mam nor her gran. They only ever had plain wedding bands that looked like curtain rings. She didn't know what her mam would say, but when Ian slipped the ring onto her finger, Bethan thought it was the most beautiful thing she'd ever seen. He must have had the proposal all planned. He even went down on one knee there beside the canal, with fish and chips paper stuffed in his pocket. It was romantic and funny, and her heart beat wildly when she realised what was happening.

Bethan ran the scenario in her head. It was the perfect proposal. Every woman's dream, although perhaps not hers until she met Ian. There was only one thing missing. Although he called her "darling", he did not utter a single word of love.

That night, Yianevan drove back to his lodgings, pushing away an overwhelming and unrealistic desire to turn the car around and sweep Bethan into his arms and off to her bed. Of course, he desired her, but it was more than that. He wanted to hold her, be with her, watch her while she slept, and wake up beside her in the morning. And he knew that Time was waiting to snuff out his happiness.

To protect himself from the pain he knew would come when they passed through the gate, Yianevan tried to place a wall around his emotions. Then he switched on his pragmatism and congratulated himself on a well-executed mission. The pennant was almost home.

*CHAPTER NINETEEN_*

Ivy looked up from the post office counter, a little disconcerted to see her friend in the shop this late in the day. A disliker of queues and large gatherings, Bethan always came at opening time. This afternoon, she wore a grin as wide as the valley plastered all over her face, clearly not so concerned about crowds. There was no-one else waiting, anyway.

"What's happened?" she smiled. "You're looking rather pleased with yourself."

Bethan opened her mouth to answer, then closed it again. She and Ian had spent the day organising a marriage licence and buying a wedding ring, and now she was practically bursting to tell her best friend her news. Although not in here.

"Are you just about finished work?" she said, putting a lid on her excitement. "I'll meet you outside, and we can walk to your house together. I have something to tell you."

Ivy held up her fingers to signify five minutes, and as the door clanged behind Bethan, her smile faded to a puzzled frown. What was going on? Not like Bethan to be mysterious.

As soon as Ivy appeared, Bethan couldn't wait any longer. She held out her hand to display her sparkling engagement ring and gushed her news of the proposal, announcing the wedding date and plans for a honeymoon in Italy, then adding a postscript that she would not be going to London to become a nurse. The exciting summary of events delivered, she drew a deep breath and waited for Ivy's expected squeal of delight.

It didn't come.

Instead, Ivy just gave the ring a cursory glance, her expression revealing neither delight nor excitement. Nor did she offer congratulations. Not even a hug. In fact, Bethan found herself confronted by her friend's expression of total disbelief.

"You're getting married?" Ivy said after taking a moment to digest the news. "To Ian?"

"Of course to Ian, silly! Who else?" Bethan answered with a laugh, although she felt a protective wall go up around her bubble of happiness. She hesitated. "Ivy, aren't you happy for me?"

Ivy had known Bethan all her life. For someone so measured with her decisions, to act so recklessly about something so important was out of character. She had never known Bethan to throw caution to the wind, and this felt... Ivy didn't know how it felt, but it was…*off*. Taking Bethan's hands in her own, she shook her head, her usual skittishness making way for a relatively unknown serious side.

"I'm sorry, Bethie. I'm just surprised. It's so sudden. I

know I should be happy, but…" Ivy looked for words. She didn't want to be insensitive, but sometimes the only way to say something is to get on and say it. "To be honest, I suppose I feel… suspicious. A few weeks ago, Ian Noble didn't exist, and the life you planned in London was becoming a reality. Now you tell me you've abandoned your dreams. This isn't like you."

And this didn't sound like Ivy. Bethan didn't remember her ever taking her hand or displaying this level of seriousness. Usually, Bethan was the sensible one. But Ivy wasn't finished.

"Why don't you give it all a little more time, carry on with your plans and see how it goes," she said. "Don't give up your ambitions, not yet. Besides, I've been counting the days until you left the village."

"Counting the days?" Bethan echoed. She had come here expecting to share her good news, but her heart sank in the face of Ivy's frank disapproval.

"I didn't mean I was looking forward to it, Bethie," Ivy said. "The idea of you going off to London and Australia was so exciting." She rolled her eyes and attempted a grin. "I'm going to be stuck here forever because this place, dilapidated and grimy as it is, feels like home. When the changes come, I'll deal with them, at least until Mam pops off. Now you've turned all your plans on their head to marry a man you hardly know. Marriage has never been your dream."

Ivy was right, Bethan had to admit, but that was until she met Ian. Perhaps she should have included Ivy a little more, so she got to know Ian too. That was possibly a mistake on her part.

"How can you say I 'hardly' know him?" she said. "We spend every moment together, although I will admit he's different when we're alone." She smiled, hoping to reassure her friend. "He's actually rather funny. He makes up stories. We chat…"

"Funny stories aren't much to base a lifetime commitment on."

Bethan was at a loss at how to respond to Ivy's obvious disapproval. Having her judgement challenged was an unfamiliar experience, but to ask Ivy how she could possibly understand seemed harsh. She gently withdrew her hands.

"I don't know what to say. We're in love. Isn't that the only thing that matters?"

Ivy raised an eyebrow. "Ian told you he loved you?" Then she held Bethan's gaze as she waited for the answer that didn't come.

"I didn't think so," she declared. "He's too economical with words."

Bethan's response came with a sigh. "Ivy, you know how shy he is. Some people don't express emotions. He might find it hard to say."

"Hard to say? Bethie, he found the words to ask you to marry him! Be honest, what do you know of his background? He can't even make sense of our street signs, and he doesn't speak one word of Cymraeg."

"Cymraeg?" Bethan exploded. "You think I shouldn't marry him because he doesn't speak Welsh? Ivy, do you want me to point out that we're having this conversation in English? And *you* only speak Welsh to your mam and the postman."

Ivy agreed with that. "True enough, and I don't understand what happened because you used to love our language before you went away to that fancy English school. And what about Ian's foreign accent? He won't even tell you where he was born."

"Ian lived in a community, and he doesn't talk about his family. That's his choice."

"Oh?" Ivy said. Again, that raised eyebrow. "A community? Where? Look, Bethan, think about Ian's pale skin, his eyes, and, like I said, his accent. He might have fled an institution or escaped from prison abroad and not seen the sun for years."

It occurred to Bethan they were discussing, or perhaps arguing, about the merits of her marrying Ian on the post office steps. The very place she first set eyes on him. She would have laughed if it wasn't so upsetting.

"You're being ridiculous! An escaped prisoner? You're just looking for reasons to stop me from marrying him. And what do you know about accents, Ivy Price? You haven't even been out of Wales."

"I've been to Cardiff!"

"*Cardiff?*" Bethan snorted. "Cardiff isn't outside Wales, and it's full of English people."

Ivy's response was not what Bethan expected, and it rattled her to know her friend had been making observations about Ian behind her back and that she believed meeting him had clouded her judgement. Also, before today, she and Ivy had never argued.

Ivy couldn't hold her tongue over such an important

matter even in the face of her friend's disappointment, but Bethan's rigid defence of Ian and angry voice made her soften her approach. She lifted Bethan's hand and admired the beautiful engagement ring. It looked expensive, and Ivy could only dream of owning one like it.

"Bethie, I don't want to stop you from marrying Ian," she said with a conciliatory smile. "I'm just saying you're giving up a lot to stay in a place only weeks ago you couldn't wait to leave. And Italy for a honeymoon? Why not London or Anglesey? Italy is a long way away with someone you just met. Besides, how can he afford it?" She nodded at Bethan's hand. "For that matter, how could he afford that ring? He must have pots of money, even though he drives around in a car that looks like a rusty bucket."

"He's not a stranger, Ivy," Bethan said. "And he'll be my husband. I'll let the council buy the house for whatever price, and we'll probably travel with his work or maybe live in London, so I'll still be leaving."

"You'll need a passport for Italy."

Bethan shook her head. "There's no time. Ian's adding me to his."

Ivy wasn't sure of the legalities, but it sounded like Ian had taken control. She had the means to check the passport requirements at the post office, but she'd see to that later. Meanwhile, Bethan's eyes had filled with tears. This should be a joyous moment, telling your best friend you are to be married, and Ivy felt terrible for spoiling it. She gave Bethan a hug. Time to dial back her disapproval. Bethan wasn't a child.

"Have you told Mike?" Ivy asked, pleased that Bethan

returned the gesture.

"Yes," Bethan dabbed at her eyes. "We'll be here for a few days after the wedding. Ivy, you will come, won't you? It's in two weeks. I chose Wednesday because it's your day off."

They were friends again, and Ivy nodded.

"I wouldn't miss it for the world, Bethie. I want you to be happy."

Bethan's delight in announcing her approaching nuptials suffered slight tarnishing under Ivy's reproof, even though she knew it was only because she was protective. She just wished she'd kept her views to herself because they also promoted her own self-doubts. Doubts she pushed away because of a deeper sense this eclipsed all her other hopes.

Despite Ivy backtracking in declaring her views, her scepticism continued to torment her. She appreciated that the mine was only a tiny part of his job, or so he said, and that he mainly worked out of town, but even Bethan didn't know his schedule. When questioned, Ian repeatedly responded with a vague "across the valley", as though the words lived in his mouth, rehearsed, ready to pull out at his convenience.

There was too much strange sequencing of events for Ivy's liking. First, Ian Noble, a stranger with no past, at least not one he cares to share, arrives in the village, makes a beeline for the level-headed Bethan, and proceeds to sweep her off her feet.

Could it be Bethan was his only reason for being here? That he saw her and stayed. Who knows? Then again, Ivy thought, how would someone not be attracted to such a pretty, educated girl. Plus, she was worth a few bob if you considered that spruced up old miner's cottage she owned. Ivy was prepared to admit that Ian was pleasant enough, but she was used to people showing who they were, so the whole Ian Noble mystery didn't sit right. Bethan appeared oblivious, which was worrying on its own. No man had ever turned Bethan's head, although some had the idea of trying. So why Ian? Why now?

After a sleepless night and unable to quell the niggle of suspicion that grew into a tide of worry, Ivy decided to visit the mine. Mr Trevor denied any knowledge of dedicated Coal Board surveyors in the town, but they would only report to him if they were carrying out work at the mine, and they weren't due for another couple of weeks. If this Ian Noble was part of the final surveying team, Mr Trevor assured her he wouldn't know of him just yet.

Ivy accepted the explanation. Maybe Ian was part of the survey work for the council at the new factories being built across the valley. He would probably go to the mine after that. It made sense, sort of, in a roundabout way, but it didn't satisfy her. The person best placed to clear up the mystery was Ian Noble himself.

Ivy had never visited Mrs Jenkins's beautiful, whitewashed cottage, set in gloriously cared for gardens with tall hollyhocks waiting for the summer to show their flowers, and a carpet of daffodils on either side of the stone path. The villagers referred to the house as a cottage, but that was a misnomer because it was more like a small manor house.

Mrs Jenkins wasn't a Llanbleddynllwyd native. Related

to the mine owners of olden days, she was bequeathed the dwelling when the last one died in the 1920s. When her husband passed away, she turned it into a boarding house for visiting Coal Board men, rather than rattle around the place like a pea on her own. Most prospective lodgers only stayed there once. After that, they preferred to take a room at the pub, citing their hostess's incessant talking. Ian seemed to tolerate her, and seeing as he was so quiet himself, that added to Ivy's suspicions.

In her heart, Ivy wanted to find Ian without blemish for Bethan's sake, but he was just so *mysterious*. Add to that, he'd obviously made sure not to let anything slip to Mrs Jenkins, or it would be around the village by now, spread by those few who would listen, although Ivy had never heard a word spoken of him.

She pulled on the doorbell then stepped back, fearful of leaving a shoe print on the quarry tile step Mrs Jenkins kept shined to a brilliant red with a dense layer of Cardinal polish. While she waited, Ivy noticed the brass step nosing, polished to such a high sheen she could see the reflection up her skirt. It made her wonder how, with all this cleaning, Mrs Jenkins had any time to gossip.

The lady of the house opened the front door and wafted out onto the step amidst an aura of lavender-scented furniture polish. Upon seeing Ivy, she folded her arms under her ample bosom and set her face in a frosty caricature.

"Ivy Price."

Ivy knew Mrs Jenkins's opinion of the Price family, and it was beyond her why her mam was always so gracious about the old busybody.

"Yes, Mrs Jenkins. Is Mr Noble at home? I would like a word."

Mrs Jenkins sniffed. "I disapprove of lady callers. Mr Noble is mindful of my rules."

What an old dragon. Still, Ivy was here now, and she was determined to speak to Ian.

"Mrs Jenkins," she said firmly. "I am not a lady caller. It's just a word. I can speak to him out here on the doorstep if you prefer."

Mrs Jenkins did not prefer. Ivy Price was a little fast and loose by all accounts, and she wasn't keen on such a girl chattering with one of her houseguests, let alone a decent gentleman, on her doorstep. With a huff, she stepped back, signalled Ivy to wipe her feet, and admitted her into the hallway. Then she pointed to the parlour, a stern warning on her thin lips.

"Wait in there. When Mr Noble comes down, leave the door open. I'm just in the kitchen, and I'm watching you. Make no mistake."

Ivy mumbled her thanks. She didn't know what Mrs Jenkins supposed she would do. It was little wonder the old woman's mouth was so wrinkled, with her lips constantly pursed in disapproval.

In the parlour, she perched on the edge of the sofa and looked around. The brown TV set took pride of place at the side of the bay window. She heard Mrs Jenkins had one, but Ivy thought TVs looked like giant wirelesses, with a pane of glass to watch the stories through instead of just listening to them. She'd seen them in Mike's shop, but no-one else in the village could afford one. Besides, even if they had the money, her mam wouldn't have something with moving pictures in the house.

A grandfather clock sounded the passage of time. Tick. Tock. Tick. Tock. Ivy counted the seconds until she heard Ian speaking to Mrs Jenkins as he came downstairs. Fearful she had made a dreadful mistake in coming here behind Bethan's back, she jumped to her feet, and when he entered the room, her courage fled. Facing him now, she didn't know how to start the conversation.

Yianevan waited for Ivy to resume her perch on the chair before seating himself opposite. He half expected this. Bethan told him about Ivy's less than enthusiastic reaction to the wedding news. She didn't trust him, and she was here to see if he had an agenda.

"Ivy," he said, offering her his best smile, aware of her discomfort and trying to set her at ease. "What can I do for you?"

Ivy took a breath. "Bethan told me you're getting married."

"As Bethan's best friend, I expected you to be the first to know."

"That honour went to Mike because I was at work, but *as* her best friend, I am here to tell you I don't trust your motives."

"My motives?" Yianevan laughed, revealing his perfect teeth. He reminded Ivy of a toothpaste advertisement. On that alone, she could see why it would be easy to fall for him.

"You make me sound menacing," he said. "Ivy, my intention is to make Bethan happy."

Yes, well, being handsome wouldn't let him off the hook, so with her courage back in place, Ivy got into the swing.

"Is it?" she retorted loftily. "How would I know? How would Bethan know? First, you arrive here from God knows where and take the best woman in the village, then she tells me you're whisking her off to Italy on a honeymoon." Ivy shook her head fiercely. "I said to her, I said, Bethan, Italy? What's wrong with Anglesey?"

Yianevan envied Bethan having such a good friend. He'd never had a friend, at least not anyone who cared enough to defend him, other than his mother. Ivy needed reassurance, and if Bethan knew she was here, she would want him to offer it. But he couldn't give too much away.

"Bethan doesn't wish to live in the village, Ivy," he said. "She never has. I thought you knew that, so I am not 'whisking' her away from something she will miss, and I chose Italy because it's somewhere she dreams of visiting."

Ivy didn't know that. Bethan had never told her, and to hear it from Ian, quite took the wind out of her sails. He sensed this was something Bethan had not discussed with her friend.

"We all have these dreams, never believing they'll happen," he said. "I want to make this one come true for Bethan. It's the perfect destination. I'm sure Anglesey has many merits and would have been delightful. I simply did not consider it."

Ivy sniffed. "I've never been there. Bethan says she's going to Italy on your passport. I'm not sure that's legal."

Ivy thought that would be her ace, but of course, he

had an answer.

"Only as a temporary measure until we can get one of her own. I have already contacted the authorities, and there is no legal requirement for a married couple travelling together to have separate passports."

Righto, Ian Noble, Ivy thought. What about this one?

"I went to see Mr Trevor up at the mine. He's never heard of you."

Enquiries about his identity had concerned Yianevan ever since he met Bethan, and so far, he believed he got away with it. It seemed he underestimated Ivy's tenacity. Fortunately, he recently decided to keep track of the mine's closing works.

"That's not surprising," he answered, thankful he'd shown that foresight. "The closing surveys aren't yet due and might not even involve me. The NCB will send word if I am required."

"You gave us all the impression, at least in the beginning, that you worked part of the time at the mine. Bethan says you are always too clean to go underground."

"Not all mine work is underground, Ivy. Bethan knows that."

Ivy tried to read into everything he said to see if he avoided her eyes or hesitated with his answers, but he didn't. What does a liar look like, anyway?

"You have it all sewn up, don't you, Ian? Why won't you tell her, tell us, where you come from? Why you are here?"

"You are reading far too much into the situation, Ivy," Yianevan said, making sure his smile looked as placating as he hoped his words sounded. "I prefer not to speak of my home, but I will tell you I plan to take Bethan there following our honeymoon. She will have the life and all the opportunities she deserves. I promise you she will be happy beyond her wildest dreams. That is my aim."

Yianevan knew humans always sought an unwavering gaze when detecting truth or lies in an opponent. Ivy would see he was telling the truth; it was just that she could not comprehend if he were to elaborate.

Ivy felt she had no choice but to believe him. He'd said all the right things, and she could hear Mrs Jenkins banging pots around in the kitchen to make sure her unwelcome visitor knew she was keeping an eagle eye on the proceedings, even if she couldn't hear the conversation. She began to feel a little foolish. Still, she had one more parting shot.

"You know, Ian, right now I feel daft for coming here, but I bet when I get home and think about everything you said, I'll find you didn't say much at all. You are very clever."

Yianevan dipped his head at that nugget of wisdom. He hadn't given Ivy enough credit.

"I understand your concern for Bethan," he said without addressing her comment. "Her happiness is as close to my heart as it is to yours."

Ivy gave a tiny laugh. "Is that an admission of love? If someone asked me to marry him, I would expect to hear that first."

Yianevan knew he left out an essential part of the proposal, but there was nothing he could do now, so he couldn't give Ivy a straight answer. "I know it concerns you that Bethan and I haven't known each other long," he said instead.

Ivy nodded. "And it reminded me of something Bethan once said. If you've been waiting at the bus stop for a while, don't be tempted to take the first bus that comes along." She tried to dredge up the exact words from her memory. It went something like that. She just had to hope Ian understood. He didn't at first. It was too nuanced for him, so he offered what sounded like a sensible reply.

"Because you might not reach your destination?"

"That, and because it's worth waiting for the one that will take you where you want to go."

Ah. Yianevan saw it now.

"You believe Bethan is taking the first bus?" he said with a grin. "As far as I am aware, she has not been waiting for the right bus—or man, if I understand the metaphor—to come along at all!"

With that response, Ivy's pained expression said it all. "There isn't a girl in Wales not waiting for the right bus, Ian. You don't know much about women."

He couldn't argue with that. "I only need to know about Bethan. She will be happy. I promise you."

That sounded sincere. Either way, Ivy had done all she could by coming here and confronting him with her worries. Had he said anything sinister, she would have returned to Bethan and owned up to the visit. But he hadn't. In fact, Ivy couldn't really fault him. He was strange, not like a lover, but she supposed not everyone wore their hearts on their sleeves.

She stood up. "Ian, Bethan mustn't know I went

behind her back."

"I can keep a secret," he assured her, "but don't count on Mrs Jenkins."

"Well, how about I organise a reception at the Prince of Wales after the wedding? Then, if my visit gets back to Bethan, we can say it was about that. Has she organised anything yet? She didn't say so."

Yianevan opened the front door. "That sounds like an excellent idea. I will tell her to expect a surprise."

Ivy stepped down onto the path, avoiding the highly polished brass outside the door. She paused before turning.

"I'm still not sure I trust you, Ian Noble," she declared, "but you are marrying my best friend. She says she loves you, so I will put my worries aside for now." She raised a finger in warning. "Just remember. I'm watching you."

He believed Ivy had been watching him from day one.

"Thank you, Ivy," he said. "I respect that."

Closing the door, Yianevan headed for the stairs, only to find Mrs Jenkins's indignant face peering at him through the bannister.

"I don't like girls like that coming to the house, Mr Noble," she said tartly. "What did she want?"

"Please don't trouble yourself, Mrs Jenkins," he said, giving her a winning smile. "It was nothing."

She couldn't press the point, so with her curiosity unsatisfied, Mrs Jenkins went into the parlour to dust off the chair where Ivy sat. She liked Mrs Price, but not the daughter so much, a bit free and easy with her favours, so the talk went.

In the days following the proposal and Ivy's visit, Yianevan realised putting his emotions on hold wouldn't work because Bethan transformed from "proper" to affectionate and tactile.

During their crossword sessions on the sofa, she would sit with her legs over his lap. She would come up behind him in the kitchen, stroking his hair and kissing the back of his neck. Other times, instead of a simple peck, she would nibble his lower lip, and he had to control the delicious tingling that spread throughout his whole body. He wondered if she realised or if this was how she assumed she should express affection, in which case she would be entirely innocent of the effect. Whatever the explanation, it was gloriously unbearable. And according to what he read in the old magazines, not how most women behave.

Bethan held nothing back in displaying her affection for him, and never once did she ask him if he loved her in return. One day, he had car trouble and arrived at Bethan's over an hour late. She threw herself into his arms and smothered him in kisses, unmindful of his greasy hands, then proceeded to extract a promise that he would never worry her like that again.

To make it up to her, he suggested they go back to Llyn Deron to see the sunset. They took Peekybarks and lashings of hot cocoa in a thermos to sustain them. Their only light was the sun's brief halo over the tops of the mountains as it heralded the fleeting end to dusk. Then they brought thick blankets from the car to wrap themselves in to watch the night sky and wait out the hours until sunrise.

Yianevan couldn't help himself. He loved it. He loved it all, and he loved Bethan, yet the feelings never formed themselves into words. Often, when she snuggled close to him on the sofa and murmured that she loved him, he wanted to say it back, but it was almost like trying to say something in Welsh, and he hadn't managed that either. He told himself that not giving in kept the mission in mind, stopped sentiment, and made him focus clearly on retrieving the pennant. All other considerations had to be secondary. He could not stay here, munch on spicy Peekybarks, and do crossword puzzles for the rest of his life. It could never be. The reality was he could not let the pennant remain on a planet once invaded by Lyrans.

CHAPTER TWENTY _

On the morning of the wedding, Yianevan came down from his room to thank Mrs Jenkins and tell her he was moving out. She was quite overcome and demanded to know what she did to warrant such an abrupt departure. Then, to make matters worse, Mike Trent showed up on her doorstep wearing his Sunday best on a Wednesday morning and asking for Mr Noble. She purchased her TV from Mr Trent's shop, and she didn't even know Mr Noble and Mr Trent knew each other.

Unprepared for her response, Yianevan tried to offer an explanation. He didn't need to read her "chak" to understand she took this as a personal slight. Mike told him he shouldn't have left it to the last minute, so as Mrs Jenkins sank into one of the parlour chairs, and ill-equipped as he was to deal with a tearful female, he hastened to assure her she had provided the most excellent and comfortable lodgings. Then, prompted by Mike, he lied by saying he had received sudden notification his assignment was at an end.

Mike flicked his eyebrows to encourage him. That was

good, but a little more grovelling wouldn't hurt. So Yianevan also spoke of her excellent cooking and how he would remember her Bird's Custard with fondness. He added Mike was only here to escort him across town.

Mrs Jenkins loved the fuss Mr Noble made of her, so she gave herself a few moments longer to recover. When they finally got to the front door, she thanked him for being such a considerate house guest.

Once they were in the car, Mike and Yianevan looked at each other and grinned.

"How did you live with that woman?" Mike laughed. "What a drama queen!"

"She's not so bad if you can avoid the meals," Yianevan said, although he felt relieved that he wouldn't be returning. "And I keep myself to myself."

That's a fact, Mike thought. This was only the third time he met Ian since Bethan first introduced them, and today, he was acting as the best man at his wedding.

On Mike's suggestion that it might be a gracious gesture, Yianevan stopped by the florists in the new town and organised a bouquet to be delivered to Mrs Jenkins. Mike waited in the car, but had he also gone into the florists, he might have saved Yianevan from making a social gaffe. He chose a box of Black Magic chocolates to accompany the flowers, unaware the brand typically symbolised romance, sophistication, and courtship.

Whether or not Mrs Jenkins misinterpreted it, the token saw his sudden departure forgiven. For the rest of her long life, Mrs Jenkins considered Mr Noble the most gentlemanly, not to mention the most handsome of all her guests.

From his extensive reading of women's journals, and despite Bethan's enthusiastic displays of affection since the proposal, Yianevan believed the wedding night might prove a little more challenging. Although he suspected Bethan possessed a deeply sensual side, until now, kissing and cuddling were as far as physical contact went. He knew that she had no past encounters with intimacy, at least not as Bethan, so she might not have any particular expectations. He couldn't deny his desire for her but resolved to be sensitive and tender. Either way, it didn't matter how this night turned out, he doubted he could be happier than at this moment, and he believed Bethan felt the same.

He needn't have worried. As soon as they were alone in the cottage, it quickly became clear Bethan didn't read any magazine that spoke of demure and shy brides. Her affectionate outpourings quickly spilled over into unbridled passion and unabashed delight at discovering her new husband's body. To kiss anywhere other than the mouth hadn't occurred to Yianevan, but Bethan seemed inspired to kiss just about everywhere. She showed no desire for tenderness. No desire for sensitivity. This was new and unexplored, and she loved him with all her heart. Why hold back?

The newlyweds spent the night in so much delicious pleasure and laughter, Yianevan wondered if he had woken in Bethan something of Phildre's alleged wildness.

He was still smiling when she fell asleep snuggled close against him, her lovely face relaxed and calm in rest, her hand curled over his belly, keeping him near. They had neglected to close the curtains, so the moon crept in to lend a supernatural light to the room, but Yianevan dared not sleep for fear of missing a moment of the time he had left with her. Her breath felt warm against his skin, and in a while, her rhythmic breathing settled him. He ran the wedding back through his mind, concluding with a silent chuckle that Mrs Jenkins's stash of magazines should be thrown out because the information was so outdated. Not once in the ceremony did Bethan vow to obey him!

But the peace was fleeting. Reality intruded and snatched away the precious moment. Yianevan tried to take it back, just for tonight, but his purpose for being here was having none of it. It demanded to be heard. It demanded his attention. Yes, Bethan was here beside him, the honeymoon arranged, and soon they would access the gate. He'd even checked out a map that showed a hiking trail that wound its way to the summit of Vesuvius. If Bethan or the pennant were connected to the gate, it would reveal itself. Bethan would manage the hike easily, and hopefully, his graft would last until then. The encroaching toxicity of this planet as the fungal spores from the soil seeped into his pores were already poisoning his blood. He felt the changes daily. When the contamination reached critical saturation, catastrophic organ failure would bring a swift end. Dying here was not an option. The interface could administer an antidote to the toxins if he got as far as the ship. But that was another concern. He hadn't heard from Corky since before he proposed to Bethan.

Yianevan swallowed hard against the bitter sadness at what was to come. He didn't want that reminder. He wanted to fight against the temporary nature of his time with her even though he knew it was a fight he would never win. Yes, the pennant would be returned to its proper place, but so would he, and so would Bethan. There was little chance she would remember him once they went through the gate, so she wouldn't have to face the heartbreak of their separation. She loved him now, but as he faded from her memory, so would her feelings.

It would be different for him. Never having lived other lives here, he remembered where he came from. This day, this special night, would be forever burned in his memory. Having Bethan beside him, holding her in his arms, was the fulfilment of a dream he had since he met her. Now, in a matter of days, he would have to let her go. When he arrived here, overflowing with arrogance about saving the galaxy from the Lyrans, how could he have known this beautiful human would capture his heart? Now he faced the prospect of a life without her and the pain of knowing these last days would be all they would ever have.

He kissed the top of Bethan's head. She stirred and tightened her embrace. Her arm felt cool, so he reached across to pull the sheet around her. As he did, he felt fluid dripping across his upper lip.

Fumbling around for the box of Kleenex on the nightstand, he wiped the moisture from his nose. There was sufficient moonlight for him to see the pale viscous fluid soaking into the wad of tissues. A Noble's blood was vastly different to human blood. Never deep red, it had a lighter, pinker hue and was considerably thinner. If he didn't want to fabricate a problematic explanation, he would need to be up and about before Bethan in the morning. The tissues needed to be disposed of, and he had to make sure not a trace of his alien blood remained on his face.

Yianevan groaned at what this meant. They were scheduled to leave for Pompeii in four days. He had to survive at least that long to get Bethan to the gate.

The day after the wedding, Bethan received a cursory reply from the Alice Maud Hospital, acknowledging her withdrawal from the student nurse program. The letter required the last word as it advised her in lofty tones that "The Alice Maud does not accept married women as students".

Becoming a nurse had been a long-cherished ambition, a step to independence, but the pompous wording made her almost glad she had withdrawn. She didn't need them because right now, with Ian beside her, Bethan felt there was nothing in the world she couldn't accomplish. They had made no definite plans about where they would live after the honeymoon, but Ian told her travel would be involved and not to worry. Her tame and ordered life had taken on mystery and excitement beyond her wildest dreams.

She tossed the letter onto the hallstand and went into the kitchen, where Ian and the cat were engaged in what had lately developed into a mutual fan club. Yianevan forgot he disliked cats but still believed himself not entirely converted. Although this one was quite the entrepreneur in securing food and shelter, so he revised his opinion to "enterprising" rather than opportunistic. Also, this animal had an engaging personality and language, with its definite inflexions of purrs, meows, and slurps, that he found far easier to deconstruct than Welsh.

Bethan forgot the letter as the newlyweds planned their honeymoon. She managed to fish out an old atlas to work out the locations and the places they would visit. It would be the trip of a lifetime, the first of many, and Bethan couldn't wait to start her new life. Also, just before the wedding, she had accepted the council's offer for the house. Everything had fallen neatly into place. As her mam always said, it must be destiny.

Just before dawn on the second morning after the wedding, Yianevan awakened to excruciating pain burning through his chest. Disentangling himself from Bethan's arms, he slipped out of bed, taking care not to disturb her for fear of her seeing his distress. He stifled his agonised groans as the pain spread throughout his body and stumbled down the stairs to the outside lavatory. Once there, he fell to his knees and hung his head over the toilet bowl, stifling a scream as a sharp cracking sound from his ribs answered his violent retching.

Exhausted, he collapsed in an anguished heap beside the toilet and gingerly pressed himself around his middle. At least one rib had cracked. Brittleness in the bones was one of the final symptoms of the spore's poison leaching through his body.

Time had run out.

Although the graft had offered him some protection, it was not enough. He only needed a few more days, but the spores were no respecter of time, nor did they grant wishes. Only mocked him that he got so close.

Wiping his mouth, Yianevan struggled to a sitting position and leaned back against the stone wall in a vain attempt to cool the burning pain throughout his body. At this stage, his only chance at survival lay with Corky, who could wash the fungal spores from his blood, but Corky's continued silence might mean the condition of the gate led to him being abandoned. He closed his eyes and thought of Bethan.

All this, everything I did, he murmured. *Everything I took from you was all for nothing. Bethan, I'm so sorry. Please forgive me.*

One thing was for sure, his legacy would not include Bethan finding him dead on the toilet floor, so summoning every ounce of strength he had left, he crawled back inside and up the stairs to the bedroom. Raw, angry pain accompanied every effort until he fell to his knees beside the still sleeping Bethan. He granted himself a moment's rest before struggling into his trousers and shirt, but he couldn't muster enough energy to put on his shoes. He needed that strength for one more task he had to accomplish.

Against Bethan's throat lay the pennant. He had to take it. If by some miracle, Corky was still monitoring him, he would register his dying moments. So, with that hope, Yianevan needed the pennant to be in his possession. Clutching his chest, he rolled onto his knees, trying to regulate his breathing. The delicate chain glinted in the light from the window, so with a quick movement, he snapped it with the blade of his pocketknife. Bethan's eyelids flickered.

"Hello, you," she murmured. "You're up early."

Yianevan willed his voice to sound natural. "One or two things to finish, my darling. I won't be long."

Bethan managed a sleepy smile. "It's not even light."

"I'll be back soon," he said. "I promise. Go back to sleep."

Bethan sighed and turned over. Yianevan waited for a few moments until her breathing became even, then struggled to his feet. There was little chance he would ever see her again, so reaching down, he lifted her fingers to his lips, kissed them for the last time and whispered the words he somehow never found the courage to say.

"I love you."

Fighting to stay conscious, Yianevan staggered out to the car and headed toward the countryside. Hunched over the steering wheel, he drove for several miles along a country lane, but failing vision and searing agony throughout his body caused his foot to slip from the controls. He slumped forward. He could go no further.

The car slowed and drifted through a hedge, sliding into a ditch on the other side, where it stalled, concealed from the road. Yianevan's chest contracted, crushing his lungs, and the heaviness in his body felt as if he was turning to marble. Death would come any moment now, and he would welcome it. Better to die than live without Bethan. The mystery of Ian Noble would deepen when they found his body, and he imagined her grief, a widow before she even got to be a wife. The charm would be returned to her, and she would forever wonder why he cut it from the chain while she slept.

With his oxygen-starved mind in turmoil, Yianevan pulled in desperation at the door handle and tumbled out into the field. He took one more breath. On this Earth, it was to be his last.

He awoke flat on his back on the bridge of his ship with the interface panel hovering above him.

"Noble, I regret I could not return you as soon as you manifested symptoms. I could not locate you until you turned up on the spiral sensor. The gate has become more unstable, and I expect its imminent collapse."

Yianevan rolled onto his stomach. His body still hurt, but he had enough strength to crawl into the command chair. Corky was right; that was close.

"I thought I was dead," he groaned. "I didn't think you were monitoring my life signs."

"Not for several hours, Noble," Corky said. "The spiral searched but only discovered you as you approached death. I have purged your body of the spores, but your skeletal system is fragile and will remain so until we can rebalance mineral depletion over the next few hours. Noble, you cannot return to the surface. If you do, you will succumb to the toxins."

Corky told him that the moment the spiral registered Yianevan's plight, Lieutenant Phildre disappeared from sensors. So even though Yianevan had retrieved the pennant, he had lost Bethan.

"Corky," he said. "Show me the gate."

Corky complied, noting the Noble's use of a name rather than "Interface".

A full day and a half had passed since Yianevan first visited Earth. Vesuvius appeared quieter, and although Chief Jardin specified the initial stage of the eruption was alarming in its pace, Yianevan recalled the accounts he read of the event in Earth's history books. They suggested a slower progression. If the Lyrans found a way to employ this pennant in creating the Monk's Gate, it might also influence time flow in the surrounding area. When Bethan caught the pennant, it set up a whole new dynamic, disrupting local time and pulling her into the well. Now, without the pennant on the surface, local time appeared to return to normal. Yet, the gate remained. Without further study of the pennant's language, there was no way of identifying these secrets and their connection to Bethan and the gate.

Corky expected to begin an analysis of the gate now the Noble's concerns about Lyrans inhabiting that timeline were allayed. They may have entered the portal at a separate time, but there was little evidence so far. However, Corky elected not to press the issue as the Noble appeared deep in thought, even though he now required further orders upon which to act. Instead, he stood by, ready to assist as the Noble took a deep breath and stood, a promising sign considering he had been at death's door only minutes earlier. Corky hadn't instilled a spore antidote in years. Nice to know he still had the knack.

"I should have tried to get to the gate sooner," Yianevan said, gritting his teeth against the pain in his ribs and supporting himself on the command seat. "I wasted time."

"Would Lieutenant Phildre not comply?"

"It wasn't that Corky," he said with a groan. Speaking hurt. "Social conventions prevented me from inviting her to Pompeii. Unlike their counterparts in the ten sectors, these humans are more simplistic, with formalities and cultural systems that are difficult to navigate. I stayed with the marriage concept and used Pompeii as leverage for a honeymoon destination."

"Honeymoon, Noble?"

"A ritual a couple engages in following their marriage."

"And she did not wish to take part?"

Yianevan took another cautious deep breath, just to check. "Yes, she wished to take part. I was surprised she even agreed to my marriage proposal. Her friend didn't trust me and even went to the trouble of challenging my intentions."

"Interesting, Noble. Did her friend manifest signs of being Lyran? There could be a time crossover."

An image of Ivy flashed in Yianevan's mind. If she was Lyran, then they had regressed.

"No, she wasn't Lyran, neither is Beth.... the interventionist. As far as taking information on a Lyran war council from the future back to my homeworld, this mission failed."

"I disagree, Noble," Corky said. "You failed in extracting Lieutenant Phildre, but that outcome was always doubtful. You have established there is no Lyran civilisation in at least one timeline, which is reassuring. May I suggest we now turn our attention to deciphering the gate before it destabilises? Perhaps now would be an appropriate time to alert the hierarchy and enlist their scientists' help."

Yianevan wasn't sure he would ever alert the hierarchy to the gate. The pennant was the focus now, and he believed it had some direct or indirect influence. He was sure that once proximity to the pennant was severed, the gate would cease to exist. That wouldn't happen until after they left orbit. So understanding the gate involved deciphering the pennant, and he didn't need his family to know for now. At least not until he knew why a Noble pennant sought out Bethan and why Corky's sensors could only locate her while it was in her possession. The pennant saved his life because, until he took it from Bethan, Corky had indeed lost sight of him.

Once more lost in thought, he touched his lips. He would never again kiss Bethan, breathe in her perfume, or hold her in his arms. That pain was greater than any agony the spores brought. Hours would have passed on Earth by now, and Bethan would be out of bed, wondering why he hadn't returned. When he held her fingers to his lips—for him only minutes ago—he felt the wedding ring, a symbol of love and commitment on that world. Bethan had willingly given herself to him. She held nothing back.

And all he offered in return was deception.

Bethan would have had a happy life if she had never met Ian Noble. She would have become a nurse, joined her brother in Australia and perhaps even married, continuing to wear the pennant as a charm, none the wiser, and never remembering her other self. Instead, she gave up everything for Ian Noble. A phantom. A falsehood.

Corky had spent enough time around organics to recognise the Noble's facial expressions. Anguish, and not just from the pain of the toxins. Lieutenant Phildre had that look when she was hungover, and Chief Jardin often had that look about Lieutenant Phildre.

"Are you experiencing regret, Noble?" he asked. "Your heart rate accelerates when we speak of the lieutenant. I must remind you there could never be a long-term outcome, as your time on the planet was limited. Are you in distress?"

Yianevan walked from the command centre without responding. His joints creaked, and stinging pain burned into his muscles as he moved, but he was grateful. It reminded him of his regret and loss. His heart was entitled to beat a little fast because, yes, he was in distress. He knew what it was like to be happy for the first time in his miserable life, and now, forever lost to him, was the reason for his happiness. Recovering the pennant didn't even come close to compensating.

CHAPTER TWENTY-ONE _

Yianevan watched the eruption's aftermath through the viewport in his quarters, a cup of Birn in his hand. His lips barely touched the liquid before its bitter, rugged scent assaulted his senses. Before he tasted its far superior cousin, whisky, he had enjoyed the mellowness Birn offered, a mellowness he now sought in the hope it would dull the ache in his heart. It wasn't just that Earth's whisky had spoiled him. No amount of liquor would dim the pain of remembrance. He still felt the slender delicateness of Bethan's fingers against his lips, damp and warm from being tucked in the blankets. And he told her he loved her in a whispered admission of the absolute truth. Perhaps, had he declared his love before, it would ease her grief at his disappearance. He would never know.

He arrived on the planet unrehearsed, a foolish hero focused on uncovering a Lyran plot against the ten sectors. What possessed him? He never sought heroism before. So, was his desperation to delay his return to his homeworld the only factor that made him go to the Earth unprepared?

None of it mattered now. Even with the pennant in his possession, he felt only overwhelming loss. Bethan's beauty, her gentleness, stirred feelings he'd never known before. The scent of her skin as he held her naked body in his arms was a universe away from the cold duty of the Noble betrothal awaiting him on his homeworld.

The memory of their wedding repeated in his mind. He had no right to that joy, and it was fitting that he would be tortured with a tantalising glimpse of happiness. All he had with Bethan, all he would ever have, were his memories and a regret destined to be a constant companion for the rest of his life. Images of her bewilderment when they discovered his car haunted him, her desperate search for answers, and her sorrow at losing all her hopes and dreams. These would never be purged from his mind.

Maybe in retrieving the pennant, he saved Earth from a terrible fate, but its language would have to be deciphered for him to learn if that was true. Would it be worth the sacrifice? He planned to recover the interventionist to determine her involvement with the gate, then when he learned of the pennant, to retrieve them both. Now there was just the pennant, and it was a poor prize against what he had lost.

Picking up the cup of Birn, he tossed the contents into his mouth, and as the rough liquor hit his throat, his face crumpled in revulsion. He deserved to feel disgust. If he could, as a penance, he would deny himself any pleasure until the day he died, and he wished with all his heart Corky had only saved the pennant.

Yianevan held the faintest hope that Bethan would

follow through with their honeymoon plans and discover the gate. However, as the anomaly no longer registered her, the possibility it would guide her came into question. It would mean Bethan might always wonder why her treasured "charm" went missing the same day as her husband.

The interface seldom interrupted leisure moments or disturbed the crew in their quarters unless it felt necessary. Yianevan wanted to be alone with his thoughts but could not ignore the urgency Corky injected into his vocal processor, requesting he attend the bridge. Shouting was a trick Corky learned from his human crew to get attention, although it sometimes backfired, earning him a stream of insults and invectives.

In this case, Corky's disturbance was warranted. A single data tile, enlarged with a highlighted central image of the anomaly, greeted Yianevan as he entered the bridge. He instantly recognised the emerging pattern, but given the shroud of secrecy and scarce data, he doubted the interface, or any other technology, would have it in their database. Neither he nor the interface spoke for several minutes as they studied the intriguing pattern.

"A plexus fragment," Yianevan said finally. "A Waino plexus."

Of course, he had seen the language before. This was just a small part. Bethan's pennant contained the entire text, so someone had initiated that sequence at some historical juncture in the past. This proved a connection between the pennant and the Monk's Gate.

"I have no precedence of either this situation or this

language, Noble," Corky continued, "but there is no doubt it is …."

"… Noble technology." Yianevan and Corky finished the sentence together. There could be no doubt the Waino plexus precluded the gate from being of Lyran origin. Waino was the creator of the calming pennants, and his creations were at the foundation of all Noble technology. They did not include complete images of pennants in an interface's database, and the programming only had fragments of the plexus that identified the Waino signature. So while Corky read it as Noble technology, he couldn't decipher it. And that was intentional. A ship could be stolen, and its interface stripped by another species trying to discover Noble technology to usurp their position of power. The Nobles never took those kinds of risks.

Yianevan no longer believed Lyrans were in Earth's future, but this confirmed that all the events of the past few weeks had the pennant at their heart. Yianevan understood neither the pennant's purpose nor the reason for its creation, but its existence had created a myth that warranted only cursory remarks about time travel in the Noble archives. That made Yianevan wonder why his hierarchical ancestors denied its existence.

"Corky," he said. "Check among the redundant files where you found the neurotryptojag information."

"Can you be more specific, Noble?"

"Mention of a pennant, but unique, unlike a calming pennant or those used in phase and energy technology. Something with the markings of this plexus."

Corky returned a negative search result.

"Nothing, Noble. I do not believe I can add any information to what you already know. I do not have full records of any pennant."

Yianevan had considered employing the interface to help him decipher the pennant, but first, he would search the archive on the Noble homeworld. The pennant was hiding out in time for a reason, and he needed to know why.

Corky awaited further instructions, but none were forthcoming. That was expected. This Noble liked to do things his way without interference, and now he was back, Corky wondered if he should just power down all systems except for life support. His presence wasn't called for, but first, he had an idea, which he implemented without referring to the Noble, believing he would approve. Once completed, he told Yianevan what he had done.

"Noble," he said. "When you learned we could not retrieve Lieutenant Phildre, your biosigns registered the emotion of regret. I checked on the diverse behaviours human societies exhibit during stages of grief. Using the criteria from the human colonies on Mar'Ayan in the Hlet system, and for the sake of completeness for the lieutenant, I created a situation that will allow her to believe that you are dead. She will live her life as if you never existed. Humans prefer a determination that their spouse is deceased when the situation calls for it."

Yianevan groaned. "What did you do?"

"The lieutenant accepted that you worked at the mine, so as it was being dismantled, I initiated a minor cave-in. I have ensured no-one will suffer as a consequence." Then he added. "You will be pleased to hear the effect on the gate was insignificant."

Yianevan was stunned. For all its human-like foibles, Corky was still technology. Killing off a spouse wasn't a distraction; it was a disaster. While he knew that lack of closure to their time together would be unbearable, there would still be no physical body to bury and no way for Bethan to mourn. It wasn't any better than him going missing. Corky's diversion would only bring more distress to Bethan. Ian Noble had intruded into her life, made her love him, disrupted her plans and abandoned her. What else could he do to cause pain? Corky found that "what else". He could only stare in dismay at the interface.

Corky waited for affirmation, but when it didn't arrive, he asked the Noble if his assessment of the situation had been mistaken. He did not receive a reply.

"My intention was to improve the lieutenant's position," Corky said, curious why the Noble's heart rate and blood pressure became elevated. He checked the biosigns. Several hormones that only came into play during anger or arousal coursed through the Noble's bloodstream, indicating high levels of rage, although there was no reason for such an emotion. Appraisal of situations and resolution was written into the interface program and, in the main, much appreciated.

"It is unfortunate we lost Phildre," he said, "but we have vital information about the gate. Information that will be required by the hierarchy. It might be..."

"Corky," Yianevan roared. "Not another word! And stop helping."

Yianevan didn't plan on telling the hierarchy anything. Someone in his family knew it was the basis of the mythical Monk's Gate while not claiming the technology as their own. Why? What other secrets did the hierarchy keep? What else did he not know about his own people? "Monk's Gate" seemed an inapt name now that he knew the Lyran Monks had nothing to do with it, and Yianevan didn't follow the reasoning behind the deception. Corky dated the plexus before the Lyran war, but why would the Nobles build such a device only to abandon it? They must have created the pennant to generate this fissure in time, but why here, of all places, on a planet with toxic soil?

Yianevan knew the calming pennant's construction patterns became lost in prehistory, and not one artisan now lived who could recreate them. That was why they were such a precious and protected commodity. Were the Nobles seeking to improve their technology and attempted a new form of pennant? Or was it a time experiment gone wrong?

Yianevan rolled the pennant between his fingers. Whatever the answer, someone on his homeworld, in the not-too-distant past, still knew how to construct one.

He could not identify a single Lyran in Bethan's village. Not Mike, not Ivy, the butcher, the postman, the librarian. They weren't planning to take over the galaxy. The Nobles made grandiose claims of protecting the human world from Lyran sabotage, which had formed the basis of his earlier theory that Lyrans existed there. Now he knew that was a lie; suspicion for the existence of the Monk's Gate and its reason for being must fall on his own people.

There were still two more days before his father

expected him home. Yianevan knew he held the source of the gate in his hand and that once he left, it would no longer appear on sensors, so he decided he would wait the full two days. Bethan's timeline unfolded more rapidly than it did on the ship, and he now speculated that her dream of Pompeii might compel her to travel there.

"Corky, where is the interventionist now?"

Since the Noble's earlier unexpected "human" outburst, Corky had busied himself with mundane tasks like diagnostics. This was the first time the Noble had spoken to him since the incident.

"Echoes of her coordinates only, Noble," he advised. "No exact location."

"Very well. I see you dated the plexus fragment to before the Lyran war. What is the possibility this technology is presumed lost?"

"Unlikely, Noble. There is no mention of it in my data store, but someone could have erased the data or failed to enter it during my programming phase. I would speculate a structure of this magnitude has a point of origin, a generator. I just cannot locate it."

Yianevan knew where that generator was. In his pocket.

"Why would my people generate this portal on an inhospitable planet?"

"I cannot say, Noble. Given your experience, the soil toxins are still active in the future and present a danger to the Nobles. I do not understand their rationale."

"Perhaps they meant it as a prison for Lyrans."

"Again, unlikely, Noble. We did not take Lyran

prisoners."

Yianevan knew that. Nobles brought back some technology from the war, but they didn't save any of the Lyrans, who became an isolated and broken race that fell into extinction.

"Why would my people allow one of their own creations to become a Lyran myth?"

"If I may correct you, Noble," Corky said, "the Monk's Gate is a Noble myth. Not Lyran. Its existence is first mentioned by the Nobles. The Lyrans didn't survive long enough to create myths about this planet."

Well put, Yianevan thought. The Noble hierarchy had revealed their proclivity for subterfuge. Was it possible the real danger to the galaxy might come from his own people?

CHAPTER TWENTY-TWO _

A desolate mewing woke Bethan, and she wandered down the stairs, still half asleep and her mouth open in a wide yawn. As she passed the end of the bannister, her hand touched Ian's heavy coat. She frowned. That's odd. He never left the house without it, regardless of the weather. She checked the hall rack. He hadn't taken his hat either.

Puzzled, she went into the kitchen, lit the gas under the kettle, made some toast and opened the back door to let in the cat. It was then she noted Ian had left without eating breakfast. Was that something he regularly did? She supposed newlyweds had lots to learn about each other. Perhaps he was in a hurry, but leaving his coat, not eating breakfast, and not letting in the cat? He opened the door to it whenever it appeared, regardless of the time of day, a habit he developed leading up to their wedding. Each visit resulted in an exclusive smooch session between him and the moggy.

Now, the cat looked for Ian but, seeing he wasn't in the kitchen, realised it wouldn't get the sweet nothings to which it had grown accustomed and allowed itself to be tempted by the saucer of milk Bethan put on the floor.

As she munched her toast, the sleepy, predawn encounter from earlier ran through her head. It was too dark to see what Ian was wearing, but she was positive he only had on a shirt and trousers, not even his suit jacket, which he also wore everywhere. She hated that the sheets on his side of the bed felt so cold that morning when she woke. After only two nights, she already missed him beside her. It didn't take her long to get used to having him around, and she hated he had to head off to finish his work only a couple of days after their wedding. It would have been much nicer if he stayed with her, cosied up in bed, but she supposed she had the rest of their lives for that. In a couple of days, they would leave for Italy and a few glorious weeks to look forward to.

Lost in thought and from habit, she reached up to fiddle with her necklace. Startled to find it not there, she looked down and patted her chest around the area under her neck, then checked down her nightdress. Where was it? Even the chain was gone. It was definitely there last night. Running back upstairs, she checked over the unmade bed. Nothing. So she knelt to fish around on the floor, and found the chain on the rug with several links broken.

Bethan sat back on her heels, thinking of ways the chain might have broken. Making love with Ian was certainly energetic. Last night, perhaps more than the first. She flushed when she thought about the indescribably delicious feelings of passion Ian aroused in her. Where did her boldness come from? It just bubbled up, and she went with it. Luckily, Ian seemed delighted. Before her own wedding night, she hadn't even considered what happened after the ceremony. It hadn't interested her. Now she could see it would be one area of their relationship that held no secrets. Maybe the chain broke then. It was rather delicate, but not even a link had snapped in all these years. But then, she had never shared her bed, and these were her first passionate encounters. The chain may have been a casualty.

Bethan flattened herself out on the floor and reached under the bed, feeling around with her hand. The charm might have rolled under when the chain broke, but the bed was too heavy to move alone, so she would have to wait until Ian came home when they could search together.

By nine, he hadn't returned. At ten, she wondered what could have delayed him. By eleven, more to distract herself, she popped down to the office to see if there was anything Mike needed. She left Ian a note to drive over and pick her up.

Bethan took Mike a bottle of rum—his favourite tipple, a thank you for all his kindness, then made morning tea for the last time. Mike was very sorry to see Bethan leave because he didn't know how to replace her. There were few young people in the village, and the young girls from the local estate seemed more interested in factory work because it was more sociable than working in a stuffy office with a middle-aged man.

Mike was also relieved to see Bethan getting away from this environment. Not a man who showed his emotions, he felt a certain amount of relief when she first told him of her nursing ambitions. He hated to lose her, but she was wasted here and destined for greater things, so it surprised him when she abandoned those plans and married Ian Noble instead. It wasn't that he thought Ian came second to Bethan's ambitions. It was just that he shared Ivy's concerns about his secretiveness. What could he say? Bethan was an adult. He could only wish her well.

A repeating siren distracted him as they chatted, so he went to the window to check it out.

"Is that the pit alarm?" he said over his shoulder.

Bethan joined him. She had only heard it once before when the pit was still operating, and then no-one was injured, but its insistent wail chilled anyone who heard it. People were running down the street, even though it was a fair distance to the mine.

"Why would the alarm sound?" she said. "I thought there was only closing up activity at the pit?"

Mike thought that too. "It's just a team making it safe, drainage, and such. I don't know. Ian might know what's going on."

At the mention of Ian's name, an icy premonition gripped Bethan's heart. A sudden and terrifying sense of loss and dread.

"Mike," she said, her voice trembling with fear. "I don't know where Ian is. He went out before it got light."

Mike had wondered why Bethan turned up alone but didn't ask. Now he wished he had because this was mighty peculiar.

"Ian went out. Why?"

"He said he had a few things to finish."

Police car sirens blasted past, and Bethan's hand went

to her mouth. Mike put two and two together and placed his hands on her shoulders.

"Wait a minute," he said, looking into her ashen face. "You don't think Ian is at the mine?"

Unable to utter a word in her rising terror, Bethan looked at him in wide-eyed fear. How could she know where Ian was? He never told her. Mike gave her shoulders a gentle shake.

"You mustn't jump to conclusions, Bethan. You said yourself he doesn't go there often. I thought they might keep him apprised of what's happening there. I didn't mean to imply…"

He stopped rambling; her expression told him he was wasting his breath, so he grabbed his coat. "I'll drive you to the pit. We'll set your mind at rest."

It didn't matter the pit was no longer in use. There was something about the wail of the pit siren that throughout history, had the power to fill a wife with dread. It shouldn't have the same effect now, but to Bethan, she knew it heralded disaster. She tried to reassure herself Ian seldom needed to go underground. He never mentioned that he had in all these weeks, but any collapse would be no respecter of persons if he happened to that day.

Mike drove through the lines of spectators heading for the pit, and Bethan wound down the window. An air of anxiety rippled from one person to the next, igniting memories from when the pit alarm meant disaster. She jumped from the car when they reached the colliery, where the curious crowd gathered, waiting to learn the reasons for the alarm. Mr Trevor emerged at the top of the steps and held up his hands. The crowd silenced in anticipation, and Bethan could have heard a pin drop.

There had indeed been a collapse, and several workers, all former well-experienced miners involved in boarding the mine, had become trapped. The fire brigade asked volunteers and ex-miners to descend into the pit to move rubble and free the men, but water seepage created complications. Because of this, they would treat the collapse as they would any other, but Mr Trevor assured the crowd all would be well. Then, as was the tradition in these situations, he called out the names of the dozen men trapped. Bethan held her breath as he read the names in alphabetical order.

Ian was not among them.

Mike smiled and handed Bethan the keys to his car.

"I told you," he said. "Now, I'm going to stay in case they need an electrician. I expect they'll find something for me to do." He helped her into the driver's seat, but she still looked pale. "Don't worry. Ian's probably at home waiting for you."

Bethan managed a weak smile. Mike didn't know she left Ian a note to collect her from the office. He hadn't turned up, so he hadn't read it, which meant he hadn't gone home nor heard the pit siren. Otherwise, he would be here to help. Still, it made sense to leave. She would be better waiting in her kitchen than here, where she would be in the way. Besides, Mr Trevor would never overlook someone working underground.

Ian wasn't at home, so Bethan waited in the kitchen,

watching the minutes on the old mantle clock tick by. Then she drove Mike's car back to his office and dropped off his keys. She waited for the bus but ended up walking home, hoping the fresh air would sweep away some of her foreboding.

Late afternoon turned to twilight, and with still no sign of Ian, Bethan took to pacing the floor. Out in the hallway, she held his coat to her face and tried to breathe in his scent. There was none, just the fibrous aroma of the woven fabric. It felt like the man who wore it had never existed.

The boiler was lit, but the kitchen felt cold and unwelcoming. Fighting feelings of utter helplessness and to keep herself busy, Bethan made a pot of tea and sat at the kitchen table to wait. And wait. Fearful of moving in case she missed his key in the lock or a messenger with news, she sat in front of the cold teapot until eight o'clock, when she heard a knock on the door. It was Ivy.

"I saw Mike," Ivy said, shocked by Bethan's tear-stained face and dishevelled hair. "He said you were here. I just wanted to stop by and check Ian got home."

Bethan couldn't help herself. Just having someone to speak to about her fear was enough for her to collapse into Ivy's arms.

"I don't know where he is. I had the most awful feeling when I heard the sirens. Oh, Ivy," she sobbed, "it was like a sixth sense when I heard that sound…."

She couldn't finish, so Ivy steered her into the kitchen and sat her down at the table.

"I didn't think Ian ever went down the mine," she said.

Bethan shook her head. "I don't think he ever did, but

you know how he was talking about his job. Ivy, I'm so worried. What if today was the day he did go into the pit?"

"Mr Trevor would have read out his name, Bethie, so Ian couldn't have been there. Anyway, it was all a bit theatrical as far as I was concerned. They only sounded the alarm to alert the fire brigade because the phone wasn't working. Six of the men are out, and they just reached the others when I left."

Bethan felt wretched. Ivy tried to convince her not to worry, that Ian would soon be home, and she hoped with a darned good explanation, but all Bethan could do was bury her face in her hands, trying to speak through her tears.

"What if Ian *was* down there? What if Mr Trevor missed him?"

Ivy hated to see Bethan distraught. Whatever Ian was playing at, she cursed him for his thoughtlessness. There was no way they'd miss him if he was in the mine, but repeating that would fall on deaf ears, so instead, she hugged her friend and stroked her hair.

"Mike said you didn't know where Ian was going, only that he had a couple of things to clear up. That doesn't mean he was at the pit."

Bethan felt anger at herself that she had given up asking Ian about his work and where he went. Then she felt angry at him because his answers were always vague, and his pronunciation of the towns so terrible it confused even her. If he had been just a little more forthcoming, all this could have been avoided.

"I'm not sure, Ivy," she said. "I know he spent a lot of time on the other side of the valley. If that was the case, he should have been home by now if he was only doing a few things to finish up. He could drive that distance in less than an hour."

Ivy didn't know what to say, but all her uncertainties about Ian flooded back. Why would he worry Bethan like this? She didn't understand but prayed for Ian's sake she didn't see him before Bethan did because Constable Marley didn't take kindly to violence in his village. Right now, Ivy battled murderous thoughts.

None of this would help her distraught friend, though, so Ivy remained calm, held Bethan's hand, and helped her drink a few pots of tea before supervising her into bed. Too distressed to care, Bethan made no protest when Ivy wiped her tear-stained face with a wet flannel, took off her shoes and tucked the eiderdown around her trembling body. Ivy knew Bethan wouldn't sleep and would listen for Ian's key in the front door, but it was almost midnight, and Ivy couldn't leave her mam alone any longer. With a gentle warning to rest, Ivy kissed Bethan on the forehead and promised to look in first thing in the morning.

As Ivy predicted, the night crawled by as Bethan strained her ears for any sound that Ian might have arrived home. In moments of fitful sleep, she dreamed of Ian's fine hair brushing against her face, stretching herself across his smooth body and giggling at the newness of intimacy. Other times, all she could do was stare into the darkness, too afraid her sobbing would make her miss the sound of his car so she could run down the stairs and throw herself into his arms. And each time she reached for the comfort of the little charm that had always hung around her neck, its absence brought fresh weeping.

Bethan didn't wait for Ivy's visit. Instead, she walked to the Price's house to let her know she was okay, declining an offer of breakfast but agreeing to return if she needed anything. She then continued on to the grocer to see if there was any more news from the day before. Mr Griffiths had a telephone, so he was generally the first to hear.

"Everyone's up, love," he announced. "Storm in a teacup, I'd say. Two men went to hospital but no severe injuries."

"How could the mine collapse, Mr Griffiths?" Bethan asked. "I thought the shafts were secure."

"Well, that's what everybody thought, Bethan. Seems something got missed. The boarding and sealing were complete, and the coal board was about to carry out the final inspection."

Bethan didn't want to hear that. "The final inspection? Would they need a surveyor?"

Mr Griffiths twisted his normally cheerful face into a frown. He knew little about the pit because he avoided it as a youngster. On the other hand, a surveyor sounded reasonable, and the villagers considered him an authority on most things, even when he wasn't.

"Yes, Bethan," he agreed. "I think that sounds like a job for a surveyor. The board would have had their men there, but only local lads were underground."

Bethan felt her fragile composure slipping. Ian only acknowledged his contract was ending, not what it involved. Would it have been the final survey? Bethan found it impossible to coordinate her breathing in this state, and her voice came out strangled and strange as she thanked Mr Griffiths and turned to leave. He then paid attention to her dishevelled appearance and the wavering in her voice. Young Bethan was near to tears, so he changed his tone from conversational about the pit collapse to that of a man who saw the distress in a woman he'd known since she was a baby.

"Bethie? What's wrong, girl?"

"My husband didn't arrive home last night." Bethan took a deep, calming breath before continuing. "I've not heard from him."

"Oh, lass," he said, "that is a worry. Look, I expect there'll be a perfectly good explanation. Try Constable Marley. He's been at the mine most of the night, and he'll have a list of the casualties and the volunteers."

Bethan managed a smile. "I'll do that."

The bell above the door clanged noisily as she left, and the grocer watched the unhappy woman turn in the direction of the police station. Alfie Griffiths had this shop for decades and knew every man who worked at the pit. The only one unmarried was Jacob Barton. He didn't know any of the coal board people who occasionally came in for cigarettes or newspapers, but that was the extent of his involvement. Maybe Bethan asked about the surveyors because she married one of them. Well, she kept that quiet. He hoped her husband hadn't just up and left her. Who would do a dreadful thing like that to a lovely girl like Bethan Davies?

Bethan had known Constable Marley for years. His bright red, handlebar moustachioed face greeted her from behind the counter at the police station, his bright eyes twinkling under bushy eyebrows. A man of boundless energy and tireless devotion to Llanbleddynllwyd, he didn't look as if he'd been up all night assisting a rescue.

Constable Marley's greeting to his unlikely visitor boomed out with a Welsh accent so strong, the villagers liked to say that when he spoke, every window in the village rattled, and when he sang in the church choir, the steeple needed to be replaced. Indeed, the constable was loud, but that voice drove fear into any miscreants daring to enter the village to cause mischief, especially those who didn't speak Welsh. Constable Marley had a habit of slipping into a fiery version of the vernacular when apprehending a villain but was kindness itself when the situation demanded, such as this one.

Bethan's tired, red-rimmed eyes and pale cheeks alarmed him, so he hurried around to the front of the counter to take her arm and draw her to a chair. She looked fit to drop. Something was amiss, that was for sure.

"Bethan Davies. Come and sit down. What has happened?"

"I'm Bethan Noble, now, Constable Marley." Bethan held up her hand to show her wedding and engagement rings. "I got married on Wednesday."

Constable Marley didn't think Bethan looked much like a blushing bride, not with a tear-stained face and a trembling hand holding a drenched handkerchief against her mouth, so no doubt this had something to do with the new husband.

"Well, young Mrs Noble," he said. "I can't congratulate you with your weeping and eyes all red. Tell me about it."

Through her tears, Bethan told him about Ian's work, his leaving early the previous morning and not returning. When she finished, Constable Marley shook his head. Her story confounded him because he'd been over at the pit, and the board men hadn't arrived. Dai Trevor even mentioned the final inspection wasn't due for another week.

"Are you sure, Bethan?" he said. "Only local boys were involved."

"Mr Griffiths said the surveyors were there, too."

He wished she said that to start with because he knew otherwise.

"Then you've got nothing to worry about!" he said, squeezing her hand. "Old Alfie's got it wrong. The surveyors aren't due until next week, although I expect they're on their way now, given what's happened. There weren't any there yesterday, I promise you, Bethie."

Bethan didn't believe it. Constable Marley must have made a mistake.

"Ian wouldn't just go missing."

Well, that was a different matter. A man might go missing for other reasons.

"Your husband can't be in the mineshaft, Bethan," he said. "We accounted for all the boys, but my concern is why your husband wasn't at home with his new wife. Married two days, and he's off to work?"

Bethan shrugged. "He had a contract and needed to

finish up a few things. I didn't mind. I planned to pop into the office and see Mike, anyway. That was where I heard the pit alarm."

Constable Marley frowned. There seemed to be some curious circumstances here, so he asked Bethan how often Ian went to the pit and where else he worked.

What could she say? She had to admit she didn't know and only guessed he was part of the new estate construction, adding that Ian went out the day before around the time of the early shift at the mine.

Constable Marley listened with increasing suspicion. It sounded like Bethan didn't know much about her husband.

"It's not usual to combine local council and coal board," he said. "I'll check first thing on Monday. Now, you go through the volunteer list, and I'll ring the hospital. Ian Noble, you say? What does he look like?"

Constable Marley made it his business to know everyone who stayed in the village, and from Bethan's description, it sounded like Margaret Jenkins's house guest. He also recalled Mrs Evans telling him about a man who helped her when she fell, taking her home in his car with all her groceries. The tall, pale man, whose name he had not known prior, had only lived at Margaret's house for the last few weeks, so he hoped Bethan knew him before that; otherwise, it was a pretty rushed marriage. Now though, was not the time to ask Bethan about her courtship, and it wouldn't be right to judge the man involved. Not until he had more evidence.

He poked his large fingers into the dial on the phone, half hoping Ian Noble was at the hospital. If not and discounting the acts of kindness and his own reluctance to judge, he wondered if perhaps the bastard had just run off.

Bethan listened to the one-sided conversation Constable Marley had with the nurse.

"Thank you, nurse, thank you," he said, nodding and huffing into the telephone. He concluded with, "Yes, I'll tell her," before replacing the phone in the cradle.

"Like I said, Bethan. No-one other than a couple of local men. All I can say is, your husband wasn't in the mine when it collapsed."

"He's not on the volunteer list either," Bethan said, placing the single sheet of paper on the counter. "Constable Marley, this can't be a coincidence. I don't know what to do because he said he wouldn't be gone for long. I only know that if something happened, he would do everything he could to let me know. That's why I am afraid he was below ground, and somehow, he got overlooked."

Constable Marley nodded. He understood. "Now, Bethie. Did he have a car?"

"Yes, a brown Austin. It was old, and I don't know the registration number. There was a dent in the front bumper." Bethan gave the constable a sad smile. "I don't think he ever washed it, either."

Constable Marley chuckled. "Can't expect a surveyor to keep a car clean!" He didn't want Bethan to lose hope and assured her he would do everything he could to find out what happened. "I'll get the heddlu over at Llanfrydd to look out for it," he told her. "Meanwhile, you are not to worry. There's bound to be a perfectly good explanation."

Bethan closed her eyes. She doubted there was a

"perfectly good explanation", but if the police were looking out for the car, it might give them some clues.

"Jacob Barton was on the casualty list," she said. "Do you know if he went to the hospital?"

"Yes," Constable Marley replied. "Wide awake when I last saw him. I believe they sent him home last night. Might be worth a word if it sets your mind at rest."

Bethan knew the Barton family well, and Ivy always hoped Jacob would notice her. The three went to the same primary school, and Mrs Barton was friends with her own mother and Ivy's. It might be a good place to start.

CHAPTER TWENTY-THREE

"Ian Noble?" Jacob looked up from the couch, his thin face a mess of scratches and his foot swathed in bandages. His mother clucked around him like an old hen, and he shushed her out of the way. "I've never heard of him. I didn't even know you got married."

"On Wednesday."

"Oh, well, congratulations, but I haven't seen a surveyor in months. What does your husband look like?"

Describing Ian wasn't likely to yield results because he hadn't mixed with people in the village, but Bethan had to try.

"Late twenties," she said. "A shade over six feet, light brown hair, and his skin is quite pale, like he doesn't get much sun. His eyes are very blue."

"Well, I guess I wouldn't be looking into a man's eyes," Jacob said, "but I haven't seen anyone like that at the pit. Coal board men are short, fat, and balding, not to mention later than middle age. Sorry, Beth."

Bethan attempted a smile, then cringed as her next

words flowed without thinking.

"Thank you anyway, Jacob. I'm sure there is a perfectly good explanation."

She nodded towards Jacob's bandaged ankle. "I hope you feel better soon."

Jacob lifted his foot to show her his injury was only minor.

"We weren't deep, and this is only a sprain. There will be an investigation because someone said it was a deliberate act. You know, sabotage. Can you believe it? Someone removed a single strut. Who would want to sabotage the mine? We've all known each other since we were kids. Why would any of us put our friends in danger?"

Bethan couldn't imagine who would do that. But Jacob was right. It wouldn't be anyone with a connection to the village.

"I suppose if it was deliberate, they need to know," she said as she refused Mrs Barton's offer of tea.

Jacob had not asked, and Bethan provided nothing more about Ian's disappearance, but he wished her luck as she left.

What a horrible situation to be in, he thought, married one day, and abandoned the next. He expected to hear all the details the next time he bumped into Ivy. Strange, she'd not mentioned the wedding.

Bethan didn't go straight home. Instead, she went to the park and sat on the odd seat that faced the bakery wall. There, she wept, uncaring of anyone who saw her, until she was all cried out. The pithead rose like a tombstone from the valley floor, and she couldn't bear to look at it, so she turned away to still her unpleasant imaginings. More than twenty-four hours had passed since she last saw Ian, and try as she might, she couldn't stop the terrifying images that ran through her head of him lying at the bottom of the mine shaft. He would be hurt, unconscious, or worse, and no-one believed he might be there. She'd been foolish not to press him for information about where he worked when he went out, but he should have volunteered that information. Why was it such a big secret, anyway? She was his wife, after all, and it was just work. He went missing at the same time as the cave-in. How could she not put two and two together?

If it weren't for Ivy, Bethan wouldn't even have left her bed over the next two days. She convinced herself Ian was dead at the bottom of the pit and somehow got overlooked. That could be the only explanation. Ivy pointed out that Ian's car would be parked there if that were the case, but Bethan, inconsolable, would not see reason.

Constable Marley stopped by on Monday to tell her he had enquired at the council and the coal board as soon as their offices opened that morning. Each advised him Ian Noble was neither an employee nor a subcontractor. Bethan took the news calmly but still insisted that the cave-in had something to do with Ian's disappearance.

Constable Marley offered to take Bethan to the mine to be reassured by Mr Trevor, but Bethan preferred to make her own way. As soon as the constable left, she changed her clothes and took herself off to the pit head. To disguise the days of weeping proved an impossibility, and she knew she looked a mess, but her head was in such turmoil, even if she plastered on layers of makeup, nothing would hide her blotchy cheeks and red-rimmed eyes.

The mine manager watched from his window in surprise as his late good friend and workmate's daughter trod the gravel road towards his office. Nevertheless, she was a welcome visitor because he hadn't seen Bethan in a few months. He heard she was off to London to be a nurse, which was not surprising because Bethan was a bright young thing, even though she kept herself to herself.

"Bethan. Sosej," he beamed, using a family term of endearment he often called her as a child. He stood back to let Bethan into his office, and as he did, his big smile faded. Although delighted to see her, he'd never known Bethan Davies so *sombre*. Mud spatters covered her shoes and the backs of her stockings, but she didn't seem to care, and with her face pale and sad, she looked a pitiful sight. He couldn't imagine what had taken place.

"Bethie, are you alright? I'll get you some tea."

He didn't think she'd even have the strength to hold a cup, but he went to turn on the gas burner anyway, even just to give him a moment to get over his shock at her appearance.

Bethan didn't want tea. She was all tea'd out. She needed to get straight to the point of her visit while she felt able to find the words.

"I was here on Friday after the alarm," she said. "I thought my husband might be working here, but you didn't read out his name. He's a surveyor, and he told me that a small part of his work was for the board. Constable Marley spoke to them this morning, but they've never heard of him.

My husband told me a few days ago he had been carrying out geotechnical testing across the valley, but the council haven't heard of him either."

Ian had explained geotechnical testing to Bethan. It sounded important, so she couldn't understand why the council wouldn't know of someone who worked for them in a significant capacity, even if he was a contractor.

"He went out on Friday morning, around dawn," she went on, as Mr Trevor sat beside her with a box of Kleenex, just in case that brave facade crumbled. "He told me he would be back soon. When he didn't come home by eleven, I went to Mike Trent's office. That's where I heard the siren." Bethan bit her lip. "Mr Trevor, I was terrified."

"Lass, I didn't even know you got married."

Even to Bethan, it seemed so long ago.

"On Wednesday," she said. "He would never deliberately cause me this worry. Do you know anything about contract surveyors? Could he have gone down the mine and got missed in all the chaos?"

Dai Trevor's brow furrowed in confusion. A contract surveyor? Now, where on earth would she get a notion like that? The board had their own on the books, and they only sent them when needed. He didn't know about other surveyors, but it sounded reasonable to be contracted to the council because of that big project across the valley. All he knew was that council contractors came from Bristol or London, so Bethan's husband must have been one of them. Unfortunately, his answer would only deepen her confusion.

"I haven't seen a surveyor here in weeks, Bethan, and

I'm not expecting another visit for a few more days. The council might need to recheck their list of contractors."

Bethan shook her head. "Constable Marley says they know the name of every subcontractor, and they didn't know an Ian Noble."

"Ian Noble?" Mr Trevor sat up. "Young Ivy Price came up here asking about someone of that name."

Bethan didn't understand. Why would Ivy come here to ask about Ian?

"When was that?"

"Oh, about three weeks ago. I told her I'd never heard of him. Bethan, what's going on?"

"I don't know, Mr Trevor," Bethan admitted. "I don't know where Ian is. He left the house around the time of the first shift on Friday morning, then there was a cave-in, and now he's missing. It all seems too much of a coincidence. Is the board going to open the mine to investigate?"

She had presented Mr Trevor with a conundrum. He seemed sure he had everyone up from the pit, and Bethan was almost certain he didn't. Almost, because a tiny niggling worm in the pit of her stomach now challenged that conviction.

Mr Trevor knew the board was unlikely to go to the trouble of opening the pit. They would just make it safe and go ahead with the closure, but he hesitated to tell Bethan.

"We haven't run the early shift for weeks," he said. "There's no need. Besides, the mine's flooded right now, so the board will need to wait. All the men are out, so they're in no hurry. Look, love, we accounted for everyone who went down."

He watched as tears spilt onto Bethan's cheeks. Only once in the past had he sat here with a grieving widow, her husband buried in a cave-in, and he hoped he would never witness such a devastating loss again. Although he knew for sure it hadn't happened now, it didn't make Bethan's distress less real. It would almost be kinder to let her think her husband was in the mineshaft because it appeared the alternative would be just as devastating. He offered her a handful of Kleenex tissues and hoped he could soften his next words to try to lessen the hurt.

"Bethan. It may be your husband has run off. Some men don't realise the responsibilities that come with a wedding ring."

She looked up at him, her face a picture of misery. "He'd know that after two days?"

Mr Trevor had to concede it seemed unreasonable. That soon after the wedding, the delights of marriage rather than its responsibilities were the usual consideration. There must be another reason for the man's disappearance. It was a long shot, but in the past, a couple of journalists for some of the London newspapers turned up after problems at the pit, asking questions about the Clean Air Act and other unrelated issues. They paraded themselves as from the National Coal Board, erudite and plausible in their manner, and giving false names to get on mine property. They even fooled him, but it hadn't happened in a while. No-one was harmed, but none had gone as far as marrying a local girl.

Mr Trevor decided that if he ever met this Ian Noble, he might just punch him in the jaw. What kind of man would marry a girl as sweet as Bethan, then just up and leave two days later? It was the only answer. Ian Noble had walked out. He had to be one of those blasted reporters who singled out Bethan, and because she was such a decent girl, he had to marry her to get his way. Then he discarded her. Some of those reporters were true scallywags. He thought he'd seen the last of them, but it was a lamentable fact that Bethan wouldn't be the last to fall for a glib bastard's lying tongue.

He gave her a sanitised version of his theory, but she just kept shaking her head. Ian wouldn't do something like that. Then he suggested she check the wardrobe at home for his clothes. Bethan sensed Mr Trevor's growing judgement of Ian. It was the same for Ivy and Constable Marley. Even Mike when he visited. She and Ivy had checked the wardrobe together, despite Bethan telling Ivy that Ian had no time to unpack. The wardrobe held only the shirt he wore to the wedding and his suit jacket. Ivy also found his shoes under the bed. Next, they opened Ian's leather valise, which he brought into the house on the evening of their wedding. She hadn't asked about the rest of his luggage, assuming it was in the boot of his car, and she forgot to mention it the next day.

The valise was on the bedroom chair where Ian left it, but she found only a few Sherlock Holmes novels and one change of underwear when she opened it. The only other items of clothing he left behind, apart from his shoes, suit jacket and wedding shirt, were his beloved coat and hat.

Bethan would find no answers here, so she thanked Mr Trevor for his kindness and began the walk back to the village. He watched her go, saddened to see the light dimmed in one of the village's shining stars.

Constable Marley had already listed Ian as a missing person and widened the search for his car, but Bethan went to the police station in case there was any news. There was none, and she didn't expect it anyway. Concerned to let her go home in such a state, the constable escorted her to the Prices to be looked after by Ivy.

"You could petition the mines department to open the shaft," Ivy said as she settled Bethan at the kitchen table.

"The coal board doesn't know who Ian is, Ivy. Besides, they're waiting for the water to drop before finishing the boarding. If Ian were in there, he would have drowned by now. Mr Trevor thinks he just walked out on me."

"Walked out?" Ivy exclaimed. "After two days? Those first few weeks after the wedding are the best of all!" She paused before adding, "So I've heard."

Since Ian went missing, Bethan had done much soul-searching, but there was no reason to suspect he was unhappy. She said so to Ivy, who nodded, but still felt she needed to ask.

"Bethan, I know it was only two days, but were things okay in the bedroom?"

Never one to engage in such private topics, Bethan was so numb it didn't even feel like a personal question.

"What can I say?" she said. "Ian and I got on in every way. He was the first man I was ever with. I think it was the first time for him, too, because he's never kissed another girl. He didn't even kiss me until the night he proposed."

Ivy picked up her teacup and made her face disappear

into it as far as it would go. She didn't want Bethan to see her expression of disbelief.

Ian Noble, she said to herself, *you are a bloody liar!*

How could someone with those looks never have kissed another someone? What was he up to? Feelings of murder were again tying her innards in knots, so she could only hope she never set eyes on Ian Noble before anyone else did. If so, Bethan would likely be visiting her in prison. However, it was time to face the music and confess her visit to Ian before the wedding. She just hoped it had not contributed to his disappearance.

"Bethie." Ivy pushed a wayward lock of hair from Bethan's face. "I did something bad. With everything that has happened, I think I should tell you."

Bethan sniffed and blinked away tears. Nothing could be as bad as what she was going through. Her friend had gone to see Mr Trevor to ask about Ian. It was understandable. She almost wished she had done it herself, but that wasn't part of the confession because Ivy's face revealed this went beyond a simple admission of guilt.

"I went to see Ian the day after you told me you were getting married."

"Why?"

"I was suspicious. I just didn't trust him."

Bethan knew that. "You didn't know him like I did, Ivy. And he never told me about your visit."

"Well, he was jolly good at keeping secrets," Ivy pointed out. "I asked him what his intentions were, and he said he only wanted your happiness."

"Didn't you believe him?"

Ivy had to admit Ian had been convincing that day.

"Yes," she said, "I did, but looking back, he seemed to only say what I wanted to hear. You were so happy. What choice did I have but to accept his word? I told him I would be watching him."

Bethan wondered how it would feel to know almost no-one, and those who did, mistrusted you. Poor Ian.

Ivy felt genuine remorse for going behind Bethan's back, but all this proved she was right to be suspicious.

"I'm sorry, Bethie," she said, cupping Bethan's face in her hands. "After the visit, I persuaded myself he was sincere, but with all that secrecy, it was just too much. And now this. I can't help wondering what it was he wanted. Surely not to break your heart. What about his family? Can you reach out to them?"

It would have been so much easier if Bethan knew where to find Ian's relatives, but as she couldn't draw Ian out about them, there was no way she ever would. As for Ivy feeling the need to investigate Ian before the wedding, she understood. She was just being a cautious friend, but it was sad she didn't trust the judgement of the person who knew him best.

"Ian was, is, a mystery," Bethan said, "and so is his family. I don't know where they are. Europe, I think. I might have to accept that Ian wasn't at the mine on Friday, but Ivy, no-one recognised Ian from my description. Now I feel like I'm searching for a ghost. I can't even organise a funeral or get a death certificate."

"You might be asking the wrong people," Ivy said. "Of course he's not a ghost, and applying for a death certificate is premature." Then, after a moment, she added, "I think it's worth insisting the coal board check the mine, just to set your mind at rest."

The authorities would take some convincing. Ivy knew it, and so did Bethan. If the Coal Board hadn't employed Ian, and Mr Trevor had no knowledge of him, it was unlikely they would investigate. They didn't even need to say it.

CHAPTER TWENTY-FOUR _

Yianevan knew Bethan would be too stricken by grief to go to Pompeii only two days after he disappeared, but he had already formulated a plan that might encourage her in that direction.

"Corky, if we direct the spiral into the gate just once more, not to search for the lieutenant, but towards the bank repository, what is the likelihood of success?"

"Unknown, Noble," Corky answered. "If it destabilises the gate further, we could lose the opportunity for research."

Yianevan understood, but the spiral alone had less effect on the gate than his presence. It might work.

"I want to give the interventionist the means whereby she could access the gate before we leave orbit. I expect the currency you made accessible to me during my time on the planet has remained in the bank."

All Yianevan's account identification, including his passport, was in the pocket of the trousers he wore when he disappeared. If Corky could modify these accounts via the spiral, he could transfer his wealth to Bethan in the same way he set them up. If the transaction proved successful, instinct and curiosity might lead her to Pompeii. He outlined his plan to the interface.

Corky realised the Noble would discard any protest. Thus, compliance would be a prudent and less time-consuming course of action rather than stating the possible consequences.

"This world's legal and financial systems are not automated, Noble. What you propose would involve a wider application. For my sensors to examine such data through the narrow lens of the spiral, I will need time."

"How much time?"

"Sixteen hours, Noble."

Sixteen hours. Years may have passed in Bethan's time. He nodded.

"Do it. Hopefully, one further visit from the spiral will not be counterproductive."

Corky completed the initiative in exactly sixteen hours, gaining access to a time a few days before Ian Noble's departure. There still needed to be physical evidence, which Corky provided by implanting various official documents into the bank records via the spiral. The gate appeared to tolerate the spiral's presence but did not yield any information on the lieutenant.

While Corky worked, Yianevan allowed himself a meditative state to ease his agony and heartbreak. He held the pennant in the palm of his hand, where its presence brought some comfort, perhaps because Bethan kept it so close to her heart. If his plan worked, she may yet return to her own time, even though she would never be part of his life again.

Now he had time to examine the pennant, he expected to decipher the language without difficulty. But he couldn't. He felt as if he should understand it, so he blamed the turmoil in his heart and mind for the pennant refusing to allow him even a glimpse into its secrets.

As Yianevan turned his thoughts inward to still the dull ache of grief in his heart, he wished he could use the pennant's power to bridge the gulf of time that divided him and Bethan. He imagined her lying on the bed or sitting in the kitchen with a pot of tea, waiting for his return, and wished he could brush his lips against hers just one more time. But time had proved it was not a creature he could hunt and capture. It moved on without regard for his pain.

The hazy afternoon sun slanted through Bethan's bedroom window. Lying on her back, she watched the dust fairies as they floated above her head. They were multiplying by the day because she hadn't lifted a duster nor run the hoover over the rugs since Ian left these three weeks since. She spent most afternoons on her bed, wondering why her grieving heart kept beating and why the world, which once held so much promise, continued to turn.

Ian's coat still hung over the bottom of the stairs, and his hat was on a peg on the coat rack. To remove them would be to admit he was never coming home. His shoes were still under his side of the bed, adding to the mystery by making her wonder how he ventured out into the chilly morning in his bare feet.

Mike asked her to come back to work to keep her busy, at least until she decided what she wanted to do next. She appreciated his kindness, but how could she decide? Not yet. Ian had been in her life for such a short, glorious time, and now he was gone she felt lost, as if her world had slowed, almost to a stop.

Apart from a few personal clothing items, he had left behind little evidence he ever existed, but his presence was everywhere, throughout the cottage and inside her heart and mind. He occupied every waking thought, and as it had thousands of times since he disappeared, that first visit to the lake was always the memory that haunted her.

It was the day the sunset took his breath away. The day he discovered tea with sugar, and the day she read poetry in a language he didn't understand but listened to politely. It was the day he told her about the firefly planet. They just didn't have enough time to build memories together.

Sleep had become a rare visitor at night, but now, burdened with weariness and sorrow, Bethan allowed her eyelids to droop. A few minutes of respite from her mourning would be welcome, and she dozed there on top of the bedclothes. In her sleepy state, she smiled as she felt something brush her face and the sensation of lips pressing against hers.

Alarmed, she sat up and raised a hand to her cheek. What touched her? A frantic scrabble around for a spider or a fly that might have been sharing the bed with her revealed nothing. Besides, that wouldn't explain the icy coldness of the kiss.

Shaking her head to chase away the fog in her brain, Bethan swung her legs over the edge of the bed and stared down at the crumpled state of her dress. Tiredness had clouded her focus, and now she was imagining things. There was no spider. There was no fly. She fought the urge to lie down again and instead pulled straight the messy tangle of sheets.

This won't do, she announced to the room. *Ian isn't coming back. You may never discover what happened to him, but you are still here, and you must carry on.*

She ran her finger over her lips where the kiss still lingered. Wherever Ian is, she thought, perhaps he is thinking of her. If he really was dead, maybe this was a message to tell her goodbye and stop waiting for him.

The following day, Bethan rose at dawn and headed downstairs to the kitchen. A bird sang a melancholy solo outside on the wall, and an early shower pitter-pattered against the window. A familiar, forlorn mewing sent her to the door, and she invited the fat tabby cat in for a saucer of milk. As she waited for the water to boil for her pot of tea, she sat at the table and penned a note to the Alice Maud Hospital, explaining her current marital status and adding a humble request they reinstate her application as a student nurse.

CHAPTER TWENTY-FIVE _

The summer of 1961 saw London swelter through a mini-heatwave, and the lightweight cape the hospital insisted its nurses wore when outside in uniform left Bethan feeling sticky and uncomfortable. Now qualified, she no longer had to live in the nurse's home and rented a spacious bedsit with her friend, Doris, but she had to walk half a mile to get home. In addition, the day had been long, and she was desperate to get out of uniform and soak in a bath. She had received her state registered nursing badge a year before but took another year to gain some theatre nursing experience before heading to Australia in time for Christmas.

Her flatmate greeted her at the door, waving a telegram. Anticipation of the bath evaporated in the face of Doris's desperation to learn its contents. She didn't even let Bethan take off her cap and cape before pushing the telegram into her hands.

"This arrived today, Beth," she said, unable to contain her excitement. "It looks official. Look at the name. It's addressed to Mrs B Noble."

That was odd, because Bethan never used her married name. She turned the telegram over a few times.

"It's from Hambly's Bank," she said. "Why would they be sending me a telegram?"

"Open it and find out," Doris urged, handing Bethan a letter opener.

Bethan frowned. "I don't bank with them. There's a branch in Llanfrydd, run by the postmistress."

Doris wasn't interested in trivia. Telegrams always brought important news, and Bethan was frustratingly slow in getting to it. "Who cares!" she exclaimed. "Just open it!"

Grinning at her friend's impatience, Bethan sliced open the envelope and read the two lines contained inside.

'Mrs Noble. Please contact our agent on the telephone number below. You will hear something to your advantage.'"

Each sentence was punctuated by the word STOP. The contents only added to the mystery, so she handed the telegram to Doris, who read it twice before her excitement took a nosedive.

"What does that mean? 'Hear something to your advantage?'."

Bethan couldn't explain it. She'd never had any dealing with Hambly's bank. The only thing to do was call the number in the morning and see if they could shed any light. Doris, however, would brook no hesitation. This mystery needed to be solved without delay! So Bethan found herself steered out to the hall payphone, with Doris insisting she wouldn't sleep a wink until she knew what was going on.

Listening in as close to the receiver as she could

without bumping heads with Bethan, Doris only got snippets of the conversation. She strained her ears to hear but only got Bethan's occasional "yes" and "uh-huh" and the final signing off with an agreement to be there at nine the following morning. Bethan replaced the receiver and frowned.

"So?" Doris demanded, wide-eyed. "What did they say?"

Bethan shook her head. "I'm still puzzled, Doris. It seems my husband left me some money. The agent is meeting me at his office in Oxford Street. Apparently, this only came to light now that Hambly's bank is being taken over by one of the big banks. It's very strange."

Ian told Bethan he was financially secure when he arranged their honeymoon, but she couldn't recall if he said *how* secure.

"He organised the trip to Italy," she told Doris, who was dying to hear all about it, "but I was distraught after he disappeared, and it didn't occur to me to cancel the arrangements. Could this be some kind of repayment?"

"Would they bother tracking you down for something like that?" Doris couldn't see anyone going to the trouble. "Did they tell you the amount?"

"No, only that it's 'a significant sum'."

"That doesn't sound like a refund on a holiday."

Doris had a point.

"No, it doesn't," Bethan agreed. "Ian didn't tell me how much he had in the bank, and to be truthful, I never asked. He wasn't very forthcoming about personal things, anyway."

That unmodern attitude earned Bethan a raised eyebrow from her friend, and she gave Doris a sideways grin. "I know, I know," she laughed. "I don't think like that. It was just the circumstances."

"You said you never asked him."

"It never occurred to me."

Doris laughed. "How very traditional of you."

Yes, Ian had that effect on her, but right now, she didn't know what to think.

"Gosh, Doris," she said. "I don't know whether to be shocked, excited or both!"

Bethan arrived promptly for her meeting. She announced herself to the receptionist, who directed her to an upstairs room to wait for the agent to arrive. She sat on an oversized chair with a slippery seat across the desk from where the agent would soon tell her news to her advantage. The room had the tangy smell of stale cigarette smoke and polish, and through the massive sash windows, Bethan could see the tops of the red London buses carrying shoppers down Oxford Street.

Mr Peters, the agent, arrived late with a profuse apology and a vague reference to London train schedules. He told her he currently represented a firm of solicitors acting for Hambly's Bank in Cardiff. He then offered another apology on behalf of the firm regarding their oversight in not discovering this matter earlier. It seemed the bank previously could not trace Mrs Noble and placed the file in the "too hard" basket. It only came to light when Hambly's was audited. He then proceeded to empty the contents of his briefcase onto the desk, changing his spectacles before finding the relevant file. When he did, he shuffled several sheets of paper into a neat pile.

Bethan waited for him to finish his ritual. If not for the buses and the room's musty smell, she was reminded of sitting in Matron's office a few years before, answering questions about her brief marriage. It was a daunting experience, designed to make a trainee nurse feel rather insignificant. Sitting here now, presenting herself to someone about to change her life, was much the same. She wondered if Mr Peters enjoyed prolonging the suspense, although there is only so much paper-pushing one can do, so she had no choice but to be patient until he completed his task.

At last, he peered at her over his spectacles, steepled his fingers, and told her what she came to hear. Despite his officialness and grandiose paper-shuffling, Mr Peters found delivering good news the most satisfying aspect of his work. Of course, he sometimes needed to organise a cup of tea for a stunned recipient. Today, Mrs Noble, who for the moment had lost her voice, was that beneficiary.

Bethan's mind was in turmoil. Ian had secrets, and she may have learned them had he not gone missing, but how could he have so much wealth and not tell her? Mr Peters presented her with a letter from the Cardiff branch of Hambly's bank, which confirmed the sum of money held, awaiting her instructions. There was also a handwritten apology from the bank manager, who advised the difficulty in locating her. Unable to focus, Bethan gave the documents a cursory glance, then pushed them back across the desk, where Mr Peters pushed them back again with the advice they were hers to keep.

Two cups of tea later, Bethan felt sufficiently recovered to accept direction to the bank currently absorbing Hambly's, to open an account. Tucking the signed documents into her bag, she somehow walked from the office without her knees buckling. She seldom needed to go into central London, and the way she felt, she was glad it was her day off because there was no way she could have concentrated. Above her, the sun shone, the sky was blue, and wherever he was, for all his inexplicable ways, Ian was looking out for her. It had been five years, and although she no longer cried herself to sleep, Bethan still loved and missed him. This money meant never wanting for a single thing in her life. She'd never felt rich, even after the council bought her house at a much-reduced sum when she was desperate to escape the village and the memories. Now, her future was assured, but she resolved not to squander the money as she made her way to Lyon's bakehouse for a chocolate éclair and yet another cup of tea. A treat for someone on a nurse's salary.

Doris burst through the door of the flat when she finished her shift, flopping down on her bed and propping herself on a pillow before uttering her first demand.

"Do tell!"

"Three hundred and seventy thousand pounds!" Bethan replied. She had repeated the sum to herself over and over since leaving the bank, but still couldn't say it without becoming breathless.

Doris sat up and pulled her pillow in front of her as if cuddling it would help Bethan's words sink in. A look of utter disbelief spread all over her face. It took a moment to reach her jaw, which, not unsurprisingly, dropped in shock.

"Say that again?" she gasped.

"Three hundred and seventy thousand pounds. Doris, I can't believe it!"

In danger of hyperventilating, Doris fanned herself with her cushion and marvelled at how Bethan could look so calm?

"Bethan, you're a millionaire! I can't believe Ian never told you he was rich."

"I don't even know if that's all he had," Bethan said, trying to recall Mr Peters' explanations. "It's just what he left me, and I'm hardly a millionaire." She grinned, still in an "it's not sunk in yet," mode. "He wore nice clothes, although he didn't have many, and his car was a bit of a wreck. As a joke, I once said that he must have found it dumped in a barnyard, and he didn't deny it. He paid when we went out, but I would never have considered him wealthy. The money isn't an inheritance. It's just a bank transfer made out to me."

"You can leave your job and go to Australia now."

That hadn't even occurred to Bethan.

"What?" she said. "That's nonsense. I love nursing. No, this money is wonderful, but it can stay in the bank, and when I get to Australia—it's only a few months now—I'll decide then. It's all too new and exciting and somehow…" Bethan suddenly didn't feel quite so thrilled. "Sad and final."

Doris patted the bed beside her, inviting Bethan to

come for a hug. Since they met, Bethan seldom spoke of her husband. A picture of them on their wedding day sat on the nightstand, but Doris supposed losing him the same week they married must be the worst kind of grief. Then to endure all the mystery surrounding his disappearance.

For Bethan, the layers of memories of those few weeks with Ian tempered her feelings about her new wealth. The money would set her up in Australia, perhaps even buy a house or a flat, but knowing it was there and that Ian wanted to be sure she was okay made her miss him even more. For him to set this up, it was almost as if he knew their time together would be short.

The final paperwork showing the transfer of Ian's money arrived within a week, and Bethan sat for a long while with the deed in her hands. The date of the transfer, two days before the wedding, and Ian's signature drew her gaze as she tried to remember how he got to Cardiff and back without her knowledge. He couldn't carry out a transaction like this over the telephone, and according to the paperwork, it did not involve the agent over at Llanfrydd as an intermediary. Besides, the deed had a Cardiff stamp beside the signatures, so Ian would have to be present. Except he didn't go to Cardiff that day. They spent the afternoon and evening together, and he couldn't make a round trip like that during the morning.

On impulse, Bethan opened her files, pulled out her marriage certificate, and laid the documents out on her bed. Ian's signature, just above hers on the marriage certificate, bore no resemblance to the signature on the documents.

A bewildered Bethan greeted Doris when she arrived

home.

"What is it?" Doris asked, glancing at all the papers strewn across the bed.

"I don't know, Doris. I'm a bit confused. Would you cast your eye over these?"

"Of course. What are we looking at?"

"Documents from the bank and my marriage certificate." Bethan held up the transfer deed. "This was witnessed at the bank in Cardiff, and it's dated two days before my wedding."

"I see that. Is it significant?"

"Yes. Ian didn't go to Cardiff that day. It would have taken him hours, even by train."

Doris agreed that was odd, and a bank wouldn't make a mistake with a date.

"What has your marriage certificate got to do with it?"

Bethan set the two documents side by side.

"The signatures don't match."

Doris picked up the papers and inspected each one. Sure enough, the signature on the marriage certificate was different.

"Does Ian have any other family you could ask?" she said. "Your marriage certificate says his father's name was Evan Noble and that he was an archaeologist. Perhaps you could find out where he is and ask him."

"I don't think Ian told him about me."

Doris remembered the story. "I know you said they were estranged, but you could track him down. Perhaps your friend Lincoln could help. He's a detective."

Bethan rolled her eyes, dismissing the suggestion.

"Yes, but he asks me out every time I see him." She looked again at the bank documents. "On all these, Ian's signature is identical. The only difference is on my marriage certificate. Doris, I know it sounds silly, but could these documents be forgeries?"

"Witnessed by the bank?"

"I told you it would sound silly, but what if this money isn't Ian's?"

Doris popped the kettle on their little gas burner. It was probably nothing.

"You're overthinking, Bethan," she said. "It's just the shock. I'm going to make a cup of tea. Want one?"

Why did people think tea was the answer to everything? Even so, Bethan said yes.

"The only way to find out is to ask Lincoln," Doris said. "It might cost you an evening out with a handsome—yes, I have noticed—pleasant man who is crazy about you. I'm sure you can make that sacrifice."

Bethan had to agree that someone like Lincoln might shed a little light on the predicament, so putting aside her earlier dismissal, she skipped the tea and instead walked down to his office at Scotland Yard.

"Is Detective-Sergeant Ablett available?" she asked the desk constable, but before he could buzz through, a door opened.

"Hello Bethan, I saw you pass the window. Of course, I have time for you." Lincoln escorted her into his office with a quick glance at his colleague. "It's okay, Constable."

For weeks, Bethan hadn't returned his calls or answered his notes. He was getting the message she wasn't interested, so this visit came as a surprise, although the file in her hand suggested this wasn't a social call.

It was true Bethan had been avoiding him. It was just that he was so persistent. Doris was right. Lincoln was handsome, tall, green-eyed, educated, and since they met a year before, he did not hide his interest, but Bethan believed that attraction needed to go both ways. Although Lincoln was pleasant, his attitude towards women belonged to the nineteenth century. He would jump at this chance to take the lead, and she needed the benefit of his expertise in this.

Also, Lincoln had one significant flaw. He wasn't Ian.

He pointed to the folder. "An official visit?"

Bethan nodded and handed him the file. "I hope you don't mind looking at these documents for me. I only found out a few days ago that my husband left me a tidy sum of money, but there's something not quite right."

Lincoln examined the marriage certificate, then the bank documents. He looked up.

"The signatures?"

Bethan nodded. Lincoln then asked how well she knew her husband's handwriting, but all she had were the notes Ian sent her and her memories of crossword puzzles. That was about it. Not much to go on.

"Well," Lincoln said, "There are four signatures, and the only one that differs is the one on your marriage certificate. Could your husband have changed it? People do that sometimes."

No, she told him, that didn't make sense. Why would he change it just for the wedding? She pointed to the transfer deed. "See this date? That was two days before we got married. Ian didn't go to Cardiff that day."

Lincoln studied each document again. He wasn't an expert in banking, but these looked in order.

"Is there a copy of a will?"

"No," Bethan said. "Besides, they wouldn't act on a will until they got a Presumption of Death certificate. It's been five years, so I still have two years before I can apply for one. According to Hambly's Bank, this is a simple transfer of funds."

Lincoln scratched his chin and clicked his pen a couple of times.

"The easiest way to sign over funds would have been for you and your husband to go to the bank together," he said. "He could have made you a signatory to the account or even opened a joint account. Lots of married couples do it. I didn't know him, so I don't know his motivation. It seems a complicated way to go about things."

Yes, Ian was complicated, more than she initially thought, but as she needed Lincoln's help, she admitted that she and Ian never discussed finances. Lincoln was a firm believer in men governing household accounts.

"I take no issue with that, Bethan," he said, a little too pompously for Bethan's liking. "Many men do not discuss financial affairs with their wives. However, Hambly's appear satisfied your husband is, was, the account holder. So the first question is, why did the transfer take five years? And second, is there other money in the account?"

"The bank had problems finding me because my other bank account is still in my maiden name," Bethan said. "I didn't think to change it, and most people don't know my married name, anyway."

"This clause here mentions your husband requested a delay in the transfer."

"What?" Bethan took the paper from him. "A delay? We were just married, planning a life together. Why would he arrange for a delay?"

Her brain scrambled about, trying to make sense of this new information. She hadn't read the documents at the bank, but they may not have known why Ian asked for a delay unless it was recorded somewhere else. Perhaps she didn't possess all the information.

"I didn't ask the right questions at the bank, Lincoln," she said. "I'm sorry, but I was speechless when they told me the amount."

He understood. "I'm not surprised. This is a fortune. The transfer was due to be made days after your wedding. Bethan, only you would know his reasoning. He may have planned to leave."

Lincoln's words stung, resurrecting a common opinion in Llanbleddynllwyd once word of the wedding and Ian's subsequent disappearance got around.

"That's just it, Lincoln. I don't know his reasoning. I spent the first few weeks after he disappeared convinced he was lying at the bottom of a mine." Bethan's mouth tightened. "I will never accept he left me. He wouldn't." Then she added a little self-consciously. "We were in love. I can't accept he planned his disappearance."

Lincoln knew no decent woman would accept her husband leaving without explanation. The documents added to the layers of questions around Ian Noble's disappearance, which he knew was investigated, albeit by a country copper. Now Bethan had sensibly turned to him with her concerns.

"Are you thinking this money did not belong to your husband?"

"Something like that," Bethan responded, wishing she didn't have to admit her suspicions. "Or these documents are fake. If I knew his family, I would speak to them, but I only know his father's name, Evan Noble. The registrar gave the marriage certificate to me on our wedding day, but I put it in Ian's shirt pocket. That's where I found it after he disappeared. It hurt to look at it, but now I feel like it's a piece in a jigsaw puzzle."

"Where was Ian born?"

"He wouldn't tell me, and I don't even know where he lived before Llanbleddynllwyd." She hesitated. "If they had found Ian's body, all this would be academic."

Lincoln disagreed. "Not really, Bethan," he said. "The money would have been the proceeds of a will, but this is a transfer made before your marriage, and he made it in your married name, which was strange considering the marriage had not yet taken place."

This Ian Noble was confident, supremely so, and Lincoln didn't trust him. There were no bones about it. He knew he was leaving, but Lincoln found it hard to believe the man suddenly developed a conscience about his plans and decided to make financial restitution.

"I'm sorry, Bethan, but I think your husband planned his disappearance, at least in the beginning. You once mentioned his accent. Did you ever see a passport?"

"No, he had one, I know that. He put my name on it when he arranged our honeymoon."

Lincoln knew some couples did that, less so now, with women claiming more independence. If Ian didn't have an English passport, the issuing country might have required a photo of the wife, but on enquiry, Bethan shook her head. No, she didn't need to provide a photo, so that narrowed it down a little. Lincoln would have to find out where Ian Noble's passport was issued.

Bethan felt like an absolute fool. Almost as soon as she accepted Ian's proposal, she handed over all the organising to him, and now she could see the secrets piling up. Ivy warned her, and she didn't listen. She vowed to be independent, but she willingly gave over all her control to her husband.

Lincoln put the documents back in the file. "Let's assume your marriage certificate bears Ian's authentic signature," he said. "I'm no writing expert, but with the others, I've never seen such exactness. Each of Ian's signatures is the same colour ink, which is fine because I would expect an educated man to have his own pen—" he dropped his own elegant pen onto the file, "—I can't even tell if it's a fountain pen or a biro, but it looks as though the bank witness used the same pen. Now, why would that happen?"

Bethan couldn't see his point. "Maybe they shared it?"

Lincoln smiled. "Unlikely, Bethan. A small bank would treat customers with this amount of wealth like royalty, and they are meticulous about etiquette. The bank manager would donate a pen if Ian had forgotten his, but he would not ask if he could borrow it back to witness the signature. It's just not how it's done. I'd like to check with one of our handwriting specialists."

Bethan had to quell her sense of panic, not just because of the reminder of Ian's secrecy, but because it might lead to something she wouldn't want to know about him, something shady in his past. She should just go home and forget it, maybe give the money to charity, seeing she didn't trust it. She'd managed on her salary so far, but if the money *was* Ian's, and he wanted her to have it, she would be rejecting his last gift to her. The indecision gave her a headache, and she closed her eyes, feeling her anxiety growing.

Lincoln placed his hand on her shoulder. "Don't worry. I'll get to the bottom of it."

But Bethan couldn't shake the feeling she'd opened a can of worms. "Is it possible to keep it between us for now? It'll probably be nothing."

Lincoln had a few suspicions, but that was his nature. However, he didn't want to worry her just yet.

"I know someone in East Ham who used to work for the police," he told her. "We keep in touch. He's thorough."

Bethan brightened. "Can I come with you? I would like to hear what he has to say."

Lincoln shook his head and held the door open for her. "Not today. He only needs to examine the signatures. When it's done, I'll contact you. Come on, I'll take you home."

CHAPTER TWENTY-SIX _

Four agonising days passed before Lincoln called to tell her he had a result. He protested when she insisted on going with him but gave in when he realised it would be an opportunity to spend time with her. When he arrived to collect her, he found her pacing the pavement outside her bedsit.

They met with the handwriting expert in a dingy café in East Ham. Lincoln didn't introduce the man to Bethan, not that she wanted to shake hands with him, because he looked and smelled like he needed a bath. The entire exercise felt underhand and seedy, but she supposed Lincoln knew best how to handle these types, although she couldn't imagine this man ever working for the police, at least not in any official capacity.

Of uncouth speech and demeanour, the man smoked endless cigarettes, lighting the next on the embers of the one before. He blew smoke out of his nostrils, and sometimes he opened his mouth to make smoky "O" shapes with utter disregard for Bethan's wrinkled nose and vain attempts to waft away the smoke with her hands. He laid the cigarette in the overfull ashtray only once, and that was to push an entire jam doughnut into his mouth before slurping tea to wash it down. Once he'd wiped the jam from his chin with his finger, he replaced the cigarette between his lips. Bethan found herself willing him to get on with whatever he had to report, but he refused to speak until he finished his sickening ritual.

Finally, the man set the file in front of him. "The examples on the bank documents," he said, tapping the folder. "Those ain't signatures."

Bethan leaned forward. "What do you mean?"

The man's leathery face creased as his mouth curved between a sneer and a smile.

"Well, little lady, what I mean is, to my expert examination, I found no pen pressure. Nor pen lifts. Whatever made these signatures did not use a writing implement because while I found a perfect likeness across each document, there was no ink bleed. Every signature on these documents is made by the same… I dunno, technique, process. I can't tell. It ain't possible to reproduce such precision in freehand, so it don't hold up to scrutiny. Only a machine could make such a precise duplication, but not any machine I know. That's my best guess." He gave a dismissive shrug. "Paper's authentic, though."

Bethan sat back. "You just said expert examination and guess in the same paragraph. So which is it, an expert summary or a guess?"

"I'm telling you what it ain't. Not what it is."

Lincoln agreed it was confusing. Frank never delivered

such ambiguous reports, so he placed his hand over Bethan's. Better let him deal with this.

"Could it be a forgery?" he asked.

The man closed one eye against the curling smoke from his cigarette.

"I can tell a falsification, detective," he sniffed. "That's why you brought it to me. This ain't a forgery. It's nothing. Not even as identifiable as the 'x' of an illiterate man. You're asking me to analyse the signature of this good lady's husband?" He glanced at them both, then removed the bank deed from the file and held it up. "Well, detective, I've analysed it. I can see it, but that ain't a signature."

"And the marriage certificate?"

"Real enough," he conceded, "but no similarities between it and the bank documents. Not the same hand—" He smirked as he put away the bank deed and offered the file to Lincoln. "Nor machine."

Then he lifted his cup in a hail Lincoln understood. He'd done his work and delivered his report, so the interview was at an end. When the waitress returned with more tea, the man pulled a tatty flask from his pocket and emptied its contents into the cup. Lincoln handed him a manila envelope, and the man grinned so widely, they were treated to a view of his nicotine-stained teeth.

As soon as they got outside, Bethan stopped Lincoln with a fierce whisper. "How can we trust that man? He looks like a reprobate, and he was *drunk*!"

"Bethan, wait." Lincoln sighed. He knew she would react like this. That's why he wasn't too keen on her accompanying him. "I've known him for a long time, and you wanted it kept between us, didn't you?"

Yes, her expression told him, *maybe, but for decency's sake…*

Lincoln raised an eyebrow in response. "Engaging an official handwriting analyst would presume I have something under inquiry and not just doing a favour for a friend."

"But Lincoln, you *paid* him. Surely I…"

"Please don't worry about that, Bethan. I realise Frank is an acquired taste, but he wasn't always like this. He went to Oxford."

"He did not!"

Lincoln laughed at her stunned surprise. "Yes, he did, but he dropped out. Later on, he joined the police as a document analyst but suffered brain damage during the war. His mental health plagues him, and he gets into the drink, but his analytical skills are matchless when he's sober. When he analysed those signatures, I promise you he would have had a clear head. A few of us use him when we don't want things on the books, and it helps him a bit with money."

Bethan couldn't believe her ears. "What about his accent? He sounded local. Not Oxford-educated."

"Frank's an Essex boy," Lincoln said. "Not so proper, anyway. The Eastenders would suspect someone with an educated accent, plus they wouldn't accept ex-police force. He's lived here since the war, so his accent is second nature now."

Bethan shook her head in disbelief. She'd learned something today. "Well, that's a lesson to never judge a book by its cover. Or their accent!" It occurred to her, briefly, just how close that was to home.

Lincoln grinned. One thing he adored about her was her lilting Welsh voice.

Back at the car, Bethan and Lincoln sat in silence. She accepted years ago that Ian never went to the mine or was involved with the local council, and she knew Constable Marley agreed with Dai Trevor that Ian had deserted her. Lincoln, however, didn't have the benefit of hindsight or experience with Ian's secretiveness, so he mulled over growing suspicions he knew for sure would set the cat among the pigeons. He waited for Bethan to speak, hoping she'd give him a lead-in.

"The mine manager told me about London reporters who went to the mines looking for a story," she said, dredging up all sorts of information she had largely forgotten and might be irrelevant, anyway. "They lied about their identity."

"Did any of them end up marrying a local girl?"

Not that Bethan knew of. "It seems like a rather extraordinary length to go to. And to what end? I'm no-one special."

Lincoln would have taken issue with her last point, but not right now.

"Ian must have had an agenda, Bethan. Did you ever catch him out in a lie?"

"Never!" she exclaimed, leaping to Ian's defence and regarding Lincoln in wide-eyed dismay. Then, she took a reality check. "Well, not a lie, more that I never caught him out in the truth. He seldom spoke about himself, and on the surface, he seemed quite a simple soul, someone who just wanted a quiet life, only…"

"Only what?"

"He didn't tell me about his past or his family. And he used to study me. Watch me." She laughed. "I know that sounds creepy, but he was so attentive. My friend, Ivy, called him mysterious, but later I found out she didn't trust him. To be honest, until all this happened, I didn't think he hid anything important from me. I just can't believe he had an agenda."

"And you had no idea what he was doing in Llanbladylalaland? Sorry, I can't say it."

"Neither could Ian. He said he was surveying."

"Surveying what?"

Another admission. "I don't even know that," she said. "Llanbleddynllwyd had been in existence since Roman times. After the war, the local council erected prefab housing across the valley for returning servicemen in anticipation of a housing project. It affected our village because we didn't have the infrastructure to handle an influx of families. They concentrated on creating industry, then started building houses again. I assumed it involved Ian because he used to say he was working on the other side of the valley. That was where the new estate was being built. They were also building shops and a swimming pool. It was an extensive project."

"So that would have been local government. Where did the mine come into it?"

Bethan thought back to her first conversation with Ian at the dance. After all these years, she realised she'd been the one making assumptions.

"He never said that he worked for the Coal Board, at least not directly. I made that assumption, and he, well, he just agreed."

"Did he keep surveying equipment in his car?"

Bethan didn't know. She had never checked.

"Okay," Lincoln said, reading her expression. "What kind of car did he drive?"

"An Austin A40."

"It's unlikely a car that size would carry all the equipment an independent surveyor would need," Lincoln said. "It would have to be an estate car or van."

A farmer had found the car abandoned in his field two weeks after Ian went missing, and Constable Marley told her they had to force the lock on the boot because of rust. They found only spiders' webs and chicken feathers inside, and upon checking the chassis number, they discovered it didn't belong to Ian but to a deceased farmer, so they didn't know how he came by it. She told Lincoln what she knew.

"It seems the Welsh police would agree with you because Ian didn't own that car," she said. "He knew a lot about rocks, geology, the sorts of things surveyors need to know."

Lincoln hadn't said so, but Bethan wondered if he was judging her. She looked out the window at the passing traffic and murmured, "You think I was foolish, don't you?"

"I don't think you were foolish, Bethan."

"Yes, you do, like my friends back home. I wasn't looking for a husband when I met Ian because I had my life mapped out. My friend thought there was too much mystery surrounding him, and perhaps I should have listened. He seemed sincere when he and I were together." She paused, not wanting to sully Ian's memory. "I know he cared for me."

"I have to say your husband was a man of many secrets."

Yes, Bethan agreed. Now more than ever.

"Look, Bethan," Lincoln said. "I know I agreed to keep this between us, but to be honest, I'm worried. Ian may have been an agent."

"What?" she laughed. "That's absurd. No!"

"You said he had a foreign accent."

"Is that all you have to go on? If it is, you would need to suspect half of London. Lincoln, if Ian was a spy, his accent wouldn't be so blatantly on display!" But now, she wasn't so certain. "Would it?"

"How do you know that was his real accent?" Lincoln said. "To be blunt, if he's not at the bottom of that mineshaft, where is he? Why did he leave? The two events are very coincidental. You told me that yourself. Add to that the differences with the signatures? And a stolen family sedan when he should drive something that would take all his gear?"

"Thank you for that litany of suspicion, Lincoln," Bethan snapped. "If he just wanted to go missing, he would need money and wouldn't have left everything he had to me."

"No?" Lincoln knew he'd upset her, so he tried to make her see his reasoning. "Bethan, he might have needed to divest himself of his finances. There might be other bank accounts with other funds, even other women he's left high and dry."

Bethan's head pounded. All she felt right now was anger. It was a mistake to allow Lincoln to bring all this drama!

"So, what are you suggesting, Lincoln? That Ian is a philanderer who is going around leaving his wealth to his endless streams of women! Shame on you!" It was laughable, considering she was the only woman Ian had ever kissed!

Lincoln had never seen Bethan's fierce side, and he raised his hands in defence.

"Okay, have it your way, but I will check to see if there are any other bank accounts in his name and any currently in use. I will also ask Interpol to check on passports."

It was becoming what Bethan feared, bigger than Ben Hur, and now she had started, Lincoln seemed determined to finish it. He didn't know Ian but now wanted to paint him as a criminal, a person of interest to the government. Bethan couldn't allow it.

"Ian was a good man. He kept some secrets, but not espionage. I'm sure of it."

Lincoln tried to feel sympathy, but Bethan once mentioned a rumour about sabotage at the mine. And it happened on the exact day Ian Noble—if that was his real name—went missing. A cover-up? A coincidence? No, there was more to it, but he didn't have time to explore now. He was already overdue at the station. Time to get Bethan home and himself back to work.

"Well, you might be convinced," he said as he started

the car. "I'm not sure I am, and from what I've heard today, I think it warrants further investigation. I'm sorry, Bethan."

He just caught Bethan's muttered, "*I wish I hadn't told you,*" as he joined the traffic. Having been in the police force for many years, Lincoln believed criminal activity came to light sooner or later. Be sure your sins will find you out, as his mother used to say. He still believed it, but now, Bethan had hunched herself as far to the side of the passenger seat as she could get, forging a barrier between them. He'd said enough for one day, and he also cursed himself that his professionalism got in the way of something he wanted. Bethan.

She went to jump out of the car when they arrived at her flat, but he stopped her.

"Do you know, Bethan?" he said, hoping she wasn't too angry with him. "Today is the longest I've spent with you since we met. The offer for dinner still stands."

Bethan didn't dare turn to look at him. Had she done so, he would have seen a face set in cold fury. The entire afternoon had been an emotional whirlwind, and he was asking her out to dinner? How could he understand what it felt like to be a presumptive widow after only two days of marriage? Then to find out your husband was not what he appeared to be and now suspected of being a traitor? She didn't know whether to cry or slap Lincoln for his insensitivity. Instead, she slammed the car door and stalked up the steps to her flat.

Lincoln watched her. At least she didn't say no. It would have to do. Bethan always found a reason to put him off, but time was running out. He might end up following her to Australia.

CHAPTER TWENTY-SEVEN

"Hello Doris, that looks dull."

Bethan kicked off her shoes and threw herself down on the bed to wonder what Doris found so engaging in the pages of a telephone directory.

"I'm doing it for a reason, Bethan," Doris said, not looking up. "Evan Noble was an archaeologist, right? Look." She shoved the book under Bethan's nose and tapped on an entry. "There's an archaeological institute only a short walk from the hospital. You should go after work tomorrow to see if anyone is listed."

"He'd have to be a member, or at least known to them."

Doris nodded. "It's an elite profession, so I expect he was registered somewhere. What did the handwriting expert turn up?"

After such an emotional day, Bethan didn't feel like talking, but Doris was unlikely to stop asking until she did.

"Put the kettle on," she sighed. "I'll get some aspirin, then we'll talk."

Doris listened to the account of the handwriting expert's deductions and the parting conversation with Lincoln. Doris's face took on a thoughtful expression throughout, and it remained even after Bethan offered up every detail.

"I hate to say it, Beth," she said, "but I'm starting to not trust your husband."

The vacuum in Bethan's brain that started earlier was on the verge of splitting her head wide open. Aspirin wasn't cutting it, and she needed to flush out all these thoughts, lie down in the quiet and sleep. Doris, however, was having none of that. She waited for Bethan to convince her Ian was to be trusted. Unfortunately, no reassurance was forthcoming. Instead, Bethan made it worse by telling her Lincoln didn't trust Ian either.

"I don't believe Ian was involved in anything shady," she said. "And he knew so much about geology. He couldn't have made it up."

"Are you sure?" Doris asked. "What do you know about it?"

Bethan hadn't considered that. "Nothing," she confessed. "Ian was good at making up stories to make me laugh, so I would never have known. I was told reporters from the London papers sometimes lied to get mine access, but our village was not that important. I don't know why anyone would trouble themselves, but the pit manager assured me it went on in the past, so perhaps Ian *was* glibber than I thought. In one of my letters to the coal board after he disappeared, I asked if the mine manager ever mentioned any reporters. The phone at the pit was out of commission for weeks, so no one could check it."

Doris remained sceptical. "Perhaps Ian sabotaged it so they couldn't."

Bethan just didn't understand why people were so quick to see Ian as a villain. She shook her head. "You sound like Lincoln. One man involved in the pit collapse said the lads thought the cave-in was sabotage."

"Was it?"

"An Act of God was the informal conclusion. Anyway, Lincoln now wonders if Ian was working for a foreign government."

Doris's eyes grew to the size of saucers. "A spy!? How exciting!"

Instantly, she regretted her burst of enthusiasm when Bethan's slow blink told her it was not only not exciting but also unnerving.

"Sorry, love," Doris said, dialling down her delight. "I read too many Ian Fleming novels."

The day had drained Bethan. Too tired to fire up again in Ian's defence, she let the words come out without giving them too much thought.

"Well, there's Ian's accent, Doris, and the Cold War…"

Bethan stopped mid-sentence. What was happening? Why should that be grounds for suspicion? Was she giving in to the doubters? She refused to believe what all the signs were edging towards. "I only remember his gentleness, Doris," she said, "and he was so funny…."

Doris waited for her to say more, but her eyes had taken on a faraway look, lost in memories. She prided herself on her patience and would wait for Bethan to open up again. She didn't have to wait long.

"Ian was clumsy in the way he asked questions and hopeless in social situations," Bethan said after a moment. "He was interested in what happened elsewhere in the world, and we had many long discussions, always with me taking the lead, so I assumed he knew nothing of current affairs. Then, of course, I realised someone with his education should have known more, but our conversations were so lively, I was never suspicious of him." She laughed, an out-of-place laugh in a serious conversation, but Bethan knew Doris would never believe this part. "I was the first woman he ever kissed. Let me tell you, it was obvious! He didn't fake that! A spy would be more confident, more self-assured. I would have known if he was leading a double life."

None of this convinced Doris. "Don't spies have to be good actors? I mean, it would be essential for a role like that. You told me you met only a matter of weeks before you married. It's not much time to get to know someone."

"I know," Bethan agreed as she lay back against her pillows. "I felt at home with him. It was as if we'd known each other all our lives."

"I've had that experience. Let me tell you, it fades."

Bethan closed her eyes, hoping that Doris would leave her alone now and let her drift off and get rid of her headache. Something was not right here, and it needed investigation, but Lincoln's appraisal of the situation had to be wrong. No matter what, she could not reconcile herself to Ian sabotaging the mine or exposing people to danger.

Why would he? And why would he engage in something so criminal as espionage, in Llanbleddynllwyd of all places?

Now Bethan had to face the prospect of Lincoln's investigations. If they found Ian alive, it would mean he *had* deserted her and prove to all those people who thought badly of him that they were right.

The minute Bethan got off duty the following afternoon, she headed straight to the archaeological institute without even bothering to go home and change first. The institute's secretary was obliging but not very helpful because Bethan could not tell her where Evan Noble had worked. Several individuals called Noble had registered in the last century, but none with that Christian name. One retired archaeologist was Ewen Noble, living in Bethnal Green. The secretary believed him worth a visit, suggesting he might be a relative or perhaps a misspelling of the name. It was a long shot, but Bethan found herself increasingly desperate for answers.

Mr Noble's housekeeper gave Bethan a chilly welcome and advised her the "old man" didn't need a nurse and that she was perfectly capable of caring for him. Bethan assured her she was not there in an official capacity but that the archaeological society had given her the address. The housekeeper grudgingly admitted Bethan and made her wait a full ten minutes before announcing her to the "old man".

Bethan was unprepared for his welcome. He took her hands and drew her to a chair near the window, his eyes bright with unshed tears as he told her he hadn't had a visitor in years.

"I thought you were a nurse come to give me an injection," he said, his false teeth chattering up and down against his gums as he spoke.

Bethan extricated her hands from his. He looked in his nineties and smelled of urine and neglect. "I am a nurse at the Alice Maud, and I came here straight from work. The archaeological institute suggested I visit because I seek information about Evan Noble. It's not a common surname, and your name, Ewen, is very similar."

The old man tapped the back of his hand against his mouth, creating a sucking sound. His face puckered in thought. Then he closed his eyes and sank down in his chair. After a few minutes, Bethan thought he'd fallen asleep, but just as she considered giving him a nudge, he sat up, wide awake.

"Hmm. Evan Noble, you say? Well, he's not related to me, although most of my relatives are dead, and I don't recall any archaeologists among them. I'm sure I've heard that name before. Do you know any of the sites where he worked?"

"I'm afraid I don't," Bethan said. "I only have a name, and the receptionist suggested it might be you because of the similarities in your Christian names."

The old man's eyelids fluttered as he mulled over the information. "Hmm. Evan Noble. Evan Noble. Evan Noble," he chanted before huffing out his breath. He shook his head. "I've heard that name, Sister. I just can't remember where."

Bethan had a suggestion. "Perhaps if you tell me where you worked, I might remember something my husband told me. I was married to Evan Noble's late son." She wondered at the chances of two archaeologists with the same name working in proximity or even meeting by chance, but if he'd heard the name before, it was worth waiting for him to remember.

"I'm very sorry to hear of your loss, Sister," Mr Noble said. "It is a tragedy to lose someone dear. As for me, I researched the Romans around Lincolnshire and made it to the continent a few times in later years when I worked for the British Museum. When do you think this Evan Noble was born? Were he and I of like age?"

"I'm afraid I know nothing at all. His son would have been early thirties now, so at a guess, his father might be fifty-five or even sixty-five."

"That young? Well, he'd still be in the field." He chuckled. "We archaeologists spend so much time amongst relics that we don't notice when we become one ourselves. I'll give you a few names that might give you some leads."

The man scribbled in a notebook, then tearing off the sheet, he folded it and handed it to Bethan.

"These fellows may help."

Bethan smiled. "Thank you, Mr Noble. I've taken up enough of your time."

"No problem at all, Sister. It's been a pleasure. I hope you'll come back. It gets very lonely here."

As Bethan turned to leave, he suddenly lifted his hands to his wispy-haired head.

"Wait, wait. I know!"

Relief flooded Bethan as the man's expression went from faded recollection to realisation. At last!

His face lit up with boyish glee as he pointed to himself.

"Noble! That's *my* name!"

Then it was over. His face eased into confusion, and his eyes narrowed in mistrust as he jabbed a gnarled finger at Bethan.

"You got my first name wrong! Have you come to give me an injection?"

Bethan unfolded the piece of paper. It contained nothing more than the scribblings of a man who no longer had his mind. She thanked him and left, not even glancing behind as the housekeeper slammed the door. How stupid of her to think she would find answers here.

A light drizzle fell, so she debated between hailing a taxi or waiting for a bus. No one would notice her tears of disappointment in the rain, so she wrapped her cape around her and managed a couple of miles before she couldn't take another step and stopped a black cab.

After her experience with the archaeological society, Lincoln suggested trying the birth records at Somerset House to see if she could find a record of Ian's birth. She told Lincoln she doubted Ian was of British parentage and wouldn't find anything, but Lincoln thought it was worth trying because of his English-sounding name.

The registrar entered Ian as "full age" on the marriage certificate. Ian told Bethan he was twenty-seven, but that could have been a lie because she remembered speculating about his age when she first met him. It was all she had to go on, so he would be around thirty-two or thirty-three now.

He only ever said his birthday was in March.

She searched the relevant indexes but found no matches, then tried the years before and after, then either side of those. The assistant denied her request to check adoption registries, and after hours of fruitless searching, Bethan gave up. She deliberated about stopping by the police station to update Lincoln and see what he turned up about Ian's passport, but she could not face him and his suspicions. Not with her brain fried by the births, deaths, and marriages indexes. A bowl of soup and a rest beckoned, and by the time she got off the bus, weariness had driven all other thoughts from her head. So, when she spied Lincoln waiting on her doorstep, her cherished plans of a quiet lunch evaporated. Her instinct was to tell him to go away, but that would be rude, especially after slamming the car door the other day, so she forced a smile and invited him in.

"What transpired at Somerset House?" he asked, perching on the end of Doris's bed. There was something inappropriate about being in a woman's bedroom, even if it was also the sitting room.

"It was a waste of time," Bethan declared, not trying to hide I-told-you-so from her voice and showing her irritation that he turned up unannounced, even if he was helping her. "Ian's accent must mean he was born overseas."

"I don't understand how you can marry someone and not know where they were born."

Bethan gave him a scalding look.

"Is that a criticism?"

Lincoln allowed himself an inward groan. He kept putting his foot in it.

"No, sorry. Look, Bethan, you know everything about me, and we're not even courting. You wouldn't need to check up on anything, yet the man you married—and I presume you trusted him before—appears to have no history. I heard from Interpol. Ian Noble did not have a passport, not from any country, so he must have given you a fictitious name."

"Then he gave the bank a fictitious name," Bethan said drily. "If he falsified identification to get an account, don't you think the bank would have been suspicious? I don't believe it."

"Falsifying documents isn't difficult for foreign government agents, Bethan."

Of course, she knew that. She sat down on her bed and sighed, wishing all this would just go away. Let things go back to how they were before Ian's money.

"He didn't have fancy gadgets like spies have in the movies, Lincoln," she said, helpless to find an explanation for this turn of events. "His car was barely roadworthy, and he didn't even wear a watch."

Wearing his detective hat, Lincoln hadn't turned up on spec. He was here for a reason, and not just to see Bethan. There was another stone he wouldn't leave unturned. "I was hoping Ian had a watch," he said. "Do you have anything else? Something that might have his fingerprints?"

Bethan only had a pair of cufflinks she gave Ian as a wedding present. He'd put them away when they got home that night, and she hadn't touched them since. She opened a drawer and handed the box to Lincoln.

"I polished them before I gave them to him," she said,

"so I rubbed off any prints from the jeweller."

Lincoln opened the box. These would be perfect.

"Can I take them?"

Bethan nodded.

"Thanks. Now, about Ian's accent. Could he have been American? Or Russian?"

She just didn't know. "I'm not sure. He couldn't pronounce anything in Welsh, and even since coming to London, with all its overseas visitors, I haven't heard an accent like Ian's. I think he was European."

"It's fine. The FBI has a database. If our forensic team can get a fingerprint, we can cross-reference. They're very accommodating." His voice became cautionary. "Bethan, the enquiry is about to become official."

In other words, Lincoln was taking it out of her hands. Had Ian not left her the money, she would have continued with her life and not come under scrutiny. If Lincoln was wrong, it would show that Ian, in his own clumsy way, was only trying to be mindful of his wife's future welfare. But, if Lincoln was right, part of her, a huge part, didn't want to know.

"What about me?" she asked. "Am I under suspicion?"

"No," Lincoln assured her. "Ian may have just been a con man, and you one of his victims. The bank considers the transfer to you legitimate, so my hands are tied there until we get an official report on those signatures. And we only have your say-so that he had a passport."

"Can you tell me the basis of the investigation? Do you still think he's a spy?"

"I need to take the documents and have them analysed

by one of our team at the Yard, Bethan, to get an official opinion on the signatures. If it concurs with Frank's conclusions, the bank will consider a charge of fraud, but we don't know Ian's true identity. There is also the question of theft of a motor car and creating a false persona with intent to deceive. The latter alone points to him being a foreign agent."

Bethan's shoulders slumped. If Ian wasn't who he said he was, perhaps it was best she hadn't changed her name. Lincoln understood this news was unwelcome, but there was no easy way to spare her from what was coming. Her husband was not who he appeared.

"Bethan," he said. "Your marriage is valid, even though Ian falsified his information. When this is over, you can get it annulled."

Stunned, Bethan slapped her hand down hard on her bedside table, making Lincoln jump.

"I don't want my marriage annulled! How could you even suggest it?"

Lincoln seemed to make a habit of overstepping his bounds, but he had a job to do.

"I think you were part of the subterfuge, Bethan. I'm sorry."

He stood, knowing he had outstayed his welcome, but he hated to leave her like this, grey eyes flashing and that beautiful mouth set in a ferocious line. Also, judging by her frantic searching around the room, she might just be looking for something to throw at him.

At that moment, Doris walked in with a bright smile, her cheeriness causing her to miss the bristling atmosphere.

"Hello, Lincoln," she said. "Are you and Bethan going somewhere nice?"

"A late lunch, Doris." Lincoln's quick response backed Bethan into a corner. "I suggested a drive as well."

"How lovely! Lucky things. It's a perfect day. Have fun, Beth!"

Doris stood grinning at the two of them, so Bethan grabbed her document file and tossed it at Lincoln, who caught it with a sheepish grin at Doris. Bethan then snatched her jacket from the bed and followed Lincoln out to the car. She was so furious, they were outside the city centre before she said a word.

"You've got a nerve," she snapped. "You deliver a list of suspicions against my husband, and then you toss in, 'but it's okay, Bethan because you can get your marriage annulled!' "

"I didn't mean…"

"Yes, you did! Ian was real to me. My marriage was real, and I don't need you to tear it down."

"I wasn't tearing…"

"Yes, you were. You're fixed on Ian being guilty of a crime. Any crime."

"He stole a…"

"Yes, I know he stole a car. I know he lied when we got married, but Ian Noble was only his name, not who he was." Bethan folded her arms. "You don't know anything about him."

"It seems like no-one did." And after delivering that line, Lincoln wisely shut up.

Bethan looked out the window. Going for a drive was

a bad idea. She wasn't hungry anymore and she didn't want to be part of this investigation. She was fuming at Lincoln and wished herself anywhere but here. What was the name of that planet Ian told her she lived on? The one with the fireflies. Chabin, yes, that was it. If only it were true.

By the time they arrived at a café with river views, Bethan's temper had levelled out, and she allowed Lincoln to ask her a few questions about Ian. He took care to show respect for her feelings and not treat her as though she was just any witness in any investigation. He'd waited for a year to get her to spend time with him, and although this wasn't his idea of courtship, it might lead to something down the track.

And for Bethan, allowing herself to answer Lincoln's questions highlighted the inconsistencies in Ian's story. He came to her house most evenings after work, but he never looked as if he'd been traipsing through muddy fields, even when the rain had been bucketing down all day. His hands and fingernails were never dirty. He never got sweaty or grubby, and he always wore his worsted coat and homburg hat. Apart from geology, their major topics of conversation were astronomy, current politics, and society because he claimed he liked to know about changing events. They never seemed to run out of things to discuss, and Ian could talk for hours about the life of a rock or the origins of the universe. But did any of this mean he had an agenda? Or, as she once thought, seeking an escape from some tragedy in his life? Maybe she should suggest that to Lincoln, who gave it a moment's thought.

"Perhaps he was a bigamist," he said, the ungracious

response earning him a fierce glare from Bethan.

"*Or* he concealed his real name because he was running from an unhappy relationship. Have you thought of that?"

He hadn't, and he was again straying into sensitive territory. He just couldn't see another way around it.

Bethan huffed, her angst returning. "I don't know why I bother trying to convince you!"

"I'm sorry, Bethan," Lincoln said, hoping she would see reason. "I don't mean to keep putting my foot in it. There could be myriad explanations, but I doubt any of them are legal. Think about it. If you didn't want to be found, where better to hide out than in an obscure village? I might have gone along with your idea of fleeing a tragedy if it wasn't for his disappearance, the money, the passport, and the signatures."

"Well, the money's going to charity," Bethan declared. "I want no part of it."

Except Lincoln would not support that decision. "If Ian's fingerprints come up on the FBI database, they will freeze that money. You won't be able to access it, and this might prevent you from going to Australia."

Bethan looked at him in disbelief. "You said I wasn't under suspicion."

"You're not under suspicion, Bethan, but the money might be. If Ian was working for a foreign government, and that's not official, not yet, then MI5 will want to hear about it as a matter of national security. Right now, he's at the level of a fraudster, and you are one of his victims, but once I get the fingerprints back from America and the document report, that might change. Meanwhile, I'm reviewing a few other avenues."

"What avenues?"

"The usual; aliases, bank accounts, that kind of thing."

"I would have sensed *something*," Bethan said again. "He was a fish out of water in company, but I put that down to him being a quiet type."

"All part of the act," Lincoln said with grating authority. "His existence was an enigma, even you have to admit that."

She wasn't going to admit it, even though she agreed. "Giving me this money draws attention to him," she said. "Why would he do that?"

Lincoln didn't know why. Perhaps it was all part of the subterfuge. "The life of an agent comprises secret agendas and lies, Bethan. They don't care …"

He was about to say they didn't care about the people they hurt, but Bethan bowed her head. She didn't want to hear anymore, so time to change tack. Time to make soothing noises.

"Whatever else Ian was," he said, softening his tone. "I'm sure his feelings for you were genuine."

He didn't realise how hollow and insincere his words sounded. Neither did he see Bethan's stony expression when she heard them.

*CHAPTER TWENTY-EIGHT_*

Bethan was relieved to find the flat empty when they got back. She didn't think she could face going over the day's events and contend with Doris's glee at her having lunch with Lincoln. Then there would be a demand for information about her visit to Somerset House. Doris was a wonderful person and an amazing friend, but she loved drama! And the sad part was that neither Doris nor Lincoln saw how much Bethan was hurting.

Bethan ran a bath and wandered back out into the bedsit to collect her nightclothes. A good book and relaxing on the bed in her pyjamas sounded like an excellent strategy for the rest of the evening, but as she walked over to her bed, she kicked a large piece of folded paper. Her marriage certificate. It must have fallen out when she tossed her document folder to Lincoln earlier, and Doris didn't notice it after they left. Bethan groaned because she knew Lincoln would use this as an excuse to call back as soon as he realised it was missing. He was only trying to help. It was just…

Bethan sighed. She didn't want to think about Lincoln. She planned to toss the certificate into the drawer for when he came to collect it, but something made her hesitate. Could she have missed some tiny detail? It wouldn't hurt to check again. So, despite having studied the certificate many times over the past few days, she reread it from one side to the other, allowing her gaze to linger on the details of the two fathers.

Husband's father: Evan Noble. Rank or Profession: Archaeologist.

Wife's father: David Davies. Rank or Profession: Miner. Deceased.

The last attempt to find Evan Noble hadn't turned out so well, but Bethan supposed that in nineteen fifty-six, he must have been alive and well somewhere; otherwise, Ian would have told the registrar he was dead. Of course, that was assuming the name wasn't just something Ian plucked out of the air.

She folded the document and placed it in the drawer on her nightstand. Ian looked out at her from the picture she kept there, the one Mike took on their wedding day and had framed. He'd been reluctant to give it to her after Ian's disappearance, but Ivy convinced him. Bethan was glad. It was one of the few things she had to prove to others he once existed.

So many sad memories came after that day, but this photo always made her smile. What on earth possessed her to wear sunshine yellow? It was so bright, but she liked it at the time and planned to wear the dress and jacket ensemble when they went to Italy on their honeymoon. Ian told her the hat looked beautiful against her dark hair, and he complimented her on every little thing she did that day. Even at the modest reception Ivy organised, he took every opportunity to catch her eye, smile at her, touch her hand, and brush against her shoulder, not even minding that Ivy and Mike were present. He had never been so public with his affection before, and when they were finally alone, their passion for each other opened like a floodgate.

Bethan picked up the frame and ran a finger over the photo, delicately tracing Ian's outline. He looked so dashing, so handsome, smiling at the camera. They were both so happy that day, and no matter how she looked at it, Ian did not behave like a man plotting to abandon his wife nor leave her a fortune at some random time in the future.

She slept little that night. Unable to still her thoughts, every likely scenario to explain Ian's disappearance ran through her mind. It wasn't the first time she did this, but now it felt like she must have missed something of importance, some tiny detail that would explain everything. When her chaotic thoughts allowed her respite, she dreamt of the burning mountain and the tiny baby in her arms. The pain in her feet caused her to cry out as she ran, the stark images unfolding as they always did, ending after her audience with the prefect and the vision of a dark sky and tall ships in the bay.

Tonight though, the dream lacked one crucial element. Her charm. Even though Ivy and Mike helped her clear the house, she never found it. The three of them searched the bedroom inch by inch, but it turned out that on the day she lost her husband, Bethan also lost her cherished bead.

The thought stayed with her when she woke the following morning. She was due at the hospital at eight, so there was no hurry, but as always, the dream of Pompeii left a vivid impression. She hadn't had the dream in years, not since before her wedding, and didn't understand how no longer possessing the charm in her waking life could have manifested. How can dreams know what happens when we are awake? Bethan felt foolish for even entertaining the idea, but it was just that the dream never varied before, and she either carried or wore the charm. Last night, although all other features remained the same, she was aware it was missing.

The first time she showed him, Ian admired the bead as a pretty piece of jewellery. He later remarked on its uniqueness, so perhaps finding the chain broken on the floor only hours after he said goodbye might not be a coincidence. Could Lincoln be right? Could Ian have planned to leave? Perhaps he took the charm as a memento, although she couldn't imagine why, not if he was so callous. And why not the chain as well?

It didn't occur to her before now that Ian might have the charm. Even after she searched for it amidst the dust under the bed with Mike and Ivy, no-one thought Ian might have taken it. She didn't even report the missing trinket to Constable Marley because a link between the two hadn't entered her mind. In hindsight, perhaps it should have. She didn't know the charm's age or history, so it could be the sole reason Ian Noble turned up in the village from nowhere. The chain was long enough for the elegant filigree bead to nestle inside her bra, so it was never on display.

Even Ivy had never noticed.

Did Ian have prior knowledge of the charm? Perhaps Mam or Dad, the only other two people who knew she wore it, mentioned it to someone while they were alive, and the story got back to some foreign museum or government. Could someone high up believe it to be valuable? And how would they get it? Send the utterly charming Ian Noble to wheedle his way into her dull, unsuspecting life and snatch it from her while she slept. That's how.

If the charm had something to do with Pompeii, then it would explain Ian's fascination with the Pompeii dream and his insistence they go there on their honeymoon.

Bethan caught herself staring out the window, lost in analytical and condemning thoughts. She shook her head. What on earth was she doing? If Ian didn't have her to defend his memory, he had no-one. He could be innocent of any wrongdoing, and she hoped she was just reacting to all the suspicious talk about him. Still, if she could find out more about the charm, about Ian's link to Pompeii, she might get answers that would prove or disprove all the theories, and she wanted that more than anything.

Lincoln told her to tell him if she recalled any minor details. So, heading out to the hallway payphone with a handful of change, she lifted the receiver, prepared with the charm story and her dreams. She stood for a full minute before replacing the receiver in its cradle. None of this proved Ian was a foreign agent or any type of criminal. Earlier, she had been remembering their wedding and Ian's happiness. He seemed to have not a care in the world. That part, at least, was not a pretence because no-one was that good an actor. And whatever else came of this, abandoning her was not part of the plan.

Convinced now of Ian's link to the charm, Bethan wondered if he was simply trying to return it to its rightful owners. But then, why not just ask? Why not confide in her? Not that she was sure she would have given it up, but if he had a good reason, then who knows? She didn't believe he married her just to take it from her, and if he was involved in something criminal, he might have disappeared to protect her.

If she were to tell Lincoln all this, which might be nonsense anyway, he might see it as giving weight to the argument. It would take his investigation in a whole new direction and implicate her because she had the charm for a long time. She couldn't explain how it came into her possession, her only clue being she caught it in the Pompeii dream, and that would be too vague to satisfy an official enquiry.

It was time to make her own decisions. Bethan went back to her room and picked up her wedding photo. Ian smiled out at her. She longed to hold him again, tuck herself under his arm in that old double bed of hers that was too short for him, and ask him why he vanished into thin air. All she had to hold onto were memories. Memories and questions.

I never stopped loving you, she whispered. *But please understand, I have to know the truth. I have to find you.*

Bethan only had a five-hour shift to get through, then she would get the bus to Oxford Street to the only travel agent she knew of. Booking a flight to Italy was a long shot, but she had no other channels that might give her a lead.

The hardest part was sitting in Matron's office to ask for immediate leave, citing personal reasons. As expected, she got quizzed, but Bethan managed to not give her full reasons, saying only her urgent attention was required concerning her late husband's will.

Bethan contributed much of her spare time to organising hospital volunteers, so Matron felt she could be generous and grant one of her best nurses a few days, with the expectation she would be back on the wards in a week. She also reminded Bethan why they did not accept married women as students. It complicates things, Matron said, alluding to Bethan's current predicament. That was for sure. Bethan had difficulty convincing Matron all those years ago they should reinstate her. She certainly didn't need reminding.

On Sunday morning, Bethan left a note for Doris to say she needed time to think, then took the train and a taxi to London Airport. She had another message delivered to Lincoln to say she would be back before Saturday. It read:

Dear Lincoln. I know you believe Ian was involved in some kind of underhand activity, and these past few days, you have presented some pretty powerful arguments. You almost convinced me—almost. But, Lincoln, you didn't know him, and if the situation were reversed, he would move heaven and earth to prove my innocence. So I need to follow my instincts because I believe now, thanks to you, Ian is not dead and that he took an assumed name for reasons I aim to find out. I'll contact you in a few days. Bethan.

Lincoln read the note in dismay. Late on Saturday

night, he received irrefutable proof that Ian Noble, as Bethan knew him, did not exist. Not anywhere on the planet. Ian Noble was a phantom.

Bethan's room at the hotel in Naples overlooked the bay, and the moment she saw it, fragments of her dream surfaced. The bay looked peaceful, with little yachts bobbing about on the blue water, quite unlike the ash-laden and devastating aftermath of a volcanic eruption. Across the bay, Vesuvius lay sleeping in the summer haze.

Before dinner, Bethan visited the concierge to ask about tours of Pompeii. He suggested a local guide, as access to the ruins was restricted to specific days, and only certain guides were allowed. She liked that idea. A local tour guide would have substantial knowledge, and if she was the only one, she could ask questions. She thanked the concierge and went to the dining room to sample Italian cuisine for the first time.

As luck would have it, when the guide arrived the following day, he turned out to have more than just local knowledge. An Englishman who now lived in Naples with his Italian wife, Alfred was a former archaeologist who had worked at the Pompeii site until injury forced him to give up archaeological digs. He then turned to writing thriller novels with modest success, but not enough to retire altogether. Still, his credentials allowed him into sections of Pompeii not open to tourists, which was precisely what Bethan needed if she could get him on side.

The tour was fascinating, with her guide equally fascinated because his client appeared to know her way around. She even moved ahead of him as he described some architecture or artefact.

"Have you been here before?" he asked after she strayed yet again to settle in front of a ruin. "You seem familiar with this place."

Bethan apologised. "I didn't mean to wander off. This will sound strange, but I know this ruin."

"Do you?" Alfred glanced at the pile of rubble. "What do you know about it?"

"Master Tullius, a merchant, lived here."

As far as Alfred's knowledge went, they had not yet identified this ruin. They didn't find mummified remains here, but with the amount of damage the building suffered, that didn't surprise him. Either way, despite Mrs Noble being an intelligent woman, she wouldn't have this information unless she was an archaeologist herself, and she told him she was a nurse.

Bethan took a few steps forward. There was little of the atrium left now, but she recalled so many details. A fountain stood in the centre. The mosaics on the floor, not yet having succumbed to the burning ash, had at first provided cooling balm to her blistered feet. The panic-stricken father who begged her in his fear and desperation that she should save his child had emerged from a doorway across the atrium. A doorway long crumbled into ruin. She told Alfred what she remembered of the architecture but did not mention the baby in case he thought her deluded.

Alfred had spent twenty years studying the ruins and twenty years since his injury, reading every book written about them. He found Bethan's description of the atrium's layout detailed and intriguing, but she could have been describing almost any atrium in Pompeii. She spoke of an elegant shrine in this ruin that sounded like Lararia. They found these tributes to the gods in most atriums, and Alfred informed her that fountains were also a commonplace aspect of plumbing. Bethan pointed out the different areas, making grand, sweeping movements of her arms as if she were about to suggest some serious interior decorating.

To Alfred, the strangest of all was Mrs Noble's lucid narrative, communicated in the first person. As interesting as it was, he wondered why she set her story from the perspective of a child experiencing a volcanic eruption. When he questioned her on her comments about falling ash, she identified the AD79 eruption, but it seemed to have progressed at a speed greater than history recorded. When she finished what seemed like a somewhat whimsical piece of fiction with elements of fact thrown in, Alfred didn't know what to say. It sounded like something someone would put in a novel, but Bethan took his silence for disbelief.

"I didn't make it up," she said defensively because she recognised even as she spoke, it was a fantastic claim on its own. It was clear she sounded fanciful, but it didn't matter if he believed her or not. Seeing this place in real life was no different to how she had seen it so many times before. Even though it was now a ruin, she recognised the buildings, the streets, the pillars, even the low wall where she grazed her knees.

"Are there any records or transcripts from around this time?" she asked. "Master Tullius had a cousin in the

Roman navy."

The Roman fleets were not his area of expertise, and Alfred could only think of one person with that name attached to Pompeii. It seemed Mrs Noble was a mite confused, but he might be able to clear up the mystery.

"I believe you refer to Marcus Tullius, who built a temple here in Pompeii. He died before Vesuvius erupted."

"No," Bethan insisted. "This Master Tullius lived here at the time of the eruption. He might have been a relative."

If it wasn't a matter of record, Bethan didn't care. Her dream was accurate, right down to the finest detail, and she would love to have the time to find out how and why. But for now, that research had to be put on hold while she investigated the more pressing mystery surrounding Ian. After all, that was why she was here, and she only had a few days.

She handed Alfred a sketch of her teardrop charm. The squiggly filigree detail hadn't turned out quite right, but she spent a good hour reproducing it as well as she could.

"Have you ever seen an artefact like this?"

Alfred examined the drawing and shook his head. "Never. It doesn't look Roman. Or Greek. So not something I would expect to find here. Do you have any background?"

"No," Bethan said. She might as well come clean. "I have very vivid dreams, Alfred. The most vivid is of this house and of these streets. I know it is unbelievable, but I can only tell it like it is. In all the dreams, I hold this object." She pointed to her drawing. "It's made of metal, and in real life, I wore it on a chain around my neck. It went missing the day my husband disappeared."

Alfred was far too polite to make assumptions about the absence of the lady's husband. Few women travelled here alone, but Mrs Noble appeared to be on a mission. He chose the brief response.

"I see. May I inquire where you obtained it?"

Bethan pulled a face. "I don't know that either. I caught it down by the Sarnus, as if someone tossed it to me. Alfred, another question, I'm afraid. Have you ever heard of an archaeologist called Evan Noble? I believe he might have worked here. I'm not certain, but he may have had his son with him."

Interesting that she used the old Roman name "Sarnus" for the river, Alfred thought. It had been "Sarno" for centuries.

"Evan Noble?" he said. "A relative of yours?"

"My father-in-law. My husband implied he visited Pompeii many years ago, so I wondered if he was here with his father."

Alfred tried to think if he'd heard that name. It didn't ring a bell.

"They don't let children run around the site, and I can't say I know the name." Then he had an idea. "There's a technician, a field archaeologist who's worked here since before the first world war. Canadian guy. If anyone knows, it would be him." He smiled. This was one strange lady. Pleasant, but a little wacky if you ask him. That's okay. He didn't mind wacky. She might just feature in one of his future novels!

"I have other commitments for the rest of the day, Mrs

Noble," he said. "If you wish, I can collect you tomorrow, and we'll see if we can locate him. Meanwhile, enjoy Naples. It's a delightful city. I'll drop you off at the funicular. You'll have the rest of the afternoon to explore."

Bethan took Alfred's advice, but her restless anticipation about what she might discover the next day hampered her enjoyment. She decided against the cable car and instead went to a market where she picked up colourful scarves to take back for Doris and Ivy. The hotel wasn't far enough to catch a cab, but it was a tidy walk, so she was ready to flop face down onto her bed and take a nap before dinner by the time she got back to her room.

Late that night, she sat at her window in her pyjamas and watched the harbour lights reflecting on the bay. It seemed extraordinary to have walked the streets of her dream and now see a clear moonlit sky bejewelled with twinkling stars. What a stark contrast to her memory of this place, fearful of the future as a lost child, with the sight of monstrous, creaking masts waving against a blackened sky and, looking down upon the scene, a moon shrouded in grey ash.

CHAPTER TWENTY-NINE _

To Bethan, it seemed she and Alfred zigzagged the entire length and breadth of Pompeii the following morning to track down the technician. It was on a day when the site allowed tourist groups, so they spent half their time fighting their way through sightseers who showed scant regard for the antiquity upon which they stood. Noisy families jostled to take photos, carelessly dropping still burning cigarette butts onto the ancient ground, and in one case, a young man spat out chewing gum. The desecrating behaviour and the tourists' disrespect appalled Bethan, but Alfred was less emotional.

"It's not their story," he said, "so they tend to not get sentimental about it. People nowadays care little about preserving history." He called out to another guide, and after a brief exchange in Italian, he took Bethan's arm and steered her away from the tourists.

"Come on. Luca's at the far end."

Luca looked as old as Pompeii and as much of a relic. He wore the skin on his face like a wrinkled, leathery pouch, his eyebrows drooping down like two hairy caterpillars that trapped the beads of perspiration trickling from under his hat. His short, creased, brown arms poked out of his shirtsleeves like a pair of gnarled bony spindles, yet his hands and fingers were deft and slim. Years of kneeling to carry out his work had resulted in knobbed and calloused knees, and as he stood at Alfred's greeting, he only reached Bethan's chin.

Luca looked like a local, despite Alfred's assurance he came to Italy from Canada to avoid the first world war and stayed to hide from the second. Somehow, and Luca was thankful for it, the world forgot about him.

Luca's English was occluded by a significant Italian accent that had embedded itself over the years as his native tongue fell out of practice. He listened with interest about Evan Noble, but he had nothing to offer.

"There's been no one of that name," he said. "I'm sorry. I've been here longer than anyone, and I remember just about everyone who's been through these ruins."

Bethan felt a sense of hopelessness. After Luca, she had no idea where she could find more information. In coming to Pompeii, she was sure she would find answers but hadn't considered what she would do if she found none. Like everything to do with Ian, she didn't always show presence of mind. She didn't want to give up, but maybe this was the universe telling her it was time to walk away.

"Thank you, anyway, Luca," she said. "I came here in the hope someone had heard of him. Dreams I have of Pompeii intrigued my husband, Evan Noble's son, and I wondered if it was because his father worked here."

"That's right, Luca," Alfred chimed in. "Mrs Noble has the most remarkable and detailed dreams about Pompeii." He grinned at Bethan. "She even seems to know her way around."

Luca didn't believe it. Dreaming about a place you'd never visited belonged in fairy tales, and he suggested she had seen one of the documentaries at the movies, and it stuck in her mind.

Bethan had never seen a film about Pompeii. There wasn't much opportunity back in the village, and her teachers only touched on it at school, but she wasn't here to convince him. She just needed information. She asked Luca if any of the archaeologists had brought a child with them.

"No ma'am, I'm sorry," he said, but seeing Bethan's disappointment, he realised her trip here was of some importance. Could this mysterious man with the distinctive name be like him, a refugee from the wider world who didn't want to be found? A change of identity was essential for hiding out, and he barely even remembered the name his parents gave him. He might do that man a disservice if he helped her uncover the mystery. Would he want his own whereabouts revealed if someone came looking? What should he do? The woman seemed genuinely convinced her father-in-law, this Evan Noble, had worked here. But he took a moment too long to deliberate, and the words were out before his better judgement kicked in.

"Do you know if 'Evan Noble' was his full name?" he asked Bethan. "Did he have a middle name he might have used?"

She shook her head. "Not that I know of. I've never

even met him. My husband disappeared under mysterious circumstances some years ago, and I'm just working on a few leads of my own."

Luca understood. He was right. This was important. "I'm very sorry to hear that, Mrs Noble. Do you have a photograph of your father-in-law perchance?"

Bethan only had her wedding photo, so she fished it out of her handbag and handed it to Luca. "Not of Evan Noble, but this was taken on my wedding day." She pointed to Ian's smiling face. "I don't know if my husband and his father are alike."

He stared at Ian's image for a full minute, recalling a strange encounter close to where they now stood. Despite the day's warmth, he felt an icy tingle on his skin, and the hairs on the back of his neck rose. He handed the picture back to Bethan. That chance meeting made such an impression; he even remembered the year it happened.

"Nineteen-fifty," he stated.

Bethan and Alfred looked at each other, then echoed together, "Nineteen-fifty?"

"I was working alone," Luca continued, his memory of that day crystal clear. "There were no visitors, but when I looked up, the man in your photograph was standing over me. He didn't look like a sightseer. He was dressed all wrong, so I asked if I could help." Luca pointed to the photo in Bethan's hand. "Looking out of place wasn't the only distinction. The photo doesn't show it, but you say this is your husband?"

"Yes. Ian Noble."

"The man I saw had eyes bluer than the sky. Never

seen eyes like it. Looked like someone painted on his eyeballs. And there's something else…."

Bethan held her breath.

"He looked the same as in your photograph, not old enough to be the father of an adult son. His skin was baby smooth, and he didn't look like he'd even started shaving!"

There could be no doubt. Luca was describing Ian. Alfred asked Luca if he was sure the man in the picture and the man from his encounter were one and the same.

Luca shrugged. "I'd swear on it."

Bethan tried to make sense of what she had just heard. Ian visited here a full six years before they met. Of course, there might be a perfectly good explanation. He often travelled with his work. Perhaps Luca would oblige with a few more answers.

"You said he wasn't a sightseer because of how he was dressed. What was he wearing?"

Luca wiped the sweat from his forehead with a grimy cloth and looked up at the sky, shielding his eyes. "It was like today, the sun was blazing, but this man wore a heavy coat and a homburg. Darndest thing. Not dressed for a Neapolitan summer."

"Did you see where he came from?"

"Not where he came *from*," Luca replied, pointing off into the distance. "After we spoke, he headed for the sleeping giant."

"The sleeping giant?"

Alfred explained Vesuvius was sometimes called "sleeping giant" by locals.

"That's right," Luca said. "He went that way, but that

sun was fierce, and there was a haze, so I lost sight of him. There are no roads in that direction, just the track the hikers use."

It was like Ian to wear his coat and hat regardless of the weather, but in the summer heat?

"Did he speak to you or try to engage you in conversation?" she asked.

"Yes, he asked me the year. And I told him."

Bethan looked at Alfred. "Why would he ask the year?"

These entire proceedings mystified Alfred. Perhaps the man had heatstroke. That can do funny things to your brain.

"I'm sorry, Luca," Bethan said. "I have a few more questions if you don't mind. When he spoke, did he have an American regional dialect? Russian?"

Luca confirmed the man spoke English with an accent. "I can tell you it wasn't American, though," he added. "Before I came here, I thought I would settle in the States. I travelled through thousands of counties and never found one that suited me, but I've heard many people talking many ways." Luca shook his head. "Never in my life heard an accent like his. I couldn't place it."

Bethan looked towards Vesuvius. Despite Luca's certainty about the identity of the man he spoke to being Ian, reason now told her it could not have been, not unless there was a strange genetic mutation in Ian's family that allowed them to defy the ageing process. Unless he lied about being twenty-seven. Without a birth certificate or other proof, she had only his word for it, and in the beginning, she had trouble guessing his age. She wished now she had looked at his passport, but she never got the chance.

Besides, Lincoln said his passport was a forgery. And how did Ian arrange the honeymoon? He couldn't have done that without identification, not unless he knew a way around the rules.

The third "unless" was that he never planned for them to go on a honeymoon, and it was all an elaborate ruse to get hold of the charm. Bethan bit her lip. She hoped to prove Ian's innocence, justify her confidence in him, but with all that had transpired, it might turn out she would confirm his guilt.

Although she had only known Alfred for little more than a day, Bethan needed to talk to someone impartial. Before she knew it, they were sitting in a café with cups of rich Italian coffee while she told him the entire story, including her broken necklace. Alfred didn't say a word until she finished, and she couldn't even gauge if he believed her or not. Her suspicions about the missing charm sounded absurd, even to her ears.

"Do you want my opinion?" he asked cautiously.

Bethan assured him she did indeed want his opinion and would value a fresh perspective.

He took her at her word. "Then I'm with your friends here, Bethan. Your husband sounds as though he had something to hide. You say Ian convinced you he was a geologist. I can tell you someone with your husband's knowledge could orchestrate a minor cave-in. The question would be, why? As a distraction? So he could make a quick getaway? It sounds like he had no business at the mine, or none that was obvious. As for the charm, I can number many among my acquaintance who also studied metallurgy.

They would know if the charm was ancient or valuable and the metal used in its construction. To me, the oddest thing is the bequest. Perhaps he was recompensing you for the charm or had a guilty conscience?"

"It's a possibility," Bethan conceded with a sigh. "Anything's a possibility. I just don't know how someone can look identical in a photo taken six years apart and, from Luca's description, wearing the same clothes. For weeks, I persuaded myself Ian was lying at the bottom of the mineshaft because it was the only explanation for his disappearance, at least to my mind. The charm went missing the morning he left, but until a few days ago, a link between the two events never occurred to me."

"Well, you must have trusted him to marry him. Did you know him long?"

"Less than two months."

Alfred chuckled. "A whirlwind romance, eh?"

"More like a hurricane. One that left a trail of devastation. But yes," Bethan smiled. "I trusted him."

"I married my wife after only two weeks, and we have been together for twenty-five years. It can work." Alfred patted her hand. "Bethan, your husband deceived you, perhaps not in everything, and only you can make your peace with why he behaved as he did. Now, you have picked up your life and moved on. This mysterious chapter will end too."

That might be a paradox, and she wrinkled her face, uncertain of what awaited her when she returned home. "Not if it turns out Ian was a foreign agent. My friend in England, the detective, said the police would question me about him."

"Then you answer their questions," Alfred advised. "I believe they will label you naïve and advise you to walk away. Then they will try to find out why a spy would leave such a trail. That is, if your detective friend is correct." He laughed. "I write thrillers, but I suppose it goes to show I know very little about espionage. That must be the secret to my success or lack thereof!"

Bethan managed a smile. "I said the same thing about spies and bequests. After speaking to Luca, I'm starting to believe Evan Noble and Ian Noble are the same person. I've decided I will do nothing with that money and wait until the British police give me the all-clear. Then, when I get a certificate of presumptive death, I'll reassess. At least that would tie up those legalities if the police come up with nothing else. Meanwhile, I'll continue with my plans and get to Australia by Christmas."

"That sounds sensible. This is just a hiccup, and you did get to see Pompeii."

Yes, she did, and it fulfilled all her expectations, and she still had the mystery of her dreams to explore. One day, when she was ready.

"Why don't you come to dinner with my wife and me tomorrow evening," Alfred suggested. "You would be very welcome, and your dreams would fascinate her."

Yes, well, that was the other part of the mystery, but Bethan was in no mood to socialise. She didn't even feel a need to prolong her stay in Naples, feeling she had learned everything she could.

"That's very kind, Alfred, but I think I might get an

earlier flight home. I'll see what the hotel can arrange."

Alfred understood. "I've enjoyed meeting you, Bethan. I hope you get all the answers you seek, and one day, I may read all about it in your memoirs!"

That made Bethan laugh out loud. A memoir wasn't likely!

"Alfred," she said. "I'm sorry I bent your ear with all this personal information. It's nice to speak to someone detached from all this intrigue."

Alfred lifted his hat in an action that reminded Bethan of Ian's old-fashioned charm. "My pleasure. I can assure you it will remain confidential. Often, as tour guides, our clients get very chatty. I promise you; I have heard stories to make your hair curl!"

Bethan could believe it, but she wouldn't mind betting hers was the strangest.

CHAPTER THIRTY _

Bethan scheduled a call to Lincoln and apologised for taking off without telling him. She planned to let him know everything that had happened, but when he heard she was in Naples, he made disapproving noises about being too adventurous and travelling without a man's protection. She gave his concerns a tart dismissal, telling him she felt perfectly safe the entire time and to stop being a fuddy-duddy, but before she could start her report, he told her the fingerprints turned up a negative match. He also had further discussion with Interpol. Even with their resources, they could find no record of Ian Noble other than an old bank account in his name that had no supporting documentation as to his identity. Besides that, he had no background. It was as if he never existed.

"I've been making some inquiries of my own," Bethan said, somehow not surprised at the results of Lincoln's investigations.

"In Naples?"

"Just listen, Lincoln, and don't judge. Remember the

marriage certificate said Ian's father was an archaeologist? I came to Naples, or rather Pompeii, to look for him, and I spoke to a fellow associated with the site. He didn't recognise the name, but when I showed him Ian's photo, he claimed to have met him in nineteen-fifty! They had a conversation, and the man who looked like Ian asked what year it was. Why would he do that? Where could he have been?"

Lincoln was still trying to connect Bethan's husband and his father to Pompeii.

"Perhaps his old man has some kind of sickness, and that's why you know nothing about him." It was all he had to offer. "Ian might have been ashamed."

"Lincoln, you're not listening. It was Ian the man met. Not his father. Ian was very youthful-looking. Even I had trouble telling his age. Apparently, it was the height of summer, but Ian was wearing his heavy coat and homburg hat, just like he always did. I can't help but think his interest in my dreams about Pompeii and my necklace has something to do with him turning up there."

"Wait! What?" This was new. "Your necklace? Your dreams about Pompeii?"

"Yes. I used to wear a charm on a silver chain. On the day Ian disappeared, I found the chain broken and the charm missing. When I came to Pompeii, I had it in my head that Ian needed or wanted the charm and that I might find some answers here, or perhaps even locate his father. If Ian had an ulterior motive in getting to know me, the charm had something to do with it. I made a drawing and showed it to an archaeologist, but he'd seen nothing like it."

"Was the charm valuable?"

"I assumed it was just a piece of metal, but I liked it."

"And the dream? What was its significance?"

"My dreams are vivid and detailed, but the one that most interested Ian was one I have about Pompeii. His interest, and the fact Pompeii is swarming with archaeologists, I put two and two together. I didn't find his father, but it turns out Ian has been here before."

"I noticed the marriage certificate missing from the file," Lincoln said. "Was that deliberate?"

"No, it fell out when I tossed the file to you that day."

"We'll need to give it to our handwriting analysts when you get back."

"Okay," Bethan agreed, "but I thought if I could find Evan Noble, I might find out what happened to Ian."

"And now you're convinced Ian Noble turned up in Pompeii wearing a winter coat and hat in the middle of a heatwave six years before you met him? Perhaps the heat got to the man you spoke to."

Bethan let Lincoln's scepticism slide because she couldn't explain it herself.

"Think about it, Bethan," Lincoln said. "If you're right, it would make Ian a lot older than twenty-seven when you met, and he doesn't sound like a man who would turn up on an archaeological dig not knowing what year it is. I think this proves he lied; he may have even been incarcerated in some foreign jail and lost track of time. Although that's unlikely, prisoners usually count the days. As for the charm, I'm sure that's a red herring. Now, my investigations have revealed a few things that are just as difficult to explain.

Would you rather it waited until you get back?"

"No, tell me."

"Remember that I was going to check if Ian had other bank accounts? I requested his records from the bank that has just taken over Hambly's. I can't make head nor tails of this, but that bank account, the one used to transfer the money to you, was opened in eighteen ninety-eight in the name of Ian Noble."

Today was a day for shocks. She could cope with another, even if, for a moment, she couldn't speak. Lincoln tapped the phone, unsure if the line had gone dead or if she had hung up.

"Bethan, are you there?"

"You said he didn't exist."

"He doesn't. Neither does Evan Noble. That's why I wish you'd consulted me before you went off on a wild goose chase. It makes no sense for a government to use the same name for a stolen identity. Also, if Ian was twenty-seven in nineteen-fifty-six, his birthdate would be around nineteen-twenty-nine. If we assume the man you spoke to is useless at guessing ages and Ian lied to you, even at a stretch, he would not have had a bank account in eighteen-ninety-eight. He wasn't even born."

"Perhaps his father's real name was Ian, not Evan, and it was his account."

"I don't think so. Hambly's Bank only opened that year after merging with two other banks. There's more."

Bethan closed her eyes. Oh, God. Not more.

"They sealed this record to stop it from being viewed," Lincoln said. "Now, the statutory period has long passed, and upon police request, the bank released it. A vast sum of money was donated to a housing group in your unpronounceable village. Would you believe in eighteen-ninety-eight, and expressly dedicated by one Mr Ian Noble for the benefit of clearing slums, upgrading housing and providing a park? *Except* it didn't say which of the merging banks the funds came from, and records from Hambly's were of no help."

So it appeared Ian took the name of the man who helped the miners? She remembered telling him about it, but he must have known already. How did he get access to such old funds? That would mean the money he left her belonged to someone else.

"Did you check for an Ian Noble around that time?"

"I did," Lincoln said. "I followed up on death indexes for both Ian and Evan Noble and found none that fit, but there were a few epidemics in the late nineteenth and early twentieth centuries. It is possible the Ian Noble, whose identity your husband stole, didn't end up with his death recorded, or he died intestate, possibly in obscurity overseas. No-one came forward to claim the money. Bethan, I hate to say it. Ian was either on the run, a foreign agent, or involved with something disreputable. Please come home. We can sort this out, but not if you're not here. Under the circumstances, I can involve the Italian police, and they will arrange your flight. I'm even a little concerned for your safety now all this has come to light."

Bethan didn't want any more police involved because it seemed like Lincoln had already spread the word to every law-enforcement agency in the whole world.

"No, it's alright," she said. "The concierge is arranging an earlier flight as we speak. Lincoln, I wish I hadn't started all this."

"I think it's natural to want to know the truth. It can't be easy to know part of your life might have been a lie. Send me a telegram with your flight details, and I'll pick you up at London Airport."

Bethan had hoped that she would lay a few ghosts to rest in coming here. Now it seemed Lincoln would embroil her in an espionage enquiry, or at the very least, historical fraud. She could do nothing, so she thanked Lincoln for his offer and told him she would let him know.

Her head spinning with all this new information, Bethan longed to be in familiar surroundings, so it disappointed her that the only earlier flight available meant she had to stay in Naples for another full day and night. She considered contacting Alfred to change her mind about accepting his dinner invitation, but when she picked up the phone to dial, she realised she needed to be alone with her thoughts. As she stood at the telephone, she caught the glint of her engagement ring sparkling in the light. She hadn't worn either her wedding or engagement ring since she came to the Alice Maud, preferring to store them away while her heartbreak healed, only putting them on again when she came to Naples.

If everything Ian told her was a lie, there was no real meaning in them now. Perhaps part of the healing would be to take them off, put both rings back in the drawer, and never look at them again.

Bethan didn't remove her rings. That night, she grieved again for Ian. Not the dishonest, traitorous version Lincoln believed him to be, the unfeeling scoundrel who could steal a dead man's identity. No, she grieved for the man with the bright blue eyes, the man who told her stories, taught her about rocks and stars and whose last words to her, heard through a sleepy haze as he kissed her fingers, were a whispered, *"I love you."*

In the morning, Bethan rose early and opened the window to the promise of a warm Naples day. She dressed and walked down into the town to sit in a café and watch the world go by. Then, taking out a notebook, she compiled a list of all the things she knew about Ian Noble, and when she got to the end, she realised the list contained everything she *didn't* know about him. Nowhere was there evidence of his existence or proof of his identity.

She turned over to a new page. What single definitive thing was there besides the fact that he was a living being who used the name of a man who had been dead for decades? Ian Noble was not his real name. She accepted that but still struggled with Lincoln's suggestions he was a foreign agent. Perhaps he was on the run and just a mastermind at covering his tracks? Possibly, Bethan thought, tapping her pen on the table. Except he wasn't that good at it because he seemed to leave these odd clues all over the place, particularly about the money. That baffled everyone.

The new page remained blank. She was sure of his feelings for her. She didn't doubt them even in the face of all this so-called evidence. And what about her genuine love for him? He turned her world on its head, and her desire to be with him made her abandon all her long-cherished plans. But she was happy. Maybe love blinded her. Maybe all this new information proved Ian's dishonesty, but she couldn't help that she still loved him.

Lifting her pen, she wrote his name, ensuring her elegant script did the words justice. Underneath, she wrote, over and over, "I love you" until her wrist ached. Several pages of her declaration of love, perhaps only as a memoir or tribute, started out neatly before evolving into childish scrawl and rough scribble that mirrored her sadness and frustration. She stopped when a single tear splashed onto the page. Ian had left a riddle, but he also left an ache in her heart. If he were to sit now on the chair opposite or suddenly turn the corner, smiling that beautiful smile, she would ask no questions, just be glad he came back to her.

A brochure, buoyed by the breeze, fluttered onto her table, and intrigued by its bright colours, Bethan caught it before it flew away again. It was an advert, headlined:

Tours to Vesuvius.

She looked up at the sky. It's a beautiful day, she thought, and she needed a distraction. It might be the perfect place to visit. The tour office was right across the street, so she booked a coach trip to the mountain for later in the day.

Overseas tourists packed the small bus, mainly American and German, and Bethan listened for any nuances in their speech. She gave herself a mental slap. *Stop trying to be a detective*, she told herself under her breath, as if speaking it aloud would carry more weight than if she simply thought it.

Even with all the windows open, the bus felt cramped and stuffy. Bethan fanned herself with a brochure and half wished she had checked the distance before signing up for what was likely to be an hour-long trip there and back. Just for a two-hour visit to the mountain. Not much she could do now. She was stuck with it, so she rolled her head to the side to view the passing scenery and wondered how it must have been when Vesuvius erupted in AD79. It would have affected all this land, with terrified people running before the ash cloud, just like in her dream. How many lost their lives? How many now slept deep in the earth below this peaceful place?

As they approached Vesuvius, the sheer majesty of the "sleeping giant" made Bethan dizzy. The tourists were out of their seats in a flash, surging towards the door with excited chatter as the bus rolled to a halt. Bethan always thought the mountains back home were majestic, but they didn't have the imposing authority of Vesuvius. This titan rose high in the landscape, the fate of those who dwelt below at its mercy. Ian spoke about advances in volcanology, but Bethan bet this mountain still had a few tricks up its sleeve.

An earlier tour had ascended the mountain to visit the crater, something that appealed to Bethan had she known about it. Her tour group left far too late in the day, so she would not now get the opportunity. Instead, she contented herself with exploring the surrounding area, then enjoyed a pleasant hour listening to the tour guide before wandering off alone to find a kiosk that sold cold drinks and almond croissants.

Munching her snack, deep in thought and elevated enough to see Pompeii in the distance, she estimated it would be at least twelve miles, maybe more, to the edge of the site. The trundling old bus had continued a good half hour after passing Pompeii before arriving at the mountain.

Twelve miles? Even if she was out by a couple of miles either way, how did Ian, or whoever that person was, walk that distance on what Luca described as a sweltering hot day, wearing the expensive coat and hat that Ian used to wear? It would have been unthinkable.

Bethan looked down at her strappy cotton dress. It was lightweight, but the afternoon sun still felt too warm. According to Luca, the man headed towards the volcano but couldn't see the path he had taken. Did that mean a vehicle was waiting for him? Luca said there wasn't a road, just a track.

I'm hunting a ghost, she thought, taking a deep breath. This was threatening to take over her life. *I have to stop. I have to go home, answer any questions and let the authorities deal with it.*

The bus driver cautioned that if a passenger didn't arrive back on time, they wouldn't send out a search party. He made it sound like a joke but still handed each person a card with the number of a taxi company. So clearly, it was a common occurrence for people not to turn up for the return journey.

Bethan picked up her hat and started walking back to the bus, seeking to turn her thoughts to going home the next day and getting back to work. Her route took her past the bottom of the trail, and several hikers jostled past as they descended the mountain, causing Bethan to stop to take one last look at the summit and the sky beyond. A short walk on the trail wouldn't hurt, and it seemed to call to her. She had a little time, and if she missed the bus, there was always the card with the taxicab number. Her summer outfit wasn't suited for a hike, but if she got stranded on the mountain, she wouldn't freeze to death, not if the past couple of evenings were anything to go by.

The trail wasn't even that difficult, and Bethan wondered why the hikers all seemed to wear such elaborate gear while she was wearing only a dress and sunhat. Two hikers gave her a cheery wave as they passed on their way down, but for the next half an hour, she didn't see another soul.

Bethan turned at each noise, but it was only a bird or small animal settling as the day passed into late afternoon. She wondered about turning back. That would make sense because some sections were very steep, but despite those sensible thoughts, and even after her shoes and dress got dusty, she continued to climb. After a while, the insects ceased their chirping, and fireflies lit their wings to carry them through the twilight. Below, through the brilliance of the sunset, Bethan could make out the ruins of Pompeii, and beyond, the lights of Naples, which held the comfort of her hotel room.

She did not leave the mountain, only waited until the moon rose high enough to lend its light to her ascent. She continued until her way became barred by an invisible barrier she knew was not natural to Vesuvius. The rough bushes shredded her dress at the hem, her shoes were long gone, and somewhere along the way, she had discarded her handbag to climb more easily. This place was familiar. This unseen colossus rising to the heavens. She'd seen it before. Stretching forth her hand, she felt its marble coldness. A tomb? A doorway? A gate? As she inched closer, the stars went out, the moon lost its brilliance, and there in that dark world, she heard a familiar, beloved voice telling her to step forward.

"Ian?"

The ground under Bethan's feet changed. She had stepped onto a threshold, but it felt like walking on air.

"Ian?" she whispered again. *"Is that you?*

"Bethan, it's alright. I'm here."

Her hand remained outstretched, hoping Ian might take it and draw her in to join him. He didn't, so she followed his voice, trying to make out his form through the gloom. Behind her, sturdy ancient doors closed in silence. She didn't see them, but she knew they were there because she had passed through them before. She was very little then. Just a child. And they opened onto a river.

Ahead, a single ray of light illuminated an arched, panelled window. Like the doors, it reached so high Bethan couldn't see the top. The added light revealed a gallery that stretched into eternity, with more arched windows standing like watchmen on one side. As she moved past, golden light streamed through. Fascinated, Bethan stopped to view scenes from the lives she experienced in her dreams. She saw the destitute village and her old rags. The blood-soaked brocade dress and the scenes of war. Fieldwork before the invention of technology and all the others she visited in her sleep.

At the final window, she again reached out her hand to Ian. Even though he did not take it, she felt calm because he was with her and would be her guide.

"Where am I?" she asked. "What is this place?"

"See how black the sky is?"

At the sound of his voice, Bethan turned towards the window and her dream of Pompeii. It ran as if she were watching a newsreel. A terrified child fled before a cloud of ash, a tiny baby in her arms. In the background, a mountain burned, but unlike before, Bethan didn't feel the pain from her feet or the tearing of her flesh as she clambered over walls.

"It seemed so real," she said. "But it was only a dream."

"Not a dream, Bethan. Your earliest recollection of Earth."

How could she dream of Pompeii when she had never visited there before yesterday? How could her mind tell such a story? If Ian showed himself, it would all make sense.

"Ian," she whispered. "Am I dead? Did I die on Vesuvius? It was foolish of me to climb the trail alone."

It was at that moment he took her hand. "You are very much alive, Bethan, and I am here to take you home."

A mist swirled into Bethan's mind, blotting out her memories one by one. She caught one that shone above the rest.

"Are you taking me to Chabin?" she asked.

"Yes, Chabin." She heard the smile in his voice.

Then he stepped from the shadows, and every one of

Bethan's memories, Vesuvius, her lives, Ian, and even the village, tumbled into an unentangleable mess. Her mind scrambled to extract strands to help her make sense, but they dissolved each time she tried to pull them back. The person at her side, holding her hands, looked like someone she knew, but she couldn't remember from where. His eyes were the colour of liquid gold, but no-one has liquid eyes. And his skin. Pale, like a dead man. Fear and bewilderment gripped her.

"I don't know you," she cried out, snatching away her hand and running aimlessly from left to right to find safety, but everywhere was in darkness. Panicked, she stepped backwards and fell. Arms flailing and ears ringing from her own screams as she plunged into a deep well, she heard the rush of air as she went ever deeper. Yianevan caught her and held her until her breathing slowed.

"You are safe," he said. "It's just an illusion."

Still holding her in his arms, he pointed through the last window. It had become murky and grey in the throes of surrendering its memory.

"This is the Bay of Naples from where the Romans took you to Britain after the eruption. See the ships?"

The man would not let her fall. He was here to save her, so she looked through the window. Yes, somewhere, sometime, she had seen ships that rose dark and eerie against the sky, pitching and rolling on their moorings. A soldier held her hand and kept her safe. Was this the soldier? It couldn't be. The soldier didn't have liquid eyes. She looked back along the endless corridor with its darkened windows, their light snuffed out because they were no longer part of her.

Bewildered, she pointed back into the gloom.

"Is my home back there?"

"No, you don't belong there. Not in any of those places."

Outside the gallery, a light glowed like the rays of the sun.

"A door closed," she said as she allowed him to lead her towards it.

"A construct of your mind, nothing more."

As the last of her memories melted into blessed confusion, the man drew her close and pulled her into the light. He promised to take her home.

*CHAPTER THIRTY-ONE_*

Slivers of tantalising information swirled around Phildre's mind like exploding rock as she stood in the middle of her apartment on Chabin. Struggling to organise the pieces into memories, she somehow believed she should recognise this place, even though every image that presented itself proved too stubborn to allow examination. Through the vast window, the setting sun bathed the distant peaks in dazzling shades of pink and gold, and far below, a large crystal clear lake sparkled jewel-like in the evening light. How could anyone forget a view so magnificent?

As she watched, a tiny spark of remembrance lit, and she recalled a place where she recited poetry and talked about the stars. Where was it? Not here. Somewhere else. Somewhere that held meaning. Trying to remember was pointless. It wouldn't come to her, and forcing those fragments together only seemed to make them more elusive. She didn't recall how she arrived in this apartment; she only knew it was a place of safety.

She didn't move, just waited for the dusk to turn to

nightfall. Happy little winking lights, filled with purpose, darted here and there against the blue-black sky. Fireflies? Where had she seen fireflies? But just like the memories that never lingered long enough for her to examine or provide clarity, the imagined vision of a firefly would not take shape for her. She frowned. No, not fireflies, not even insects. The flickering was too controlled, unrandom.

Those lights were ships. Yes, small ships. She'd seen them before, but where? When? There was a story about fireflies and spaceships. Where did she hear it? Maybe that was why fireflies were the first thing that came into her mind.

As the moon rose, the giant structures that stalked the dark landscape, each with broad rings threaded onto the central spire, began to glow in bright, comforting reds and blues. Those giants were the tiny firefly ships' destination. One ship turned towards where she stood, its intensity growing larger as it neared, until it became as clear as the moon. She stepped back, uncertain, as the ship rose above the window. Not tiny, like a firefly, but immense and thrilling.

Phildre turned from the window to survey the apartment. She liked the big, comfy chair with the colourful coverings. She'd searched for a chair like that, walking up and down looking for one just like it. Where was that? A place with people and rain. And these rugs scattered across the floor? She daydreamed of owning such a rug but, like the chairs, never found one that suited. A few steps below where she stood, a grand array of plants with shiny green foliage stretched in splendour around the wall and under the window. Images of another window with two lonely plants drifted in, but the picture slipped away as soon as she recognised it.

A cat rubbed against her legs, purring a loud welcome as if she had been away for years. Did she like cats? She assumed so, provided they didn't lick butter off cold toast.

This room tried hard to remind her it was familiar, but Phildre's addled brain couldn't filter out real and imagined. She looked down at the one-piece outfit that appeared to be a uniform. It fitted as if someone had made it for her. Her hair, unexpected because she imagined soft silkiness lying around her shoulders, only yielded short spikiness when she touched it.

The strange apartment became less strange as the minutes passed, yet not once did she acknowledge the man who stood watching.

Yianevan didn't speak. She needed this time to acclimatise, to reacquaint herself. She might not even know he was there or even recognise him, but he couldn't leave her alone in these first few moments. Not where all would seem new and yet so old.

An elliptical, bevelled-edged panel glided across the floor and stopped in front of her. As it spoke, Phildre felt neither fear nor familiarity.

"Phildre," it declared. "Welcome back. I have prepared Micy for you."

A cup of shimmering liquid, with an array of florals steeped within, hovered before the panel. Phildre then uttered the first words she had spoken since she woke. Her sing-song Welsh inflexion remained but she handled the language, Sector, without stumbling.

"What is it?"

"It is Micy," the panel responded. "Your favourite relaxant."

Phildre examined the unfamiliar server. It had no mouth, yet it spoke. It had no arms, yet it carried. After a moment, she accepted the cup, allowing the clear liquid to touch her lip. Instantly, her face crumpled in revulsion. Shuddering, she held out the offending cup to the panel.

"I don't drink. I don't want this."

The interface moved back, disconcerted by this comment from its mistress. Phildre loved Micy. She loved all alcoholic beverages.

Yianevan took the drink from Phildre and handed it back to the interface with a gesture of dismissal.

"Your memory will return, Lieutenant Phildre," he said, wishing with all his heart he could take her in his arms and explain everything. "It will take time. Your friends have arrived to help you."

Phildre pointed to the window. "In that ship? The one that went past?"

"Yes, in that ship."

Phildre took in the man's white hair and his slender frame. What species was he, with a face so pale? And those strange eyes.

"I know you."

"I am Yi, of House Anevan," he said. "I am a Noble, and I have been with you since your rescue."

"I don't recall being rescued," Phildre said, although she didn't disbelieve him. Right now, she didn't know the truth of anything. "What was I rescued from?" she asked. "When?"

"From a mountain," Yianevan told her. "I returned you here, to your home, and you slept until only an hour ago. I felt it wise not to disturb you. You were fortunate to have survived because you were caught in an eruption."

Phildre gave him a blank stare. "What was I doing in an eruption. Was it a volcano?"

"It is your work."

"I work on volcanos?"

Yianevan could afford friendliness, tenderness. In her current confused state, she was unlikely to recall this encounter, so he did a most un-Noble thing. He smiled.

"I promise this will soon make sense."

Phildre looked around the apartment. "I know this place," she said, then pointed to the interface. "Even that has something familiar about it. Why does my brain feel like it's stuck in a waterfall? Why is the water washing away my thoughts? Nothing seems to want to stick."

She looked up at him, lost, bewildered, silently begging him to unravel her confusion. He hated seeing her so vulnerable, and he didn't want to leave her, but there was no longer any reason for him to stay.

Phildre had fallen into a deep sleep when he got her onto his ship, so he changed her hair and clothes so she would appear as a crewman who had been missing only days. He advised Chief Jardin and Lieutenant Merris of their crewmate's safe retrieval, but he did not give details, only telling them she had suffered an incident during a spiral malfunction. He also swore them to continued secrecy regarding the anomaly. In return for their silence, he arranged a furlough on Chabin for them to help Phildre recover.

A buzzer announced the arrival of Phildre's crewmates. She blinked and looked towards the door, where she could already hear voices raised in excitement. That was Yianevan's cue to leave, but Phildre took a step towards him and caught his sleeve as he moved away.

"Please don't go," she pleaded. She sounded so forlorn. "What if I don't know them?"

Her hand felt warm as he gently removed himself from her grasp, aware it would be the last time he would ever touch her. "They know you, Lieutenant," he said. "Their presence can aid the recovery of your memories far more than mine."

He had done his duty, and there was no need for him to linger. It was over.

"Yianevan," Phildre called out as he reached the exit. He paused but didn't turn back to look at her, only heard her murmured "thank you" as he stepped aside to let Jardin and Merris pass.

As he headed towards his shuttle, the sounds of reunion reached his ears. While the interventionist was between worlds, he needed to be as far away as possible. He was her only connection from where she was before, and soon, her real world would open with all its opportunities restored.

For Yianevan, his freedom was about to end. He had put off the inevitable for long enough.

CHAPTER THIRTY-TWO _

"You are going to the ceremony, aren't you, Philly?" Jardin asked his now recovered crewmate a few months after her return to duty. "The new ship is a big deal. It's huge—" he threw his arms wide, hoping to instil some energy into his friend — "and the crew quarters are absolute luxury!"

Phildre grinned. Only the chief could come over all unnecessary about a ship. She felt no such enthusiasm.

"Only for the launch, Jar. I don't plan on staying for the reception."

Jardin knew better than to argue. Months ago, before she disappeared, Phildre was the life of the party, but since she got back, she shunned Micy, Birn and any other recreational beverages. She didn't seem to want company either, except for her cat, which now got carted between Chabin and her shipboard quarters. Whatever transpired in those few days before the Noble found her, she'd changed. She was still brilliant at her job, still had a good heart, but he often wondered about a link between the change in her nature and the anomaly.

Yianevan's insistence the anomaly had to remain their secret also bothered him. He would never go back on his word, but it made him wonder what the Noble discovered that he wasn't sharing. No-one questioned Jardin or Merris about the events leading to Phildre's disappearance, and as far as Jardin knew, the Nobles considered the matter closed.

Another point that worried Jardin about Phildre was that she began dropping hints about leaving the interventionist program to travel the ten sectors, maybe beyond. He couldn't question her abilities, but she didn't seem as settled to her tasks. In fact, he half expected her to resign at any time. The special bond between the three crew members before Phildre vanished seemed severed. And he missed it.

"I thought this launch would make Phildre come out of her shell," he said to Merris when she joined him later on the bridge. "I hate seeing her like this."

Merris rolled her eyes. That was his favourite saying, repeating it often since Phildre returned to work.

"I suppose she's in her quarters?"

Jardin nodded. "With the cat. We've been in orbit over the Noble homeworld for a day, and she hasn't even bothered going to the shipyard to catch up with her friends."

"Stop worrying, Chief," Merris said. "I keep telling you, Phildre's the same, apart from that funny accent. She's just not as outgoing. We may need to give her more time. It's only been a few months."

Jardin accepted he might be impatient, but it was like a light went out.

"Lieutenant Phildre is the ablest of all interventionists, Chief," the still-unnamed, personality-less interface cut in. "This is all the hierarchy requires."

That was another thing in a growing list of things that miffed Jardin. Yianevan didn't return Corky, so they were stuck with his interface, which they couldn't reprogram in case he decided he wanted it back. So it wasn't just Phildre who changed. Everything changed.

"You're just like the Nobles, Interface," Jardin said. "You aren't interested in her as a person, and I still reckon Yianevan knows more than he lets on."

Merris agreed. She missed Corky too. And the old Phildre, but they could speculate all they wanted about Yianevan. He wasn't giving them any more than he had already.

"Let it go," she said. "You sound like you've taken some kind of speech purgative that makes you say the same thing with boring regularity. You're becoming obsessive! It doesn't matter to the Nobles that Phildre left her personality on the planet. They're only interested in us carrying out their precious covenant."

Merris had a point. Phildre seemed to have forgotten the whole incident, or at least she never mentioned it, so he resolved that once they transferred to the new ship, so would he. He appreciated Merris's level-headedness about Phildre when he got emotional.

"We weren't there, Chief," she reminded him. "Perhaps it's better this way."

As the Nobles didn't allow foreign shipping to access their homeworld, they'd scheduled the launch reception on their orbiting pontoon. The protective forcefield that surrounded it offered spectacular and spine-tingling views of the planet below. There was also a massive observation platform overlooking the separate shipyard and launchpad.

Phildre wasn't interested in the launch, but she couldn't pass her role over to another interventionist, as she was to be part of the new ship's crew. When the Nobles organised a function that included the interventionists, they did not request her presence. They demanded. And when the Nobles demanded, there was no option but to obey. Jardin, though, loved to visit the Noble pontoon. He loved the grand parties that followed official functions; parties the Nobles didn't attend, so crews didn't have to endure their frosty presence. There was a time Phildre would champ at the bit to get to one of those receptions, but this evening, she hung back, subdued in her dress uniform and feeling out of place.

Jardin handed her a drink. "Not alcoholic, Philly," he said with a grin. "Just fruit punch."

"Thanks, Jardin." Phildre looked around. "There are so many people here. It's just a launch."

"Yes, but what a ship!" Jardin laughed, eyes wide with delight, not understanding her apathy. "With the improved safety protocols, we can get closer to the planet, and we will never risk degradation of the spirals. Not like what happened to you."

He continued to chatter with undisguised enthusiasm about the new ship until his words became background noise. Phildre didn't believe the spiral report for a minute, but without more information, she couldn't decide between what was truth and what was suspicion. To distract herself in those early days, she concentrated on her work and filed away all the other puzzling and confusing images, hoping that in time, they would disappear. They didn't, which made her resurrect her suspicion that there was more to it. The official report and what others told her about herself before her disappearance was all she knew, and they agreed she had returned much changed. She didn't know what it felt like to be Phildre and saw in their expressions they thought she was a dull facsimile of her old self.

Jardin couldn't stay still, so when he saw she had become vague, he excused himself.

"There are a few people I'd like to see. Come with?"

"No." Phildre edged towards the exit. "I'll stay here and prop up the wall, then go back to the runabout when the launch is over. Don't rush. I've got stuff to do."

"If you're sure?" However, Jardin was already waving to someone across the room, so Phildre gave him a gentle shove.

"I'm sure. Go."

The elder Nobles were present for the launch. No doubt the hierarchy knew about her rescue, but it was months ago, so old news. Besides, the hierarchy paid little attention to their interventionists, provided they did their job, and Phildre resumed her duties as soon as she got cleared. There were a few questions from the tribal ordinaries, none she could answer, and no doubt her Noble rescuer provided most of the details. Either way, she heard no more about the incident, although not a day went by that she didn't think about it.

Fleet directives were strict in that no-one approached a member of the Noble hierarchy, but one male Noble stirred up a vague reminder from when she stood in her apartment just after her rescue. Strange and disturbing images haunted her then, and she felt like a shadow that needed a body to attach itself to. She still did, particularly when those images came to disturb her. The man who stood with her the day she returned home was a Noble. She was certain this was that man. The striking similarities between Nobles, male and female, didn't matter. As she watched him, Phildre knew this Noble was Yianevan. The Noble who was in her apartment.

When he turned briefly and met her gaze, Phildre remained steady. The temptation to walk across and address him was strong, but it would bring a reprimand from her superiors, not to mention Jardin's furious admonishment afterwards. Besides, what would she say? More than that, what would *he* say? It would doubtless just be an awkward reunion. So she stayed put, deciding that if the opportunity presented later, after the launch, and if they were in proximity to each other, she might respond if he spoke first. Otherwise, it would mean hanging around to catch him before he left, even if she could get his attention. If anyone knew what happened in those hours before she arrived back on Chabin, it would be him. The report made it out to be a simple recovery following an atmospheric effect on the spiral's sensors, resulting in her being tossed away from the spiral tray. A plausible explanation of how it happened followed, including why she suffered short-term memory loss. Happily, her memory of her work and life returned quickly. She even remembered how she consumed large cups of Micy and Birn mixed with other herbs. Strange that she couldn't stand it now, not in any combination, and Merris told her she used to be a party animal. That was another thing that had changed, along with her accent, which she rather liked. So unless her brain was shielding her, something profound happened on that mountain.

There were other thoughts as well, confusing thoughts that presented like memories, each with many layers. Phildre wanted to understand them but didn't feel confident confiding in either Merris or Jardin. Now, those thoughts filled her head every day. Sometimes, they invaded her dreams, robbing her of sleep with their demands to be heard. The only one who might help was the Noble, Yianevan. She might also ask why he didn't return Corky. Did Corky know something? Did he undergo illegal data isolation? She hadn't bonded with the new interface, and she wasn't interested in humanising it. It functioned adequately as a support to her work. She didn't need to be its friend.

Phildre hadn't seen the new ship since its completion, only given the impressive specs a once over. However, the launch was dramatic, and even her current contemplative frame of mind couldn't stop a little thrill of admiration for Noble design skills. The ship raised from its dock in quiet elegance, the gleaming hull reflecting the pontoon lights as it turned full circle. Many of the ten sector delegates present gasped in admiration. It was beautiful, and Phildre couldn't deny that to be part of the crew was a privilege. With many years left as an interventionist, the human planet, her distant ancestor's home, would offer countless opportunities to save the world from the Lyran sabotage. This new ship, of a sleeker design, with more effective phase technology and far more comfort, would allow closer access to the planet. If required, it could land, all without the inhabitants ever knowing. The crew would never miss a significant event, and her mishap—if it was a mishap—at the volcano would never be repeated. Except she was no longer sure that was where she wanted to be. Her colleagues saw her as dedicated to her work, but the truth was, as they often reminded her, she was different.

Launch over, speeches delivered, she abandoned the idea of lingering to speak to the Noble. He would probably consider himself too lofty to revisit their acquaintance, anyway, so she shelved her concerns and troubling images and headed for the runabout to wait for Jardin. It was likely to be a long wait, but that was fine because she had a few things to do before going to the new ship.

The fixed spiral took her to the pontoon's lower level, close to the shuttle docking area. The central atrium was silent and deserted, with only one of the private waiting bays occupied. As she passed, she saw the Noble she recognised earlier, gazing out at the planet below, lost in thought.

Phildre hesitated in the doorway. She could barge in and interrupt him in his musings, and if he didn't want to speak, he could just tell her to go away. If she didn't do it now that the opportunity had presented itself, then when?

As she deliberated, the Noble's chin lifted, and he turned. Emboldened by his acknowledgement of her presence, Phildre stepped into the room. There would be no going back now. If this was a mistake, then like all the risks she took in her work, she would deal with the consequences.

CHAPTER THIRTY-THREE _

Yianevan had returned to his homeworld amid the fanfare befitting a prodigal son. The clan father had kept the knowledge of his son Yi's disobedience confined to the Marisene—the palatial province of the Noble hierarchy—as far as he was able. With twenty years passed, he believed that most had forgotten his son's delinquency and only welcomed his return as heir.

The lesser Nobles conducted separate ceremonies to rejoice in the heir's age of majority, resulting in Yianevan's father delighting in the manifest material gifts of sumptuous textiles, technology, even books, hoping they would stimulate his son's values of duty and commitment to race and clan.

Yianevan's brother was among those who rejoiced. Bo was relieved to see the heir alive and well. He did not aspire to the rulership and had Yi died, he would have been the first consideration. Far too attached to his indulgences in food, hunting and his Amuses, he had no aspirations of being anything other than the overlooked son. However, his greater fear was that Yi would reject his birthright, resulting in Bo's dispossession and expulsion. His father had made this condition only since the death of his second wife, the heir's mother. When Yi initially ignored the request to return, Bo spent many days and nights trembling in fear. He didn't leave his chambers until he received word, via the Grielik police, that his brother had been informed of the expulsion threat and had agreed to the clan father's demands.

The threat made little sense to Bo as the second-born son. The clan father had the power to make Yi's exile permanent and name any son or grandson he wished as heir. Indeed, before the mother's death, the clan father showed no interest in Yi other than the occasional police check that he kept to the conditions of his exile. Bo observed his father's growing obsession with Yi's return, to the point he wondered why the police were never sent to bring him back all those years before. After all, it wasn't the first time his wayward brother fled in a stolen ship.

The elder sister, Aaris, believed her son a more worthy candidate for succession, but Bo feared her influence. Driven by jealousy and ambition, it would be a mistake to allow her anywhere near the rulership. No matter. Bo sighed, taking pleasure in being relieved of these burdens. The musings were academic. Yi was home, and soon there would be an heir with one or both betrotheds. He could sit back, relax, and not squander another thought on the proceedings.

Yianevan endured the celebrations with neither comment nor complaint. He accepted his father parading him to both his sib and the other Noble houses across the face of the planet and anticipated a time when he would cease to be a source of fascination. Having acknowledged himself as heir, he was now bound to take over as clan father, but he would not tolerate a life of behind-the-scenes obligation. When he succeeded, he would instigate a more open and honest exchange with the ten sectors.

For now, though, he would not speak of change. Steeped as his father was in the old ways, bonded to the traditions, unless it suited him otherwise, if his son showed he might not live by those rules, he would not yield his power. The clan father's vision for the homeworld would not be abdicating in favour of a dissenting son, and he had strong views on preserving the Noble mystique. It was far better he believed that time out in the ten sectors had cured his heir of his rebellious ways.

For Yianevan's father, a man who celebrated the excesses of his position, the actual act of rulership was of far less importance than hunting, eating, games, drama, and theatre, all of which were given the same weight. A few other hierarchical houses within the Marisene, although loyal to House Anevan, numbered many scientists and engineers who worked to safeguard the Noble hierarchy's claim as the most advanced civilisation in the ten sectors. They took no glory for themselves. That was not the hierarchy's way, and they frowned upon any hierarchical Noble who tried to laud any individual achievement or invention as their own.

As a young man, Yianevan viewed the hierarchical lifestyle, House Anevan's especially, to be a meaningless and self-indulgent existence. He preferred to spend his time at the other houses in the Marisene, observing their scientists at work and sometimes helping his mother in her own workshop. He held that if the ten sectors viewed how the mighty ruling family of Anevan lived, it would be exposed for its shallowness and indolence. It was a life in stark contrast to the free and productive lives of tribal ordinaries who were at liberty to choose their own paths. They didn't suffer pressure to provide an heir, and even though they still lived in sibs, there were no true boundaries apart from moving off-world. From the ranks of tribal ordinaries came educators, philosophers, historians, and academics. Work opportunities abounded according to knowledge, from simple farm work to implementing the advanced technology channelled from the Noble hierarchy and lesser houses. Only those technicians involved with the police or interventionist fleets spent time away from the planet. And in most cases, the hierarchy didn't interfere.

Not that Yianevan hated his world. How could he deny the beauty of its waterfalls, sweeping archipelagos filled with wildlife, deep lakes and rolling hills? Throughout, vast mountain ranges and volcanos that in centuries past had baptised the new inhabitants of this world with fire, rose high into the landscape, offering exciting challenges for young people to conquer and claim.

The Nobles brought the volcanos under control with the pennants, and now the world was calm, its climate temperate and its pastures yielding and fertile. The only region left untended was the Southern Climes, an area of microclimates where those who "sinned" against the hierarchy would find themselves banished at the whim of House Anevan.

Yianevan was lucky not to be living or perhaps dying there himself, but he supposed as heir, he had some immunity. It was known to be a harsh and hostile place, and though such things could not be measured, he heard rumours that many of the banished took their lives rather than trying to survive in such an environment. It was where the clan father would have delivered the gentle and nervous Bo had the heir not returned. Bo would have been among those who could not survive.

The Marisene was the first area the Nobles settled when they arrived on this planet aeons before. Forced to flee persecution by their origin ancestors, they crossed galaxies to establish a homeworld where they could live in peace. As the largest single region, the Marisene became the central estate for all levels of hierarchical houses. Members of lesser houses and tribal ordinaries were admitted to the Marisene only upon invitation, such as for employment or betrothals, and always under the watchful eye of House Anevan.

The sprawling palaces that dotted the Marisene landscape gleamed a brilliant white with mined stone from northern quarries. Hierarchical sibs favoured mosaic flooring crafted from gemstones, with handwoven textiles and sumptuous furnishings to add luxury and grandeur. Throughout, holographic waterfalls, almost impossible to distinguish from the real thing, cascaded in splendour from man-made cliffs in every quarter. The Nobles' lavish tastes in food were catered for by dedicated farmland tilled and tended by tribal ordinary farmers and horticulturists.

Elsewhere on the homeworld, the lesser Nobles and the tribal ordinaries were free to live as splendidly or humbly as they wished. The hierarchy placed few constraints on the ordinary peoples' enjoyment of any technology developed by Nobles. The only exceptions were space-going vehicles. Besides the maintenance fleet used by selected tribal ordinaries to maintain the interventionist and police fleets, the Noble hierarchy kept several research vessels for their most senior scientists. Apart from these, the hierarchy restricted off-world travel to avoid contamination or infiltration by the ten sectors.

The ancestors who built House Anevan's palace set it high on an island hillside, where views of the sparkling sea on the western edge swept across to the dense, dark forests in the east. It also afforded high ground in the event of insurgency by the lesser houses or ground attack by an enemy. To Yianevan's knowledge, no house had ever tested the theory behind that paranoia.

Although he saw the beauty of the world, he took no joy in being born into a ruling house with so little vision and substance. Was it enough there was no war? Was it enough the only progress came with technology? The culture had stagnated, and he could not live life in the same way as the generations before him, not after knowing the wonders that existed beyond the walls of the homeworld. By the stars, he only wanted peace, but he could not be peaceful here without change. He wanted to be the first to offer a genuine hand in friendship to the ten sectors, allow them access to the homeworld, and create a freer and progressive society for his people. Perhaps then, he would not feel so "cloistered".

A rueful smile came to his lips as he remembered Bethan's words to describe her life. Memories of her disturbed rather than calmed, and he had yet to find a place in his heart where knowing she was out there in the galaxy did not bring pain.

The clan father had engaged the two betrotheds, so Yianevan couldn't even look upon his chambers as a sanctuary once the excitement following his return died down. He spent each day from morning ablutions to late evening in the company of his sib, joining in pointless activities designed to prevent him from solitude. He predicted it would be this way for some considerable time, so he had no option but to prepare himself to lose his privacy, his quiet, and live without the peace he knew with Bethan.

Following tradition, each woman would present in his chamber on consecutive nights. The clan father was eager to seal a marriage between his son and both women, a pledge that would not happen until a male child resulted from the coupling. Yianevan knew nothing of the women who would attend, only that one was from an equal house and one from a lesser.

It didn't matter because attraction or emotional connection were not requirements of a betrothal. They were designed only to produce an heir and continue the posterity of the house. Yianevan believed betrothals would make for a somewhat distant and bland affair with no relationship other than that required to procreate. If a man or woman wished for a deeper connection, they could take an "Amuse", a casteless distinction that permitted liaisons between any consenting adults, from tribal ordinary right through to Noble hierarchy. However, tradition restricted the unions in that there could never be a child, no status, and no absorption into either sib. For him, taking an Amuse would enhance loneliness rather than assuage it.

In a betrothal to a hierarchical male, a woman from a lesser house stood to gain considerable status for her child. Most accepted these assignments because of the personal benefits they provided, particularly if they were career motivated, but for a woman of the hierarchy, betrothal meant only absorption into another ruling house. So unless a woman wished for motherhood, a clan father's offer of betrothal to an heir would often be declined in favour of an Amuse, or even multiple Amuses.

A month following his return, Yianevan waited in his chambers for his first betrothed's presentation. Instead, his little sister, born years after he left, slipped through the door with a cheeky grin. The girl, Kerys, was the breath of fresh air he needed when he arrived back. Now, almost eighteen, she had been an unexpected addition to the sib, as Yianevan's father had already past eighty years. Bo's mother was older than expected for a female to make another venture into motherhood, but his father rejoiced in the daughter, and Yianevan understood why. Kerys was a delight, and it appeared she had bonded with him, although she shouldn't be here under the circumstances, and he needed to send her away.

"I am awaiting my betrothed, little sister," he said with a smile but did not invite her to linger.

Kerys ignored him and climbed onto his divan.

"I know," she said, "but Yi, I have waited all my life to meet you, and we have scarcely spoken."

"That's not true, Kerys. We speak together often."

"Yes, but we are always with the sib, and I want us to be friends."

"We are brother and sister," he teased. "We are not meant to be friends."

"You mean like Aaris?" Kerys screwed up her face. "I am not like Aaris. I respect you and your rejection of our traditions. When I was small, I made up stories about your travels."

Yianevan lifted an eyebrow. "How so?" He was about to say she was only seventeen, and how could she know anything about his early life, but his rebellion and first escape attempt came at the same age she was now. It would be patronising to contradict her.

"I don't like that there are people around me all the time," Kerys said, her voice edged with irritation. "I want to spend my time in the archives, studying and reading. Father engaged a tutor from Tribe Bul because he wishes to encourage what he calls my 'lively mind', and I have a study area. He also granted me access to the shipyards, but I may not fly a shuttle on my own. I love science, especially engineering, but I will never go further into space than the shipyards because I'm hierarchy."

Yianevan understood her frustration. He'd felt those same things himself. He still felt them now that he'd returned, but where his sister's sentiments were of longing, he only felt loss.

"Our father is reasonable," he said, choosing his words with care so as not to inflame an already tense situation if those same words got back to the clan father. "He is not always so indulgent or obliging. Be thankful."

"Thankful?" Kerys sat as far back on her heels as she could. "*Thankful?* That we are born into a life where tradition suppresses our individuality and tramples our freedoms?"

"That is dramatic, little sister," Yianevan said, meeting her complaint with firmness, although she was only expressing his own secret thoughts. "Your studies in science may lead to great knowledge to share among all people. You may invent and discover amazing technology."

She looked at him in disbelief. Then gave him a slow, wide-eyed nod.

"You are so *right*!" Her voice rose, fuelled by passion, resentment, and the tiniest hint of sarcasm. "*My* knowledge, *my* creations, *my* work, will be handed to the lesser houses and the tribal ordinaries because that is the hierarchy's way. Is that fair when those achievements are mine? Yi, study brings purpose, but when my ideas are to be applied by someone anointed with greater liberty, how will I remain in the shadows?"

"Development of technology is not the destiny of House Anevan, Kerys," Yianevan said evenly. "The most capable scientists are from the other houses, both lesser and hierarchical. The only glory our father seeks is tribute from the ten sectors. That is no secret."

His sister folded her arms and glared, but he dare not encourage her, at least for now, so he would have to suffer her indignance.

"Brother," she said. "I think you deliberately misunderstand. I do not seek glory. Only a point to my existence. Until I am twenty, I am encouraged to education, but even if I am offered betrothal to a lesser house, as hierarchy, I will always be bound by hierarchical rules. There is no escape." She tried to temper her tone because she wanted to show her brother that she was too old for petulance. Even so, she grumbled. "I may as well be like Aaris and have no passion."

Yianevan didn't misunderstand. He just wanted to protect her.

"Aaris has passion," he said. "It simply manifests in an ambition that will benefit no-one but herself."

"She is an embittered hag who does not hide her opinions. She wastes her existence."

"And that is what will happen to you unless you change your attitude. Kerys, we are Noble hierarchy. We cannot change what we are." *At least not yet*, he added silently.

Kerys would have scowled, but he was looking directly at her, and she still wanted to impress him. But that statement was what she would expect of a defeatist. Something the younger, quieter brother Bo might have said. How disappointing to hear such tame words fall from her rebellious brother's lips. What had happened to him to turn him into a docile pet? He had been absent for twenty years and had yet to see things were not as he left them.

"Our world is not the same, Yi," she told him, showing far more wisdom than Yianevan did at her age. "It has changed. The people have changed. I *will* see the galaxy, with or without the clan father's sanction, but I hope you will be ruler by then, and we will see some relaxation of these archaic rules. The alternative is I will go mad. Do you wish that on your conscience? The entire population of the Noble homeworld lives with freedoms and choices that we as hierarchy are denied."

"We limit off-world travel, Kerys," Yianevan pointed out. It was a fact she would be aware of and part of her frustration. "It comes only by sanction of House Anevan, even for those who travel within the ten sectors. The tribal ordinaries work within the bounds set by the hierarchy, so even they are not free."

"*You* went off-world."

Yianevan grinned. "I was a thorn in the hierarchy's side. Our father was glad to be rid of me. I do not counsel you to follow in my footsteps."

"Don't worry. I can be patient."

He felt for her. His responses sounded weak, but he had little choice for now, not while he needed to gain the clan father's complete trust. Yianevan had resigned himself to ruling, and it was only from that position could he make any of the changes Kerys demanded. In the weeks since he returned, he had seen for himself the difference in the attitude of the lesser houses. Reform would take time but would not come at all if his father suspected him of opposition to established rule. Kerys's feelings wouldn't change, even though the reforms she desired might not come soon enough.

"You know the tribal ordinaries live by their own accords, Yi," she said. "We younger hierarchy envy them. Look around House Anevan, House Numij, any house within the Marisene, and you will see more and more of the youth seeking ownership of their achievements. Do you understand, Yi? The hierarchy must change if it wishes to stay relevant."

He recalled his own youthful impatience. At least Kerys was not taking it to the same extremes. "Things will be different, little sister," he promised. "I only ask that you be patient and not voice these notions in our father's hearing."

She searched her brother's face for signs that he spoke the truth. Then nodded her agreement. She said everything she needed to say, at least for now, and hoped her brother would prove to be a kindred spirit. He was so much older and had seen so much more. Perhaps he knew better. Still, she could be patient, as he asked, at least with him. She jumped down from the divan.

"I'll try. Now, I'd better go. You should be busy making a grandchild for the clan father."

Kerys slipped through the door just as the betrothed arrived, carrying a tray of ceremonial wine. The vibrant liquid contained an aphrodisiac that Yianevan had doubts would work on him in his present frame of mind. Anticipation of what the evening required turned him to thoughts of Bethan. Whatever transpired here tonight, whatever duty called for, no other woman would ever take her place.

With a smile, the betrothed offered him a cup of wine.

"Yi," she said. "I am Willa, of House Eiled."

Willa had fewer compound retinas, suggesting ancestral inbreeding with tribal ordinaries. She was of slighter build than most Noble females, her skin pale with a soft sheen the colour of moonlight. Her silvery-white hair, never cut under Noble tradition, draped in elegant braids and loops over her neck and shoulders.

As expected of betrotheds on the first night, Willa had painted the inside of her mouth with gold pigment and wore a sheer flowing gown of purple. As nudity held no intrigue for Nobles, tradition considered covering the body with jewelled colours enhanced arousal. This ensured, along with the aphrodisiac, the coupling would prove effective, but as the convention was incumbent on both participants, Willa found it curious that her betrothed was not only unpainted but dressed in daytime attire.

The clan father informed Willa of the heir's historical rejection of protocols. While his appearance was a little startling, she settled herself beside him on the divan and raised her cup, waiting for him so they would consume the wine together.

He did not drink. Instead, he placed the cup on the table beside him, and for a moment, Willa could only blink in bewilderment at this second conspicuous infringement of custom.

Then she also placed her cup on the table. This was leading somewhere. So far, the heir was living up to his reputation as a non-conformist.

Yianevan felt a flush of guilt for his dismissal of tradition. It wasn't Willa's fault, but the memory of Bethan would always be between them.

He knew about House Eiled, a lesser house whose abilities in medicine and botany were widely regarded throughout the homeworld. His own mother was also one of their daughters. It was a house on the verge of extinction, so this betrothal would considerably boost its fortunes, but the hierarchy also considered it politically more progressive. That alone made it interesting his father would choose someone such as Willa. Not when he did not yet trust his own son's motives.

"Tell me about yourself," he said.

Willa had been betrothed before, so she wanted to make sure she understood what the heir desired. Or desired first. She had dressed to arouse, braided her hair, offered him wine fortified with an aphrodisiac, but perhaps not enough to persuade him. She smoothed the coverlet on the divan in invitation and smiled.

"Don't you think we should…?"

His reply was unexpected. "I'm disinclined tonight," he said. "I would prefer we just talk."

Disinclined? Willa had never considered the prospect of engaging in conversation in preference to coupling at the first meeting.

"Disinclined, Yi? Can you even say you are disinclined? I must ask. Is this a rejection? Is that why you placed the wine on the table?"

Yianevan sighed. "I am not rejecting you, Willa. No doubt the clan father apprised you of my unorthodoxy. It is only that I would prefer to get to know the woman with whom I am to found a dynasty." He smiled. "We have no obligation to tell my father what transpires here tonight."

Willa conceded this was certainly unorthodox. The clan father had made her aware that he disapproved of his son's actions in the past but assured her his rebellion was now resolved. Armed with that knowledge, she should have expected the unexpected.

He watched Willa puzzle over the situation, half expecting her to walk out. That would have left him with some explaining to do. Instead, she grinned.

"I must admit, the betrothal invitation came as a surprise," she confessed. "I am not generally in your father's view. House Eiled abides far distant from here, far lower on the social level. However, I will admit to being intrigued by your rebellion when I learned of it." She leaned her head to one side. "I found it rather entertaining."

Entertaining? He would have considered his disdain for tradition off-putting.

"Intrigued?" he said. That word lightened his mood, and he laughed. "Entertaining? That's very gracious and far better than feeling obligated, as I have been told my other betrothed feels. She is of similar rank to me and will know more about the folly of my youth. My father refers to my past as disloyal and rebellious, so I am surprised he found any woman to accept the betrothal."

"He believes you are reformed," Willa told him. "I know your other betrothed took some convincing from her family."

Yianevan knew that, and he would face her when the

time came. For now, he would get to know Willa, beautiful, educated, everything a clan father would demand for his son. But he didn't know her yet, and she wasn't Bethan. Even though no woman would fill his heart again, he had little choice but to accept Willa into his life. He invited her to join him at the window seat, where he prompted her to tell him her story. That, and no other diversion, would be the order for tonight.

She told him of her first betrothal, which resulted in twin girls and a cleaving to a man she cherished. An older man, but in a rare move for Nobles, they cleaved only to one another and shared a deep bond. His death had left a scar, and as she was not a woman to take an Amuse, she had been alone for ten years. There had never been a sister-wife to help with the children, and as her own sib was small, she placed her career as a physician on hold.

When the clan father presented this opportunity to her, and with the two girls now growing up, she allowed her personal ambitions to direct her to accept. She had developed a keen interest in certain viruses that resulted in cyclical pandemics within the ten sectors but was limited in her research. Now, her work had stalled, and to regain momentum, she would need to spend some time off-world. As her heritage was not hierarchical, this assignment to the heir would not only permit her to continue studying but might provide the possibility of access to the affected worlds. Of course, the hierarchy would impose some limitations, but Willa felt able to work within those parameters. Besides, she did not wish to leave her daughters for long periods, anticipating that when she and Yianevan had a child, with his vast, extended sib, she could enjoy motherhood *and* her career.

When she finished, Yianevan laughed.

"You are quite the mercenary, Willa! You know we will expect you to share in the care of a child during its infancy?"

She gave an elegant shrug. "I am inclined to motherhood, Yi, but I hope to share a child with a sister-wife. I look forward to being in a family again, but motherhood alone does not fulfil me. After dedicating myself to my daughters and sib for ten years, I would like to return to my research. Satra is Noble hierarchy and immerses herself in the hierarchical lifestyle. As an academic, it does not appeal to me."

"Satra?"

"Yes, your other betrothed." She frowned. "Am I the first?"

"Yes, she declined that honour. I didn't know it was Satra. We knew each other as children."

Willa bit her lip. She had made an uncomfortable revelation. "Then I am sorry to have revealed it. Satra is traditional, and as her house is aligned with yours, I would expect her to be presented before me."

Yianevan couldn't care less about the tradition of the betrothed announcing herself. Was it meant to be a surprise? Foreplay? Names were something you could pick up and put down at will. They didn't tell the world, any world, about who and what you are.

That evening, besides lively conversation, there was no other exchange between Willa and Yianevan. Later, after she left, he stretched out on the divan and enjoyed these moments of solitude. Throughout their few hours together, he found Willa's manner easy and saw the possibility of friendship. He respected her for wishing to continue her career, even though he teased her about being a mercenary. She made no apology for her inclination away from tradition, and he enjoyed her candour while envying her freedom to reserve her time from the sib and their shallow excesses. As heir and soon to be clan father, that liberty was denied him. For now, the world would expect him to be wherever the sib congregated, just like his father and his father before him.

During the evening, Willa told him she believed the hierarchy needed to be less precious—a good word—about mingling with other species. Further, she thought they needed to ease their control of all Nobles who spent time off-world. Her views were not treasonous or radical, and he saw the same inclinations in his little sister. He even heard similar rumblings among the lesser houses. It seemed change would come even without him, although he was unsure how anyone would implement it without resistance from the hierarchy. The dissatisfaction he felt twenty years ago had spread to others, taken root, and grown. Headstrong and reckless, he hadn't realised then that he was not alone.

Satra attended Yianevan the next night. Tall, slender, and striking in feature, but with a cold and perfunctory manner, she gave the traditional introduction, drank the wine in a single gulp and laid on her back on the divan to await him. He felt an obligation to drink the wine because joining with

Satra might prove ineffective if he didn't. It was over quickly, and Satra stood, adjusted her untraditional, copious layers of clothing, and left without another word.

He watched her hurried departure, desperate to be free of him. Then he laughed out loud. Tradition. Duty. It was all so absurd.

Rolling off the bed, he changed his clothes, then hoisted himself through the window to make his way to the observatory garden. Spreading himself out on his back on the grass, he gazed into the night sky. What would Bethan think if she could see him now, attempting to conceive a child with a woman who could barely tolerate him?

He knew from where Satra's resentment stemmed. Kerys told him she had taken a tribal ordinary Amuse to whom she had become attached. Her sib insisted she took the assignment to the clan heir and threatened to dissolve her relationship with the Amuse if she did not comply. It was understandable she would be resentful, but a hierarchical clan father's word was law. So even Willa's concern about Yianevan rejecting her on their first night wasn't valid. He didn't have that power.

The next morning, as dawn spread fingers of light across the hills, Yianevan stood and stretched. Although his muscles ached from sleeping on the grass, he had spent a pleasant night out here. The heavens were breathtaking, and he wearied his eyes by staring skyward to search for Earth, making postage-stamp-sized grids to narrow down the parameter. He could have located it easily in the observatory, but that wouldn't be the same as a memory of Llyn Deron and Bethan's nearness as he pointed out the stars.

As they often did when his thoughts turned to her, he suffered the realisation that no matter how much he wished for it to be otherwise, the real Bethan existed only in his heart. She was now Phildre, back in her real world. Could there even be a place, in that vast expanse of time, where Bethan still loved him?

Kerys fell into step beside him as he entered the courtyard.

"Did you like Satra?" she asked.

He placed an arm around her. "You are bold, little sister, and you interest yourself far too much in business that does not concern you."

"Really?" Kerys stopped walking and slapped his arm away. The action stunned him, and he turned to face her.

"If you had liked her," she snapped, "you would smile when I say her name. But you don't."

Yianevan didn't understand her attitude. "I must accept whomever our father engages."

"No, you don't, Yi," came her fierce retort. "If you make yourself wretched for his sake, you will disappoint me and prove you are weak, as Aaris says. Only you can bring transformation, so don't condemn those who prayed for your return." Then she turned on her heel and headed toward the waterfall.

He watched her stalk away. Was he too compliant, too tractable? Perhaps, but he wasn't ruler yet, and might not be for years if his father didn't trust him to uphold tradition. He had to live the lie a little longer, and neither his little sister nor this homeworld should look upon him as a saviour.

Like Yianevan, Willa realised that a successful betrothal went further than an aphrodisiac. That was why she understood his preference to at least foster the beginnings of a relationship once she got over her surprise on their first night. At their next meeting, she found him on the window seat when the door slid open to admit her to his chamber. Tonight, his dress remained untraditional, making her wonder if this was to be another evening of conversation only. He didn't greet her, just took the cup from her hand and set it on the table. Then he released the two ties that held her gown in place. As it fell away, he placed his mouth against hers, and in response, she held her soft, warm body against his. His thoughts went to Bethan, and ashamed, he pulled away. Willa understood neither the kiss nor his confused, apologetic expression when he stopped. To encourage him, she smiled gently and took his hands in hers.

"What's wrong, Yi?"

"Nothing," he said. At least nothing he could admit to, so drawing Willa to the divan, he kissed her again.

"Is this a prelude?" she asked, touching her lips. "You know you don't need to."

"It's a kiss, Willa," Yianevan said. "It's something other species…humans, do. I learned it while I was away, and I… well, I find it pleasurable. We can perform it as an act of affection or a prelude to procreation. I'll show you."

She laughed then. "I see. Am I also to be your Amuse?"

"You enjoyed a devoted relationship with your

husband, much more than a basic coupling."

"We were each other's Amuses, Yi, and I have never heard of 'kiss'." She moved closer, ran her fingertips down his neck, and pressed a shallow area under his collarbone, a point of heightened sensitivity on a Noble male. His expression gave nothing away. Perhaps to kiss was his way of igniting desire. No matter, she was well-schooled in the passionate arts.

CHAPTER THIRTY-FOUR

In those first few weeks, the clan watched for signs of restlessness, so Yianevan kept his feelings close to his heart, presenting as a man resigned to his destiny. His father realised his son was unsettled, but he had satisfied tradition, which was all that mattered. Appearances were paramount, and he would adjust. Besides, the alternative would be unthinkable to someone with a conscience, such as Yi, and that was the fact of the matter.

Because of the clan father's mistrust, the sib granted Yianevan little solitude. In daylight hours, he remained in the sib's company, which meant that Bo, Kerys, and their mother, along with Aaris, her husband, and her children, were always with him, giving him little opportunity to devote any time to the study of the pennant. Often, the wider clan joined them, which included aunts, uncles, cousins, and their extended families.

Most nights, Yianevan found comfort in Willa's company. They established a friendship that often saw them neglecting the rituals for which she became his betrothed.

Satra, meanwhile, chose only to accept an offer of a visit to appease the clan father, and she never once asked for Yianevan's attendance in return, which Willa did, often. Yet, she understood when he declined so that he might spend time alone.

Aaris confirmed to Yianevan what Kerys said, that Satra preferred her Amuse, telling him that Satra didn't wish to be tied to a weak fool like him. She also liked to challenge him that there was still no sign of a child with either woman after weeks of coupling. She took to childish taunts.

"Do you know what it's for?" she would say. "*Did you lose it out in the ten sectors, brother?"*

Yianevan ignored her lame attempts to provoke him, although he was worried about the lack of conception. The physicians reassured him, but he had thought at least Willa would have conceived by now. Perhaps they needed to engage more in intimacy during their hours together and less in conversation, in discussing her research, and their many hours in the gardens and observatory.

Weeks more passed before the family relaxed its surveillance on their favourite son. Weeks in which there was no sign of an heir. Yianevan did his duty by Satra, albeit with increasing difficulty, but the only moments that approached happiness were with Willa. He continued to find his raucous sib and restricted privacy a challenge. His attempts to spend time alone didn't go unnoticed, and often, Kerys spotted him in the secluded area of the gardens, seeking at least a few moments of solitude, far from the encroaching clamour of community. She made every excuse to bend his ear about her constellation of plans for the

Noble homeworld and the changes he must make if the hierarchy remained. Other times, he would hide away in the archives, where the buzz of his loud, jovial sib gave way to blessed peace. If Aaris discovered him there, and she usually did, she delighted in drawing him back to the family on the pretext it was the clan father's wish.

When he became clan father, Yianevan knew he would have support. Willa spoke as Kerys did but as an older woman, took a milder, more mature attitude. She was well-considered throughout the lesser houses, and her father was a wise leader. Willa and Kerys' expectations for the future of the hierarchy were not without merit, although Willa's focus seemed to be more on the inclusivity of other species. However, she accepted the need for subtlety. This was not an egalitarian society, and Yianevan knew many Noble houses would reject embracing different cultures. It would be difficult to strike a balance, but he felt ready to find that balance. For the first time, rather than viewing his life as a prison, he felt a growing anticipation to lead the homeworld into a new age. It would not be like the bumbling fiasco he created on the human world. He had grown in wisdom since then.

Meanwhile, because of the demands on his time, he made little headway in understanding the pennant. He managed only snatched moments late at night or in the early hours, and so far, the archives had yielded nothing. The filigree patterns made sense on an intellectual level, but the initiation process that might arise within the plexus escaped him. He noted tiny "scars" on the filigree that interrupted the flow of the language but didn't comprehend their purpose, nor could he understand them. Nevertheless, they appeared to be an integral component of the language. He decided against the use of any deciphering tool which might leave a signature and further deemed it unwise to attempt activation near the Marisene in case it projected a Monk's Gate-like anomaly.

Coupled with the historical lies that arose from the discovery, Yianevan decided he had to do all in his power to keep the pennant concealed, even though he didn't know how he would ever find time to dedicate himself to its interpretation. It occurred to him he always needed time. More time on Earth. More time with Bethan. So, to gain extra time, he sacrificed sleep, taking to rising before the morning bell sounded and spending those stolen moments in the tranquil setting of the archives. Unless Aaris came looking, it was the only place his family would leave him in peace, if only for a short while. He considered enlisting Corky's help but still hadn't revealed the pennant's existence to the interface. Corky remained on Yianevan's ship, which now never left the planet other than to go to the pontoon or shipyards. Otherwise, Yianevan only used it to visit provinces or other Noble houses outside the Marisene, and when he did, Bo and Kerys always accompanied him.

One sib lived in an area abounding with hot springs, a place he frequented with his mother when he was a child. It didn't hold the same fascination now, but as the hierarchical family were so welcomed, Bo wished to linger to socialise and enjoy the waters.

While they waited, Yianevan and Kerys discussed hierarchy politics. His sister always made grand assumptions about the reforms he would make when he ascended to rule, even though to protect her from her own eagerness, he didn't reveal that he would make any of a significant nature. He doubted Kerys spoke of her dissatisfaction to their father, but he still cautioned her not to make too free with her words, at least none where she mentioned his name.

As expected, she met his caution with protest.

"Willa agrees with me," she said. "And Aaris wants change, too."

"Aaris has her own agenda," Yianevan reminded her. "If I died out there in the ten sectors, Bo would have become heir, and if he ascended, Aaris would most likely become regent. He's afraid of her sharp tongue, and he is not a leader, so he would accept her counsel for the sake of peace. His peace. There would be division and possible civil war if he listened to her. She does not show all her hands, Kerys. Do not trust her."

"Our father is not as steeped in tradition as you believe, Yi," Kerys said. "When it suits him, he ignores it and makes his own rules. While you were exiled, did you know he considered making Bo his heir? He changed his mind when your mother died."

"I did know, and also that he reconsidered."

"Why was that do you suppose?"

"Because traditionally, the eldest son succeeds and, as I said, Bo is not a leader."

"He knew that when you left."

Fair enough. It was an intriguing question why the clan father changed his mind about Bo and insisted Yianevan return. A question not so far answered.

"Then I don't know why," Yianevan said. "As you are across all the information, perhaps you should be clan father."

"Don't mock, Yi," Kerys grinned. "Aaris believes hierarchical daughters should be in the line of succession. I agree, although my views are far more encompassing. We need to open up to the rest of the ten sectors, but you know as well as I do, no hierarchical council will hear such a petition. Sometimes change needs a revolution."

"Sister," he groaned. She would not let up until she drew him into conflict with the hierarchy. "Please grow up a little more before you become a revolutionary."

"*Brother*," she drawled in response. "Does that mean you plan a revolt?

"It means that Aaris pretends to be moderate to win over the disgruntled. Kerys, I know of her whisperings about me to the other houses and that our father ignores her politics because he considers her views foolish and born only from envy. Jealousy has not clouded your vision, as it has our sister, but even I cannot transform your dissatisfaction into a utopia overnight."

"I would join a revolution if it would bring freedom from our traditional constraints."

Yianevan felt a ripple of concern about Kerys's zeal. She needed to temper her enthusiasm.

"Would you?" he said. "Will conflict offer a quick solution? Aaris has no interest in benefitting the planet, and we won't need a war if we change our world a little at a time. Not if we use a discerning hand and sensitivity to the people's desires."

Kerys looked impressed. "A democracy. I like that, but if there comes a day when hierarchical females can rule, I am in line, and I will order freedom in all things for everyone. Even those who don't choose it. So, Yi, if you don't wish for Aaris to make regent, you must have your own son, or until then, make sure you don't die."

"I'll try, little sister," Yianevan sighed. "On both counts, I will try."

CHAPTER THIRTY-FIVE _

One evening, during one of Satra's rare visits, she wasted no time finding a reason to become contentious before storming out. It didn't matter to Yianevan. He'd barely said a word but felt grateful she left before she treated him to one of her shrewish displays of dissatisfaction.

Glad of the respite, he poured himself a cup of Birn. The pungent aroma made him grimace, and he lamented that the rugged taste no longer satisfied, doubtless stemming from nostalgia for whisky. Still, it might dull the aftermath of Satra's presence and remind him that he needed to come up with a palatable formula to make Birn smoother and more like its human world counterpart.

With that in mind, Yianevan picked up the wine cup and wondered if blending the two drinks might change the texture. Of course, it would be unwise to add too much; the added aphrodisiac might just give him a sleepless night, but as he weighed the possibility of such an experiment, a tiny glint on the wine cup's rim caught his eye. With a chuckle, he lifted away a fragment of crystal-like residue and rolled it between his thumb and forefinger. How long had Aaris been adding this to his wine? He expected her to attempt something far more sinister. It would have delighted her to use the disagreeable, and most likely highly complicit, Satra as her agent.

The following morning, immersed in further fruitless searching of the archives for any mention of the mysterious pennant, Yianevan missed the ablutions bell. Aaris found him surrounded by an array of data tiles. She pushed them out of her way.

"I thought to find Willa attached to you like the scales on a gossicle limpet fish," she said with her trademark sarcasm. "I marvel, as you seem so fond of her, she has not yet conceived."

Yianevan viewed her through the holograms that had collided in a pile as she flicked them to the side. "What is your interest in my affairs, sister? I am engaged with far more diverting topics than your gossip."

"I am interested only in seeing you fail," came Aaris's tart reply. "I am sent by our father. He requests your attendance."

"Did he say why? I spoke to him only last night."

"He did," Aaris replied. "He tells me all, but you will have to attend him to find out." Aaris liked to think she sounded superior, but to Yianevan, she lacked any grace or style. It made him wonder how the lesser houses received her covert campaigning against him. He shook his head. "When I am ruler, I will tell you nothing. I may even have you banished."

Aaris didn't believe her brother had the stomach to carry out such a threat. "You could have stayed away," she said. "Our father would have come to terms."

"And leave our brother to take his anger? I would not have Bo outcast because of me."

"He based his conditions on your sentiment, Yi," Aaris told him. "He knew how to manipulate you into returning, even though he has a worthy candidate to succeed in my eldest son. I expected to hear of your death out there in the ten sectors. Then I believe father's good sense would have prevailed. He would have made my son heir over Bo and appointed me, as the boy's mother, regent until his majority. That is our way. And our father is old and close to abdication."

His sister wanted power. Yianevan knew that. If she could not rule, then she would have succession pass through her own children. It was there she would have the most influence. He did not realise before he came back the extent of her appetite. Her son was still in his youth, with his majority many years hence. Long enough for his mother to twist his mind.

He shook his head. "I am sorry to have spoiled your petty ambition, but I have no intention of dying,"

Aaris sniffed. "Pity. I rather hoped you'd fall into that volcano on the human world. I expect you didn't just to spite me."

Not in the humour for a juvenile trade of insults, Yianevan removed a scrap of lint from his pocket and placed it on the bench. Aaris peered at the tiny twist of fabric.

"A gift?" she sneered. "How sweet."

"In a sense," Yianevan said with a smile. "Your gift to me. I am returning it."

He opened the lint, and the crystal remnant glistened accusingly. Aaris glanced down but made no attempt to deny her involvement. Yianevan couldn't help it. He burst into laughter.

"Tarpir residue? Is this the best you can do, sister? Render me infertile?"

Aaris shrugged, unruffled he had uncovered her plot. "You should thank me. You don't want a child, anyway."

"So say you to the lesser houses!" Yianevan saw her mouth tighten. She didn't know he was aware of this brand of her slander. "Aaris, it is not for you to decide." He planted his hands on the bench, forcing her to make strong, unwavering eye contact. "Know this, *sister*. Your son will never be my heir. If I remain childless, it will not strengthen the position of you or your children. You are treacherous, serving only your own desires, and now the Tarpir is revealed, I look forward to fatherhood."

Aaris's golden eyes glittered hard and cold. Unrepentant, she stepped close enough for him to feel her breath. She would not pretend, nor would she back down.

"I speak the truth to the lesser houses, Yi," she spat. "Our father is a fool to have you succeed him. Twenty years in the ten sectors have done nothing to quell your rebellious spirit. You are not to be trusted. Mark these words, brother, House Anevan will sink into ruin under your rule."

"Oh? And who *should* rule, sister? You? Women do not rule in the hierarchy, and the houses will not be worn down by you or your son. Only the clan father of House Anevan can decree a change in succession. Therefore, inflaming the lesser houses' opinion against our father or me will not further your cause."

Aaris's lip curled. "A woman can rule as well as any man," she snarled. "You must know Satra has had enough of you and your weak ways. She wants father to offer release so she can return to her Amuse."

Yianevan disengaged. He did not wish to argue further because it would get them nowhere.

"Then I wish that hapless Amuse luck," he said. "Why doesn't she resign from the assignment? It is her right. I would spurn her if she wasn't father's choice."

Instead of coming back at him with a snide retort, Aaris's earlier steeliness faltered. He'd touched on a point that disconcerted her.

"She can't. It's some agreement between her father and ours. I don't know what it is." The confusion was momentary, fleeing as soon as she regained her imagined superiority. She would not let her fool of a brother witness any vulnerability. "I only know you are not worthy of her," she stated. "She was glad of the Tarpir. Her Amuse is twice the man you are."

Yianevan didn't care, but he couldn't resist pointing out that Satra's Amuse was not the heir. She could have satisfied her clan and kept her Amuse into the bargain.

"Now, sister," he said, keen to finish the exchange. "Do I need to look over my shoulder in case Tarpir becomes something more ominous?"

"I will neither confirm nor deny your suspicions,

brother. No-one overhears us here, and our father trusts me over you." She gestured to the data tiles. "What are you studying? Means of escape?"

"Nothing of interest to you."

"Everything you do interests me. Is that the ancient language of pennants?"

She would give him no peace, so Yianevan flicked along the array of tiles. This was a common study area, so it would not arouse her suspicions.

"How *dull*," she scoffed. "Perhaps I should report to the clan father you are stuffing your mind with trivia. If you seek banality, then find Crane, the historian from Tribe Bul. He's responsible for the organisation of many of the archives here and is the authority on pennant language. He was deadly dull as well, like these tiles. You won't remember his droning on and on about pennants, but as the elder, I do."

"I might do that," Yianevan said as he dimmed the tiles and discarded his search history. "Now, I will go to see our father."

The clan father awaited his son in the garden. Alone. It was a minor concession, not one he cared to repeat too often, as he deemed Yi's sentiments about privacy nothing more than self-indulgent rubbish. He knew his heir did not enjoy the social nature of the Nobles and that he privately referred to group activities as "orgies", although none of the group meals or other activities involved sex. That was one of the few things Nobles undertook with just one other, or two or three, depending. All other events took place with the sib, and that was just how Yianevan's father liked it, keeping family where he could see and hear what they had to say. It didn't apply to him, of course. He had his own historical secrets he didn't care to share. At least not yet. All in good time. The younger ones, like Kerys, still needed to learn obedience, but she was too young to do any harm. Aaris, though, meddled too much where she had no business meddling. The clan father conceded his eldest daughter showed wisdom in one thing. The sentimental Yi could prove an unworthy ruler, although he possessed other attributes far more valuable.

Satra's father, the ruler of House Numij, and the other senior advisors to House Anevan knew the truth behind the clan father's insistence on his recalcitrant son's return to the homeworld. And it had nothing to do with taking his place as ruler of House Anevan.

Years before, the heir's mother had secured a ship with the clandestine aid of House Eidel and sent the boy out into the ten sectors. Wearied by many years of Yi's rebellion and attempts to flee the homeworld, at first, the clan father felt no loss, despite his concern the difficult youth might throw the Nobles' secrets wide open to those worlds suspicious of them. Never in history had an heir been granted leave from the homeworld, but at the time, he was glad to be rid of the complicated and argumentative Yi. He had been considering the Southern Climes — he did, after all, have another son placed to be heir—but no clan father had ever condemned his child there.

As he always did when Yi went missing, he sent the Grielik police to find him. The mother saw to it he had a head start this time, and even on a tracked ship, it took almost a year. The police discovered him disguised as a Chabin native and, according to them, maintained his belligerent attitude. Under his mother's direction, he had not identified himself so far as a Noble.

Upon learning this, the clan father allowed the exile under certain conditions. He'd dealt with Yi's attempts at escape over the years and didn't want the problems the boy caused, so he exacted penalties and restrictions on the exile, including disguise, which the former heir accepted without question, even though it meant he could not approach the homeworld again. House Eidel, the heir's mother's house, wielded considerable influence among the lesser Nobles, and returning Yi to send him to the Southern Climes would be an act he could not keep from them. Had the Grielik police returned with news of his son's demise, he would have met it with indifference, at least in private. It would be a different story in public, but he would have had to meet expectations. Now science had uncovered vital and previously unknown information, the clan father's indifference gave way to an insistence the heir return and take his rightful place in Noble society.

"My son," he said as Yianevan approached. "Aaris advises me you remain in solitary pursuits?"

"I was alone for many years, Father. It's not an easy habit to break."

"And you have been back among your people for over six months. Apart from your brother and sister, you avoid gatherings. Yi, we are a community, a social people. You must embrace your world and keep your sib close. There is peace of mind in keeping your enemies in plain sight. I promise you." It sounded like a warning.

"I find the passage from singular to many difficult to navigate," Yianevan said. "Six months against twenty years will take adjustment. The sib fills my days with activities that do not stimulate. Their conversations are superficial, and their constant chatter is nothing short of cacophony. I do not know how you bear it. None will engage in one-on-one exchanges, so I seek my own company in the archives or the observatory."

The clan father had kept a close eye on his son. While no longer openly rebellious, he still lacked conformity and loyalty to House Anevan. He paid only lip service to the customs the clan father used as a cover for a much different purpose. It may work to his advantage.

"The hierarchy lives as directed by the laws of the origin ancestors, Yi," he said. "They understood better than we that pursuit of knowledge, development of technology for the benefit of all our race, is the duty and right of all Noble hierarchy. They also saw that individual achievements fostered resentment, which led to discord. Because of this, they made it their sacred law that members of the sib congregate together, that none should be alone, and thus there can be no secrets. Therefore, those laws safeguard us by forbidding personal achievement. Those inclined to study and achieve pass what they learn to lower houses or tribal ordinaries. Our way protects us from rivalry. I trust that when you ascend, you will uphold these customs?"

To answer would call for a lie. Fortunately, the clan

father did not wait for a response. He could not read his son's chak, but he had a lifetime of gauging who he could trust and who he could not. He would know when to reveal the truth. It was not yet. But soon. It had to be soon. He had waited long enough.

"I do not wish to argue our laws," he said. "You are well-versed in them. Tell me, how do you find your sister?"

The question was bewildering and unexpected, but Yianevan read nothing in his father's tone how he should answer, so he assumed it was Kerys of whom he spoke.

"She is a delight, Father," he said. It was the truth. "We get along well."

He received a grunt in response. "I do not speak of Kerys. I speak of Aaris."

Aaris?

"Father, Aaris is unchanged since we were children."

The clan father clapped Yianevan on the shoulder, then threw back his head in uproarious laughter. "You mean outrageous? Ambitious? Treacherous? Yi, you must know of her disappointment that you did not perish out in the ten sectors?"

That was no secret, but Yianevan didn't see how that fact could place Aaris alongside humour in the same sentence.

"It is academic, Father," he replied with a puzzled frown. "I am here and of full age. I do not need a regent."

"That will not hinder her ambition, Yi," the clan father said, still grinning. "She thinks I do not hear of her whisperings, but I have eyes and ears in every corner of the Marisene."

That's good to know, Yianevan thought. The clan father's paranoia must have grown. Perhaps it was because of Aaris's dealings with the other houses or his father's lack of trust in his heir. He would check his own chambers for listening devices at the first opportunity.

"Do not underestimate your sister," his father said, setting aside his mirth. "When you ascend, she plans her own rebellion. Even now, she seeds the lesser houses and anyone within the Marisene who will listen, with promises to protect them from your plans to admit the ten sectors to our world. I doubt her first attempt at usurping you will come to much, but you must be vigilant. Even I am at the mercy of her whims."

His father would know he would never discuss his plans, illegal or otherwise, with Aaris, although it bothered Yianevan that his father had any inkling of his intentions. In such situations, denial was the safest course.

"I don't understand, Father," Yianevan said, maintaining steady eye contact. "I have never discussed such plans, nor any plans, with Aaris. She is driven by her own vain desires and wishes to excite the lesser houses against us. Let us be honest. Our people, the hierarchy, the lesser houses, and the tribal ordinaries, all have their internal system of governance. They abide, without question, by the wider laws concerning succession, technology, and contact with the ten sectors. Tell me, what is there to govern? You spend your days in idle pursuits, Father. What would Aaris gain if she were to rise against me, us, and be victorious? A sterile leadership, devoid of meaning."

The heir made valid points, and the clan father had

heard them before, but the day would soon come when it would no longer matter. What concerned him was that Aaris had an inkling about the Noble's continued surveillance of the human's planet. Nothing specific, but she knew House Anevan was not sitting back, rotting in its own indolence.

"Yours is the opinion of a spoilt child too long apart from his sib," he said. "House Anevan is as our forefathers decreed, and I see no need to allow a female to rule. Meanwhile, Aaris covers her designs by painting you in wrongdoing. She fails, for now, because most houses do not perceive you as weak, despite her scaremongering. They believe your fractious days are past, and I am glad they did not hear you speak as before, or they might turn to her words and politicking. No, the senior hierarchical houses are confident you will rule as our household has always ruled." His father made a slight bow of acknowledgement. "They foresee some trivial changes because you are right; we have a sterile and colourless rulership, and that is how I wish it. All clan fathers institute change to their landscape. It is what makes us leaders. My son, your sister's ambition will be part of my legacy to you, but you must remain strong against her. I brought you here to declare my intention that in one year, I will abdicate, and you will ascend. It is critical to me that before that time comes, you have produced an heir."

That was looking less likely. "I'm afraid Satra dislikes me."

No matter. Satra was unimportant. The clan father only introduced her because House Numij held their knowledge of their history over his house. Of course, Yi was ignorant of this. Now, it had backfired, and she could go back to her Amuse.

"You would be happy with just Willa?" he asked.

"I find her grounded, Father. I believe I need that in a wife."

"You need that in *life*, Yi," his father laughed. "It is also my preference that Willa remains, as she is the only woman of childbearing age left in House Eidel. Soon, it will pass into extinction."

The clan father rested his hand on his son's shoulder. "My son, allow yourself to settle back into your traditions. The sib must surround men such as we. Perhaps if your mother had not been complicit in your escape from the homeworld, you would not be so dissatisfied."

"I am grateful to her," Yianevan said, "and also grieved you felt it necessary to threaten Bo."

"You refused to return!" his father exclaimed. "Yi, you are no longer a wayward youth! It is time to face up to your responsibilities. I am an old man, and your brother is unworthy."

Yianevan didn't answer. There was little point in arguing over what might have been. He just wished he could learn what prompted his father to change his mind about his exile. His mother's death? He doubted it. His father didn't suffer sentiment. Yianevan would never have set foot on this planet again, and he knew his father knew that too.

Concealed behind a wall, Aaris tried to listen in on the exchange. She didn't pick up much because Yianevan's voice was like the rest of him. Soft. And the clan father kept his voice low, but his joviality as he returned to the sib showed the meeting with Yi went well. She wondered if the clan father divulged any information about the human planet to her brother. Finding Yi neck-deep in historical data tiles about pennants piqued her interest, so telling him about Crane might not have been a good move. There had to be a link between her father's secret and Yi. Some, if not all, came down to pennants and quite possibly the extinct House Waino.

After leaving his father, Yianevan went to his ship to enlist Corky's aid in locating Crane, but Corky couldn't help. Addresses weren't part of his programming. There were records about Crane's notable contribution to philosophy and history, but he otherwise appeared to have dropped off the map. However, there was one glimmer of hope. Kerys's tutor was of the same tribe as Crane. He went in search of his sister and found her with her friends. He took her aside.

"Your tutor is Tribe Bul, isn't she?" he asked.

"Yes, why?"

"There's a teacher I wish to contact. An expert on pennants."

"Pennants?" Kerys grinned. "Yi, you need to get out more."

He ignored the comment. "His name is Crane. I tried the interface, but nothing showed. Will you ask your tutor?"

"Of course," Kerys said. "I've heard of him. He didn't contribute to the tribe by fatherhood because he consecrated his life to teaching and study. It seems too much going on in that head for anything to go on with other parts of his body! You might not locate him because I hear he doesn't want to be found. He's ancient."

"Will you try?"

With a smile, and because she respected him, she assured him she would.

He didn't have to wait long. Kerys arrived at his chamber later in the day. She didn't ask for admittance, simply overrode the controls, as she often did, and took a running leap to bounce on the divan beside him. Yianevan frowned.

"No respect for privacy, little sister?"

"Not on this planet, brother," Kerys giggled. "I didn't ask the tutor outright because I think you're keeping a big secret. Instead, I steered the conversation around to Crane, and she told me where he lived. It's remote, but the interface will find the coordinates."

She leaned across to open the interface, but Yianevan stopped her.

"No, I will check with the interface on my ship."

This was definitely a secret! "Yi, is this something our father mustn't know about?"

Yianevan didn't want to raise suspicions. Reading about pennants is one thing. Going on all-out research is another. Lies worked well in the past, so he would try one now.

"Father told me I spend too much time in inactivity. I have promised to change and be more sociable, but I was in the middle of a project, and it pleases me to finish it."

Kerys eyed him. She might be over twenty years younger than him, but she wasn't a fool.

"You're up to something, Yi," she said with a

suspicious grin. "Don't worry, I won't say anything, but I will expect an explanation later. Crane lives in a retreat in the north, but don't go as yourself. He won't want the others to think he's courting the hierarchy because the scholars don't have a very high opinion of us. Cover your hair, take the time to grow ocular prostheses, and act like you know where you're going. Otherwise, they'll think you just drifted in and escort you out."

It was clear Kerys had researched this, so Yianevan agreed to her directions.

"And another thing. Don't take your own ship. Take a tribal ordinary internal shuttle. They won't bother tracking it."

"Yes, Kerys."

"Shall I come with you?"

"I would prefer to go alone, and Kerys, I appreciate your silence."

She nodded. "It is as I said, brother. You and I are kindred spirits."

CHAPTER THIRTY-SIX _

A day later, Yianevan spiralled from a single occupant light shuttle onto the outskirts of the cantonment where the historian lived. He wore the garb of a tribal ordinary and had generated optical prostheses the previous night to cover his compound retinas. If the dwellers gave him a passing thought, it would be to speculate at the youth of a visitor in a commune of ancients.

Despite Kerys's insistence to head straight to Crane's abode, Yianevan was so taken with the beauty of the cantonment he slowed his pace to admire the architectural work of art the occupants created. Many scholars lived here, but so did many former engineers, and it would be logical for each dwelling to gleam with high-end technology. Instead, the structures wove upwards and side to side in an extraordinary labyrinth of graceful terraces and gravity-defying courtyards. A few dwellings faced lakelands and waterfalls. Others had views of rolling hills and mountains, but all the shutters were open to the beauty of the day.

He located the building where Crane lived, a twisting

turret of red walls that gleamed like rubies in the morning sun, and climbed the picturesque stone steps, brushing against trailing flowers that spilt their fragrance from overfilled flower boxes. A yellow trumpet-like flower, the colour of sunshine, hung from a vine and nodded in the breeze as he passed. Its sunny radiance reminded him of Bethan on their wedding day, and he lifted the bloom to run his finger across its petals and breathe in its sweet perfume. The temptation to pluck it might have overwhelmed him, but he also couldn't bear that if he did, it would soon wither and die.

Crane lived in the topmost apartment. The door was open, with a simple screen to deter insects and local wildlife. However, Yianevan had noticed a few rodents of a common species that roamed throughout the provinces and were often troublesome and mischievous inside a home. The door scan took a moment to decide Yianevan was not insect-infested flora or unruly fauna before admitting him without fanfare or announcement into a large chamber cluttered with books. Against the walls, stacked in a precarious tower, ancient data tile readers teetered dangerously over storage cases, benches, and historical paraphernalia. There was almost no room to step, and it would be at your peril if you did.

Therefore, Yianevan didn't move.

A frail figure, wearing a long black tunic, his sparse, wispy hair sticking up in comical tufts and a back stooped with age, worked at a grimy counter heaped high with pans and yet more books and data tiles. Every item was so thick with dust, it would have been years since they were last viewed. Or cleaned. A testament to their age. The man's back was to the door, and he neither looked around nor acknowledged his visitor, who lingered in the doorway, partly because of what he might step on and partly because he was unsure of his welcome.

The moments ticked past as the man continued with his tasks. Yianevan realised he was being ignored, so he cleared his throat to draw the man's attention, then spoke up.

"Good morning."

The greeting earned Yianevan a heavy sigh from the man, but he didn't turn. "What do you want?" he demanded instead, slapping a bunch of herbs onto the bench. "I'm doing my best to die here, but I keep getting disturbed."

Realising he had intruded, Yianevan turned to leave. "I apologise," he said. "I can return later."

At that, the man glanced over his shoulder. "Return?" he scoffed. "There will be no 'later' to return to. This potion—" the man held up a small cup "—holds my eternal rest. I have chosen my time. I have earned it, and my time is now, but it won't happen if people keep walking in."

Yianevan knew of this ritual, and he should have recognised it. At his suggestion it might have been sensible to lock the door, the old man turned and waved Yianevan into the room with an impatient sigh.

"The door lock malfunctioned."

As the man moved from the bench, Yianevan saw a large pan filled with a colourful collection of herbs and petals the tribal ordinaries used in the ritual of eternal sleep. This practice was respectable, and Yianevan even knew of a few lesser Nobles who availed themselves, although most Nobles considered taking one's own life a disgrace. The process took several days of an infusion of herbs, ingested each night until the blessed "relief" occurred while one slept. He believed he had never seen anyone as ancient as Crane, so to "relieve" himself of life seemed reasonable, and he was glad he had arrived before the herbs did their work.

"I am sorry to have disturbed your ministrations," Yianevan said. "I seek advice, and I will not detain you for long. Others spoke your name with veneration as a man of knowledge."

Crane spluttered a short laugh. "Veneration, you say? I'm astounded anyone remembers me." He shuffled across and squinted at his visitor through rheumy eyes. "Hmph. Yi. House Anevan. I heard you were back."

Yianevan looked down at the wrinkled face and took in the tufty hair, once long and lustrous like his own. The man could not see chak, yet he had looked right through the disguise.

"I'm sorry," Yianevan responded. "I don't know you."

"Well, I know *you*," Crane said, shoving a bony finger into Yianevan's chest and looking him up and down. "Is this trickery to entrap an old man?"

"I altered my appearance to not draw attention," Yianevan said. He understood how the old man would see it, but he didn't set out to deceive him.

Crane gave him a wobbly grin. "You couldn't fool me, Yi. I held you when you were an infant. I watched you grow, but I didn't stay beyond your childhood."

Yianevan had no memory of this man. In all honesty,

his childhood was a blur in his haste to be removed from it, but when Crane smiled a smile that only lifted one side of his mouth, he felt sorry he didn't remember. It was one of those quirks one would talk and laugh about when reminiscing with one's own children. The smile trembled on Crane's cheek for a few seconds before his face fell back into place.

"It's not surprising I have moved from your mind," he said, plucking at his sleeves to drop them over his arms now his herbaceous task was temporarily abandoned. "You were the most restless of children. How you found your way back to the Noble homeworld is a marvel." He pulled in a shaky breath. "Why are you here? Given the trickery, I would say not with your father's sanction."

Crane didn't look as if he needed help to end his life. A man of alarming frailty, each shuffle he made on his spindly legs threatened to send him to the floor, where Yianevan was sure the venerable historian would shatter into thousands of bony fragments. It would be prudent to get straight to the point, so Yianevan opened his hand.

"For this."

Nestled within his palm was Bethan's pennant.

If Yianevan had concerns about Crane's frailty, the old man's shocked expression was sufficient for him to fear he would cause his demise. Crane may have failing eyesight, but he recognised the pennant.

Composure lost, he sucked in his breath, murmuring long since unspoken words from the ancient traditional language of the Nobles. He stumbled backwards, hands flailing as he tried to find some support where he might not have to rely on his weak legs to keep him upright.

Yianevan was at his side in an instant, guiding him until he could ease him onto a divan. He poured a cup of water and helped the panicked man take a few sips until his breathing became even, and he regained his composure. When he did, Yianevan's help got flapped away in a flurry of gestures.

"I apologise for my distress, Yi," he said, pulling Yianevan down onto the seat beside him. "This was unexpected."

Crane uncurled his visitor's hand to reveal the pennant, brushing the teardrop filigree with the tip of his finger. After a moment, he exhaled a sigh, a mix of reverence and fear.

"To see this…" he whispered, searching Yianevan's face. "Tell me, heir to House Anevan, by what means did you come by it?"

"I took it from around the neck of an interventionist."

"Took? Please do not tell me it was surrendered."

"Not surrendered," Yianevan assured him, although he didn't understand Crane's concern. "She wore it as an adornment, and I removed it as she slept."

Disbelief and wonder gathered up the wrinkles on Crane's life-weary face. "I never expected its return, even though generations of hierarchy searched. Now, just as I am about to die, I find it in the possession of an heir." He fixed his gaze on Yianevan. "Perhaps the worst hands to hold such a pennant?" Then he nodded sagely to himself a few times. "We shall see."

Yianevan didn't understand. He had come to this remote place to speak of the pennant's language and seek knowledge about the Monk's Gate, but the old man's reaction told him there was more he had to learn. What he hadn't expected was this sense of fear.

"No-one knows I have it in my possession," he told Crane. "I am convinced this is at the foundation of the Monk's Gate, and I suspect the catastrophes taking place on the human world are not of the Lyrans' doing. I cannot explain why I feel that revealing the pennant to my family might have consequences for the humans."

"Ah!" Crane's eyebrows shot up. "You fear for the humans? Yi, this has consequences for the *galaxy*. The human world was the last known resting place of this artefact."

This pennant, his homeworld, and indeed the hierarchy were bound together. Before he left this place today, Yianevan vowed he would know how and why. Crane had the answers to both.

"Crane," he said. "I must know the purpose behind its creation and why the portal it generated was presented to the ten sectors, and our people, as a myth."

Crane spent many years of his life around House Anevan. He knew their ways, their ambitions. The answers the heir sought with such eagerness were indeed secret, but his knowledge came from a different, more unexpected source. He knew he had given away much with his reaction, but if the boy was like his mother, Crane had nothing to fear. If he favoured his father, it would not matter what transpired, so he must rely on his intuition. In a few hours or days, he would be at his eternal rest and what would be, would be, and no-one could hold him accountable for that which was said within these walls.

The dust had now settled around them from the kerfuffle when the heir revealed the pennant, and tiny sunlit specks floated in a lazy haze through the air before Crane's eyes. It occurred to him that soon those eyes would be dark. His voice stilled. Yi of House Anevan would never hear the truth, only lies from the lips of the clan father. He clasped the hand in which Yianevan held the pennant.

"Yi," he said, his voice earnest, his skin thin and cold against Yianevan's fingers. "Your house is driven by greed and ambition. The pennant gives them the means to steal from time itself. It is called Irrinait, from the language of our origin world, meaning 'yet to be'. This atrocity has taken billions of innocent lives." He released Yianevan's hand and waited for a response, reading only questions in the heir's eyes. Questions that would demand answers. "The Lyrans were but one race to suffer under its power." Then, taking courage, he lifted the teardrop-shaped bead from Yianevan's palm, its elaborate plexus glinting as it caught the light from the door. "Formed from a calming pennant, it does not calm. It destroys." Crane leaned forward and whispered a warning that chilled Yianevan to the bone. "This must never again fall into the hands of House Anevan, lest other civilisations meet the same fate as the Lyrans."

For a moment, Yianevan didn't know how he should respond. Bethan had worn this around her neck, and now Crane was describing it almost as a weapon.

"I don't understand," he said at length. "The Nobles

were not the cause of the Lyran decline. They were a species doomed to extinction."

Crane grunted and sat back. "So history says."

"The ten-sector council endorses the historical account," Yianevan said, although he knew records could be "fudged". "The Lyran civilisation suffered from the Monks' extravagances, their lack of care regarding climate and their failure to address declining fertility. If we wiped them out, by this—" he pointed to the pennant, "or by any other means, the act would be witnessed by the ten sectors and boundary worlds, and they would hold us liable. In the same way they would if we acted aggressively against any other race."

Crane knew an attempt to hold the Noble hierarchy accountable for any trespass was laughable. Not one world in the ten sectors would challenge the Nobles because to do so could mean technological suicide. Of course, it was understandable the heir would defend Noble versions of history. It was all he knew, and deconstructing it was part of his path to the truth. He needed to open his mind. In fact, Crane needed to strip it back to its bare bones.

"You came here for knowledge, Yi, did you not?" It was a pointed remark, delivered with the unmistakable voice of an educator. "Yet you contend with what I say. You must allow a different truth into your mind and heart because only then can you decide which truth will lead you. You are correct when you say Lyra was a society in decline, but it was not a ten-sector world. It lay far beyond the boundary, so the council had no stake in the ordinary Lyrans' welfare and concentrated only on the Monk Cartel—not without good reason—because of their piracy. We knew little of the ordinary Lyran people because no-one ever asked. Apart from the occasional freighter out at the boundary, few witnessed the Lyrans going about their business, trying to survive."

Yianevan agreed. "We think of Lyrans in terms of the Monk Cartel," he said. "They held the reins of government on their own world."

"We don't know that. The ten sectors never sent a delegation there. The region was too dangerous, and the Noble hierarchy only complied with the ten sector's request so they could ingratiate themselves and display their superiority. All the Nobles had to do was control the Monk Cartel and the other pirates."

"At least that part of history is true," Yianevan said. "We subdued them."

Crane snorted a laugh. "Not from the point of view of the boundary worlds. Our interference drove up their crime rate. And don't hang on to your precious history. It is not a legacy in which to invest pride."

Yianevan knew he shouldn't add unnecessary and possibly incorrect historical subtext. He was just eager to learn how it all came together.

"Are you saying the Monks were minor players?" he asked. "Were they not the scourge of the ten sectors? Does this mean their involvement with the human world was similarly exaggerated?"

Crane let out one of his rickety breaths. "The Lyrans are not answerable for the catastrophes on the human world, but there are none left to speak of it."

He waited for a moment for his words to impact, but again, there was no reaction apart from a slight furrowing of his guest's brow. The heir already had his suspicions.

"Outside House Anevan, outside those involved," he added, "I am the only one who knows the story. If your father knew I knew, he would not have tolerated my existence, but he needn't trouble himself. I've repeated it to no one. When you stepped over the threshold, I assumed he'd found out and sent you to kill me! You would have saved me the headache of gathering and preparing all those herbs! I killed a few flowers on the way!"

Yianevan lifted his hands to show he bore no weapons. "Crane, I am not an assassin. Besides, my father doesn't trust me."

"Of course not!" Crane laughed. "You are unpredictable. A rebel. But one day, he will tell you about the pennant. He'll give you the more sanitised, palatable version, but he will draw you in. Only then will you learn the truth. You say that is what you seek, so I will give you the truth now, Yi, House Anevan, Yianevan, Noble." He went through all the titles. "It will forever change you. But first—" he placed the pennant back in Yianevan's hand, "I wish to know how the pennant came to be an accessory about the neck of an interventionist."

If Crane was right, and he was seldom mistaken about people, the heir had taken a considerable risk coming here. The sib would wonder at his absence, and may even search for him, so he must be genuine and unaware of the story about to unfold. Now he had sought the truth, the homeworld would lose a son. A son, were it not for the pennant, might have brought, in peace and friendship, the change and freedom so many Nobles and tribal ordinaries now sought. A son who was already part of the history of the pennant.

Yianevan began his story with Merris's discovery of the "smudge", then the interventionist's steady life signs, followed by the interface's discovery of the time portal. He also told Crane about the graft he used to protect himself from the effects of Earth's soil fungi. He recognised it as one of Yianevan's mother's creations.

"She told me not to tell anyone I had it because the plant is scarce," Yianevan said. "But it allowed me to visit a few worlds where the soil toxins were present."

Crane nodded. "Your mother enjoyed getting her hands dirty. Anything to do with the soil! Did you know her research was under your father's direction? He wished to allay toxicity effects in the soils of several worlds. The human world in particular."

Yianevan didn't know that, but he could guess why it would be advantageous. "It seems she succeeded," he said.

"Of course!" The old man chortled in delight and appreciation for Yianevan's mother. "She was brilliant. And she told no one. Well, except me. And you."

"Why would she tell you? I thought only I knew of the graft."

"Your mother told me everything, but I will come to that later," Crane said with a gentle smile. "She didn't tell the clan father because she wanted to keep the galaxy safe. She was a wise woman and knew there must be worlds on which the Nobles could never tread."

"You have a low opinion of the hierarchy."

"I have a low opinion of your house, Yi, and others who ally themselves. Apart from that, I am loyal, albeit a tribal ordinary. Now, continue with your account. You determined you had stumbled upon the mythical Monk's Gate, and it swallowed the woman?"

"That is what I believed. In the beginning, I thought she might even be Lyran. I wondered if the Monks had constructed the gate as an escape route to the future, or even a retreat, a place to regroup until they could rise once more." Yianevan shook his head. Was his entire history a litany of lies? "Of course, like everyone else, I believed the myth."

No shame in that. There was a time when Crane believed it himself.

"The clan father of the time thought it prudent to extend the lie to his own people," he said. "Not just the ten sectors. How did you locate the interventionist?"

Yianevan explained how her life signs remained at the anomaly's centre, then related the interface's initial resistance to his directions, only adjusting its reasoning programme after protracted argument. He grinned as he remembered Corky's protestations.

"It still thought me delusional," he said, "but at least it allowed itself better comprehension of my line of thought. It sent a spiral through the anomaly with a sensor tether, attuned to the interventionist's biosigns. At first, the interface couldn't determine the timeline, only that she had been there at some point or left an imprint, as though she were living many lives. There was evidence of a chronological timeline that the interface analysed, settling on a time in the planet's future. Initial attempts to place me at her coordinates failed."

Yianevan's earnest retelling further allowed Crane's trust to grow. He could have left the interventionist and reported her as missing, wiped the biosign registry and fabricated some explanation. Many Nobles could lay claim to such acts in the past, believing other species to be disposable. This boy, this heir, was unlike his father or grandfather. He did not possess their ruthlessness, their cruelty.

"Why did you not leave her and report the anomaly to your father?"

The question and the inference he would abandon an interventionist without trying to solve the mystery surprised Yianevan. Was it not clear?

"I needed to understand her connection to the gate. If I located her, I believed I would find the Lyran hiding place."

The response earned him an indulgent stare. Crane kept a store of these stares for students who didn't give enough forethought to their actions.

"Lyrans look like humans, Yi. How would you know the difference?"

"I assumed I would recognise Lyrans by their behaviour," Yianevan said. "That when I discovered them, I would find them amassing weapons, building an army. I am ashamed of my arrogance, but at that point, I believed the woman held the key to Lyran activity or the possibility of a war engine within the gate. Had I discovered such activity, perhaps I would have notified my father."

Again, that indulgent look. "Assuming you could get back."

Yianevan admitted he took a risk. He explained the interface's modifications to the spiral. "They worked whenever it needed to extract me, but it could not identify the interventionist when we finally located her."

Crane was no engineer, but he saw on a spiritual level how that could happen. "I expect she became too integrated into her lives. If you had lived other lives while you were there, as it seems she did, it is likely the spiral would not have recognised you either. You had one signature; she had many."

Yianevan hadn't considered that. "I assumed she would be the same woman who left the interventionist's ship."

"She is, fundamentally," Crane said, "but if she passed through other timelines, how could she come out the other side unchanged? You must ask yourself about chak. Is not the ability to read it supernatural? And why cannot a Noble read the chak of another Noble? Did Time design it that way? Perhaps chak, including our own, has a deeper, more spiritual meaning and is far more connected to time and destiny than we believe. I would say most definitely in the interventionist's case because she could not be Lyran."

Yianevan never understood nor accepted the historical reasoning for the evolution of Noble's compound retinas, which were attributed to reading the intent of their enemies in their dark warring past on the origin planet. Nowadays, there seemed no point in reading how the previous week's events or a species' anxiety levels affected them. It was little more than a party trick. Perhaps Crane was right. Chak might indeed play a more significant role.

"It took some attempts to find her," he continued. "On the last two occasions, the spiral placed me in a small village where the interface detected her signature, but each time decades earlier than her projected time. As I observed from the spiral, I remained phased. The conditions of the humans there shocked me, and I wondered if the interventionist might not have survived, and I was wasting my time."

"Did you feel compelled to help the unfortunates?" A memory of the heir's mother came to Crane's mind. Kind, generous and always ready to assist the tribal ordinaries. Was her son the same? To his great relief, the answer came swiftly and with not a small measure of indignant surprise.

"Of course I helped," Yianevan said. "How could I not? When I returned to the ship, I asked Corky what we might do."

Crane tilted his head. "Corky?"

"I'm sorry. The interface. The interventionist gave it a name."

Crane had never heard of such a thing. Perhaps humans were sentimental about machines.

"Very well. Continue."

"Corky channelled funding to aid the village. He researched their financial institutions, social structure, and currency to provide relief to the people. The transaction required identification, so the interface extrapolated Ian from my name and Noble from our race. I became Ian

Noble. When I found the interventionist, I saw the change those funds instigated."

"I'd like to meet this 'Corky'," Crane said with a grin. "He sounds a character. So, after carrying out your good deeds, you located the interventionist?"

"Yes, decades later and living a life normal for her status and time, with only vague memories of her childhood there. The difficulty was she had relocated far distant from the gate's coordinates. I also realised I was not dealing with Lyrans, yet still believed the gate to be Lyran technology."

In Yianevan's shoes, Crane would have believed that too.

"But you were confident that you were in a future place despite the time period's undeveloped appearance and technology?"

"Yes, without a doubt. I even read of the volcanic eruption in their history books. The interface encountered communication issues as the gate destabilised, so I decided to leave. Before I could, the interventionist showed me the pennant and told me of her dreams. One specifically mentioned the volcano, but in each, she held the pennant. I believe she acquired it as she entered the anomaly. After that, I dared not leave until I retrieved it."

The Noble's experiments with time involved placing Irrinait either in the subject's hand or under the skin. Crane knew that, but the heir wouldn't be aware.

"It is possible," he said. "How did you convince her to return?"

Yianevan thought he would never get over his foolish reliance on women's magazines.

"I didn't," he said. "There were social conventions…" He cringed at his own folly. "Suffice to say, I entered a marriage covenant with her because I believed, wrongly, that under the rules of that society, a wife was compelled to acquiesce to her husband's will. I informed her that following the marriage, we would travel to Pompeii, the region of the gate."

Crane smiled. "Informed her, did you? She did not hit you over the head?"

Yianevan had to laugh. He got it completely wrong. "I made a mistake. I trusted old information about a woman's compliance, but she agreed to go. We just never got that far. When the graft failed, I took the pennant and fled. Corky found me and administered the antidote, and meanwhile, the gate appeared to 'peel'. Soon, the plexus became visible. It was identical to this pennant, so I assumed it generated the anomaly."

Yianevan placed the pennant on the bench between them. In its dusty surroundings, it looked benign and unthreatening. So much history and violence in a tiny bead. Bethan called it a lucky charm. Not so lucky for the Lyrans.

"And you realised the technology belonged to the Nobles, not the Lyran Monks?" Crane said after a moment. "Now, you want to know why the hierarchy lied."

Yianevan wanted the entire story, but frustratingly, Crane appeared not ready to deliver it. Instead, he asked what had happened to the interventionist. Yianevan felt a ripple of impatience, but he wasn't the master here, so he answered.

"She assumed I was dead and continued with her life.

Then, before we broke orbit, she made it to the gate of her own volition. Some Earth years had passed, although on the ship, it was a matter of days."

The Noble scientists from centuries before had observed such phenomena. Crane found it interesting that she discovered the coordinates on her own.

"Did her dreams give her insight? Drive her?"

"I believed, given the means, she might go to the mountain, perhaps to learn the truth about me and her dreams. Given she does not remember that life, we did not discuss it when I took her back to her home. Corky detected her at the gate. When she hesitated, I went to her."

"What did you see within the gate?"

At this further delay, Yianevan allowed his impatience to get the better of him. "Crane, does it matter?" he snapped.

"It matters to me!" Crane snapped back. "You tell me your story. I tell you mine."

Yianevan sighed. He was the one who sought Crane out. "Very well. It was as if the spiral moved downwards through a mist. When I walked back with Bethan, her mind composed and projected a cathedral with many windows, each playing out a vignette of her past lives."

Crane smiled. Not "interventionist". Not "the woman".

"Bethan?"

What could Yianevan say? He shifted a little. He had been so careful not to reveal her name, to give away more than necessary. Now it was out in the open, there was no point in trying to hide it any longer. He covered his heart with his hand.

"She is here if you must know. This is not what you would expect from the future ruler of House Anevan."

No, not what Crane would expect. But Yi would never become ruler.

"Does she know you took the pennant?"

"No. She remembers nothing."

Crane clasped his thin hand over Yianevan's arm and gave it a gentle but urgent shake.

"Yi, your father must never learn that the portal on the human world opened."

"Then tell me why!" Yianevan was almost at the point of dropping to his knees and begging. His whole life pivoted on learning this truth. "Tell me why it is a danger to the galaxy."

Crane had kept the secret of the pennant for decades to protect Yianevan's mother. After her death, he kept it to protect her memory. In another day or two, at least after the final infusion of herbs, he would not be here to witness the outcomes, and until the heir turned up, he was unsure he even cared. Now, while death would still be a welcome visitor, the legacy of this heir would remove the threat of House Anevan. Perhaps this would be Crane's last word.

"My knowledge comes with a warning, Yi," he said, his watery eyes widening. "I will tell you what I know, and for you, it will rewrite history, but more than that, so will it write your future."

Yianevan lifted his chin. He was ready.

Crane doubted it.

*CHAPTER THIRTY-SEVEN_*

When a boy learns the history of his people at his father's knee, how could it be anything but the truth? A father does not lie. A father does not deceive his son. Unless he is the clan father of House Anevan. A liar. A tyrant. All Nobles, save those select few that House Anevan kept close throughout the centuries, were deceived. Were it not for the mother sending her son into the ten sectors in an act of boldness and sacrifice, Crane wondered what would have become of the boy. Never had an heir left the homeworld, but the mother knew more about Waino and the time pennant's history and much more about the power of chak than the father or any of his sib. Many years into her son's exile, and in fear for her life, she told her closest friend the hierarchy would soon demand her son's return, and he would be at the clan father's mercy.

As Yianevan waited for Crane to begin his story, the birds and insects outside hushed their melodies, the daily sounds of the community faded, and Yianevan's mind and heart opened to the narrative with no distraction. It would be a narrative that told a horrifying saga of lies and treachery committed by the House Anevan, from as far back as the unreachable Ancestral Homeworld of the Noble's origin.

He learned from Crane that in ancient times, House Anevan was not only a lesser house but the lowest of all until their status became elevated by the marriage of one of their daughters to the heir of Waino the Elder, ruler of House Waino. That house was equal to the hierarchal houses, and from there came the artisans who created the calming pennants, the mysterious technology that influenced the fortunes of many of the worlds in the Ancestor's sector.

"The hierarchy on our origin world were benefactors of all the other planets in the region," Crane told him. "Their technology, as a result of the pennants, was superior, but while they did not share the designs of their subsequent inventions with other civilisations, the Ancestral Nobles employed their discoveries for the good of everyone. They helped many planets to become self-sustaining, and as a result, enjoyed the respect of all worlds in their galaxy, far distant from here."

Yianevan knew instinctively something had brought this altruism to an end. What developments furthered the story? Crane held up a cautioning finger before he had the chance to ask.

"Ah, I know what you are thinking. For generations upon generations, this cooperation endured. But always, darkly, secretly, House Anevan plotted access to greater technical knowledge and education. I do not know how such a lowly daughter became part of a hierarchical sib, but she became a willing instrument in the drama to play out."

"As a go-between. A spy?"

Crane nodded. Exactly. "The development of the calming pennants, over many generations, underpinned all technology and every source of power. It made our Origin Ancestors great. Strong. But they were not cruel overlords. Their warring past was but a distant memory. The pennants united the different houses, but no-one except Waino artisans knew the secret, and those artisans appeared perhaps once in a generation. The pennant structure could be neither studied nor copied, and as today, the ability to construct them is a mystery."

"That is why we protect the pennants we have left," Yianevan said. "House Waino is no more."

Crane drew his eyebrows together and made a throaty sound before proceeding. "Yes, well, I'll get to that later. Despite the cleaveship of the daughter to House Waino, the status of House Anevan did not rise much above the tribal ordinaries of our own society."

"I do not understand. Are tribal ordinaries a construct of our own world? Did they not exist on our origin world?"

"They did not. The Origin Ancestors shared their world with a humanoid race who possessed similar genetic attributes. While interbreeding became accepted, the Origin Ancestors did not permit cleaveship and never acknowledged a mixed-species child as a Noble. They referred to the humanoid spouse as an 'Amuse', never destined to take the place of a betrothed or a wife or husband."

Crane watched the different emotions playing out

across Yianevan's face. The heir didn't shake his head or challenge, and Crane believed he would be open to the answers he sought. Gratifying, because everything he knew about his people and their origins was about to be turned on its head.

"A section of House Waino became swayed by the treachery of House Anevan's daughter," Crane continued. "The lowly clan father of House Anevan whispered treason in her ear, that if a pennant could truly displace energy into the past, as was rumoured, then a Waino artisan might construct one that could move into the future."

Crane flicked open a detailed holographic image of a calming pennant. A remarkable piece of technology, these small, indestructible beads were vital to the power, not only in a functional sense but in preserving a position of superiority within the ten sectors. He told Yianevan that House Anevan became convinced the future held technology that would place them in a position of power. The Origin Ancestors uncovered their plot and placed sanctions on them because, as far as they were concerned, the future is a place better left undiscovered.

"Wouldn't that have confirmed the rumours that part of a pennant's power lies in displacing time?"

Crane nodded vigorously. "I should say it did! And the Ancestors' opposition served only to inflame House Anevan's ambition because they now wanted to learn the secrets of the pennants."

Yianevan took a moment to catch up on the family dynamics. "And the husband the daughter corrupted, was he one of the rare artisans? That would have played directly into my ancestors' plotting."

Crane gave him that lop-sided grin. The heir got it. The son of Waino did indeed become corrupt, persuaded by House Anevan. When he became Waino the Elder upon his father's abdication, he changed the language of a calming pennant without House Anevan's knowledge. The refashioned plexus filigree also changed the pennant's shape.

Yianevan pointed to the bead on the bench. "Is this the very pennant?"

"It is not. You are ahead of me. Waino the Elder plotted to test the pennant on an inhabited moon outside the Origin Ancestor's home system, but the daughter tattled to her father. House Anevan threatened to expose Waino if he didn't include them, claiming it was their initiative. However, none of them anticipated the result. The changed form made the pennant unpredictable, and it blew an almighty hole deep into the moon's crust."

"The opposite effect of a calming pennant?"

"Waino's actions puzzle you as well. I can see it in your face. An artisan who initiates a pennant changed by his own hand. It should have been easy. Am I correct? Then I will tell you that when it re-emerged, the ensuing catastrophe swallowed an entire city."

Waino's common sense had fled, either in enthusiasm or foolishness. It made no sense to Yianevan. "The trial of a prototype of any description requires careful planning," he said. "Waino crafted the new pennant from the template of a calming pennant, so assumed it would behave alike, except the energy displacement would be future, not past. Instead, where a calming pennant would mitigate, the altered pennant brought catastrophe. How could he not have considered such an outcome?"

"Because being an artisan didn't stop him from being an idiot," Crane answered with a derisive snort. "Waino meddled in power he could neither predict nor control. I have heard it said Time itself imbued House Waino with empathy, allowed its power to be used when they created the calming pennants, but only seconds into the past. Where this covenant with time originated, we do not know. It may be the truth. It may be a myth. If so, how did the first Waino discover how to displace time? There are no records. Not even fragments of artisanship exist. But if it is true, then the future may not have wished for its secrets to be revealed to unworthy explorers."

Yianevan looked around the cluttered chamber, with its years of dusty knowledge stacked against the walls, almost to the ceiling, and at its heart, the ancient historian huddled on the divan. If the answers to those questions weren't here, he didn't know where he might find them.

"Crane, forgive me," he began. "While I accept that a calming pennant displaces to the past and that the Waino line had a remarkable ability, wouldn't the backwards displacement result from research, not some kind of agreement with a—" he searched for words to describe the essence of time. "I suppose I can only say a supernatural entity. For every being, time flows to the future regardless of our actions, yet the past follows us like a shadow. I know the future exists because I have been there. I admit that I find it hard to understand how something so unfathomable possesses a directed consciousness."

He waited for Crane to respond, but the old man burst into laughter. "Well, that was deep! I'm sure I asked for it, but it's a question for one of those metaphysical types out at the boundary." He reached up and flicked his ears. "I just repeat what I hear."

"I apologise," Yianevan smiled. "Perhaps I am thinking aloud. I distracted you. Please, tell me what happened when they discovered Waino's error."

"The Ancestors evacuated the survivors. It was known the event was unsanctioned, but it generated hostility towards the Ancestors. The unrest and mistrust that followed shifted the dynamics of their galaxy."

"If the Ancestors were so revered, could they not make restitution?"

Crane didn't have an answer. The historical account concealed by one of the lesser houses recorded that the Origin Ancestors confiscated the pennant and placed House Anevan and House Waino on trial. The first trial ever to take place in recorded history. At its conclusion, House Waino and House Anevan were placed in stasis and despatched into the cosmos, along with a number of other humanoids and dozens of other houses implicated in the conspiracy. Did that constitute restitution? Perhaps.

Yianevan always believed his people fled persecution. Another lie from House Anevan.

"How long did the outcasts remain in stasis?" he asked.

Crane had pondered this before, not that it was crucial. Although centuries would have gone by, it would have only seemed like a single night before they awoke in an unfamiliar galaxy. The time they spent searching for a home following their stasis revival was long enough for those who took power to shape a story that would suit themselves.

"I don't know," he admitted. "The ancestors ensured the exiled would never navigate back to the homeworld or the origin galaxy. When they awoke, they did not recognise the stars, and the interface's memory of previous star charts had been erased. They were close to the ten sectors, still in its infancy then, and found refuge. In my view, the ancestors made a grave error."

"Do you mean in their distance calculations?"

"No, I think they got that right. The further the better, if you ask me. I meant in judgement. The ancestors should have either confined or executed Waino the Elder." Crane tapped his temple. "Waino kept the knowledge of the pennants up here. The Origin Ancestors knew it, but they still chose to export their problem."

Yianevan agreed. That was an error. "They continued their experiments here on the homeworld, though, didn't they, and discarded them because of the possibility of diverging timelines? I have seen a brief mention of time travel in the archives. When I dig deep enough," he added.

Crane gave one of his disparaging snorts. "Discarded? Truly, Yi? Your forebears might have caused mayhem in our origin sector, but do you think House Anevan would let it rest?"

"So why didn't the Origin Ancestors recognise its potential?"

Crane thrust his face forward, the skin over his cheeks flushing pink as it tightened with mild irritation, as if he were berating a student.

"Did you not listen? Experimentation reduced their position in their galaxy. They believed the future might hold possibilities, benefits, but it might also be a dark place. A place no being should visit before their time. I agree with them. House Anevan was not driven by curiosity. They were not interested in a glimpse of what the future held. They wished to control the ultimate power. Time. Then they would reap whatever they could from the future and make themselves strong." Crane raised his gnarled fingers into a menacing claw. "They would dip their greedy hands into the well. It would make them *invincible*."

Yianevan fell to silence at the old man's passion and restrained anger, then watched as he lifted the pennant and rolled its filigree surface between thumb and forefinger.

"Magnificent," Crane whispered in reverence as if he feared that speaking too loudly might cause it to wake and unleash destruction. "Exquisite when quiescent but brutal when roused." He held it up to the light, tilting his head as its contours sparked in the gloom. "Much like a volcano."

He smiled then and turned his attention to Yianevan. "I often wondered how you would turn out," he said. "And here you are today, a protagonist in a terrifying story. You swore a crew to secrecy, interfered with a database, fraudulently gained money, married a woman because you knew you could bend her to your will, and arrived here in disguise. There may be more to add to that list." He placed the pennant back on the bench and took a deep breath. "Perhaps you have inherited your household's kinship with deceit? Perhaps I should not trust that you will not inform your father that I know his secret?"

Yianevan felt the trust issue was already sorted, but Crane was not a man easy to know. So, he answered cautiously, but with humour. "Old man, do not have uncertainties when you have handed over sufficient to incriminate yourself."

Crane eyed him for the briefest moment, then laughed. "Little tests, Yi. Just to be sure. I like to keep people on their toes! So tell me, what was your report to your father when the interventionist returned?"

"That I located her at the base of the mountain."

"Hmm. Her life signs must have emanated from the portal because she kept the pennant in her possession. Perhaps she had an affinity?"

That was Yianevan's belief, too.

Crane rose from his seat to busy himself at his herb-laden bench. Yianevan caught a muttered, *"How strange"*, but didn't answer when he asked what he meant. Crane was elderly, and they had been speaking for many hours. He may need rest.

As he regarded his host's weary shuffling amongst the array of pots and pans, displacing dust and powdery herb residue, Yianevan wondered if the man felt he had given too much away. He now knew the clan father was aware of the pennant's existence and that much of his society was built on lies. Again, he felt that nip of impatience. The visit took many more hours than he anticipated, but Crane had been gracious, and although the chronicle was long, a condensed version would see Yianevan without vital information. He was eager to hear more and did not want a delay.

"You would be one hundred and sixty, one hundred and seventy years old," he said as the minutes stretched. "I am prepared to sit here while you age further."

Crane turned with two trays of food and wine in his hands. He offered one to Yianevan.

"I started my herbs and have no more than two days left, Yi. I will not age enough now to make a difference. Make yourself comfortable while you wait."

Humbled at his own impatience and misjudgement, Yianevan accepted the plate.

"I thought you had perhaps reconsidered and feared I would speak to my father about our meeting."

Crane pushed a crust of bread between his lips. "I do not fear for myself, Yi," he said, puffing out a few crumbs as he spoke. "Your father can't hurt me, but if he learns Irrinait is in your custody and you have kept it from him, my fear is for you."

"Explain."

"Are your betrotheds pregnant?"

"Not yet. It has been several months."

Crane spoke through mouthfuls of his meal. "Then I advise you to ensure they don't. Your father will use that which is most dear to you to ensure your compliance. The remnant of House Waino also plays a part in this, and your father knows he can use your sentiment against you."

That was a puzzling comment. "There is no remnant of House Waino," Yianevan said. "The house is extinct."

Crane put down his plate, muttering and shaking his head. Then he drew an ancient ramshackle interface to his side. It had long since lost its vocal processor and resorted only now to visual, but it was enough to project the plexus language of a calming pennant. More detailed than even the most high-tech hologram, it highlighted the perfectly cohesive plexus, which rotated and wove together its thin filaments as it would during an initiation sequence. As it neared the end of the simulation, it glowed in brilliant hues of gold and purple.

It was not unfamiliar to Yianevan, even though he found it quite beautiful each time he saw it. He had performed these initiations countless times aboard his ship when using the pennant's power structure for performing maintenance. The hierarchy permitted only those from the homeworld to view this sublime ballet. For any other species to view a pennant, even in its inactive state, was to violate a sacred law, a law upheld by every Noble and tribal ordinary. When used for calming the human world catastrophes, the precious pennant was permanently housed, protected, its mystique maintained, even from the most trusted interventionist.

Crane changed the interface image to reflect the time pennant lying on the bench.

"I watched you recite the language of the calming pennant under your breath," he said. "It is second nature to you." He pointed to the image. "Can you read this language?"

So far, although he knew every curve, every turn, and even knew what the sequence would be when he finally learned the secret of activating it, Yianevan had to admit he could not. He deftly traced the pennant's flow from pinnacle to axis. Crane was right. It was magnificent.

"I understand it on some levels, but I don't know *how* I understand it," he said, his voice soft with wonderment. "I even spoke to it as if an incantation or plea might work." He raised his hands in resignation. "Crane, it speaks to me, but I can't hear what it's saying. On an intellectual level, it makes a sense I cannot translate. I know this sounds like the rambling of a crazy man, but it goes further than just wishing to know its secrets. No matter what I do, it does not respond."

"How fortunate for the homeworld," Crane replied with a wry grin as he pushed the image away. "In your fumbling efforts to understand, you might have opened a hole in the planet, which would have heralded your discovery. What did you make of the scars?"

"I am not ignorant of its nature, Crane," Yianevan said in his own defence. "I seek only to gain a better understanding. The presence of the scars adds yet another dimension to my confusion because they appear to be placed as 'blocks' at the end of a sequence. This is why I sought your knowledge."

"And my knowledge is history," Crane said. "The language of Irrinait is not for me to know. When House Anevan started on their treasonous path, Waino the Elder's first theory was to broaden the language of a calming pennant, thus changing its form."

"But this is not the language of a calming pennant."

"I am aware," Crane replied with a sniff. "May I remind you I am the foremost expert on the language of the calming pennants? No, when he arrived here, Waino the

Elder reworked a calming pennant to take the place of the one confiscated. As expected, the pennant shifted to accommodate the extended language. Waino tested it in the Tivanale system."

"Tivanale is uninhabitable. At least no-one would be hurt."

"I am not sure that would have been a consideration. However, Irrinait did not respond to the test, and House Anevan became impatient. It was then, already having placed itself as the high-ranking ruling house, they gained complete ascension, installing itself above all hierarchy, after the traditions of our origin planet. House Waino conceded, and the other lesser houses followed. And the rest of us who had fewer compound retinas? Or those who had the ancestral eyes of our humanoid forebears? We became tribal ordinaries."

"Even though we have a common ancestor?"

Crane picked up his plate and resumed his meal, waiting until he stuffed his mouth before speaking again.

"I'm not sure we do," he mumbled. "The strength of the Noble genes certainly made us Noble lookalikes!" He laughed then and inhaled a morsel of his dinner, resulting in a protracted bout of coughing. He then sensibly waited until he'd finished his mouthful before continuing his explanation. "In the uncertain times that followed, and fearing House Anevan's power, Waino refused to make any further refinements to the time pennant and would not hand it over. House Anevan took two of his children and executed them before Waino's eyes. Still he would not budge, even though he lost more family members until he met his own demise in mysterious circumstances. Perhaps the lengths House Anevan would go to stirred a conscience in him, or perhaps regret from his previous genocide on that moon. We will never know. Whatever his reasoning, as the only man who could fashion pennants, the art died with him. His children did not inherit the gift."

Yianevan understood now why history recorded the templates as lost. They were not lost. They brought them to this planet in an artisan's memory and knowledge, which he had once used to drive his ambition. Inexplicably, he reconsidered.

Crane watched that understanding dawn. He had built a picture of House Anevan's ruthlessness and hunger for power. Now that he understood, he told Yianevan that generations after Waino the Elder's death, his descendant, named rather unoriginally, Waino, revived his forefather's interest in time travel after discovering the hybrid pennant concealed in a wall in his family's archives. He recognised the language enough to see the potential and become curious. However, the record of the catastrophe caused by the original changed pennant was contained only in sealed texts belonging to House Anevan, so the unsuspecting descendant was unaware of the danger of his interest. In innocence, and with the full knowledge and concealed delight of House Anevan's ancestors, he took up the experiment, believing them only to be a diverting pastime and using only fragments of information. Waino the Younger was a practical man, but he found the language on the changed pennant too full of whimsy and poetry, so he revised the plexus.

Yianevan stopped Crane with a question. "This Waino was an artisan?"

Crane shrugged. "He'd never built a pennant, but he understood the plexus. Remember, this was only the second 'time pennant' ever fashioned. The Tivanale system once again hosted the test."

"Successful?"

"Nothing happened. The hybrid pennant could not initiate alone. The changed plexus required an unaltered calming pennant, working in tandem."

"Using its energy to the past as a springboard to the future?"

"That's as good a theory as any because I doubt anyone else knows. Waino the Younger saw himself as a scientist, not an artisan, so he assumed his sense of empathy was scientific instinct. He didn't allow it to guide him. However, he had foresight enough to realise the combined power of two pennants may cause local destabilisation. Under the hierarchy's direction, which of course was House Anevan, with full knowledge of the power of the pennant, but choosing not to disclose it, they selected a planet with a civilisation outside the ten sectors for the next test."

"The human world?"

"No, Lyra. Their soil was also hostile to our race, so they sacrificed a tribal ordinary to set the two pennants on the surface. They did not retrieve the 'sacrifice'. He and a small Lyran community were swallowed by the ensuing well. Telemetry sent back images of an uninhabited world, so the Nobles hailed it as a partial success in that it made clear the expected Lyran extinction would indeed take place."

"Even though they would not have been able to determine a time scale?"

"It was in the early stages. One minor success at a time. A spiral recovered the calming pennant, but the Waino pennant disappeared, turning up hours later at the site of a catastrophic underground earthquake that destroyed half a continent in an area not given to major seismic events."

"And more Lyrans perished?"

Crane's tone sounded eerily matter of fact. "Half of their remaining population plus animal and plant life."

"And the ten sectors council did not investigate?"

"Why would they?" Crane replied. "They thought of the Lyrans as pirates and not part of the ten sectors. It was well known that they were a race in decline. Even if the Nobles were seen in the vicinity, no one would ask questions. No, the Nobles faced troubles of their own. Waino the Younger's horror at the genocide. House Anevan restricted contact with other civilisations unless with their express permission. Therefore, Waino the Younger focused on his work at home. He did not travel off-world and did not pilot ships. House Anevan chose not to inform him the world upon which the test was to take place was inhabited, and as a result, he refused to be involved in any further testing. As the only one able to read the time pennant, he called a halt to the experiment."

"Did anyone else try?" Yianevan asked.

"Of course they did, but none were successful. In retribution, House Anevan systematically executed Waino's large family until he agreed to resume the tests to save those left. This time, the hierarchy selected an even more distant world, but it had to be inhabited so they could measure technological advances."

"Earth."

"Earth?"

"Yes, the people on the human world call their home 'Earth'."

"I wasn't aware of that," Crane said. "That world was neither charted by the council nor in a numbered sector. Few other than Noble ships could reach it in a reasonable time. When they arrived, they found three Lyran freighters in orbit. On each, they discovered many humans, all abducted from the surface."

"These would have been the last of the human slaves seized by the Lyrans…"

Crane slapped his hand down hard on the bench, startling Yianevan.

"Am I wasting my breath!?" he snapped. "The Lyrans did not abduct and enslave humans. That is all part of the lie. The planet was too far for regular Lyran incursions. They had made that journey only once before, in ancient times, when a return voyage in one of their freighters took fifteen years. This was the act of a desperate people trying to rebuild their civilisation."

Yianevan made an inward retreat from the scolding and held his questioning. When Crane indicated he may now make an enquiry, he asked how the Lyrans knew about the human world, or even how they knew humans were compatible.

"*We* knew of that world, didn't we?" Crane replied sharply. "Lyrans had the technology to chart the skies. They weren't fools!" Then he softened. "I'm sure our ancestors shared knowledge of the corridors we passed through to get here, and no doubt, someone from Lyra recorded that information. Then, when they saw the declining fertility on their world, they searched for ways to improve their species' chances of survival."

"What happened to the humans?"

"The Noble hierarchy removed them and destroyed the Lyran freighters. There was never any war. There was not even an exchange of fire. They just blasted those Lyrans into oblivion. The Lyrans' behaviour was unethical, but they were trying to save their species. Remember I said 'freighters', Yi? The Monks did not use freighters. These were cargo ships, possessing less than spacenormal speed and piloted by ordinary Lyrans."

This was remarkable information, and Yianevan wanted more.

"So…" he began.

Crane didn't hear him. Instead, he struggled to his feet. Yianevan imagined him a mild man, but the atmosphere rippled with the old man's sudden and unexpected anger. "No, not just ordinary Lyrans," Crane repeated, raising his voice. "*Desperate* Lyrans. Do you not understand, Yi, heir to House Anevan? Your ancestors lied to the ten sectors, to everyone." His face turned crimson, and his watery eyes flashed. "Your household fabricated and maintained this lie for generations." Foam and beads of spittle flew from his lips as he snarled his words, pointing to Yianevan as if he were personally responsible. "They sacrificed thousands of tribal ordinaries and humans to their ambition and decimated the Lyrans." Crane's bitter, angry voice filled every corner of the room. "If your father gets his murdering hands on Irrinait, billions more lives will be lost. House Anevan is a house of lies! It is evil! I should have torn it down!"

The emotional outpouring exhausted the old man. He rocked on his heels, then slumped back into his seat, leaving Yianevan to wonder at this strange and sudden outburst. Crane clearly harboured deep resentment for House Anevan. It was indeed a house of lies, but perhaps that extended to many hierarchical houses. His father did not possess the pennant, so who would he have murdered in its name unless Crane referred to the sins of generations of clan fathers?

When his father abdicated and he became ruler in his stead, Yianevan resolved there would be no more lies. House Anevan would be a house of truth. He just didn't know how he would reveal its true history to the homeworld without bringing about a civil war.

It took Crane some time to compose himself. Time where he tried to mop the moisture of contempt he felt for House Anevan away from his mouth and brow with a rag, but it was an impossible task.

Outside, the community slept, night insects started their chirping, and an uneasy peace fell on the room. Yianevan had been away from the Marisene for a full day and part of the night and wondered what questioning he would face when he returned. After a long silence in the darkened room, Crane told the interface to provide light. Then he smiled an apology.

"I did not believe I could still feel such anger," he said, his voice still hoarse and emotional. "Perhaps it is good that I do not take it to my eternal rest."

Looking somewhat fragile in the light, Crane seemed calm. Yianevan asked if he would prefer to rest awhile, but Crane wished to continue,

"Some human females were pregnant by the Lyrans. There was also the question of technological contamination. It might have affected the future timeline the Nobles were keen to explore, so after debate, they kept them on board while deciding whether to keep them, use them in tests or…" Crane's voice wavered. "Execute them."

Yianevan measured his reply. He didn't want to say anything inflammatory that might upset the old man's delicate composure. "And they conducted the tests?"

Crane bent his head. "Yes, by inserting an advanced optical transponder into an unwilling human. They made a pocket in her abdomen to contain the pennant."

"I assume it created a well?"

"You assume correctly, and the woman drawn in. They recovered the calming pennant, but the woman disappeared."

"Did they record life signs?"

"They did not. Neither was she ever recovered, but the well remained open long enough for the Nobles to see movement, technological advancement, change. Of course, the parameters were narrow, but it was progress."

"How did they retrieve the time pennant?"

"As on Lyra, it found its own way back, but days later, at the site of an aridification process. Almost an entire continent turned to sand, and as on Lyra, millions perished."

"So, whenever the time pennant re-emerges, it creates these disasters."

Crane conceded that looked to be the case. "It cannot initiate a time well without a calming pennant, but it has the opposite effect when it re-emerges. Who knows what damage it does in timelines?"

"Are you suggesting that every so-called natural disaster on the human world is due to the pennant resurfacing?"

It made sense. "I would say a percentage," Crane agreed. "It is a volcanic world, anyway. We just made it worse. But there could be no mistake; the pennant opened a portal into time, and the planet offered the ideal environment. The Noble physicists worked to expand the time well, so they might better observe or even send through a Grielik who could withstand the toxic soil. They had some success, but in all cases, the Grielik and the time pennant parted company. No Grielik was ever found." Crane paused. "I find it strange. Unlike your interventionist, they recorded no life signs. Yi, what is different about her? What is the affinity she has with pennants?"

Yianevan had no answer. He questioned that very thing himself.

"Waino knew House Anevan would not stop until they had conquered the pennant," Crane went on. "He could not have the deaths of so many on his conscience, and finally discovering his empathy for the pennant, he sabotaged it by placing a code in the plexus filigree. At the next test, the pennant failed to resurface. After years of waiting, Waino refused to construct another, so House Anevan wiped out his house apart from the very youngest, hoping they may read the language and perhaps inherit their ancestors' skills."

"I see what is happening here," Yianevan said. "Our ancestors needed to establish a permanent presence around the human world to be ready when the only existing pennant re-emerged?"

"Yes," Crane said. "That area of space is remote, but not without traffic. To ward off suspicion from the ten sectors, the Nobles formulated a reason, a ruse. A fight with the Lyrans would be accepted, and a rumour circulated that the Lyrans were abducting humans. Because the Nobles could produce those humans in evidence, it worked."

"With no witnesses?"

"None that could give an authentic account."

"So why the myth of the Monk's Gate?"

Crane thought it was apparent. "To support their reasons for a sustained presence above the planet, Yi. The ten sectors asked why the Nobles did not leave after the so-called war, so they told the council they were safeguarding the primitive humans from sabotage devices the Lyrans left on the planet. Of course, it was all nonsense. The council not only accepted the lie but hailed the Nobles as heroes. The hierarchy patrolled it themselves until they created the interventionist fleet."

"I would have thought the interface on an interventionist ship would carry the time pennant's signature even in an encrypted form."

"Oh, they do!" Crane exclaimed. "Do you think House Anevan would not want their finger on that pulse? It is there all right and will alert the clan father if it encounters the pennant. Otherwise, the interface remains in ignorance. Think back to Waino's sabotage and those scars on the pennant."

Yianevan didn't need to think back. It was clear as day.

Crane nodded. "You see, don't you? House Anevan only had the signature of the pennant's original form, not the sabotaged version, which they still do not know is sabotaged."

"When Corky first encountered the 'smudge', it did not have the original 'smudge's' properties his database would have recognised. Waino didn't just sabotage the test; he made sure they would not recognise it if it ever resurfaced."

Crane grinned at Waino's cleverness. "That was his intent. He expected it to re-emerge from time to time, and he couldn't prevent any catastrophic events, but he could stop it from being used on another planet and other civilisations. The idea of House Anevan having access to the future was more than he was willing to accept. He had to make sure they remained ignorant of what he did."

"And without Waino's sabotage of the pennant, we wouldn't be here discussing it. Or our world would be much changed."

Crane's face wrinkled into a smile. Indeed.

"My father will continue to search for the pennant," Yianevan said. "It allowed tantalising glimpses of what might be, but it also destroyed what was."

"The clan father has grown impatient with awaiting Irrinait to reappear. He seeks now to construct another." Crane pointed to the pennant. "What did your Bethan call this?"

"A charm. On Earth, it is supposed to bring luck."

"Well," Crane smiled at the irony. "Irrinait is no longer there to add to the planet's natural disasters, so perhaps that is lucky."

Yianevan had one more burning question. "Where did you learn all this? While you were reorganising the archives?"

He had told the heir everything else, even revealing his passionate hate for House Anevan. So why not finish the story?

"I learned this from your mother before her death," he said. "House Anevan believe it is only they and their cohorts who have full knowledge of the history. That is not so. House Eiled, as ancient as House Anevan, also kept records. An oral history. It is a house with historical ties to House Waino. Waino the Younger was examined posthumously, and it was agreed that the ability is imbued. They couldn't learn how or predict who would be chosen, but they found a distinctive genetic profile. Your mother was the first person in centuries to be identified as a carrier. That is why she was betrothed to your father."

"If she knew this history, why would she accept such a betrothal?"

"She didn't. It is from her that your rebelliousness stems. She did not trust your father, and neither should you."

Yi's mother was the only woman Crane ever loved, and his expression of nostalgia brought a questioning look from her son.

"She and I were close," was all he would admit. "Many thought I was her Amuse!" He laughed and held up his hands. "I know, I know, I was much older, but we had such a friendship, a true meeting of minds." He leaned forward. "Yi, I must tell you. You were forced to return because the blood of Waino runs in your veins, as it did your mother."

"House Waino is extinct!" The words were out as the icy chill gripped Yianevan's very soul.

"Yi, House Anevan has scanned the blood of all newborns for the Waino marker since the death of Waino the Younger. They believed, mistakenly, that it would be apparent from birth. They have discovered it on only three occasions, and none of those children developed artisan empathy. When it became known your mother carried the marker, your grandfather approached the matter of a betrothal to your father. House Eidel vehemently opposed it, but your mother knew House Anevan would get their way, fair means or foul. To protect her family, she joined with your father. She hoped you would not carry the marker, and at birth, you didn't. Later, when you showed your contentious side, she protected you, but she could never have known that when she sent you away, you would return with the time pennant.

"During cloning 'experiments' on your mother, your father discovered that the true artisan marker shows only in adulthood. He believed his only legacy from your mother was an insolent child, and had she not saved you, you might have been removed to the Southern Climes. When he learned of your potential, all that changed."

"Do I have the marker?"

"You tell me."

"I don't know. Was my mother an artisan?"

"She was not. Her marker was present at birth, which appears to preclude artisanship, but your father used her cells as a basis for an artisan clone. He failed. There is no doubt in my mind you have Waino empathy, and it is only a matter of time before you look into a calming pennant and understand what other Nobles cannot."

The evidence was mounting, but still Yianevan wanted to deny it, marvelling at how such a tiny object could direct the course of a people's history, turn them towards evil. He felt he would never touch the time pennant again. Crane read him well.

"It matters not. Irrinait is not the cause. It is merely the instrument. It found the interventionist, and it found you. I would like to say it only wishes peace, but it once again appeared at the heart of a catastrophe."

Confusion crowded Yianevan's mind. He and Willa both descended from Waino? Willa wondered how she came to the attention of the clan father. It could only be because she was from House Eiled. Head pounding, he lost focus. All he could think of was purging the knowledge only yesterday he had sought so desperately. He leapt to his feet and paced the floor.

"I can't. I just can't. Crane, it is too fantastic."

That was when Crane set up a delighted cackle. "Sit down, Yi, because it is not as fantastic as your father's belief that any offspring between you and Willa will strengthen the Waino empathy!" Then he cackled again as the heir's expression went from shock to quizzical. It would be such a delight to deliver this news.

"Willa has no connection to Waino or House Eidel!"

Yianevan was stunned. Over the last day, in this dirty, cluttered room, his family's history was rewritten, and it seemed, as Crane warned him, his own future. Now, another mystery. Willa believed herself a daughter of House Eidel.

Willa's history was one of the few truths the clan father hadn't discovered. He had no sympathy for the clan father, but poor Yi, he had learned much today and took it well. Now this. Still, it should be good news.

"Willa's maternal ancestors are tribal ordinaries," he explained. "One of her foremothers is from an illegitimate pairing with an Amuse who claimed descendancy from House Col'imtri, now passed into obscurity. Their ancestors did not join House Waino. So Willa has none of House Waino in her blood. Some within your mother's family keep their history close to them, and they have long memories. You are the last carrier of the marker anywhere on the homeworld. There are none in House Eiled. You have not produced an heir, so it is ended. Your father has lost."

Yianevan lifted his hand to stop Crane from saying more. He buried his face in his hands.

"Forgive me," he said after a moment. "I find it hard to trust that I descend from Waino, although it would help me understand why my father threatened my brother if I did not return. Could you be mistaken?"

Nothing was cast in stone as far as Crane was concerned. "Of course, but I doubt your mother was. She didn't know you would retrieve the time pennant. Now, I pray you will have made your escape before your father discovers you are in the early stages of your artisanship."

Escape? Yianevan's mind reeled, and his skin prickled. *Escape?* Abandon his people. He looked squarely at the old man, who watched him with some bemusement. He'd delivered shock after shock this day. Why should this be any more unexpected?

"Crane, I can't *leave*."

"Yes, you can," Crane said evenly. "You must. Yi. Time has chosen you."

"Our world is changing!" Yianevan cried out in his confusion. "You must have heard the rumours. I need to lead our people. If what you say is true, we must hold my father accountable and purge the sins of House Anevan."

"Settle down, Yi," Crane said, taking Yianevan's hand and drawing him back to the divan. "You are a weapon. Do you not see it? It is not just that you possess Irrinait. You told me earlier that it speaks to you, yet you deny empathy. This desire to lead our people into a new era is a temporary madness. You are not a leader. From childhood, you craved simplicity, yearned for peace." He placed the palm of his hand against Yianevan's chest. "Tell me, why does your heart beat? For Bethan? For me? For your people? Yi, this is not the heart of a revolutionary. It is the heart of a saviour."

At the mention of her name, Yianevan closed his eyes. "Is she in danger?" he asked.

"If this was ever to come to light, then yes," Crane said. "But she cannot be your focus. You are now responsible for taking the pennant as far away as possible, even across galaxies. You must never try to initiate a sequence. Keep it quiet. Keep it out of sight, and do not allow it to lure or tempt you."

Yianevan felt peals of laughter bubble up inside. Or did he wish to weep? Perhaps he would feel relief if he let out his fear and desperation in a desolate, primordial wail? He only knew he wished he could bury the pennant and forget it until his father was gone, but that would risk catastrophes on the homeworld if it re-emerged. Even if he could keep the pennant secure, the clan father could still exploit the Waino empathy, even though Yianevan didn't have a clue how to construct a pennant, because if he did not comply, his father would use the people he loved against him. Whatever he chose, stay or leave, Kerys and Bo would still be sacrificed.

He tried to find a place for his emotions. So much rested on him, he wondered how he would ever face his father or his sib again.

"I'm not a hero, Crane," he said. "Your own words describe the ruthlessness of my House. If I have this marker, my father will use my brother and sister as leverage to ensure I do his bidding. Either way, they will be the victims."

"I should not have presumed to tell you what you must do, Yi," Crane replied. "If you leave, you will never rest because your House will forever search for you, but you must choose between your sib and protecting the galaxy. Believe me when I tell you that the interests of your brother and sister are not best served by you or Irrinait remaining on the Noble homeworld. It is too great a risk. You took this artefact from around a woman's neck before you even knew its meaning." Crane took the pennant from the bench and placed it in Yianevan's hand. He held his gaze, those wise old eyes urging him to make the right choice.

"Now, it is your responsibility. Your decision. Will you choose Bo and Kerys? Or will you choose to save countless worlds, perhaps even time itself, from falling to the rule of House Anevan?"

CHAPTER THIRTY-EIGHT

Yianevan knew he would leave. Except he could not think of a single avenue to achieve it without his father tracking him. The shipyard traced all ships that moved off-world. His own probably doubly so. Even Corky could not disable those systems, but how could he guard the pennant if he stayed? He did not know what his father would do to ensure his compliance, even if he never learned he had the pennant. Yianevan only knew he would somehow be forced to reveal his empathy and perhaps fashion a new one. Also, Crane told him it was not only his father in on the conspiracy. Did Aaris know? He doubted it, but no-one snooped or meddled as much as she. If the universe had an agenda that involved him, and despite his past scorn of metaphysical abilities, he now hoped Time, or one of its mysterious allies, would come to his aid.

That night with Crane, Yianevan also learned his father's repeated attempts to clone the Waino marker caused his mother's death. He cursed House Anevan and their lies until his anger exhausted him, and he settled into an all-consuming silence. His father had climbed across the body of his mother and the bodies of every Lyran who perished to reach his goals. He would never forgive him.

There, in Crane's dusty quarters, the regrets Yianevan had buried deep for all these years resurfaced. As a headstrong, angry young man desperate to break free from the constraints of his existence and what awaited him in the future, he accepted his mother's urging that he must leave. Blinded by defiance and selfishness, he shed his obligations when he should have remained and protected her.

Crane would not hear of it. He told him of the mother's goodness and wisdom. She wanted only to spare her beloved son the wrath of the clan father. Yianevan was not the only youth who resisted tradition, but only he showed his dissatisfaction so forcefully by sustained rebellion over so many years. Had he been a member of a lesser house, it might have been overlooked, but he was House Anevan. And they never overlooked. At least not until now. Crane also reminded him why he came back. Saving his brother was an act of sacrifice, but while his fury at his improvidence still raged, Yianevan would not be comforted.

Crane adjourned the story until the heir's outpouring of despair subsided. He suffered that same sorrow himself when he learned of the mother's death, and he suffered it now watching her son, but there was no easy way for the boy to understand why he had called the clan father a murderer.

When he settled, Yianevan asked Crane what more he needed to know. Crane obliged by showing him data tiles of

Waino the Younger's many theories of time. Some of them he could attribute to Bethan's existence on the Earth. Age appeared to have no bearing. He knew she had been a child at Vesuvius, and she had mentioned being older as she viewed despondency in her village at a time of disease. Neither could explain Bethan's apparent affinity to the time pennant nor her unusual sensitivity to calming pennants. They agreed that given the number of would-be interventionists not approved, those who were successful required a degree of sensitivity. He also felt sure the time pennant established her where she was most likely to be found. Yianevan would never know whether it mirrored other timelines or was an echo of the lives Bethan would have lived if the Lyrans had not abducted her ancestors. Pondering the possibilities reminded him of Bethan's comment, made one day as they discussed her dreams. She said she always had a sense of living out her life in a play. She was right.

He arrived at the Marisene and brought the shuttle down at the far pastures, away from the palace. He then automated it to return to the tribal ordinary hangar bays. As soon as he cleared the shuttle, he ran until his legs no longer held him. His lungs bursting with exertion, he fell to his knees, tipping forward to flatten himself out on the dewy grass. The early morning dew distilled into his clothes and chilled his body, and he rolled onto his back to look at the sky. Grey clouds, heavy with the promise of rain, drove angrily above him, and the crisp wind whipped his shirt into sail-like billows.

Yianevan didn't care about the cold. He knew he could

not stay, yet he didn't know how to leave. Crane extracted a promise that he would not try to initiate the pennant and must seek refuge as close to the edge of the galaxy as he could. Even beyond. He would keep travelling, changing ships to throw off any pursuit, and bury the pennant on a distant world in an uninhabited system when his life neared its end. Crane followed his instructions by declaring Irrinait must always be concealed, and Yianevan must resist the increasing, fierce desire to know its secrets.

Bo found him and assumed, because of his soggy, unkempt appearance, that he had been there since the previous morning. The sib questioned the heir's whereabouts, but the clan father, although irritated by his son's absence, was otherwise unconcerned. Yi's ship was in its hangar, his hunting rods were gone, and he decreed his son had taken a respite from Aaris's carping. He would return soon enough. Willa was the only one who checked his chambers but guessed he was seeking solitude somewhere. Neither she nor anyone else considered the long meadow because it was a considerable distance without sensors. Bo only discovered him by chance while using a hunting drone and took a carriage out when he located him.

Yianevan told Bo he went walking, then spent the rest of the day in meditation, lost track of time, and when night fell, he chose not to return. Instead, he stayed out in the open to enjoy the spectacle of the heavens. Bo didn't question him. He had already learned his brother's habits were a little peculiar, quite unlike other Nobles.

The only one who commented on his return was Kerys, but Yianevan told her he would speak to her another time. Not even his father made mention, only telling his son he had excused Satra from her betrothal. He considered calling through to Willa that night, but his emotions felt too raw for even her gentle company. However, with little interest in her brother's emotional state, Kerys did not plan on granting him any peace.

He knew it was his little sister when the entry to his apartments opened. Stretched out on his face on the divan, he didn't look up, only cursed that he hadn't changed the door lock. She would have overridden it, anyway.

He needed time to think, to construct an escape plan, but none of that, nor his desire for solitude, was likely to trouble Kerys. She would want to hear about his visit with Crane because she expected everything that couldn't be shared with the clan father had to be shared with her. This time, she had news of her own.

"Yi, wake up." She dug her finger into his back. "Can you keep a secret?"

He groaned and turned over.

"If you hadn't noticed, little sister, I speak to few people."

"Yes, well, I know you talk to Willa, but you mustn't even tell her. Now, I kept your secret, so you must keep mine. Yi, I invented something, and I'm not going to tell anyone!"

"You're telling me."

Kerys was too excited to interest herself in trivial details. She lifted her hand, and a holographic disc in her palm threw out a model of a spinning cone before them, then a second, then a third, all linked by a tether.

Yianevan propped himself on his elbow. "What is it?

"You know the Z34 system?

He knew it well. "Three moons, all with mines," he replied.

She gave him a wide grin. "And what do mines need?"

"Miners?"

Kerys enlarged the cones to view the underlying premise of her invention.

"Of course they need miners, Yi," she said. "But those mines have to use manual labour because of the instability of the minerals. Working underground in that environment causes all sorts of diseases."

Yianevan was tired, but this intrigued him, so he rubbed the weariness from his eyes.

"Is your invention to deliver medication?"

His sister's grin widened. "No, silly. It's for dispersion. This model isn't to scale, but a trio of these get buried deep below the ground. That would make nine cones. See here?" She pointed to the revolving neck of the funnel. "Intense vibration generated by compressed Seriomik particles diffuses upwards into the cone. That vibration pushes the minerals before the shock waves, except those waves are calibrated, so they don't cause instability. It's more like the minerals get caressed to the surface. Then they get collected in here." She pointed to a catcher contraption. "Clever, eh?"

It was indeed clever. Impressive even, provided Seriomik alloys could be located. They were scarce. No doubt more thought was needed.

"I suppose that was the simple version designed for someone of my intelligence?"

"Yes," Kerys replied without subtlety or argument. "It's only in its early stage, but it has potential, don't you think? By the time it's perfected and I've developed a prototype to test, you will be clan father, and I can petition you to use it on Z34."

"You propose to ask my permission?"

"Well, if it remains Noble technology, we can't just send it out into the galaxy. We must keep some control. Besides, what if someone misuses it?"

"How?"

"There is a volatile phase. Look…" Kerys stretched herself across the divan and opened Yianevan's interface, loading her narrow info into a local file. Together, they stripped the image to its core and reassembled it, then identified areas of weakness in the three rods that supported the angles of the cone. As they analysed, Yianevan saw a potential that may hold an answer to his dilemma. Kerys had unwittingly devised a unique explosive. Thankfully, she hadn't homed in on it.

"This is the only part I've built," Kerys said. "I have a few ideas, but the two components aren't compatible. I need to find a solution to avoid the volatile state."

Yianevan asked her if she had mentioned the invention to their father.

"What!" she burst out. "No! I can't tell him! He'll give it to the lesser houses to develop. I need to do more research, and I want to build it myself."

Good, Yianevan thought. Knowing Kerys, she would not give up the invention and only explore the volatile component, not the explosive potential. Besides, she was interested only in its mining application.

"It looks quite sophisticated," Yianevan said, covertly wiping the local data. "Did you keep a record of your research?"

"Not on a tile," she grinned, knowing that would not keep her precious research safe. "But I have a great memory."

She continued to chatter about her embryonic vision for mining while Yianevan made a few calculations in his head. Kerys proposed the use of tretilic components from obsolete Ca'Anastran lightships. In the past, tribal ordinaries used them as emergency patches in phase technology, but they were unstable. Kerys had hit on a way to ensure their volatility. One he could exploit. He even had a quantity of these components in the hold of his ship.

"Please don't tell anyone about this," Kerys said as she wriggled from the divan. She didn't even mention his visit to Crane.

"I won't," he promised. Then, as soon as she left, he climbed through the window and made his way to his ship.

How swiftly Time presented a solution for him to leave the homeworld.

Corky greeted him. "Noble, are things proceeding well?"

The interface had isolated all preceding conversations and continued to do so. It was just the two of them. It became such an effective co-conspirator that even the best programmers would not uncover evidence of what passed between interface and Noble.

"No, Corky," Yianevan said. "Although, I have an idea

for an explosive that might move things along."

He described Kerys's invention, where he wanted it employed, and with Corky's help, drew up a schematic of an explosive device.

"There is a quantity of this metal in store, Noble," Corky said. "It does not have an application in weaponry, but there is the potential to set up an explosion that would disintegrate this ship. Secondary damage might occur to the pontoon at that distance, but I estimate it will hold."

"What about searchable and analysable residue?" Yianevan knew there would be an investigation, and he needed them to find nothing of value.

"In the quantity you propose, Noble, the residue would not be quantifiable."

"And if they search for organic particles?"

"The detonation will have a nucleus at the point of the Ca'Anastran compound. The resulting cascade would obliterate any organic on the ship."

"Is there any chance it could blow an organic out into space?"

"Not if that organic is you, Noble. If you are on the ship when it explodes, not even a cell will be left to analyse."

"Me? Why do you say that?"

"I assume you plan to stage your death at the new interventionist ship launch and effect an escape from the Noble homeworld."

Yianevan was almost prepared to swear this interface could read chak. He had to tell Corky the truth. "You assume correctly, and I need this by then. Can it be done?"

"Yes, Noble, but there is no guarantee it will work."

And Corky had so many quirks. Yianevan sighed. "Why didn't you say so?"

"You didn't ask for probabilities, Noble. I did mention this was only a 'potential'."

"Alright, what are the probabilities?"

"As with all contingencies, Noble, it will work, or it will not. As we cannot conduct a test on a mixture of compounds and alloys never constructed in this manner, there is no way to arrive at a conclusion."

"Corky, are you avoiding the question?"

"Yes, Noble."

He thought so. "Very well. Are you sure that if it does work, the ship will disintegrate?"

"Affirmative."

"Well, if it doesn't, I will return to the surface, and no-one will be any the wiser."

"Yes, Noble."

Yianevan wagged a finger at the interface. "It must succeed."

Corky didn't answer. The plan had merit and many dangers, but there was no point in arguing.

The next morning, Aaris waited for Yianevan to join the sib at morning bell.

"Did you see Crane?"

Yianevan feigned forgetfulness. "Crane?"

"Do not perceive me as a fool, brother. You were missing for a day and a night. I ask again. Did you see Crane?"

"I was in the long meadow. Was Crane planning a visit out there?"

"You wished to further your research about Waino."

"Waino? Ah, you mean the pennants? No, it was just a diversion. Now, sister, this conversation is as pointless as any we hold. Please excuse me."

Aaris watched him walk away. He was too cheerful, and that made her suspicious. His mood had shifted, and it infuriated her to think he had gained knowledge to which she was not privy. What was it? It hadn't come about after a night of useless meditation in a field, so it had to be Crane. She couldn't visit him herself; it would be too out of character for her to go missing as Yi did, but she knew others among the tribal ordinaries who could. Yi went to Crane, she was sure, and he came back changed. She wanted that knowledge, and she would get it one way or another.

If he knew what she planned, Crane would have guffawed with laughter because only hours after he farewelled Yianevan, he entered his eternal rest.

On the evening of the new interventionist ship launch, Willa was among those who watched the Noble shuttles heading for the pontoon. Not yet a wife, she couldn't attend at Yianevan's side, but that would change when she told him what she learned that morning. As a physician and mother already, she had suspected, but Yi's distraction these last days made her hesitate, and she didn't wish to give him false hope. When he returned, she would tell him she carried an heir. An heir that would secure the future of the homeworld. This child meant Bo would never come under threat, and

Aaris's son would not succeed. Neither would Aaris ever become regent. Yi would be the clan father, and his son would follow him. Change and a glorious new day would soon dawn for the Noble homeworld.

*CHAPTER THIRTY-NINE_*

The prospect of seeing Bethan at the launch filled Yianevan with both longing and dread. She would have no choice but to be there, as the hierarchy assigned her crew to the new ship. Tonight though, if all went to plan, she would learn of the heir to House Anevan's death. It would mean little to her, as the mention of his name was unlikely anywhere since she returned.

Nobles rarely appeared in public and did little to distinguish themselves from one another when they did. Bethan might not even recognise him, and why should she? He last saw her, standing confused and uncertain in her apartment, and only introduced himself as the Noble who delivered her home. Now she had moved forward with her life.

In her interventionist uniform, Phildre should have blended in with all the other humans and visitors attending the reception. She didn't. His eyes were drawn to her the moment he entered the auditorium. She had already seen him, even though she was on the far side with many people milling between them, drinks in hand, finding seats, talking with colleagues. Above all the milieu, her gaze was steady, willing him to acknowledge her. When she saw he noticed her, she dipped her head in a nervous nod of acknowledgement.

Yianevan forced himself to continue walking. In his father's company, he had to uphold the lie. Nobles did not make casual acknowledgement of other species; they held themselves aloof, superior in their technological grandeur and allowed the ten sector dignitaries obsequiousness to feed their lofty ideology.

His father sensed the son's distraction and watched him. Fearful he might draw attention to the interventionist and single her out, he inclined his head towards the clan father and joined with the other dignitaries.

There had been very few words between father and son since Yianevan learned of his mother's murder and the truth behind House Anevan. In his anger, he considered assassinating his father, but he didn't know who else was in on the conspiracy. He would have to kill them all, and he was not a killer. Either way, tolerating the clan father's presence as he made his escape plans proved almost too hard to bear. In the days leading up to the launch, he did not even see Willa, fearing she may suspect. Instead, he feigned contracting a chill from his time in the meadow and kept away from company, even from Kerys. This was his first official outing in several days.

The ceremony lasted too long for Yianevan, but afterwards, to his great relief, his father became engaged in discussion with the Grielik Chief of Police. The timing couldn't be better, and he retreated to the lower pontoon. So far, the plan appeared to be falling into place. Corky had made the preparations to the ship, which Yianevan piloted rather than taking the shuttle, and as it was the heir, no-one considered it an unusual move.

Entering the landing bay closest to his ship, he checked the position of a Grielik police transport. He and Corky had prepared for every eventuality and timed everything to the tiniest detail. Except for one. Being followed.

"Lieutenant Phildre," he said as he turned, sensing her presence in the doorway.

Phildre hesitated as she stepped toward him. "I know we're not meant to approach you, but… Are you Yianevan?"

"Not approaching a Noble is more a tradition than law," Yianevan said. "And yes, I am Yianevan."

Phildre wondered what she was doing, stalking a Noble, standing here, about to demand answers. Nerves threatened, but she would not turn tail and run.

"Of all the things I forgot," she said, "you are one of the few I remember, apart from my work."

He saw in her chak that she was uncertain. If she could only see into his, she would see that his heart struggled to beat, his lungs refusing to draw breath. He could not be this close to her. Not now. He forced his voice to sound natural, in control.

"I hear your mishap did not affect your ability as an interventionist. In part, the new ship assignment was due to you."

That information caught Phildre off guard. "I didn't know that," she said. "I thought it was a safety issue, and they didn't want me or anyone getting lost again."

"We didn't wish to lose such exemplary employees." It was glib, but he just didn't know how to respond.

Phildre struggled with what to say next. With his eyes free of optical prostheses, Yianevan saw into her emotions. There, he read bewilderment and doubt in how she should frame her questions. He also saw a resolve to learn the answers, but he had none to give that wouldn't place her in danger. Any moment now, Corky would signal that the Grielik police had boarded their cruiser to head to the Macanis system on the boundary to change crews. These cruisers went to spacelight speed without delay, and he had to be on board before then. Concealed in the cruiser's hold meant a miserable and cold ninety-two-hour trip, but that couldn't be helped. Corky had set the detonator and would deactivate all but the essential parts of his program before spiralling Yianevan to the Grielik ship. The spiral would keep him phased to avoid exposure to sensors. Corky also fixed a spiral and phasing to the active parts of his program, undetectable when he transferred within the spiral. It was a hazardous plan, and seeing Bethan now threatened to derail it.

"Noble—" she began with a formal address, but it didn't seem right. She started over. "Yianevan. I need to know what happened. Can you help me? I know you can see inside my mind. I have dreams, vivid and real."

Dreams. The telltale signs of her identity on Earth. Perhaps Crane was right. In his summing up, he mentioned it was possible her chak would not let her rest until she knew the truth, and now, back in her proper environment, it still demanded answers. She was not at peace, and he, above all, knew how hard that was to live with.

"I can see the chak, Lieutenant," Yianevan said. "I cannot read minds. As far as we can tell, you found safety at the base of an erupting volcano. We do not know how you accomplished it."

Phildre ran her hands through her spiky hair. That explanation was just… utter *gibberish!* And she would challenge him.

"How could I survive two days at the base of a stratovolcano without being carbonised? Yet I survived without so much as singed eyebrows."

"I cannot advise you," came the measured response. "The interface located you. You were unconscious, and I returned you to your home. That is the extent of my involvement."

Phildre centred her thoughts on the facts. Why didn't Chief Jardin or the interface find her before summoning the Nobles if it was so easy? She wanted to ask him, but everything that came out of her mouth sounded like a demand. It took her a second to think through before she shrugged and asked him, anyway. While she was at it, she enquired about Corky.

Yianevan had not prepared himself to be in a position where he would have to answer these questions. He believed he would never see her again, so he had to think on his feet, aware of time running out.

"I understand Vesuvius contains properties that hid

you from scanners," he lied. "It only showed your life signs, indistinct but visible. Our engineers examined the interface. We found no errors, but there seemed no reason to return it. I hope this answers your queries."

Phildre shook her head. "I am told I must accept what happened, even while I have no memory. If you can see into people's feelings and emotions, you can see I know there is more to the story."

"I see you are confused, Lieutenant, but while I cannot tell what happened during your absence, I do not believe there is more to it than an accident, which had a fortunate outcome. Dreams profoundly affect the chak, and your confusion could result from them."

His answer didn't satisfy her, just as he knew it wouldn't. She wasn't a fool, so when in a bold move, she looked him in the eye, he glanced away. Meeting her gaze was too risky. He might reveal too much. She didn't move. This Noble might see beyond plain sight, but this time, she could see beyond too. He was lying.

"I am human," she said, lifting her chin. "Flesh and blood. You and I both know I could not survive the heat of a volcanic eruption on any world. I do not believe the incident resulted from spiral failure. Neither do I believe the wild theory that a brave and reckless local inhabitant found me near the crater in a confused state, then, with superhuman strength carried me, in full interventionist gear, to the base of that mountain before abandoning me. Perhaps he realised I was a visitor from space and fled, terrified, which was unlikely. Yianevan, I have studied that volcano. It is not an easy gradient to navigate. and certainly not while being bombarded with molten rocks."

"We knew you were safe, Lieutenant. My task was to locate you. Which I did."

She would forever seek answers, or she might discover the truth on her own. If she remembered, would she speak of those memories? If she mentioned the charm, she could place herself in danger. Or would she put them down to the strange dreams and keep them private? If he told her the truth, he would expose his own people's dark secret, that they were no better than the Lyran Monks they sought to defame. And she had not mentioned the pennant.

"I'm sorry," Yianevan said as he moved towards the exit. He needed to bring their reunion to an end. "I cannot fill in the gaps for you."

Phildre shook her head, trying to remember. She didn't believe that he couldn't "fill in the gaps" and jolly well felt like keeping him here until he did. This Noble was the only one who could help. So she ignored his tacit invitation to leave, knowing he would not just walk out.

"I remember a place where the night was black, and there were strange sailing vessels with tall masts," she said. "A harbour, but the sea was rough. You were there."

Yianevan stopped. He had to know how much she remembered.

Closing her eyes, Phildre envisioned the scene now in her mind's eye. Perhaps it was just another dream, but the walk along an endless corridor with windows where the light shone through seemed too real. Each window dimmed as she passed, and there was a man's voice. A voice she knew. That voice belonged to this Noble. He could deny it all he liked, but he took that walk with her. The Nobles may have similar features, but like all beings, their voices had their own characteristics.

When she saw she had his attention again, she asked him if he spoke the language of the human planet.

"That planet is inhospitable towards my race," he said.

Not a good enough response. "With respect, Noble," she said. "I didn't ask that. I speak three other dialects apart from Sector."

"My apologies, Lieutenant," Yianevan replied. "I understand some dialects of the humans, but I would not be confident in my fluency."

Phildre could see prevarication at fifty paces. She'd get it out of him tonight because even if she had to block the exit, he wasn't leaving until she did. He was hiding something.

"Noble, I wonder if you would indulge me in a little exercise?"

How he navigated these next few minutes was crucial. He couldn't tell how close she was to remembering, so did he help or hinder? Then, from the corner of his eye, he saw the Grielik ship begin its ignition sequence, causing his anxiety to increase as the window for his escape began to close.

"Would you just say something for me?" Phildre asked. "I'd appreciate it. It's a word that keeps appearing in my dreams. A place." She knew she was crossing a line, but it was just them alone, and she wouldn't really bar his exit, but somehow, she knew he wouldn't leave.

"What would you have me say?"

"Llanbleddynllwyd."

She delivered the name of the village with the fluency of a native, then waited for his reaction. His mouth moved, but he didn't answer. So she repeated it, emphasising the syllables.

"Just say after me, Noble. Llan. Bledd. Yn. Llw. Yd."

Even under Bethan's meticulous tutoring, Yianevan had never once pronounced the name of her village with any accuracy. It had always tumbled out in an unintelligible mess, and he had no hope now. He could not get the aspiration correct on the Llan, and it always came out like Qwillan or Clan, and that was at his best attempts. The double 'd' sounds were also a problem, and his past futile attempts to place the stream of syllables together caused a spasm in his jaw. Welsh was not a language designed for a Noble's tongue.

It didn't help his anxiety. If Corky commed him now, how could he walk away with her so close to rediscovery? If she told her friends, it could get back to his father, who would know she had visited the future. And that could be deadly for her. It might also expose his escape plan even if he managed to execute it. Then he would become a fugitive.

Phildre advanced to within inches of him, repeating, ever so slowly, step by step, syllable by syllable, the name of the village.

"What is this?" he said, dismissing her advance with a flick of his hand. "An odd syntax and foreign to the tongue."

She did not back down, nor did her gaze waver. "I said it, and I assure you, it's correct. But you can't say it, can you?" Then, with a look of horror, she stepped back. What was she doing? Her pointed rudeness sent waves of mortification through her whole body. And to a Noble of all people!

"I'm so sorry, Noble," she gushed. "I don't know what came over me. That word, among others, often echoes inside my mind. I regret I used you to piece together random memories that I doubt have any meaning. You are my only link, and I don't know the meanings of these words myself. I just hear them in dreams. How can I expect you to have more knowledge?"

She drew a deep breath to help gather her shattered dignity.

"I am Phildre," she declared. "I am proud to be an interventionist, and I accept I was lost during a pennant settling, and that is all there is to it. Noble, I am sorry to have detained you."

She didn't ask him to dismiss her, and with nothing further to add, made it to the door before she stopped. Since her return, she dreamt of the volcano and people running before the smoke and ash. They called the mountain "Vesuvius". Just before, when he spoke of her rescue, the Noble named it. He could not read details of her dreams in the chak, and that volcano had no official designation, only what she heard in her dream. She turned to face him, finally sure of his deception.

"Vesuvius, Noble?"

Had his remark been careless? Or had Time designed it that way. He now discarded coincidences in matters of Time and Destiny. No matter what happened, he could not risk leaving her here. With her awakening, her realisation of all those sleeping memories, any Noble so inclined could read her chak, and right now, she did not need to be around the hierarchy. She needed to know the truth so she could save herself, and to do that, he had to unlock those memories. Without thinking, he had given himself away the moment he uttered the name "Vesuvius". He knew another.

Bethan.

She knew that name. It was in her dreams. And she knew him.

CHAPTER FORTY _

Mabubel the Merchant walked on two legs, but he didn't consider himself a humanoid. In fact, he found that description mildly insulting because he was far more sturdy than any humanoid he'd ever met. He was a beast. A massive, hairy, and fearsome colossus. Or so it pleased him to think. At least when he was on his own. Those who knew and loved him didn't see him like that. They saw him more like a big old walking shag pile carpet friend of the family. A local legend.

Robust and reliable, to hire Mabubel wouldn't cost much, maybe a meal or a few pints of local ale, so if you required something heavy to be moved, you asked Mabubel. If you needed a minder for your pets or your kids or your granny, Mabubel would be sure to oblige. Such was the scope of his "services". If circumstances called for it, he had a shady side, so if you desired your husband to disappear, or your wife, or your neighbour, or if a cartel boss had a problem with a smuggler, then Mabubel was your guy.

Of dubious parentage and questionable species,

Mabubel's rumoured exploits in the maelstrom and on the outlier worlds featured in the stories children heard at their grandparent's knee. That meant he had been kicking around this part of outlier space for at least a hundred years. The oldies said he once had three arms, but everyone hereabouts only remembered him having two, the other presumably bitten off by a monster in the maelstrom. That's where they lay in wait for anyone daft enough to venture in, along with their good mates; nightmare and giant amoebas. Or so the story went. No-one ever went in to confirm Mabubel's tales. No-one except Mabubel, and fear kept the maelstrom out of reach of even the most enterprising.

Each time he left the outlier worlds, the folk hereabouts speculated that his luck would run out this time. It never did, and he would come back with a cargo of artisan pots, carvings, and textiles that he sold for a tidy profit at the boundary, because nowhere could anyone find such exquisite workmanship.

Mabubel didn't speak of his contacts in the maelstrom or why one of his eyes lolled about on its stalk the last time he came back. The maelstrom's perilous maws were nurseries for many malevolent species, but the ship required his attention, so he stepped outside where one of those blasted creatures bit his face right through his suit. He smacked the attacking alien so hard it flew halfway across the galaxy, but the force made Mabubel's eye pop out. It still had plenty of vision left, so now and then, he stuck it back into his eye socket. No point in wasting it.

He learned a valuable lesson that day. Don't get too comfortable with the maelstrom, but he so enjoyed the speculation about what happened. And his silence only added to the myths and notoriety he revelled in.

There were planets deep within the maelstrom, eminently habitable, at least to someone of his species, although he didn't know his species. There were females on those planets, indigenous to the maelstrom worlds, who, for reasons best known to themselves, loved to fuss over the woolly visitor who purchased their painted pots and textiles and took them off to who knows where. None of those worlds ever strayed from their own planetary systems, so they never followed him. Besides, he was far better looking than most of them, so they treated him like a god. A perfect place to spend his twilight years in luxury. He might even cement his godhood with all the wealth he had accumulated.

On the day Mabubel's joints creaked a little too much, and his gut denounced the last century of poor diet, he finally decided to leave the outlier systems and enter the maelstrom for good. He enjoyed the round of farewells, tears, and back-slapping, stopping to comfort those few individuals who begged him to stay, but the decision was made, so he allowed his friends to help him indulge in a little too much of the good stuff. So good, in fact, he had to delay his departure by sleeping off his brain fog in an alley.

As dawn broke, he wandered back to his ship, his hangover bringing on nostalgic thoughts and reflection of his time on all the outlier and boundary worlds. Good times now at an end here, but new ones to look forward to in his retirement. His whiskery jaw parted in a smile, and his yellowed teeth glinted in the early light. On this planet, at least, the name "Mabubel" would pass into folklore.

As he approached the landing ramp, he made out a humanoid shape at the entrance to the hangar. Mabubel could not tell the species from the attire or system they might hail from. He peered at the figure as he approached. Ten sectors, maybe, but this far out? It had a hood covering and no escort. He couldn't detect weapons, a sign of confidence because most strangers feared Mabubel's hirsute giantism. The humanoid spoke with a man's voice, educated but with poor command of basic outlier. Mabubel had heard worse, but he got that the man wanted to be taken "out-system". This planet was as "out-system" as it got. So out-system, in fact, it was considered local, but the man insisted on a "one-way trip". Never to be found. Did Mabubel understand?

Mabubel understood, but he had planned to head straight into the maelstrom and blissful retirement. Instead, his good nature made him agree to take the humanoid male to any planet on his way, and he would eat his hat if anyone ever found him.

It wasn't good enough. The man told Mabubel he would not place his retirement plans in jeopardy. His needs would cause only a slight delay, and the maelstrom would be the perfect destination for the first part of the journey.

Mabubel protested, asking how the man knew of his retirement when they were not formerly acquainted. When the man handed him a fat purse, Mabubel's words of indignance slipped back down his throat. The monetary compensation offered was eye-popping, prompting the reinsertion of Mabubel's rampant eyeball. Years of merchandising and shifty practices meant he couldn't ignore a sum of money like that, so perhaps a teensy-weensy delay wouldn't hurt. Besides, who was he to abandon a stranger in need? Particularly one as wealthy as this. Mabubel was well-travelled, and in his more than a century-plus years, he learned a thing or two from observing people. This man had covered himself to hide his identity, but he gave himself away when Mabubel realised the man had "read" him.

Only Nobles read chak. Mabubel met one once, and he didn't like their superciliousness. In this case, the cloak worked; no-one would pay attention to someone who covered themselves around here. Behaviour was a different matter. You couldn't always disguise traits you were born with, and he couldn't remember the last time a Noble ventured into outlier space. They were too scared of getting their hands, or their reputations, dirty.

No matter. Whatever the man turned out to be, Mabubel accepted the terms, and he helped the man come aboard.

The well-remunerated delay came at the outer edges of the maelstrom, where the man instructed Mabubel to wait. The payment was such, Mabubel was prepared to wait until the stars dimmed. His guest told him, without prompting, it wouldn't take that long, even though Mabubel informed him nothing ever came this way, at least not by choice. However, he was told only to continue patient, and meanwhile, they would work together to incorporate his own interface into the ship's systems. Mabubel liked the upgrade and assumed whoever the man was waiting for knew how to find them. Judging by the risks he was prepared to take, someone exceptional was coming. Either that or he awaited valuable information. All paths out here were tricky to the uninitiated, and it would be more by luck than judgement if they ever arrived.

Even though Mabubel's easy-going nature wore a little thin after months of waiting, and his delight over his newfound wealth palled, it was not the same for the man. With tireless patience, he watched and waited. Then when sensors detected an automated long-range shuttle, Mabubel realised the man's motivation.

Love.

The shuttle's occupant, a travel-weary human female, disembarked right into the man's arms. So wrapped up in their reunion, Mabubel had to squeeze past them in the docking bay door to get the woman's luggage and disengage the shuttle.

The first item he brought across was a stressed cat in a cage. That was okay; Mabubel liked cats, self-sufficient little creatures you were more likely to find out here than a human. There was also a suspended interface in its original antique carry pouch with the word "Betty" written across the case. The woman had travelled light, just like the man, but it must have been a hellish journey because those cramped, noisy shuttles only provided basic facilities. If her expedition began in the ten sectors, the woman would have taken several months and travelled on dozens of different ships to get here. This was a dangerous passage, far more than most humans could stomach.

Mabubel smirked. He bet a few of his old pirate mates were happy to get paid off as she made her trip. Once she got on that shuttle, she would drop right off the radar. One good thing; those shuttles were disposable and untraceable. Still, Mabubel was a softie for a romance, so the joyous reunion gave his labyrinthine insides the warm and fuzzies. He took a moment to observe them with a silent, "Aww, how cute," then turned his cannons on the shuttle and let loose a barrage of missiles. That was part of the deal. He tried to tell the man it would never be found this close to the maelstrom, but the man insisted there must not even be a molecule left.

With the shuttle disintegrated, Mabubel swung the ship back towards the maelstrom and daydreamed of his favourite planet, deep inside, with beautiful people, oceans and the luxurious retirement he envisioned.

His two passengers didn't notice, but Mabubel possessed another ability apart from being able to cheat death in the maelstrom. This ability had its uses in his shadier dealings, so he never publicised that he had remarkable hearing. He only listened to his guests in the galley because he was far too polite to intrude on bedroom secrets. They communicated in a dialect they thought he wouldn't understand, and he didn't, not entirely, but he could piece stuff together. He rather enjoyed the puzzle. It became a game for him. A diversion. The conversation went back and forth. He said. She said. Mabubel liked to switch ears to whoever was speaking.

Man: Was I wrong to break my promise to Crane?

Woman: As soon as you told me on the pontoon, I knew you would.

Man: I guess Crane didn't know everything.

Woman: He knew its history. We are learning about its

future. Do you want to return to the homeworld? Are you worried about your family? About Kerys, Bo and Willa?

Mabubel got that much from earlier conversations. The Noble rulership suffered some kind of challenge after someone's sister tried to take control, and apparently, there was chaos on the homeworld when the sister was banished. The man got upset, but he didn't seem surprised. In fact, Mabubel thought it sounded like he dodged a bullet by leaving. The conversation continued.

Man: We can't go back. Not yet. When I first understood the pennant's language, as Crane said I would, I also realised the chak's relationship to time. Another lesson was the role of destiny. We have to wait.

Woman (laughing a little. A pretty sound.): Did you ask the pennant?

Man: (Mabubel imagined him smiling). Actually, I did.

Mabubel loved the pinging from one side to the other. And he loved how the couple took moments to hold hands or push their lips together. He also worked out the man had faked his death to get away from some terrible parenting. The woman gave up her job to be with him, and for now, they would steer clear of the ten sectors. That should be okay. The galaxy was a big place. Easy to get lost in. He also gathered the pair had something important in their custody, something meaningful that had scars which the man had healed. All very mysterious, but then, the universe was a mysterious place.

From the things they said, the man at least was a time traveller. Mabubel wasn't sure he believed it, but if so, good on them, although he would have thought a time traveller could have managed a quick trip out to the maelstrom and back to pick up his girlfriend. Perhaps it didn't work like that. Besides, the man needed him to get out-system and help integrate the interface into the ship, so it seems mechanical expertise wasn't a necessary qualification for someone who travelled through time. Mabubel didn't want to overestimate his usefulness, but they also needed his help to integrate the woman's interface, which appeared to resent the other interface and immediately found fault. The bickering continued with the woman as referee until they sorted out their individual differences. It was rather comical to witness. "Betty", who belonged to the woman, complained that "Corky" had too many opinionated circuits. "Corky" always dreamed up something snide as a response. It was like watching an old married couple, and even though the man disguised his eyes after he removed his cloak, it confirmed his origins. The man's interface was recent Noble technology.

The woman, Bethan, was one of the nicest humans Mabubel ever met. Her voice was always gentle, perhaps a little more so when she spoke to the man, but when she prepared meals, she always included special treats for Mabubel. She called the treats "Peekybarks", and he loved them. So did the man. And Bethan always took time for a chat. To cover his eavesdropping activities, he pretended he didn't fully understand her, but he liked her voice, so the words didn't matter.

Watching the woman and the man together, Mabubel wondered how it would work between a Noble and a human. He suspected it had never been tested. Nobles seldom left their homeworld, they didn't mix, and you rarely saw one of their ships buzzing around with their enhanced speed, even in the ten sectors, except for the Grielik police fleet. Those police were everywhere, but they left you alone if you kept your nose clean. Humans though, there were a few in the outlier worlds, more out on the boundary and quite a few in the ten sectors. They were a bit frail for Mabubel's taste. Far too easy to squish, although this woman looked quite strong and fit for a human female.

Of all his new passengers, his favourite was the cat. The two undertook a mutual grooming session each night, and he wondered if he should get a pet when he got to his new home. The people there like to brush his arms and back, so he probably didn't need one, but the little creature was so cute when it curled up, purring and warm in his lap. He was going to miss it. He learned to hide the cat from the Betty interface because it was constantly feeding it and shooing it about because no-one had found something better for it to do. Mabubel thought about getting it to clean an airlock. Of course, it wouldn't be his fault if he knocked the controls…

Still, whatever adventure the Noble, the human, the cat and two interfaces were embarking on, Mabubel thought it sounded like it would be a wild and exciting ride. He might have asked to go along once, but they weren't too far from his destination, and he grew weary. He wanted no more excitement. Well, none that involved unpredictable stuff like time travel. Although, he would miss this ship. Never a finer, faster ship built, especially with the new interface enabling spacelight. Everything has its price, even this ship that had been in his family forever. And the man offered the right price. It went a darned sight faster with the Nobles interface at the helm, and it responded like a new vessel. Mabubel wished he got his hairy hands on one earlier.

As they neared his destination, Mabubel collaborated with the Corky interface to chart the most direct route back into normal space at the maelstrom's farthest reaches. It would be difficult, trying to avoid maelstrom wildlife and rogue planets, and he doubted things would improve once they exited the maelstrom near the edge of this galaxy. Perhaps they should use whatever it was that helped them to time travel. He didn't say so. He just wished them luck.

They'd need it.

EPILOGUE _

Llanbleddynllwyd Historical Society
Newsletter for July 2021

Ladies and gentlemen. Our village is saved!

It is with great pleasure I bring you this special bulletin; believe me, it contains some wonderful news. Further to the council's proposals to demolish Collier Row because of disrepair (caused by them), an injection of funds has spared them at the eleventh hour! As you know, these miners' cottages have important historical significance, and the council has, up to now, resisted all our petitions to save them.

An unknown—at least to us—benefactor has acquired the cottages, the park, Mrs Jenkins's old house and the colliery, which was very run down. All sites will receive an upgrade and be placed in perpetual trust of the Historical Society. So don't worry; if we all fall off our perches before injecting fresh blood, the deeds have made clear what we should do! But I won't trouble you with that now.

When Mrs Jenkins's old house is restored, the historical society will relocate there as a permanent meeting place, and we will act as custodians. The pit is to become a museum, and the lower end cottages near the park are to be upgraded and sold as residences. The top end, including Bethan Davies's old cottage, will be knocked into one and turned into a bed-and-breakfast and café restaurant, something for which we have been begging the council to encourage tourism.

Friends, this is history repeating itself. An unknown person saved the village in 1898, and now, more than 120 years later, it is again the beneficiary of someone's generosity. Like many of you, I have barely set foot outside of it for nearly ninety years and never had a desire to, but we all can see how it has declined. Our young people have left to discover greener pastures, and dear friends have passed away. Together we watched the new council town spring up around us and endured the curious stares of those who thought us backward and not worth saving. Lately, we have faced eviction from our homes as the council sought permission to develop the area. Now, this will save our family dwellings and preserve our village. All thanks to our anonymous benefactor.

Councilman Birch will be at the meeting on

> Friday night. I urge you all to attend and bring your questions. This is a new dawn for Llanbleddynllwyd.
>
> Warm Regards
> Mrs Ivy Barton
> President.

Ivy took off her spectacles and rubbed her eyes. The bright computer screen made them dry and itchy, but she was desperate to email the newsletter to all the members. She'd sat on the news until it was confirmed and dared not leave the house in case she spilt the beans. She hadn't even told Jacob the whole story. Not that the old codger remembered much these days.

The solicitors for the benefactor had left Ivy with a wad of papers, but she was doddery herself and her mind not what it used to be, not that it was ever much to start with. At the time, she could only feel thankful to the donor for their goodness in coming to the village's aid. Once it all hit her like a ton of bricks, it seemed too good to be true, so she read the papers, struggling with the legal jargon. She wished the solicitor who visited her had taken more care. He was dealing with an old lady, after all. An old lady in shock.

But it was a separate spiral bound section that puzzled her most because it mentioned her in specific ways, not just as the Historical Society President. It had to be clarified. Jacob's old friend, Lew Evans, used to be a solicitor, so she asked for his help. On viewing the section, he congratulated her on her personal good fortune and explained the various clauses, but if she wished for further information, she would need to contact the benefactor's solicitor in Bristol. Still in shock, Ivy waited a week before arranging to meet with a senior member of the firm who drew up the bequest. It had to be a mistake, but it was worth the trip to find out.

Mr Bott of Weigelt and Bott, Solicitors, perused the section. When he finished, he peered over his glasses.

"I am acquainted with each section of this bequest, Mrs Barton," he said. "I can assure you there is no mistake. As you know, we have offered to continue as executors following your death."

"I have children and grandchildren, Mr Bott. If we need you, we will let you know."

"The properties listed benefit the village, and their management is the domain of the historical society. I understand you have already engaged a suitable agent?"

Ivy nodded.

"And you understand the titles of several other properties are to be transferred to you under the terms of the deed and in accordance with the instructions?"

"Mr Bott, I understand it. What I don't understand is why? These few pages tell me I own practically an entire village."

"Mrs Barton," he grinned at her exaggerated appraisal. "It is not an entire village; it is only a portion thereof. We prepared these documents under our client's specific directions, but we did not ask for justification for their wishes."

"Whoever this 'client' is, purchased a town from the

council," Ivy said. "Who does that? I know you carried out the conveyancing because your signature is on the document. Don't tell me the local council didn't come out well in profit; otherwise, why abandon their plans to expand that eyesore of a council estate? What I want to know, who is this client?"

Mr Bott made a noise between a superior laugh and the condescending snort he reserved for his most "simple" clients.

"This firm carried out that conveyance, Mrs Barton. As for the purchaser's identity, I'm afraid I am not at liberty to disclose it. The deed states expressly that the seven upper Collier Row listed properties and your own dwelling remain within the Barton family to do with as they see fit. This includes the new bed-and-breakfast establishment, all of which will receive suitable renovation before sale or rental as per your instruction. The pit, the large residence of the late Mrs Jenkins, and the park have separate provisions. Your family stands to gain considerable financial benefit."

"I will reinvest until the village is back on its feet."

"That is your prerogative, Mrs Barton. I understand you have an extensive family. Am I correct?"

Either Mr Bott had done his homework, or the benefactor knew her situation. Still, she supposed they would have to know about everyone in the village. Even so, why was she singled out?

"Your family may choose a different course in the future," he continued when she didn't respond. "However, there are sufficient invested funds to support the village. Meanwhile, with the new museum, the local tourist attractions and the excellent road out to Llyn Deron, it is well placed to generate income."

"My family will pull their weight in making sure the village recovers, Mr Bott, even if I am dead and buried, I assure you. It cannot be a coincidence this came when we were all to be moved to council houses so the developers could tear the village down. I believe as a principal beneficiary, I am entitled to know who gifted this to my family."

"I wish I could help, Mrs Barton, but my clients were clear on this."

Ivy was on it in a second. "Oh, there was more than one?"

Mr Bott gave her an indulgent smile.

"I'm sorry, Mrs Barton."

Well, she tried. Ivy didn't know any millionaires, and she might never know why someone had given her money or at such a time. She stepped out onto the pavement and put on her sunnies. All the white concrete in these towns had too much glare for her aging eyes. She pulled out her mobile phone to send her grandson a message to let him know she'd finished and bring the car around. Bristol was a terrible place to park, and Tom had to drive around to find a parking space. He sent back to tell her to stay put, and he'd be there soon and had found a splendid place for lunch.

Stay put? What did he think? That she was going to take a quick gallop around the block? Ivy leaned on her stick and looked up and down the street. She hated cities and in all these years, hadn't even made it to London. All she wanted was to spend her last days in her mam's house with

Jacob and her family around her.

Her grandson helped her into the car. As he settled her, she asked, "Tom, have I ever told you about Ian Noble? He had a car like this."

Now, what made her think of Ian Noble after all these years?

"What, Gran. An old Ford?"

"Not a Ford. An Austin. It was old, but not vintage then. More a wreck, if I'm honest. He married my friend Bethan, then went missing two days after the wedding. It happened sixty-five years ago, but I've never forgotten."

"You've got a photo of Bethan in your album, Gran."

"Yes. The prettiest girl in the village. Ian Noble came along and swept her off her feet. Then he disappeared and broke her heart."

"Isn't she the lady who went missing in Italy?"

"Oh, I have mentioned her. Sorry, sweetie, I know I repeat myself these days. Witnesses said they saw her walking up a mountain near Naples. They never found their bodies, you know. Not hers, nor Ian's."

"I suppose the police stopped looking, Gran. It's probably a cold case now."

"Constable Marley gave up after a year. A detective came from Scotland Yard looking for Bethan. Can't remember his name. Very handsome. He was quite upset. It was him who told me she was missing and that they had only found her bag and shoes. I couldn't believe it. She always cared about me, and sometimes I think I see her from the corner of my eye."

Tom smiled. Nostalgia always made his gran come

over fanciful.

"Wherever she is, I think she's still looking out for me," she said wistfully.

He reached over and patted his gran's hand. She'd just inherited an impressive amount of money and property. That entitled her to feel a little overwhelmed.

"Well, someone, somewhere is," he said.

END

ACKNOWLEDGEMENTS

Thank you so much for reading The Monk's Gate. If you enjoyed Bethan and Ian's story, I would love for you to hop over to your orders page on Amazon and leave a review. Good reviews are the lifeblood of Indie Authors, and we really appreciate your support.

I would also like to thank my awesome editors, Amy and Jo. I am so lucky to have them on my team!

My special thanks to Eluned Bevan of The Welsh Society of Western Australia who created Llanbleddynllwyd as a place name and very kindly allowed me to use it. Her help and interest have been invaluable.

If you would like to be notified about my new releases, please sign up for my (occasional) newsletter at: https://matildascotneybooks.com/

Or connect with me on Facebook: https://www.facebook.com/Offtheplanetbooks

MATILDA SCOTNEY'S BOOK MENU

Entertaining short stories for the lighter appetite:
Joy in Four Parts: A Quirky Sci-Fi Novella
Foresight: A Science Fiction short story.
Rattlebones: A short AI ghost story
We, Unseen: A First Contact short story.

Gorgeous Time Travel romance for something a little more substantial:
The Afterlife of Alice Watkins: Book One
The Afterlife of Alice Watkins: Book Two
(The Afterlife of Alice Watkins is also available as a boxed set – ebook only)

Galactic adventures/space opera for the "meatlovers!"
The Soul Monger: Book One
Revelations: The Soul Monger Book Two
Testimony: The Soul Monger Book Three
Myth of Origin: A Galactic Adventure

PICE BACH (PEEKYBARKS) RECIPE (As per the author's mother)

Yes! They really exist! Perfect for kids' lunchboxes. A delicious soft round flat cake.

(As children we called them Peekybarks, Welsh Cakes or Bakestones – because they were cooked on a bakestone, but a heavy bottomed pan will do).

INGREDIENTS

2 cups all purpose flour

1 teaspoon baking powder

1/3 cup of caster sugar (don't use ordinary granulated).

½ teaspoon ground mace (you can use nutmeg if you prefer).

¼ teaspoon salt.

About an 1/8 teaspoon of ground cinnamon.

Four tablespoons CHILLED lard (don't miss this out, extra butter doesn't work)

Four tablespoons CHILLED butter (cut in small cubes)

1 large egg (beaten)

½ cup dried currants (although I use sultanas)

2 – 3 tablespoons milk

METHOD

Combine flour, sugar, baking powder, salt, mace (or nutmeg) and cinnamon. (I use a food processor for this next part, but you can use your fingers)

Add the lard and butter and give it a whizz or rub in with your fingertips. It only needs to get to the coarse breadcrumb stage.

Add the dried fruit and stir with a spoon.

Add the egg and a little milk then work it into the mixture. It shouldn't be sticky or soggy, just a nice firm dough.

Wrap the dough and chill. It will sit happily in the fridge until you are ready, but a minimum of twenty minutes.

Roll out on floured surface to about ¼ inch thick (6mm I think)

Cut out rounds with a biscuit cutter. You can re-roll and cut out the scraps.

Lightly butter a heavy bottomed or cast-iron pan and place on medium heat.

Cook cakes on each side until lightly browned. They take around 3 – 4 minutes but if they're browning too fast, reduce the heat a little. While the cakes are still warm, I put some ordinary granulated sugar in a shallow dish and coat half the cakes on both sides. I leave the others plain to have with butter and jam. I think they're best served warm but reheating in a toaster works fine, even a microwave for a short burst.

ABOUT THE AUTHOR

Passionate about Sci Fi, Time Travel, baking and grandchildren, when my mind isn't off on some imaginary galaxy quest with my trusty chihuahua sidekick Oggie, I can be found in Australia collecting teapots and nerding about all things Star Wars.

Printed in Great Britain
by Amazon

19534829R00318